TRIPLE CROSS

TRIPLE CROSS

A KATE HENDERSON NOVEL

TOM BRADBY

Atlantic Monthly Press

New York

First published in Great Britain in 2021 by Bantam Press,
an imprint of Transworld Publishers

Printed in the United States of America

First Grove Atlantic hardcover edition: September 2021

Library of Congress Cataloging-in-Publication data available for this title.

Typeset in 11.5/16pt Palatino LT Std by Jouve (UK), Milton Keynes

ISBN 978-0-8021-5921-2
eISBN 978-0-8021-5922-9

Atlantic Monthly Press
an imprint of Grove Atlantic
154 West 14th Street
New York, NY 10011

Distributed by Publishers Group West

groveatlantic.com

21 22 23 24   10 9 8 7 6 5 4 3 2 1

To Claudia, Jack, Louisa and Sam.

Prologue

NOW KATE HENDERSON was sure. She had seen the clean-shaven man with faded jeans, olive T-shirt and fawn trainers while she waited in line at the butcher's shop on the square. And the woman with dark glasses, a lime sundress and what looked like a blue Chloé handbag had been paying for parking just in front of them when they arrived in the centre of town an hour ago.

Kate put down the giant aubergines she was about to buy, nodded regretfully at the wizened Frenchman behind the trestle table and wandered nonchalantly back along the market stalls until she was standing beneath the entrance to the Grand Cathedral, the Église Notre Dame de Bergerac. She glanced up at the clock and wove her way across the road and into the pedestrian zone beyond.

It was the kind of day the South of France had been invented for, perhaps 23 or 24 degrees in the sun, and she was grateful for the patches of shade as she turned left and wandered along a side street, gazing unhurriedly into the shop windows. She went into a store selling the most expensive stationery she'd ever seen and spent a few minutes trying out fountain pens at the counter.

When she emerged again, she didn't look back and was careful to move with the same relaxed gait and rhythm. She walked on through a covered market, stopping to buy some pastries, and finally got back to find her husband and children still at the table in the little square, lingering over the dregs of their coffee.

'Success?' Stuart asked, noticing that his wife was carrying little in the way of groceries.

'Yes. We need to go.'

'Take a seat. I'll order you a café au lait.'

'We need to go now. Don't make a fuss. Don't argue. Don't look surprised or shocked. Just get up, go in and pay, and then we'll leave.'

They looked at her, dumbfounded. 'What's going on?' Stuart asked.

She gave him a broad smile, swinging her back towards the cathedral, so that there was no chance any of her watchers could read her lips. 'Just do as I say, Stuart. And please don't ask any more questions.'

All three looked like they wanted to argue with her, to fight against this intrusion of the past into their fragile idyll, but they knew better than to try. Fiona and Gus stood at either side of their mother as they waited for their father to pay.

'It's getting hot,' Kate said. Neither answered. 'Even I might have a swim later,' she added.

Stuart returned. 'Most expensive coffee in history,' he said easily. 'Almost as bad as bloody Venice.'

Kate smiled at him and they turned down the cobbled street in the direction of the quay and the river.

And now she spotted a third shadow: she'd seen the young woman with a nose piercing and Crocs by the fig stall at the market around the cathedral. Or was she imagining things?

Kate moved faster. She took Fiona and Gus's hands and they held on to her willingly. 'Come on,' she said. She wanted to run and was starting to pull along both her children.

'What is it?' Stuart whispered again. 'What's spooked you?'

Kate shepherded them across the road, which ran alongside the Dordogne river, sparkling now in the midday sun. The quay doubled as a car park. 'Get in,' Kate said, as they reached their rented Renault Clio. She took the keys from Stuart.

'You're not insured,' he said, but she ignored him. She slid in behind the wheel, pulled the driver's seat forward, glanced in the rear-view and side mirrors.

The man in the olive T-shirt was forty or fifty yards behind her, but moving fast.

'What the hell is going on?' Fiona's voice was shrill with fear.

Kate reversed steadily, ignoring her daughter. As she turned on to the road, she watched the man get into a black Volkswagen Golf, the girl with the pierced nose joining him. 'Damn,' she said.

'What is it, Kate?' Stuart asked, as she spun around the

corner, accelerated to the top of the slope and swung right on to the narrow old bridge that led away from the town.

'I don't know yet.'

'Are we being followed?'

'I think so.' She glanced in the rear-view mirror at the Golf on their tail. 'Yes, we are.'

'Why?' Fiona asked, fear in her voice.

'Please, just give me a minute. I need to work out what's going on here.'

Kate drove through the tiny hamlet across the bridge, then accelerated up towards the cemetery. She barely touched the brakes at the crossroads, prompting Fiona to squeal in terror, then hammered up the hill towards the vineyards that criss-crossed the slopes beneath the Grand Château of Monbazillac.

She was touching 120 kilometres an hour on the straight section of the narrow road and still at sixty or more in the tight chicane beneath the village, but the Golf stayed with her. As they passed the château, Gus turned to look back down the hill. 'They're still behind us, Mum!'

'It's all right,' Stuart said calmly. 'Your mother knows what she's doing.'

Does she? Kate thought. It's starting to feel like a really long time since I knew what I was doing.

She slowed to a crawl through the village, past the pretty church, the elaborate new *mairie* and what looked like a wine shop-cum-restaurant. Then she floored the pedal on the long, gentle slope beyond it.

Halfway down through the vineyards, the speedometer nudged 140. She hit the next set of tight turns a shade more slowly, but it was all she could do to keep the Clio on the road. Fiona screamed. Gus's knuckles whitened as he clutched the grab handle just below the roof. Even Stuart's face was draining of colour.

As she rounded the final corner, Kate yanked the wheel left. The Renault shot up a gravel track and flew off the crest. She hit the brakes as it landed and skidded to a halt beneath the cover of the trees.

The Renault's dust cloud drifted away into the wood as they waited, Kate's heart pounding.

They listened.

The Golf roared into sight on the road below them, slowed for the curves and accelerated again as it emerged from the stretch of woodland into the valley.

Kate finally exhaled.

'Fucking hell,' Fiona exclaimed. 'You nearly killed us.'

'Jesus, Mum,' Gus said. 'You are the man.'

'Woman, I think you mean,' Stuart corrected. 'And, yes, your mum does know what she's doing.' He looked at Fiona. 'Mind your language.'

Kate had closed her eyes. She would not, could not, go through all this again.

1

KATE KNEW SHE was in trouble from the expression of rapture on her children's faces. No matter how often she had repeated on the plane to Bergerac that this trip did not imply any kind of formal rapprochement with their father, they were now listening spellbound to his endless reminiscences about happy times in their past.

'You totally owned him!' Gus said.

'The look on his face!' Fiona added.

The story in question concerned an argument in a ski lift in Les Arcs a few years previously, triggered by Gus's irrepressible determination to jump the queue. Stuart had faced up to an aggrieved middle-aged Frenchman with such force that the man had immediately backed down. Kate hadn't much cared for the incident in the first place, and the story didn't improve with the telling. But she didn't interrupt. The meal had already proved a minor miracle and she saw no good reason to burst its fragile bubble.

Fiona had eaten everything put in front of her without being prompted. Gus was more garrulous than he'd been for some time. He'd taken the opposite route to his sister: his pallid cheeks were fleshy from too much comfort eating, the impression of teenage puppy fat accentuated by the terrible helmet haircuts he allowed his sister to inflict on him. But his face was currently transformed by laughter. So, too, was Fiona's. For a moment, Kate could forget the stark angularity of her daughter's cheeks that betrayed the seriousness of her growing mental disorder.

After the chase this morning, they had seen no further sign of their pursuers. Aside from a brief conversation back at the rented farmhouse, in which Kate had said she couldn't think of any reason why anyone should be following them, they'd all seemed to push it to the back of their minds, perhaps because the fear of slipping into the past was too much for any of them to deal with.

Only Kate remained firmly on guard. She tried to relax as she witnessed the pleasure the rest of the family took in each other's company. She didn't like Stuart's goatee beard, or his attempt to relive his youth in tight T-shirts and jeans – he had clearly been working out in Moscow, if nothing else, while exiled there – but even she'd found herself laughing at some of his appallingly unfunny jokes, and his determination to be on good form was infectious. She realized she felt better than she had in months.

She could see, though, that Fiona and Gus considered this day as a curtain-raiser on a future longed-for reunion that must surely now be imminent. And Kate already dreaded the return journey, during which she would have to explain once again that their father's betrayal of his family and his country still made any rapprochement a remote possibility.

Kate reached for the bill. Stuart, normally so quick to pay for everything in the past – their marriage had been curiously old-fashioned in that respect – looked sheepish. They both knew he didn't have the means to pay for anything at all, these days. Kate was even coughing up for the farmhouse.

'Thanks so much, Kate,' he said.

'It's a pleasure,' she replied, with as much sincerity as she could muster.

They tipped out of the restaurant and piled into the car. Kate let Gus sit in front beside his father, who shouldn't really have been in the driver's seat. But that was perhaps the least of their problems. She tried to keep her survey of the car park discreet. There was no sign of the black Golf, or any other vehicle that might have been ready to follow them.

'Cool place,' Gus said.

'Nice food,' Fiona added, without catching her mother's eye.

'Would we be able to go to school here?' Gus asked.

'Depends if you want to start speaking French,' Stuart said. 'Though I guess it would help in the next lift-queue bust-up.'

'They have international schools, don't they?' Fiona asked.

'I think they possibly do in Bordeaux. I haven't looked into it yet, but I will.'

Stuart glanced over his shoulder. Perhaps he was looking for some sign of approval from his wife. Kate kept her counsel. She was far from ready to contemplate moving here to begin life again with her former husband. Not many people managed to betray their wife, their family and their country, and she was a long way from forgiveness.

Conversation dwindled, until it was drowned by the steady hum of the cicadas through the open windows.

They turned right past the sandstone church and wound their way through the village to a bumpy track that led past a coppice to the farmhouse, hidden in the fold of the valley and surrounded by its own vineyard.

Kate had barely removed the keys from the ignition when she noticed the dark Range Rover parked in the corner of the drive next to the swimming pool. A second vehicle stood under the trees. Both faced the exit. 'Get into the house,' she said to the others.

'I'll check—'

'Take the children inside, Stuart.'

As Kate walked towards the Range Rover, the prime minister of the United Kingdom of Great Britain and Northern Ireland, James Ryan, and his cabinet secretary, Shirley Grove, climbed out.

'Kate Henderson, as I live and breathe,' the PM said. He'd put on weight again and looked older. His cheeks were puffed and saggy. His hands were thrust deep into his pockets and he wore a curious half-smirk, like a schoolboy caught stealing from the local sweet shop. It was his political stock-in-trade.

'Good evening, Mrs Henderson,' Grove said.

'What are you doing here?'

'Good question,' the PM said. 'On the money, as always. Can we talk somewhere? Can't be overheard by your husband, I'm afraid.'

'No. We can't. I'd be grateful if you could leave.'

'We've come a long way, Kate.'

'I don't care how far you've come. I've retired. Mrs Grove can vouch for that.'

'Indeed she can. But events have a habit of upsetting the best-laid plans, as you very well know.'

'That's not my problem any more.'

'I'm afraid what we have to tell you may encourage you to change your mind.'

'I don't want to hear it.' Kate began to turn away, in no doubt that she really, really didn't. Not this time.

'You have no choice because *not* to listen to what we came here to say could prove injurious to both you and your family.' The prime minister gave a barely discernible nod towards the house.

'Is that a threat?'

'A fact, I'm sorry to say.'

'Was it your people following me this lunchtime?'

'An army surveillance team. We just needed to know you didn't have any troublesome company.'

'Why the army?'

'It'll make sense if you let me explain.'

'Just hear us out, Mrs Henderson,' Grove said. A thumbnail scratching at the sleeve of a woollen cardigan gave the lie to her calm, even impassive demeanour.

'Wait a minute,' Kate said. She went into the house where Stuart and the children sat anxiously around the kitchen table.

'What is it?' Stuart asked. 'What did they want?' He wasn't doing a good job of hiding his nerves.

'I've got to hear what he has to ask. Probably just something from the old days they need help or advice on. I'll be back inside half an hour. Don't wait up for me.'

'You said you wouldn't do this any more,' Fiona said. 'You promised it was over.' She stood and backed towards the cooker, as if preparing for a confrontation.

'And I have no intention of breaking that promise.'

'Who was following us this morning?'

'That's what I intend to find out.'

Kate left before she had to field any further questions, and squeezed herself awkwardly into the back seat of the Range Rover, between Grove and the PM. 'There's a bar in the village,' she told the driver and the personal protection officer in the passenger seat. They roared off, with the back-up car behind them.

The place was deserted, and its bearded, world-weary patron didn't bother to hide his irritation at their appearance so late. They took a corner seat and ordered a bottle of rosé.

The PM waited until the less than genial host was out of earshot before he began. 'Look, Kate, the reality is stark. Half of the world still thinks of me as a Russian spy, or agent of influence, or whatever term you want to use – a Moscow stooge, a traitor, a liar . . .'

'That's not my problem. I cleared you comprehensively of that charge in the inquiry Mrs Grove oversaw before I left MI6.'

'It *is* your problem, I'm afraid. The idea that I might be a traitor stems *entirely* from that bug you put on the oligarch's super-yacht in Istanbul all those months ago. Without you "overhearing" the "conversation" that first suggested I was a spy, this would never have emerged to tarnish my premiership.'

Kate couldn't, and didn't, argue with this.

'Besides, I read your evidence to the so-called "inquiry". It's clear to me you still believe every word you heard on that yacht.'

Kate frowned. What the hell was this? 'So you've come all this way to accuse me of lying to exonerate you?'

'Just hold your horses a minute and hear me out.'

'I don't want to go over this again.'

'I understand why you'd want to leave it all behind you. I also get why you'd hold on to the original idea. We know the Russians are trying to corrupt figures in our public life, and I accept that, from a certain angle, I seem a credible candidate – chequered personal life, opaque finances.' He gave her a sheepish grin. 'As you would see it . . .'

Kate did not smile back. She thought, once again, that this man had no shame.

'So, for the purposes of this conversation, I want to go right back to the start. The man who first tipped you off about the meeting of Russia's intelligence bigwigs on that yacht was a friend from your time studying in St Petersburg, correct?'

Kate stared at him for a moment, then got up. 'I'm really not doing this again. Enjoy your wine.'

'Wait!' He leapt to his feet, face creased with worry, a far cry from the smooth talker she'd found so easy to dismiss. 'Please, Kate . . .'

If he was faking his own concern, he was doing it unbelievably well. She sat down slowly again. 'You have five minutes.'

'We've been left with no choice but to go over old ground with new eyes.'

Kate didn't answer.

He took her silence as leave to continue. 'All right. This chap Sergei was a friend from your time as a student in St Petersburg, correct?'

'It's in the file.'

'He ended up in London and it was clear to you he was working for one of the Russian intelligence agencies?'

'Yes.'

'And his previous assignment had been in Istanbul, so when he told you these intelligence chiefs were in the habit of gathering on Igor Borodin's super-yacht in the summer there, you thought the information credible and the yacht a sensible target for a bugging operation.'

She nodded curtly. What intelligence officer wouldn't? Where was this going?

'But Sergei was your only source?'

She glanced at Grove. 'Yes.'

'Who knew of your prior friendship with him? I mean, within MI6?'

Kate shook her head. She couldn't see the relevance of the question. 'Anyone on the top floor would have had access to my vetting files. It's in there somewhere. We have to declare any significant friendships prior to joining the Service, and I did so.'

The prime minister glanced at Shirley Grove, who had aged visibly since Kate had last seen her. The lines around her eyes were thick with accumulated fatigue. She gripped her reading glasses in her right fist, as if about to use them as a weapon.

'Did it occur to you at the time that the tip-off might have been too good to be true?'

'I admitted to the—'

'I'm not interested in some crap inquiry.' He leant forward. His anger matched hers, and even in the low light, his eyes were a deep, vivid blue. She had the briefest sense of why so many women lost their heads over him. 'I travelled all the way down here to find out what you *really* think.'

She held his gaze for a moment more. Was this some kind of trap? 'Yes, it occurred to me that the tip-off was convenient, if that's what you're asking, but I trusted Sergei. I'd known him a long time. I didn't think he'd lie to me.'

'You bug the yacht and it delivers the bombshell. But you lack hard proof of my treachery. So when you're later told that a Russian defector has all the hard evidence to prove your theory, of course you'd jump at it. And the video of me "having sex" with underage girls in Kosovo looked entirely authentic and convincing.'

'I was certain it was you in the footage, yes.'

The PM didn't flinch, his gaze still locked on her. 'I'll tell you something, Kate. I may be many things, but I am *not* a paedophile. Nor have I ever paid a woman of any age for sex.' The hint of that familiar smirk suggested he still believed he didn't need to, but Kate didn't allow herself to react.

At last the waiter brought the wine, uncorked the bottle and poured. Only the PM reached for his glass.

'All right,' Kate said, wanting to be away from there now. 'I've been through this over and over again. I gave Mrs Grove everything she wanted and needed when I left MI6. I admitted I'd been set up, used, hoodwinked, fooled – pick whichever term you like. You were completely cleared. I left in effective disgrace. And the quid pro quo was that I'd be allowed to get on with my life.'

'And meet your husband here in Europe,' Grove said tersely. 'An agreement we have adhered to, despite the one indisputable fact in this whole sorry affair – that he was working for the Russians and should actually be rotting in a British jail.'

Kate didn't dignify this with an answer. 'Just tell me what you came for.'

The PM glanced at Grove again. He took another sip of his wine and Kate joined him. She was clearly going to need fortification tonight. The PM put his elbows on the table once more and leant forward, as if to impart a confidence. 'Something new has turned up. There's a mid-ranking diplomat in our embassy in Istanbul called Tess Winkelman. Not one of your former colleagues, as I understand it.'

Kate shook her head. 'Not as far as I know, but it's a big organization.'

'As part of her work, she's our representative on a body called International Women in Business, which is a Turkish government quango. One of the other members she's got to know is the Russian rep, who appears to be another mid-ranking diplomat called Natasha Demidov.'

'Demidova,' Grove corrected.

'Exactly,' he said. 'The women attended a conference up in Ankara and some drink was taken. In her cups, Demidova told a very strange story. She said she was in fact a senior officer in the Russian Foreign Intelligence Service and had originally been sent to Istanbul and tasked with seducing an agent in the rival service, their military intelligence agency, the GRU. His name was Sergei Malinsky. And the purpose of the seduction was to feed him the information that would set up the greatest hoax in intelligence history, which was that the man who was about to become British prime minister was really a Russian spy. But it had gone too far, she said. Sergei had died very suddenly on a train between St Petersburg and Moscow, apparently of a heart attack, though she said he had always been in exceptional health. Is this ringing any bells, Kate?'

Both the PM and Grove had their gaze fixed firmly on her now, but she didn't blink. If they were looking for a reaction, she was determined they weren't going to get one.

'The last thing Miss Demidov—'

'Demidova,' Grove corrected again.

The PM shot her an irritated glance before he continued. 'The last thing she said before disappearing into the Istanbul night was that Tess needed to get this information directly to me. On no account could it go through MI6, she repeated. Tess naturally asked why not. Because, Demidova said, there was a traitor right at the heart of MI6 in Vauxhall, Agent Dante, the most senior spy the Russian state apparatus had ever possessed in the UK, someone at the *very* top of the Service, a man, or woman, whom all roads led through, a mastermind who had helped plan this entire operation with the former head of the SVR, Igor Borodin, and his successor, Vasily Durov. If this information went into MI6, she said, she would meet the same end as Sergei.'

The sound of cicadas through the open window was suddenly deafening.

'You appear to have gone very silent, Kate,' the PM said.

2

KATE HAD TO fight the urge to get up from the table and run, hard, into the night. Neither the prime minister's nor Grove's gaze had left her face. She took another sip of wine and stared out of the open window at a vineyard that sloped gently down the hill.

Grove broke the silence. 'Isn't it what you always suspected, Mrs Henderson, that there was a traitor right at the top of MI6? If someone at the heart of your organization had been helping orchestrate this from the start, it would explain why Moscow has always seemed several steps ahead of us.'

Kate didn't answer immediately. 'Agent Dante,' she said. 'It certainly would be neat.'

'What do you mean, "neat"?' the PM asked.

'If everything I once thought was true . . .' Kate stared right at him '. . . by which I mean that you *were* a Russian-controlled asset, or agent of influence, then wouldn't you and your friends in Moscow cook up something like this to clear your name?'

He didn't appear to take offence at her directness. 'Yes. And that is why I need you to get to the bottom of it.' The PM reached into his pocket and pulled out a packet of Silk Cut cigarettes. 'You still smoke? I seem to remember you were once . . . partial.'

'I've given up.'

'So have I. Want to step outside and join me?'

The PM stood. Grove got up to go with him, but he forestalled her. 'We'll be back in a minute.'

Against her better judgement, Kate followed him on to the terrace that directly overlooked the vineyards, brightly lit now by the stars. She looked up. The sky down here was startlingly clear. He offered her a cigarette and she shook her head. He held the packet a moment longer and she weakened. 'That's the spirit,' he said, and lit it for her.

For a moment, they smoked in silence. 'What can I do to persuade you to join me in this quest to prove my innocence?'

'Nothing. I'm done with all that, as I think I made clear.'

'I *am* innocent, you know,' he said ruefully. 'I mean, guilty of plenty of things, of course, but not this.'

She was impervious to that schoolboy grin now. 'I'm sorry you've wasted your trip.'

'Oh, I haven't finished yet.' He'd adopted a new tone, shorn of the playfulness. 'I need your help.'

'Why me?'

'Because you have no vested interest in proving my innocence. And we require someone who knows every street and back-alley within MI6, but who is currently out-side the system.'

'Call MI5.'

'I said outside the *system*. Besides, if you come to believe in my innocence, so will everyone else.'

Kate sucked the smoke deep into her lungs. 'No,' she said, as she exhaled. 'I'm sorry, I can't. After Igor Borodin's supposed defection went wrong and those Albanian mon-sters kidnapped my children, I promised them I'd walk away for ever, and I meant it.'

'We saved them, though, did we not?'

'We did, yes. But that doesn't change the promise I made.' Kate dropped her half-smoked cigarette on to the terrace and carefully trod it out. 'I'm sorry I can't be of more help. I'll make my own way home.'

She'd reached the double doors before he spoke again. 'I said I haven't finished yet.'

Kate stopped, turned. The menace in his voice was unmistakable.

'I need your help, Kate.'

'This conversation has gone as far as it's going to.'

'I need someone whose integrity is not in question. Someone who knows every angle of this story, who is of the organization but outside it. We've taken a pretty lenient attitude to Stuart's position so far,' he said, 'but I'm afraid your continued cooperation is the price you must pay for that.'

'I'm sorry . . .' Despite the cool night breeze, Kate could feel the heat in her cheeks. '*What* did you say?'

'Your husband should be in a British prison cell. Instead, he's living it up in balmy French sunshine.'

'That's the deal I made with Mrs Grove.'

'It may have been, but times change.'

Kate had to resist the temptation to punch him. 'You utter bastard,' she said.

'If you carry out the investigation, regardless of the conclusion, I give you my word – and I will put it in the form of a legal undertaking, if you wish – that I'll leave you and Stuart alone for the rest of your lives. If not, I'm afraid we'll have to revoke his freedom to leave Moscow. He will no longer be able to see either you or the children.' He shrugged. 'I can see you're not pleased—'

'Not *pleased*? You should probably call your protection officers before I break your bloody neck.'

'Punchy.' He smiled again. 'Look, I don't blame you. I'd be angry too. We'll give you tonight to think about it. But we need to be on our way by ten tomorrow morning, so I'll spin past your house beforehand for your answer. Want a lift home?'

'I'll walk. I need a little time to process your duplicity.'

'That's the spirit, Kate. All's fair in love and war.'

Kate didn't return his grin. She set off for the farmhouse without bothering to say goodbye to Shirley Grove, whom she was inclined now to view with even deeper contempt. So much for the impartiality of the civil service.

She stormed through the village, past the church and the shuttered windows of the *tabac*. But she slowed on the last stretch of the journey past the coppice and sat for a moment by the side of the road. She toyed with the stones around her feet.

The bastard. The complete, utter, total bastard. What on earth was she going to tell the kids?

She'd have to say no. She couldn't, wouldn't, shouldn't go back. She'd promised them faithfully she'd left all the fear and terror behind them, that she would never do anything to put them at risk again. Kate thought of the video she'd been sent by the Albanians of Fiona and Gus, trussed and terrified. The fake footage of Fiona being beheaded. She stood, determined to tell the prime minister where to stick his new inquiry.

Fiona, Gus and Stuart were huddled at the kitchen table. She wanted more than anything to put her arms around them all and never let go. But the exchange she'd just had with the PM filled her shoes with lead. She dumped her handbag and went to turn on the kettle. 'Anyone for night-time tea?'

'Are you really going to do this, Mum?' Fiona had her palms pressed together, her arms outstretched towards her mother. 'Tell us what happened.'

'Nothing happened.'

'That's fucking bollocks.'

'Fiona! Seriously, please. There's no need for that kind of language.'

'You know, you're the worst liar in history. I have no idea how you became a spy in the first place.'

'It's only you I'm no good at lying to,' Kate said. 'For which you should probably be grateful.'

'Then tell us what that was all about!'

Kate popped a herbal teabag into a mug while she waited for the kettle to boil. She perched on a stool at the other side of the table from her family. It felt like an interrogation. Perhaps it was.

'What did he want with you?' Fiona asked.

'It doesn't really matter, because I said no.'

'Tell us!'

'I can't. It's a sensitive security mat—'

'Oh, my God, I cannot believe you!' Fiona stood, her gaunt cheeks red with rage.

'Calm down.'

'Do not tell me to calm down!'

Stuart clasped their daughter's shoulders and guided her gently back into her seat. 'It's all right. Let's just hear Mum out.'

'There honestly isn't much to say. He wanted me to head up another inquiry to clear his name. I said I'd already done that and hell would freeze over before I returned to any kind of government service. He insisted on coming here in the morning for my final answer. I said that was my final answer and left.'

There was a long silence. Fiona glared at her. Gus examined the table. Stuart had his hand on his daughter's arm, shaking it gently to and fro in quiet reassurance.

'What is it you're not telling us?' Fiona asked eventually.

The kettle boiled. Kate splashed the water on to her tea-bag. She glanced at the bottle of whisky Stuart had bought from duty free and forced herself to resist the urge to pour a slug into her mug. 'I've told you everything.'

'Bullshit.'

Kate breathed in deeply. If there was one thing Dr Wiseman, the psychiatrist who had been helping her navigate family breakdown, the implosion of her career and near total mental breakdown, had always been clear about, it was the need to avoid being drawn into the mental torment and drama that her daughter lived through daily. *Be calm, be consistent, be clear.* 'That was all he had to say. He asked me for a favour. I told him no. I left.'

'Bullshit.'

'It's not bullshit.'

'There was something else. You're holding it back.'

Kate moved to sit at the table. She looked her daughter in the eye. Stuart often said she was a chip off the old block and at times like this he wasn't wrong: Fiona could be a fearsome interrogator. 'No,' she said. 'That was it. Now, what are we going to do tomorrow?'

'Nothing,' Fiona countered. 'Until you tell me what it was really about.'

Kate kept her temper. 'I've told you. So let's move on to happier things.'

'You're lying.'

'I'm not lying.'

Stuart squeezed his daughter's hand. 'It's all right. I'm sure Mum's told you everything.'

Gus, who had done nothing but stare at the table, suddenly got up and darted for his room.

'See?' Fiona said. 'Now look what you've done.'

'I've told you everything,' Kate fired back. 'It was all about him being innocent, so I obviously have all the old questions bouncing around my head. Was I set up from the start? Was I suckered, tricked, made a fool of? And did I put my family in the most terrible jeopardy as a result?' She managed to make her voice ring with sincerity because it was the truth, more or less.

Fiona, her face pinched, looked as if she'd come back at

her, but ran for the door instead. 'Don't worry, *I*'ll go and see if he's all right,' she said, with heavy sarcasm.

She stormed out, leaving Kate and Stuart facing each other across the kitchen table. Just like old times, Kate thought. 'That went well,' she said.

Stuart headed for the whisky bottle. 'Want one?'

'Go on, then.'

Stuart brought the glasses to the table. He smiled at her. 'Do I, Kate Henderson, detect more than a hint of cigarette smoke?' he asked.

'The least of my problems, I'd say.'

'With the prime minister? Is that like sharing a spliff?'

'I can think of about a million people I'd rather share a spliff with.'

'You've never had one, so how would you know?'

'I don't think either of us needs to be reminded of just how wild and uninhibited I really am.'

Stuart sipped his whisky. 'I kind of feel like one myself,' he said eventually.

They waited to see if the kids would return, but the bedroom wing of the long, low farmhouse was shrouded in silence.

'Shall we go outside?' Stuart asked.

'Sounds like an invitation at a school dance.'

'If you want to look at it like that . . .'

Kate instantly regretted her flirtation. She didn't know what had got into her. 'Come on, then.'

They walked out on to the terrace. Kate led him to the pool and up the gentle slope behind it until they were well out of earshot. They had a view there of the house, the surrounding vineyard and the ancient trees of the valley. 'It's practically like daylight,' Stuart said, peering up at the moon.

'No pollution, I guess,' Kate replied. 'This is what living in the real country is like.'

'It reminds me of lying out in the highlands in the summer.'

'Apart from the drastic change in temperature.'

'You don't know what you're missing, you know.'

'I bloody do.' Summer holidays in Scotland were an issue on which Kate and Stuart had fallen out early in their marriage. 'Midges.'

'The purity of the air! Grandeur. History.'

'They wanted me to conduct another inquiry to clear his name.'

'Yes, you said. It seems a strange thing to do.'

'They have new intel,' Kate said.

'Like what?'

'I'd better keep that to myself for now, but Fiona was right. There was a sting in the tail.'

Stuart took another sip of his whisky. He sat up straighter, bringing his knees to his chest. 'Something tells me this is not good news.'

'If I don't agree to play their game, they'll stop your visits to the West. Permanently.'

There was a long, long silence. Stuart didn't move a muscle, but Kate felt the tension gather in him.

'I see,' he said.

'Do you? Because I'm not sure I do.'

'What did you say to him?'

'I called him out for the ruthless, unprincipled bastard he is.'

Stuart didn't answer.

'I have no choice, of course,' she said.

'You do. You can and will say no. You – we – have to put the children first.'

'Precisely. Not seeing you for a few months, let alone years, would break their hearts. So, even as I raged against him, I knew I had to accept. And so did he.'

'And what do *you* think?'

'About what?'

'The prospect of not seeing me again.'

Kate had not expected anything so direct. She sat up, trying to overcome a stab of irritation. Why was it that men always wanted everything in black and white? No sooner had she started to feel something than Stuart wanted it itemized. 'Shall we just not go there?'

'I was so excited in the build-up to this trip. And, wonderful as they are, it wasn't simply the prospect of seeing Gus and Fi.'

'It was probably relief at the release from a life of tedium in Moscow.'

Stuart didn't reply. He stared dead ahead. And something about his demeanour – his vulnerability, perhaps, the sincerity of his love – touched her again. She turned and rested her head in his lap. Stuart leant back against the slope so that he could cradle her more comfortably.

All Kate could think of was how much she felt like crying. Was that love, or relief, or fear, or regret at what they'd once had and might now have permanently lost?

She could hear her husband's heart beating. There was a sense of excitement at being so close to him, which she hadn't felt since they'd first become lovers half a lifetime ago.

Stuart began, with infinite gentleness, to stroke her fore-head and curl her hair in his fingers, as he knew she loved.

Kate closed her eyes. The sound of cicadas, the crisp night air, the warmth of his touch beguiled her into a peace she hadn't felt for many months.

He began to massage her neck gently and she knew she should tell him to stop. She was aware she sought some kind of clarity in these moments, or at least emotional con-sistency, but found only lonely confusion, as the comforting pull of familiarity wrestled the bitter taste of his betrayal. What wouldn't she give to turn back time?

She soaked up the feeling of contentment for a few moments longer, then suddenly sat up. 'I'm going to do it.' The decisiveness in her voice surprised even Kate herself.

'Kate—'

'No, listen to me. I have to, for the children. There's no way they could contemplate being unable to see you, and I think we can both agree that them coming to Moscow is not a good idea.'

'But—'

'I'm going to tell them the truth. I don't want to go back any more than they want me to, and I think they get that. They'll understand if they know what's at stake.' She paused, wondering at the wisdom of the headlong rush to an uncertain future she was about to embark upon. 'But it's not just for their sake. I was excited on the plane down here and not just for them. I can't make any promises, but I've always loved you and that hasn't changed. I want to give us the best shot at finding a way back, however rocky that might be.'

Stuart moved a few paces away from her and stared into

the night. 'I can't tell you how much I've longed to hear those words . . .'

Kate waited, heart sinking. 'But?'

'There's a . . . complication . . . from my side I have to own up to.'

3

KATE FELT HER cheeks redden and her heart hammer. She heard herself say, 'You've got someone else?'

'No! No! For God's sake, I haven't got anyone else!'

'Then what?'

He came back to sit beside her. 'I'm not expecting any sympathy from you or anyone else. I should have anticipated it.'

'The Russians want you to sound me out about working for them?'

He turned to face her. 'How did you know?'

'If you weren't expecting it, I certainly should have been. I guess they took you quietly aside and said that if I'd left the Service under a cloud I might be susceptible.'

'More or less word for word.'

'What did they offer you if you succeeded?'

'That's where it gets complicated.'

Kate met his gaze. 'Oh, hold on a minute. How stupid of

me. They won't let you leave Moscow unless you play along? Or, more importantly, unless I do?'

She took his awkward silence as confirmation. She stared at her hands. 'But they can't be expecting me to come and work for them. What they really want is a week or two holed up in a secure location somewhere so that they can squeeze me for every last piece of information and insight on my life and work in MI6. Do that, and they'll leave us both alone for the duration to do as we please – and probably throw in some cash to tide us over for a year or two.'

'They suggested meeting in Spain or even here in France.'

'What did you tell them?'

'That I didn't think there was any chance you'd agree to it.'

'And how did they respond?'

'They said I might be surprised, that in their view you were still in love with me, and this was your Achilles heel. With enough . . . persuasion I could get you over the line. They promised the payments could run into many hundreds of thousands of pounds.'

The mention of money unsettled Kate. Was it possible that Stuart had given this proposal serious consideration? 'Were you planning to tell me anyway?'

'Of course. Just not on our first night together.'

Kate searched her husband's face for any sign of deceit. But all she saw was the steady gaze of the generous, kind, sincere man she had once so loved. She felt, unaccountably, like bursting into tears, and cursed herself for it.

Ever since she'd left the Service, she had spent many hours cloistered with Dr Wiseman, as he mapped her mind, her background, her experience and the driving forces of her personality to eliminate or tone down the elements that held her back, and build on those that drove her successfully on. A few days ago, she'd never felt stronger or better, grateful already for the near breakdown that had persuaded her to leave her old life and commit to constructing a new one.

And now she was slipping back down the well.

'What is it, Kate?'

'Nothing.'

'I've upset you.'

'No. You've been honest. And that's what makes me feel like bursting into tears.'

'Kate—'

She raised a hand, shifted away from him. 'It's all right.'

'I know how deeply I've hurt you. I don't want to do that ever again.'

Kate stood. He joined her.

She raised a hand again. 'It's okay. I just need some time . . .' She turned.

'I'll come with you,' he said.

'I'd rather be on my own, if you don't mind. I need to think things through.'

Before he could argue any further, Kate walked on up to the dirt track that crested the hill. She stopped halfway along it and listened to the cicadas and the gentle sway of the trees in the cool night breeze. It was so clear, quiet, still.

She chastised herself for failing to see this coming. She thought of what Stuart had told her on that drive through Russia after Sergei's assassination a few months ago: that his handlers in Moscow had neglected him to the point of disinterest. Tipping him into a state of desperation, no doubt. Clearly, once they had their hooks into you, they never let go.

She walked on. There were two questions now. Did she really want to remove their hooks from Stuart's back (and, if so, why)? And how in hell would she achieve it?

There was a deserted house at the far end of the valley. The kids had come back from an exploratory walk this afternoon to say it gave them the creeps. They were both convinced it was where a serial killer kept his victims walled into a basement. If so, he had a particular talent for horticulture. The garden was very neatly tended.

She circled it until she found herself on the other side of the vines. The ground was softer there, from last week's rain, and the mud stuck to her white sneakers. She stopped again and breathed in the peace and solitude.

Why had she just chosen precipitous action instead of further reflection? A relentless hunger for absolute truth in a world of grey had made her a successful intelligence officer, but she was less certain it was a recipe for happiness.

She knew no one could force themselves out of an emotional twilight zone. Was the promise she'd just made to Stuart some kind of test, to see if she could break free from the confusion of her own heart?

Her mind drifted back to the feel of him close to her on that bank above the farmhouse. Over and over their circumstances she went, the visceral force of her emotions on a collision course with her rational mind, which warned her not to step back into the orbit of the man who had betrayed her. For a brief moment, anger – or logic – held the upper hand. She recalled Imogen Conrad's glib beauty, vanity and shallowness, and cursed Stuart's decision to throw away his marriage for a few nights in her perma-tanned clutches.

She made her way back to the *gîte*, having resolved to let Stuart know with the dawn that he must fight his own battles. But that determination melted away on the perfectly manicured lawn, already damp with dew, and she found herself walking through the house to Stuart's bedroom.

His French windows were open. She hesitated on the threshold. What on earth was she doing? Some kind of madness drove her on. Perhaps them spending time as a family, or the loneliness of her life since their parting, or the stillness of the night. She stepped into the room, kicked off her pumps and let her dress slip to the floor.

'Kate?'

She slid in beside him. She ran her fingertips across the stubble on his chin and through his still thick, curly hair.

'What are you doing?' he breathed.

She gave her answer with the urgency of her desire.

Her hands ran across his newly hardened abdomen as they slipped into the sensual routine she'd no idea she'd missed so much. Only after he had peeled off her underwear and brought her to a climax did a discordant note from the past intrude. She raised her hand as he rolled gently on top of her. 'No,' she whispered. 'I'm not on the pill. We can't.'

For just a moment, she felt his body tense, and knew well enough what he was thinking: that on the trip to Moscow a few months ago – when he had saved her life on the long drive to the northern border – she had shown no such restraint with her old friend Sergei.

She pushed him gently on to his back, her long hair brushing across his face, and kissed him again. She drifted lower, brushing her lips against his chest and his stomach.

'Oh . . . God . . .' he muttered, as the night enveloped them both.

It was not the dawn that let reality back in, but the piercing scrutiny of their sixteen-year-old daughter.

'Fucking hell,' Fiona said. Then, 'Gus!' Gus!' as she thundered down the corridor.

Kate had barely had time to disentangle herself from her drowsy husband before Fiona returned, dragging her bleary-eyed brother behind her. 'Look!' she said.

'I told you,' he said calmly. 'Why did you wake me up for this?'

But he didn't retreat. They stood there, staring at their parents.

'What?' Kate asked.

'What do you mean, "What?"' Fiona's expression was caught somewhere between jubilation and consternation as her teenage brain tried to process what this extraordinary sight represented. 'You're having *sex* again?'

Kate sat bolt upright, pulling the duvet up to her neck. Stuart did the same and they faced their children like unruly teenagers themselves, caught in the act, which Kate supposed wasn't far from the truth.

'Is someone going to say something?' Fiona asked.

For once, both Kate and Stuart were lost for words.

'Erm . . . not really,' Kate said eventually.

'Well, what are you doing? What does this mean? Are you back together?'

'We're just working things out.'

'In bed?'

'Well, yes. Clearly.'

'So you *are* an item again?'

'Erm. I don't know. Like I said, we're just trying to work it all out.'

Fiona didn't seem to know whether to cry in exultation, fury or disgust, but with an expression that lay somewhere between the three, she said simply, 'You might want to get up. The prime minister's here. He's waiting in his car because I wouldn't let him into the house.'

Fiona pulled the door firmly shut. Kate rolled out of bed and hunted for her underwear. 'They must be the first teenagers in history to be pleased to discover their parents in bed together.'

Stuart hopped clumsily into his jeans. 'Christ,' he said. 'What are we . . . I mean, what are you going to say to the PM?'

Kate felt better with her clothes on. She slipped on her pumps, then stood. 'This is what we're going to do. I'll go out and tell him I accept his offer. I'll conduct his inquiry, but only in return for a legal undertaking that all potential charges against you are dropped and you'll be allowed to live anywhere you like for the rest of your life. In the meantime, you'll go back to Moscow and tell your handlers you've spoken to me and I'm interested. I want time to think about it, but I'm prepared to consider the possibility of some kind of working relationship.'

'Kate—'

'Tell them you think I'm going to need a few days, maybe a week, and that, if I decide to go ahead, I'll meet them in a safe house somewhere in Western Europe. And let them know I'm going to want money. A lot of it.'

'Are you sure?' Not unlike his daughter, Stuart looked as if he couldn't decide whether he'd been hugged or punched.

'Yes.'

'But—'

'It's all right, Stuart. I know what I'm doing.' Kate took his brush, tidied her hair, straightened her dress and walked down the corridor. What choice did she have, except to play both sides against the middle?

4

THE PRIME MINISTER was still seated in the back of the Range Rover, phone clutched to his ear. Kate knocked on the window and he wound it down. The personal protection officers in the car behind his eyed her warily. 'Morning,' the PM said. 'I would have come in, but your daughter said she wouldn't allow me in the house.'

'Now you know what I'm up against.'

'Indeed I do. Would you like to get into the car?'

'No, let's take a walk.'

'Shirley will need to come with us.'

Kate didn't argue. She led them up the path at the crest of the hill.

'We're really going to walk?' the prime minister asked.

She turned as they reached the shelter of the trees above the vines. 'I'll make this brief. I'm sure you have more important things to do.'

'Than clear my name?' he said. 'I doubt it.'

'I'll do what you wish. I'll conduct a new investigation, whose sole aim is to determine whether Sergei deliberately misled and set me up. I have a few stipulations, the most important of which is that I want complete immunity from prosecution for my husband, and his freedom to return and live in the UK.'

'Christ,' the PM said. He glanced at Shirley Grove, whose face was entirely impassive.

'Since his treachery is not widely known outside the Service, I don't think this should cause you too much trouble. And I want your legally watertight guarantee in writing.'

'We'll have to discuss that.'

'It's not negotiable.'

The PM glanced at Grove again and, for the first time, Kate saw how anxious he was. She'd never considered the possibility that he might be innocent of the charges against him. Or did she just want the investigation to be resolved so she could rescue her family life?

'Agreed. And we'll let you have that in writing.'

'Prime Minister—' Grove said.

He raised a hand. 'That's my decision, and it's final. What else, Kate?'

'I'll need premises outside SIS – somewhere that isn't a government office. And one of my former colleagues to assist me.'

'Which one?'

'Her name is Julie Carmichael. She worked with me on the Russia Desk.'

'Isn't she a potential suspect for Agent Dante?' Grove asked.

'Not from everything you've told me. She doesn't fit the profile for Dante. She hasn't been in the Service long enough to orchestrate this kind of operation. Besides, I'd trust her with my life – and have.'

'We assumed you'd need help, of course,' the PM said. 'But from outside the Service.'

'I'm going to need someone who can access all areas without arousing suspicion.'

'All right.' The PM was clearly in a hurry to leave. 'But you'll also be working with two of ours. Mrs Grove will be overseeing the investigation and reporting back to me, by which I mean that she'll need to be in whatever premises you acquire, and actively involved. I also want to offer one of our assistant private secretaries—'

'No, thanks.'

'It's not a request. His name is Callum Ellis. He's young, but tough and bright. You'll find him useful. If you need any operational support, we'll have to call in the army. We can't risk anyone in Six or Five being tipped off, which is why I used them to keep tabs on you here. Deal?'

He offered her his hand, somewhat absurdly, she thought, but she took it anyway. 'Deal.'

Grove lingered while he marched back to the car.

'So, it's you and me,' Kate said. 'Is that my punishment, or yours?'

Grove gave her a thin smile. 'I'll leave you to contact Miss Carmichael and find whatever premises you think are most suitable. Let me know as soon as you're ready to proceed and I'll introduce you to Callum Ellis. He's a very smart young man.'

'I'm sure he is.'

'Handsome, too,' Grove said, with the hint of a smile so surprising that Kate stood rooted to the spot as she strode away down the hill.

Stuart, Gus and Fiona were sitting around the breakfast table on the terrace. Stuart poured Kate some coffee and she sat for a moment with her face tilted up to absorb the warmth of the morning sun.

'So . . .' Fiona rasped '. . . are you going to tell us what's happening?"

Kate was tempted to ask her daughter to wind her neck in, but the cadaverous expression that had become her default setting in the past six months got in the way. Since responsibility for Fiona's food deprivation and churning anxiety lay firmly at her and Stuart's door, they'd forfeited that right some time ago.

For a brief moment, Kate wondered how to sugar-coat the events of the last few hours, before deciding to give it to both her children straight. Perhaps they truly were old enough. 'Well, let's start at the beginning. I certainly didn't intend you to find us in bed together—'

'You don't have to go on about it.'

It was too late for a U-turn, so Kate drove straight on. 'I didn't fully intend it to happen, but it has—'

'Oh, man,' Gus chipped in. 'Too much information.'

'But let's just say the good news is that it looks possible that . . . er . . . we *might* . . . um . . . And that's what you both wanted to hear, right?'

Kate caught sight of her husband's idiotic grin. He looked like he wanted to run around the garden punching the air. Fiona and Gus nodded meekly, though Fiona seemed much less confident of her reaction. Or was that just Kate's imagination?

'There are lots of hurdles to overcome and, as I've already warned you, there is no guarantee we'll be able to. But . . . well, we are where we are.'

'But *what*?' Fiona pressed.

'But there is a new obstacle, which neither your dad nor I foresaw, though perhaps we should have.'

'What kind of obstacle?' Gus asked.

'The prime minister is going to rescind Dad's right to travel unless I agree to head up a new investigation to clear his name.'

Fiona and Gus glanced at each other and then, brows furrowed, stared at the table. Gus's helmet hair had not had sight of a brush on this trip and looked as if he had shoved his fingertips into an electric socket.

When Fiona looked up, her expression was defiant. 'Why you?'

Why indeed? Kate thought. 'Because he says I have no desire to prove his innocence, so if I do, it'll be widely believed.'

'Is that true?'

'It has a certain logic. There's also some new intelligence.'

'What kind?'

'I'm afraid I can't tell you that.' She glanced at Stuart. She couldn't tell him either, of course, but he knew better than to ask.

'So, if you do this,' Fiona said, 'then—'

'If I do what they ask of me, then Dad would not only be able to come to France, Spain or Italy, but the UK too.'

Their eyes widened. Fiona couldn't – perhaps wouldn't – believe it. Gus looked as if he was about to burst into tears.

'Yes,' she said, responding to the almost palpable drift in her son's thoughts. 'He could be watching you playing cricket next summer.' She turned to her daughter. 'And – when the time comes – he could walk you down the aisle in any church in England.'

'Or Scotland,' Stuart said. 'And make a very long and embarrassing speech.'

Kate smiled. 'Don't push your luck.'

'I don't believe this,' Fiona said. Now she, too, looked as if she would burst into tears and run from the table at any moment.

Was it joy or confusion she saw in her daughter's eyes? 'Don't believe what?' Kate asked.

'Everything. Everything you're telling us.'

'Isn't that what you wanted?'

Neither answered. 'Will it be dangerous,' Gus asked, 'what they're asking you to do?'

Kate again considered dressing it up – and decided against it. Perhaps the time for that really was past. 'Possibly. But not, I think, on the same scale as anything we've already been through.'

'How can you be sure?'

Kate leant forward, elbows on the table. 'Look, I understand you're still devastated by what happened to you with those horrible Albanians. It was extremely traumatic. And I'd love to be able to honour my promise to leave it all behind. But I think the cost of doing so – your father's permanent exile – is too great. And the upside is that, if I can find a way through this – and I reckon I can – we can have everything we want.'

Fiona and Gus didn't know where to look.

'You're going to have to trust me,' Kate said. 'I know I've let you down before, but I sure as hell don't intend to this time.'

'It wasn't you who let us down.'

Kate tried hard to hide her surprise. This was the first time since Stuart's betrayal and exile that she'd ever heard a word of criticism of him pass her daughter's lips. Stuart's cheeks reddened. 'She's right,' he said quietly.

'That's in the past now,' Kate said, with a confidence she didn't entirely feel. 'And now we *all* get to shape the future we want. So I'm asking you to trust me.'

Fiona and Gus gazed up at her, and Kate felt a surge of emotion as she saw in their eyes that they did. Trust her. Implicitly. She looked at each of her family in turn. 'All right,' she said. 'Deal. We play these bastards at their own game – and end up with everything we want.' She stood. 'But right now, I need more coffee.'

She went into the house, accompanied by the faintest whisper that, in the world to which she had devoted so much of her life, fairy tales very rarely came true.

5

'I CAN'T BELIEVE you didn't fucking call me!' Julie burst back into Kate's life the same way she had left it: like a whirlwind.

Shirley Grove had rented them a flat that occupied the top two floors of a handsome stucco building in Cambridge Street, Pimlico. It was close enough, as she put it, to tap back into SIS headquarters or any other part of Whitehall, but sufficiently out of the way to reduce the risk of being seen coming and going.

Kate had just sent the surprisingly stoic Grove out to buy a Nespresso machine and enough Oatly Barista milk to withstand a siege – a dubious addiction she'd acquired from Fiona.

The flat had two bedrooms, which had been hastily converted into offices, and an airy kitchen, living and dining area, with French windows that opened on to a tiny balcony overlooking the street. Julie threw herself down on to a pastel sofa bathed in the morning sunlight. She'd applied barely any make-up, or given her tumbling auburn hair more than a cursory brush, but she looked more beautiful than ever. She wore a ripped brown suede jacket with black jeans and, as she shook out her hair and her tight white T-shirt rode up, Kate spotted a new tattoo of a small dolphin just above her waistband.

'Are you going to tell me what all this I'll-explain-when-I-see-you business is about?' Julie glanced around the room. 'Ah, I get it. You're about to suggest we move in together.' She gave her a mischievous grin. 'I knew you fancied me.'

Julie's standard operating principle was that everyone found her attractive. She wasn't often wrong.

'Don't flatter yourself. I have a job for you.'

Julie's smile faded. She sat up, then stood. 'I do *not* like the sound of that. Mind if I smoke?'

'On the balcony.'

Julie stepped out into the sunshine. Kate joined her, leaning back against the doorframe. Julie offered her the pack. Kate shook her head. 'Come on,' Julie urged.

'I've quit. Sort of.'

'Which I'm guessing is going to be the theme of this conversation.'

'I need your help,' Kate said. 'But I want you to know you can refuse.'

'You know I'm not going to.'

'I was in France with Stuart, trying to patch our lives back together, when I received a surprise guest in the form of the prime minister and his lugubrious sidekick, Shirley Grove.'

'Better than that special adviser, the one you said curled up on the sofa beside him, flicking her hair.'

'I'm waiting for her to make an appearance. Anyway, he gave me an ultimatum. Either I returned to head up an inquiry to prove his innocence once and for all, or he would rescind Stuart's right to travel to Europe.'

Julie shook her head. 'I don't understand.'

'I'm not entirely sure I do either.'

'Why on earth would he ask you?' Julie finished her cigarette, flicked it carelessly into the street below and followed Kate back inside. 'And why would he want to drag it all up again? I thought he was claiming Shirley Grove's internal inquiry had successfully buried the whole thing where the sun doesn't shine.'

'I have to admit I haven't entirely answered that question myself. His political opponents – inside the party and out – are never going to accept the word of an internal inquiry as they'll assume he's had some influence. I guess he and his team have realized it's still doing him some damage. Besides, there's been a new development. A Russian diplomat has come forward in Istanbul to say that she was tasked with seducing Sergei and covertly feeding him the information about that initial meeting on the super-yacht. She claims the whole thing was orchestrated by Moscow from the start with the help of a mole at the very top of the Service, known as Agent Dante.'

'Bullshit!' Julie thought about it some more, then repeated her assessment. 'Bullshit!' She looked at Kate. *'Right?'*

'Possibly.'

'Definitely. I mean, how convenient. The PM is rightly holed beneath the waterline by the suspicion he's a Russian agent of influence, so he and his handlers in Moscow come up with a new strategy to say it's all been a giant plot from the start!'

'Yes, but what if he's innocent?'

Julie gave her a long, cool look.

Kate was having trouble sitting still. She went to her desk, which she'd pushed into a pool of morning sunlight. She sat down again. 'They're going to rescind Stuart's right to travel outside Russia unless I agree to look into this,' she repeated.

'Do you want Stuart to travel outside Russia?'

'For the children's sake, I do. Not being able to see him for the rest of their lives would break them.'

'I didn't ask about the children.'

'I want closure. Clarity. I want us all to be able to get on with the rest of our lives without continuing stress and drama.'

'A politician's answer.'

'Maybe. But also the truth.'

Julie nodded. 'All right. What do you want me to do?'

'Help me.' Kate shrugged. 'We'll have to go over everything again. I'll need you to sift through a whole series of files.'

'Done.'

'Just like that?'

'Always.' Julie smiled at her. 'Have you heard the news?'

'What?'

'Ian's got it. They've made him C. And guess who has the Russia Desk?'

'You.'

'Don't be an idiot! *Suzy*. You think Ian's going to reward

me after what I did to him? He's still telling friends I broke his heart.'

'I don't believe it.' Suzy Spencer was Kate's former deputy, who'd been attached to the Service on secondment from MI5 after the death of Rav, her close friend and ally. Suzy was, on any reasonable analysis, an absolute snake.

'Yes, you do. She let Ian shag her at exactly the right time.'

A key turning in the lock signalled Shirley Grove's arrival, followed by a huge man carrying a Nespresso machine and a Waitrose bag full of every variety of milk. He unloaded it into the fridge before offering Julie his hand. 'Hi, Callum Ellis.'

They were momentarily lost for words. He was more than six feet tall, with shaggy dark hair, a rangy beard and a chiselled jawline that framed his face, which was about halfway between those of Daniel Craig and the late George Michael. He wore chinos and a tight T-shirt, beneath which his ripped biceps seemed to be struggling to escape.

Kate caught the slightest hint of a smile playing around Grove's lips. 'You want coffee?' he asked. He had a broad Mancunian accent, with a guttural, rough rasp.

They wanted it very badly.

'Jesus Christ,' Julie hissed, as he turned away. 'You could have warned me.'

'I'd never met him,' Kate whispered. 'He's Grove's sidekick.'

'Bloody hell. She's a dark horse.'

Callum slipped into barista mode and they moved to the conference table Grove had installed in the back room.

'All right,' Grove said. 'Callum is going to need to start from scratch.'

'From the very beginning?'

'Yes.'

'My name is Kate Henderson and, until very recently, I was head of SIS's Russia Desk. Julie worked with me. We had a source I'd known from my days as a student in St Petersburg who had been posted to the Russian Embassy in London. His previous assignment had been in Istanbul and he told me he'd learnt while there that the cream of the Russian intelligence hierarchy routinely gathered on a super-yacht owned by Igor Borodin, the former head of their foreign intelligence service, in the summer months. We recruited a young nanny to work with Igor's son. She managed to plant a bug on the yacht.'

Callum was looking at her intently. He didn't seem to blink.

'That was where we overheard the suggestion that the former prime minister had prostate cancer and was about to resign. It was clear from the drift of the conversation that one of the leading candidates to replace him was a Russian agent of influence. Our subsequent investigations led us to believe very strongly that this was James Ryan. And, in the course of that process, we also discovered that my husband Stuart was working for Moscow and quietly assisting him. He is now in exile.'

Kate took a sip of her coffee. 'A few months later, we got a message from Igor Borodin that there had been some kind of coup in the securocrat class in Moscow that had left him vulnerable. He said he wanted to defect and would bring with him firm evidence of the prime minister's treachery in the form of the sex video used to blackmail him.'

'The underage girls in Kosovo?' Callum asked.

'Yes. In the course of overseeing that defection in Georgia, I discovered that my children had been kidnapped back here, apparently by gangsters Moscow had hired. I had to abandon Borodin and return to London. The defection did not go ahead.'

'Your children were all right?'

'I suppose it depends on your definition of all right, but they're alive, which is more than I can say for the poor nanny we used in Istanbul and my deputy, Rav, who were casualties along the way.'

'So this new evidence suggests that the original conversation on the super-yacht was a set-up to fool us and Borodin never intended to defect, merely to plant more damaging material in the British system in the form of this video?'

'Yes.' Kate reached for a felt tip and headed for the whiteboard at the end of the room. 'Which brings us to the latest twist. An apparent Russian intelligence agent has approached one of our diplomats in Istanbul to claim that this entire business was indeed a giant misinformation ploy conceived years ago to create disorder, confusion and bitterness within the British political system, just as we have seen in America in recent years.'

'You think what we saw in the US was *all* misinformation?'

'That's a long story for a different discussion. Some was, some wasn't. But they win either way, because we lose sight of what the truth is. And along the way, we turn against ourselves, and the consensus upon which all democracies ultimately depend is lost.' Kate scrawled 'Agent Dante' at the top of the board. 'This mysterious Russian source in

Istanbul claimed there is a traitor at the very top of SIS in London, who has helped Moscow orchestrate this operation from the start. Agent Dante. That is why we're supposed to be conducting this inquiry entirely outside the remit of our existing intelligence services – both SIS and the Security Service.' Kate looked at him. 'The question is, if the prime minister is innocent, how do we prove it? Our best chance is to find out who Agent Dante is and expose how he, or she, has been able to cause so much havoc.' On the left-hand side of the board, Kate wrote 'Cyclone'. 'So, how do we begin the search for someone who has remained successfully hidden for many years? I think here, winding back in time to Operation Cyclone.'

'Go on,' Grove said.

'Shortly after I joined the Service, I was working on an op tracking an early Al Qaeda affiliate in Istanbul – where all roads seem to lead right now – when I was approached through our station chief, Yusuf, by a young Russian KGB translator called Irina, who wanted a new life in the West. It was 1997 and the former Soviet Union was still in turmoil, so it was fairly easy to pick up KGB agents, but I dutifully passed on the approach to Ian Granger, head of the Russia Desk at the time, and thought no more about it. I assumed we'd turned her down.'

Kate stared at the board for a moment and then wrote 'David Snell'. 'Fast forward to last year and, while we were investigating the prime minister's alleged Russian links, Rav and I started to look into this guy, who had helped the PM facilitate some rather nebulous "consultancy" work in Africa after his stint in the army.'

'I'm not sure I'm following,' Callum said.

'Forget the detail. It doesn't matter right now. We were trying to work out the source of the prime minister's unexplained wealth. The key thing is that Snell told us SIS had looked into all this years ago. Rav and I were pretty dumbfounded. When I got back to the office, I discovered that the investigation had been shut down by the chief, Sir Alan Brabazon.'

Kate let that sink in. 'The obvious question was why,' she said.

'And the less obvious answer?'

'I discovered that, far from turning down Irina the KGB translator, Ian had reeled her in and touted her around the bazaars as a revelatory find. She seemed to have access to an ever-increasing supply of grade-A intelligence, including details of a KGB sting on the German finance minister, who had some pretty sordid habits.' Kate sighed. 'To cut a very long story short, Sir Alan gave this information to James Ryan, by then foreign secretary, who used it as some crude negotiating tactic with the Germans. They angrily exposed it as fake. Ryan looked a fool and was livid. Shutting down the investigation into his Africa links was the price – implicit or explicit, I'm not sure which – for keeping Sir Alan and Ian in their jobs.'

'How did you find that out?' Callum asked.

'I'd prefer not to say.'

'You have your sources?'

'I've worked for the organization a long time.'

'How does that have any bearing on what's happened in the past year?' Callum wondered.

'The truth is, I don't know. I just have a hunch that this was where it began. It's the same kind of play. It has

Borodin's fingerprints all over it. They used Irina to lure us in, set us up and then deliver the sucker punch. It worked so well, I think they ended up wanting more of the same. Only this time, they went for a much bigger, bolder plan.' Kate tapped her pen against the board. 'I think it started here, with Operation Cyclone.'

'So what you're really saying,' Grove said, 'is that Agent Dante has been in place for twenty years or more.'

'Yes.'

'How can you be sure that these events are connected?' Callum asked.

'I can't. But in intelligence work, you have to rely on your instincts. If things seem to fit a pattern, then there's a high chance they're connected, even if you can't immediately see how.'

'And Dante, whoever he or she is, is in a senior enough position to be able to orchestrate these operations within SIS?'

'Yes. Or at least to take a view on how they might pan out and help them with intelligence on the personnel involved.'

'Do you have suspects?' Callum asked.

Kate turned back to the whiteboard. 'That's where it gets complicated. If I'm right, the obvious suspects are the former head of the Service, Sir Alan Brabazon, and his successor, Ian Granger. They're the only two who have been on the Russia Desk – or connected to it – consistently throughout this period.'

Grove folded her reading glasses and walked up to the whiteboard. In another life, Stuart might have described her as not built for speed, but she was surprisingly light on her feet. 'I'm sorry to say your list isn't quite complete.' She reached for Kate's pen and, with deft but precise strokes of its felt tip, added a third name.

Henderson.

Kate stared at her name on the board. Was that what all this was about? Had Grove and the prime minister always intended to help her fashion a noose so they could hang her with it? She took a cloth, wiped the board clean and walked out.

6

SHIRLEY GROVE CAUGHT up with her on the balcony. 'What on earth are you playing at?' Kate asked.

'You know how these inquiries work,' Grove said, without turning a hair. 'Every aspect of our work may be scrutinized at a later date, so we need to cover every base. It's just box-ticking. You shouldn't take it personally.'

'So we haven't even started this investigation and you're already planning how it's going to look when you leak it?'

'I don't believe I said that.'

'You didn't need to. I get it. Your job is to clear the prime minister. Much better if the person who initiated this whole sorry business turns out to have been its architect, so I can see I make a tempting culprit.'

'My job is to find the truth.'

Kate looked up at Grove. The older woman was a couple of inches taller and about a stone heavier. 'So tell me, how am I supposed to investigate myself?'

'Don't be absurd.'

Kate leant against the balcony wall. 'I'm sorry, I genuinely don't understand.'

'You're going to investigate as we asked you to do.' Grove's irritation was beginning to show. 'Exactly as you see fit. You've identified your two prime suspects. Callum and I will pursue any lines of inquiry relating to you as and when we deem it appropriate.'

'So while I investigate my former colleagues in the Service, you're going to be rifling through my underwear drawer?'

'It's a bureaucratic exercise, Kate.'

'It doesn't sound like one. And don't call me Kate.'

Grove took a step closer. Her demeanour was suddenly softer, almost motherly. 'Come on, don't make an issue of this. I'm just going through the motions. It doesn't need to hold you – or us – back.'

'You must be out of your mind.' Kate went back inside. 'I quit.'

She was reaching for her coat when Grove played her ace. 'If you do that, we'll arrest your husband the moment he sets foot outside Russia.'

Kate faced Grove again. 'You're not as nice as you look, you know that?'

'I certainly have a job to do, Mrs Henderson. But you're wrong to identify me as the enemy, and I think you're smart enough to know that.'

'You want me to spend the next month making a rope so that you and the prime minister can publicly hang me with it?'

'I want you to spend the next month working out who

orchestrated this monstrous assault on the probity and integrity of British public life so we can expose him or her and move on. Since I think we both assume it wasn't you, I don't see the issue.'

The door to the back room had been opened and Julie stood there, with young Callum towering over her. 'Shall we go?' she asked.

Kate's every instinct told her to get out now. But she bit her lip, narrowed her eyes and focused hard on the floor. 'For Fiona and Gus . . .' she whispered to herself. When she looked up again, she was wearing her best game face. 'Let's take a walk,' she said.

'Good thinking,' Julie replied.

Early falling leaves and a few spots of rain swirled in the fresh breeze as they stepped outside. The streets in the heart of Pimlico were quiet at this time of the day, the sky grey, the air close.

'Well, that was the shortest investigation we've ever conducted,' Julie said, once they were well away from the house.

'I have to go on with it,' Kate said.

'Because of Stuart?'

Kate didn't answer.

'No one can fault your devotion to those kids.' Julie's eyes were still on her. 'Ah . . . not just the kids, then?'

'Give me a cigarette.'

'Only when you've spilt the beans.'

'I honestly don't know whether I'm really responding to their desperation that we get back together. Or—'

'You shagged him?'

Kate fished a cigarette out of Julie's packet and lit it without breaking stride. 'I'm not sure I'd put it quite like that,' she said.

'I knew you would. You're an idiot.'

'And you, have you got back together with Ian?'

'God, no.' Julie shook her head vigorously. 'I mean, he wants to, obviously. He actually sent me a poem the other day, though I know for a fact he's still with Suzy. A poem!'

'Was it any good?'

'It was, quite. But that's hardly the point. He's the head of SIS, and he's sending a junior officer lovelorn poetry. I still can't knit those two things together in my head.'

'It's all right to admit you're upset, you know.'

Kate had spoken softly and Julie drew to a halt and faced her. She didn't often allow anyone a window on her soul, still less the vulnerabilities that lay within it. 'I don't know what I feel,' she said. 'That's the truth. I'm not sure if I'm upset. And that really troubles me. I mean, what if I've lost the ability to feel anything?'

'Didn't you once tell me he was a much better listener than anyone who had ever worked for him might guess?'

'Did I?'

Kate smiled. 'You know you did. So maybe the answer for both of us is to accept that it's okay to miss part of someone but not the whole.'

Julie gathered a few leaves beneath her shoe and crushed them methodically. 'I'll tell you something. If Agent Dante actually exists, it's not Ian,' she said.

'What makes you so sure?'

'He's too much of a coward.'

'Isn't that what they play on?'

'Sometimes. But I think he'd just be way too terrified of the consequences of getting caught. He's smarter and sometimes kinder than people think, but he's not brave, and he never has been.'

'He may have had to settle for the lesser of two evils, or been flattered at a time when he felt he was being ignored by his own people – you know how complex these things are. Or maybe the vulnerability you think you saw was just an act.'

Julie threw away her cigarette, as if she'd never wanted it. 'All right. You won't want to hear this, but here goes. I don't think you should do this. Stuart's freedom isn't worth risking your health and life for, even for the sake of your children.'

'I've no choice.'

'Yes, you have. This is just you trying to keep everyone but yourself happy again. You can walk away with Fiona and Gus and leave Stuart to stew in his own juice. He betrayed you, your marriage, your family – everything you hold dear. You don't owe him a thing. Grove and her puppet-master want to stiff you – that's blindingly obvious. Every step we take, they'll be looking to twist it away from the truth, whatever that may be, and into another strand of the noose they're weaving for you. And by the time we get to the end of this affair, it'll be too late to turn back,' Julie said. 'It won't be Stuart in prison, it'll be you. Because they don't want this to go away quietly, an embarrassing page turned in the Service's history. They want the full, glaring publicity of a show trial so that everyone is convinced of the prime minister's innocence.'

Kate watched an old woman dragging a shopping trolley

very slowly down the pavement. She tried to shake the sense that Julie might well be right.

'But you're about to tell me you're going to plough ahead regardless, which leads me to the inescapable conclusion that you *are* still in love with Stuart.'

'It's more complicated than that.'

'You're telling yourself it is. You don't want to let down your kids, or destroy their fragile hope of a reunion. But I know you. There are few people in the Service more ruthless when the chips are down, and I think you're standing here because you don't want to close the door on the possibility of a future together.'

'What if you're right?'

Julie took a deep breath. 'Then we crack on and we beat Grove, the PM and their eerily handsome aide at their own game. You're much smarter than they are. It'll be a piece of cake.'

'You're a good friend, you know that?'

'I do, yes. And you're welcome. And you owe me, obviously. So give me a plan.'

'All right.' Kate slipped her hands into her pockets. Considering this as a game she could win made it seem far more manageable. 'I'll need Ian and Sir Alan's personal files.'

'How am I going to get those?'

'Grove can help. She can make it look like a routine Whitehall bureaucratic exercise connected to Ian's elevation. We'll go through each one job by job and year by year. You also need to hoover up everything that relates to Operation Cyclone and the KGB translator, Irina. A lot of it's locked away, but see what you can dig up. You'll need to see what you can get on Natasha Demidova as well, our potential SVR informant in Istanbul. I'll ask Grove to rustle up Tess Winkelman's file too.'

'Who's she?'

'The diplomat the Russian woman made contact with. Then go home. I'll see you at Heathrow tomorrow at ten.'

'Where are we going?'

'Istanbul. I want to see the whites of this woman's eyes.'

'Sergei's former lover, you mean.' Julie gave her a lop-sided smile. 'Oh, boy, this should be interesting.'

7

SHIRLEY GROVE APPEARED surprisingly open to securing Sir Alan's and Ian's records and didn't request Kate's own in the process. Perhaps she already had them. Kate also successfully blocked Grove's presence in Istanbul. She had to accept young Callum as a substitute, but that wouldn't be a hardship.

She had bigger problems on the home front. Since her departure from the Service, Kate had relieved her aunt of the need to stand in with Fiona and Gus. Rose had responded with her habitual fortitude and selflessness by taking some of the burden of dealing with Kate's mother, Lucy, whose condition and behaviour were deteriorating by the week.

So, it was no surprise when Rose's husband Simon pointed her towards Lucy's care home, where she found Rose with Jane Dillon, the long-suffering manager, listening to Lucy rant through the closed door to her apartment at no one in particular. 'Bitch,' she hissed. 'Bitch.'

'Is she talking about me?' Kate asked.

'Me, I think.' Rose rewarded her with a thin smile. 'She bit Ellen again.'

'Oh, God.' Kate's lingering fear was that her mother would be expelled from the premises and she would be forced to deal with her at home. It didn't help that Ellen, like a lot of the staff, was black, and her mother had emerged as a not-so-closet racist. 'I'll deal with her.' Kate calculated her best chance of retaining the status quo was to take command. 'I'll read her the mother and father of all Riot Acts.'

'We understand she's not in her right mind,' Jane Dillon said, 'but I can't condone assaults on our staff, or putting them at risk. I'm sure you understand.'

'Of course.'

Jane hesitated for a moment, as if about to add something, then tactfully withdrew.

'I'll deal with her,' Kate told Rose. 'You've done enough.'

'She is . . . *wearying*. I don't know how you've put up with it all these years.'

'Dr Wiseman's given me strict instructions. I'm to view her as an object of pity.' Wiseman was the psychiatrist Rose had finally prevailed upon Kate to see a few months earlier. He'd been a revelation.

'All right,' Rose said. 'Call me later.' She kissed her niece.

'I hate to ask you another favour,' Kate said, as she turned away.

Rose smiled. 'Anything. You know that.'

'I've got dragged back into something. Work wise, I mean. I was wondering if you'd be able to step into my shoes at home for another couple of weeks. I give you my word it'll be for the very last time.'

Rose frowned. 'What have you been "dragged back" into?'

Kate had debated all the way through Battersea Park what she was going to tell her aunt, who, as Head of Finance, was still a senior member of MI6 as well as a second mother to her. She opted in the end for qualified candour. 'I've been asked to conduct another inquiry.'

The surprise and alarm on Rose's face were so marked that Kate beckoned her to an alcove. They sat knee to knee. 'Look, I know what you'll say,' she said.

'You had a breakdown, Kate. And, yes, you've emerged from it stronger. But I'm pretty sure Dr Wiseman would consider any step back nothing short of madness, particularly in the new climate,' Rose said. 'I'm relatively insulated in Finance, but I'm not sure even I'm going to be able to tough it out. Ian's only been in charge a few days and the atmosphere has turned on a sixpence.'

'I'm not coming back to the Service.'

'Then what?'

Kate hesitated for only a moment. 'The prime minister is still desperate to clear his name. He thinks that, since I don't believe in his innocence, I'm best placed to prove it.'

'But you already gave evidence to the internal inquiry!'

'That hasn't neutralized his critics. He's asked me to conduct an external investigation, though it's obviously deeply confidential.' Kate often found candour became less and less qualified in her aunt's company, but she knew this was as far as she could and should go.

Rose seemed utterly bemused. 'I just don't understand. Why, after all you've been through, would you even consider—'

'He said if I didn't cooperate he'd rescind Stuart's right to travel and put out a warrant for his arrest if he leaves Moscow.'

Rose sighed. 'What a bastard. And Stuart . . . My God, how much trouble has that man been. You know, perhaps it is time you left him to his own devices.'

'I can't do that to Fiona and Gus.'

There was a long silence. 'Is having Stuart free to come and go from your life what you want? I mean what *you* want?' She raised a hand. 'Actually, park that. Let's discuss it another time. You know, it's pretty inevitable that Ian will learn sooner or later that you're conducting another investigation. He'll consider it a threat to him, one way or another, since he tends to assume anything he didn't initiate or approve is. He'll conclude it's your initiative, designed to discredit his conduct and curry favour with Number Ten.'

'He will.'

'I'll cover your back as best I can but—'

'I'm not asking you to do that.'

'You of all people know what he's like, Kate. He's already withholding more from the management committee. I don't think he actually trusts any of us.' Rose stared out at the gathering darkness. 'I was trying to find a way to tell you this, but he's attempting to block Lena's sister and her new adoptive parents coming here.'

'He can't.' Lena was the nanny Kate had recruited to put the bug on the super-yacht in Istanbul and she'd taken her death hard. Saving her sister from the dismal life that awaited her in Belgrade was the last promise she'd made to the girl before her murder.

'He can. I cleared the finance with the management committee before Alan left. I'd sent the authorization to

Erna in Belgrade and the wheels were being set in motion. I was going to tell you just before they arrived, in case you wanted to form a welcoming committee, but this morning Ian put a block on it.'

'Why?'

'His ostensible reason is a budget shortfall and he doesn't want to have to ask Number Ten for a subvention. But the real reason is that he thinks it was your "mess" and he doesn't see why he should pay to clean it up when there are so many other financial pressures.' Rose stood. 'Look, I'll suggest a meeting between the three of us and Sir Alan. Ian will find it more difficult to refuse if we act as a concerted bloc.' She kissed her niece's head tenderly. 'I'm sure you know what you're doing, but please be careful.' She fastened her raincoat and disappeared into the gloom.

Kate was very far from certain that she did know what she was doing and she had a keen sense that Rose, of all people, understood that.

She steeled herself and approached the lion's den.

Lucy was in one of her increasingly rare moments of lucidity. 'That woman is a gold-plated, diamond-encrusted bitch.'

Kate sighed. 'Which woman?'

'Rose, of course. Who else could I possibly mean?'

Oh, boy, the list is long, Kate thought. 'You mean your sister-in-law and my aunt,' she said. 'The one person who's helped keep me sane this past year. Brilliant.'

Lucy leant forward. 'Can't you see what she's doing?'

'You mean showing a degree of forbearance, selflessness and love?'

'She's trying to replace me.'

And doing a bloody good job of it, Kate thought. 'She's always been fond of us all. She's never forgotten the promise she made after Dad died. So she's—'

'She wants me out of the way so she can finally claim you exclusively as the daughter she never had.'

And it would be the least she bloody deserves. 'I'm going to have to ask you to stop this now.'

'I never liked her. Was it *my* fault she and that stupid millionaire husband couldn't have children? She always wanted to get her claws into you—'

'Be quiet!' It came out as more of a bark than Kate had intended but it had the desired effect. Lucy swallowed whatever insult she was about to hurl. 'Since you appear to have all your faculties today,' Kate continued, 'I need you to hear this. If you can't stop insulting the staff who are caring for you, you'll be booted out of this place. I can't look after you at home, so you'll have to go wherever else will take you. I've no idea where that might be, or what it will be like, but I'm fairly sure it won't be in London, which means the children and I will not be able to visit you any more.'

Lucy made the journey from acid abuser to chastened child in no more than a heartbeat – and carried off both with similar conviction. 'I'm sorry,' she said.

Kate sat down heavily on the chair opposite her. Was it better when her mother was lucid? She wasn't sure any more. She'd never been any good at riding the drastic and instantaneous personality and mood swings, which seemed to be exaggerated by her mental deterioration.

'I know I'm going to die soon.'

'You don't know that, Mum.'

'Of course I do. I may be demented, but I'm not stupid.' Lucy now seemed about to cry.

'Look, you've got to try,' Kate said. 'Really, really try not to insult or hurt anyone around you.'

'I get frightened and . . . frustrated.'

'I understand.'

'One always knows that one is going to die alone. It's in the nature of life, isn't it? The only sure outcome. I mean, even if you have someone holding your hand at the last, you still walk the final mile all by yourself. But I never expected it would be so *lonely*.'

'You're not there yet. The doctors say you may have years.'

'Of decline, incontinence, irrelevance. What kind of life is that?'

Kate tried to wrap her mind around the certainty that her mother's moments of clarity would soon disappear entirely and she would die.

'I'm sorry,' Lucy said again. 'You won't believe me, but I am. My frustration gets the better of me and then I can't seem to stop myself.'

Kate wanted to say there was nothing new in that, but she managed to hold her tongue. Normally, she'd offer to make tea and force herself to sit there for half an hour at least, but she couldn't face it today. 'I have to go away for a few days. Rose is at home, looking after the children, if there's an emergency.'

Kate left without kissing her mother. She tried to suppress the idea that it would be no bad thing if Lucy did die soon.

8

YOUNG CALLUM DISPLAYED a taste for luxury on their journey to Istanbul that was most unusual in a Whitehall civil servant. They travelled business class on Turkish Airlines and their pre-booked taxi delivered them to the shameless opulence of the Hotel Kempinski on the city's European shore.

He sensed something amiss as they waited to check in. 'Julie told me to book here,' he said. 'Apparently it was important.'

Kate smiled at Julie and took her to task ten minutes later when they met at the café beneath the palm trees on the terrace.

'Well, it is where it all started.' Julie grinned.

'You can't spend the next few weeks torturing him.'

'Oh, Lord, I can.' Her eyes sparkled. 'Besides, that's not what I have in mind at all.'

'No, no, no.' Kate shook her head. 'No. Seriously. No.'

'Now you're sounding like my father.'

'No.' Kate fixed her friend with a steady gaze. 'I really am serious. Absolutely not.'

Julie threw the cigarette packet across the table. 'Have a smoke and chill out, for God's sake.'

'I thought you were going out with Danny, anyway.'

Julie lit up. 'I am, sort of.' She shrugged. 'I mean, as far as these things go.'

'What's that supposed to mean?'

'It's none of your business, that's what it means.'

The waiter arrived and Julie ordered: 'Gin, Fever Tree tonic, lemon, ice.'

Kate said she'd have the same and they watched him weave his way back to the bar. 'This place is worth Shirley Grove's money. I've always wanted to stay here.'

'Whatever happened to the Ottoman Empire?' Julie asked, gesturing at their surroundings. She'd studied sociology at Manchester University and, despite being one of the smartest women Kate had met, liked to glory in ignorance outside her core interests.

'It collapsed.'

'I know that. How?'

'It joined the wrong side in the First World War.'

'I thought it rotted from within.'

'People used to think that. It did fall behind some of its rivals, like Russia, militarily. But it was still reasonably strong until it threw in its lot with the Germans. As even you will remember, that didn't end well for anyone.'

The waiter brought their drinks and Kate finally succumbed to the temptation of a cigarette. 'Give me what you have,' she said. 'Callum will be here in a moment.' This was the first chance they'd had to talk alone and out of ear-shot since meeting at Heathrow, so Julie knew exactly what her friend was driving at. 'Nothing at all on this Natasha Demidova. She's never appeared on our radar before.'

'Really?'

'I triple-checked.'

Kate pondered this. It was perfectly plausible that some-one might have flown beneath the radar. They certainly didn't have a record of every single member of the SVR's staff, but it was frustrating nevertheless. If the woman was a fake, the Russians would naturally have made sure she was a clean skin. The less they knew, the less able they would be to judge her motives and veracity. 'What about Irina and the original Operation Cyclone?'

'As you guessed, all closed down. The thing that's a tiny bit odd is that your part of the file is still open. The way Irina originally made contact with you at the Blue Mosque, your further meetings in the bazaar, and all your assessments of her potential are still open and intact, but there's no explan-ation of what happened next. No matter how many ways you go through the filing system, you hit a dead end.'

Kate frowned. 'What do you mean?'

'Operation Cyclone exists. There's a file, as you know. But if you read into it now, you'd think that it simply con-sisted of you being approached to assess this girl and report on her potential trustworthiness to the Russia Desk. That's it. That's the operation.'

'So someone hasn't just closed the gateway to what hap-pened next, it's now been removed from the system entirely?'

'Exactly.'

'So there's no mention at all of the way Ian took it

forward, ran with it, recruited her and used her intelligence to hold the German government hostage, with all those disastrous results?'

'Right again.'

Kate tried to make sense of this. Since the file had been closed when she'd looked into it months before, she could see no earthly purpose in going to the trouble of erasing it entirely. Unless, of course, Ian was systematically covering his tracks.

'What about today's star guest?' Julie said. 'Tess Winkelman.'

Grove had given Kate the diplomat's file but insisted it remain inside their new office in Cambridge Street. 'Nothing spectacular. Pretty strait-laced. Washington, London, Brussels, London, Istanbul. Smart, ambitious. Destined for one of the big ambassadorships at a pretty young age, I'd guess, though a bit of an up-and-down romantic life with what looked to me like a different lover in each posting, so maybe she's had her heart broken a few times or been forced to make difficult choices. No experience of Russia and no reason I can see as to why she would have been singled out.'

'Straight?'

'So it says.'

'Sorry I'm late. Ran down to the gym.'

They both looked up. Callum had changed out of his suit into chinos and a midnight blue T-shirt. He'd swept his hair back from his immaculately sculpted forehead.

'What – all the way down to the gym?' Julie asked.

He rewarded her with a grin. 'All the way.'

My God, Kate thought, he looked good enough to stop a supermodel at a hundred paces.

'Can I join you?' He gestured at their drinks.

'Fuck, no,' Julie said. 'Novices aren't allowed to drink on duty.'

'Funny,' he said easily. He gestured at the waiter, who darted over. 'A large beer, please.'

There was a moment's awkward silence as he settled his muscular frame into the delicate metal chair. 'Tell us,' Julie asked. 'How did you get your very important job in Downing Street?'

'I was with Mrs Grove at Transport.'

'So you're her man, or the prime minister's?'

'A bit of both. I left Transport to be one of the PM's advisers when he was at the Foreign Office.'

'I suppose you went to Cambridge, like Mrs Henderson here.'

'Aberystwyth. And then Harvard Business School.'

'So you always like to be a contradiction in terms?'

He smiled. 'How is that a contradiction?'

'Why did you get into politics?'

Callum gave her a long, cool stare. 'You actually want to know or is this just the game you play?'

'I want to know.'

'I was brought up by a single mum. My dad left when I was five after beating us both so badly we ended up in hospital. She was a cleaner, started her own business . . . I'll leave you to work out the rest.'

'Are you single?'

Kate almost spat her drink out. 'Jesus Christ, Julie, cut it out.'

'Very,' he said, and smiled again. He crossed his endless, perfectly toned legs. But now it was Kate he was grinning at.

'Enough.' Kate looked from Callum to Julie and back again.

'This is not a game,' she told them both. 'There's no reason to suppose we'll be at risk tonight, but the moment we try to make contact with Natasha Demidova, we're leaping into the unknown. And we have no back-up. So this is not a joke.'

Callum uncrossed his legs and gave her his full attention. He'd taken his ticking off well, even if it wasn't really intended for him. 'I understand that, Mrs Henderson.'

'There is risk. And if you've not absorbed that yet, I'm putting you on notice of it now.'

'Got it.'

'Yeah, I've been thinking about that,' Julie said. 'Is it wise to plunge into this alone? Couldn't we have asked for back-up from Five, or even the military, just not told them the reason?'

Kate's eyes flashed. 'No. We're on our own. All the way through. So if either of you have a problem with that, now's the moment to abandon ship.'

'Sounds like an adventure, Mrs Henderson.' Callum re-crossed his legs and tapped the side of his left trainer with his right hand. 'That's why I'm here.'

Callum had arranged to meet the diplomat Tess Winkelman at 1924. The restaurant had been founded by White Russians fleeing the revolution and recently been refurbished to bring a hint of modernity to the St Petersburg of the Tsars. 'Tess chose it,' Callum explained to forestall any questions, though a quick survey of the menu suggested it was a much less extravagant decision than the hotel. 'Apparently Garbo came here,' he went on. 'And Mata Hari. And Agatha Christie.'

'Together?' Julie asked.

'Yeah.'

'Really?'

'Of course not.'

She kicked him under the table.

Kate was about to reprimand her, but thought better of it. She'd played Julie's mother, older sister or schoolmistress too many times.

The restaurant's pristine chequerboard floor, tall gilt mirrors, white tablecloths and dozens of images from old Russia and Istanbul glittered in the light cast by the chandeliers. A bar was tucked beneath a wooden orchestral balcony at the far end of the room.

'From Russia with Love,' Kate said, interrupting a waiter's stately progress to demand their version of a Dirty Martini. Maybe a little too quickly: she was becoming aware that the days when she drank now vastly outnumbered those when she didn't.

Julie said she'd have the same and Callum ordered another beer. 'You want to watch her,' Julie said. 'She's a very, very bad influence.'

'How long have you worked together?' Callum asked.

'Too long,' Julie responded. 'Why do you ask?'

'You seem very comfortable with each other, which I guess is important in a world where no one trusts anyone.'

Tess Winkelman hurtled towards the table long before the waiter could do the honours. Less statuesque than the photograph in her Foreign Office file suggested, and prettier too, if you could ignore her distinctly Roman profile, she wore a fawn linen jacket, crumpled by the heat, and sunglasses instead of a hairband, though the light had been fading for hours. Vivid blue eyes sparkled as she introduced herself, though her handshake was perfunctory. She slipped her bag from her shoulder and sat heavily next to Julie, as if she'd been too long on her feet.

The introductions complete, Tess ordered water at the precise moment Kate and Julie were served their cocktails. She didn't bat an eyelid. 'I hope you approve of the venue,' she said. 'I thought it was charmingly appropriate, under the circumstances, and anyway, I come here quite often. The food is excellent.'

They ordered off the tasting menu, which offered Circassian Chicken, Beef Stroganoff and Chicken Kievsky, and kept resolutely to small-talk – the daily life of a diplomat in this ancient city, which sounded enviable – until the main course had been served. Kate took the plunge first. 'We'd be grateful if you could start at the very beginning. Leave out no detail, however apparently insignificant. We never know what's going to come in useful.'

Tess Winkelman toyed with her food for a moment. 'I suppose what strikes me when I think about it is the change in her demeanour. Either something along the lines she suggests did take place, or she's a highly competent actor.'

'Not unknown in the intelligence community,' Kate said.

'I'm sure,' Tess agreed, waving her fork. 'Look, I knew who she was, of course. As I'm sure you're aware, part of the briefing prior to taking up an appointment like mine involves instruction on known agents operating undercover for foreign intelligence networks.'

Kate wondered how it was that the Foreign Office appeared to have suspicions about Natasha Demidova that had not found their way into the SIS files.

Tess helped herself to a mouthful of chicken, chewed it slowly and swallowed. 'I first encountered her at the

Russian ambassador's Christmas reception the year before
last. But we were only introduced very briefly. Shortly after
that, I saw her at the tennis club I'd joined over in Bebek.'

'Does she play there regularly?' Kate asked.

'Every morning. And she's good. I mean, really good.
Might-once-have-considered-becoming-professional kind
of excellent. I can hit a ball myself – I once played Junior
Wimbledon – but she's at a whole different level. She usually played on the next-door court, mixed doubles, with a
woman from Slovak intelligence called Nela and two men,
who I think were also from the Russian Embassy.'

'Did you speak to her?'

'No, but . . . I don't know how to put this without sounding rather too pleased with myself, but I sensed a mutual
recognition of ability, if you see what I mean. After that,
we'd nod at each other now and then around the club.'

'But she never made any attempt at conversation?'

'No. The opportunity never quite arose. We were always
passing each other. She seemed like she moved everywhere
with purpose and confidence.'

'Until . . .'

'Well, that was the strange thing. One day her whole
demeanour changed. Now, you might say I never spoke to
the girl so how would I know her demeanour had changed,
but it did. I guess I'd seen her playing two or three times a
week for months and months, and suddenly she seemed to
move around the club in a quite different way. She played
tennis with the same four, or sometimes singles with one
of the guys. But she walked swiftly away afterwards, with
her head down – as if something terrible had happened.

'Anyway, I didn't think much about it – none of my business, after all – until we found ourselves on a weekend in Ankara with a spectacularly tedious group called International Women in Business. I have no idea what a Russian intelligence officer would be doing there, but we clocked each other during the day at one or two of the symposiums and then, after dinner with a couple of American diplomats I knew vaguely, I went for a nightcap and found her at the bar.'

'Did you strike up conversation, or did she?'

'She did. I went to order a drink and she moved to sit next to me. "On my tab," she told the waiter. To be honest, I was quite tired and wasn't all that up for an encounter with one of Putin's spooks, but there didn't seem any way out. She was drunk. And by the time I'd been there a while, very drunk indeed.'

'Intriguing,' Kate said.

'Mystifying, I thought. To begin with, I was fairly certain she was hitting on me. It wouldn't have been the first time at an event like that.'

Kate smiled.

'She appeared to be on the cusp of telling me something. And then she thought better of it and lurched off to bed. She struck me as a deeply unhappy woman.'

Julie had ordered a Barolo – the most expensive on the menu, if her performance so far on the trip was anything to go by – and they waited while the waiter replenished their glasses. Tess Winkelman continued to sip her water until he had glided away again.

'By now my interest was definitely piqued. And, fortunately, that interminable conference had a whole twenty-four hours to run, so I passed her a note the following morning inviting her to dinner. I suggested a time and a place that was well out of the way. She appeared to nod, but she never showed up. I was pretty disappointed, to be honest. I felt something quite important was about to land in my lap and had been snatched away.

'I came back to the hotel and looked into the bar, but she wasn't there either. I decided to write it off as a strange incident and headed to bed. And then, there she was, sitting on the balcony of my room with a bottle of whisky, two glasses and a packet of cigarettes on the table before her. "Take a seat," she said. I was annoyed and asked her what the hell she thought she was doing. She told me to relax. Claimed she couldn't say what she needed to say in any public space.

'So, against my better instincts, I took a seat, drank whisky and smoked, which I haven't done in years. And the story came tripping out. She said she wanted me to get a message to Downing Street that the operation to smear the prime minister had been dreamt up by Igor Borodin, the former head of the SVR in Moscow, working in conjunction with an Agent Dante at the heart of SIS. I said I found it all a bit hard to believe. Why was she telling me? I asked. Because, she said, she couldn't go through any of the normal channels. Agent Dante was so senior at SIS that any attempt to route the information through MI6 would lead to him being alerted.'

'Him?' Kate asked.

'That was what she said.'

'Are you sure?'

'Yes, but it might just have been a figure of speech.'

'Do you think she knew who Dante was?'

'She said she couldn't tell me.'

'Which means she didn't know.'

'Possibly.'

Kate nodded at her. 'Go on.'

'I asked her how she knew all this. She said because it had been her job to feed this information to one of her colleagues – a man called Sergei – who had a contact of his own high up in SIS who would likely fall for the entire operation.'

'Why?' Kate felt her cheeks reddening.

'She said the SIS officer was very ambitious. And in love with the conduit she was using.'

Kate wondered if Tess knew or had guessed that she was the officer in question.

'She said she and this Sergei had become lovers. And then he had died in mysterious circumstances while travelling from St Petersburg to Moscow. She said she was devastated and left fearing for her own life.'

'What did she want in return for this information?'

'Nothing.'

Kate tapped the table in front of her. 'Did you and Natasha become lovers that night?'

Now it was Tess Winkelman's turn to blush. 'I'm not sure that has anything to do with it. But, yes, as a matter of fact, we did.'

'Have you seen her since?'

'No. I mean, yes. We see each other at the tennis club every morning, but she's avoided running into me – or even meeting my eye.'

'Thank you, Miss Winkelman. You've been very helpful.'

An hour and a half later Kate, Julie and Callum had gathered in a corner of the terrace watching the bright lights shimmering off the waters of the Bosphorus. It was still warm and Julie was lathering herself with mosquito repellent. 'Gratuitous question on the sex,' she told Kate. 'But who'd have guessed it of old Tess? What a goat.'

'Goat?' Callum asked.

'You can talk,' Julie said. 'Your jaw almost hit the floor. You were panting at the very idea of it.'

Kate leant forward. 'Callum, in the nicest possible way, I need to speak to Julie for a minute, so would you mind?'

He uncrossed his legs and wiped the smile from his face. 'We're all in this together, Mrs Henderson. I have complete security clearance, as you know. And if we're going to come out of this in one piece, I reckon we need to decide now whether or not to trust each other.'

'With respect, I've known Julie a very long time, and we've been through a lot of dicey days together. You're young, new and very wet behind the ears.'

'I never had you for the patronizing kind, but fair enough. My observation still stands, though.'

Julie swilled the remains of her drink around the bottom of her glass, then gave him the laser treatment with her eyes.

'Please just give us a minute,' Kate said.

'No. I need to be in on it. Those are my instructions.'

'And these are mine.'

'I'm asking you to trust me.'

The distant hum of traffic and the whisper of the breeze off the Bosphorus made their presence felt in the silence that followed. Perhaps Callum was, Kate reflected, as tough as he looked. It might come in handy.

'I think we do trust him,' Julie eventually said.

Kate nodded. 'All right. But you should be warned, knowledge and trust haven't turned out to be of much value in this business to date.'

'You mean for your career?'

'I mean for my friend Rav, who was murdered in his apartment. I mean for my old friend Sergei, whose throat was cut on that train between St Petersburg and Moscow. I mean for my marriage, which is smashed to smithereens. You want me to go on?'

'No, I understand.'

'All right, we'll trust you,' Julie said. 'But you'd better make sure you don't betray that, or I'll put a bullet in you myself. Understood?'

'Completely.'

Kate leant back and gestured at Julie. 'All right, shoot.'

'Despite her taste for occasional Sapphic encounters,' Julie said, 'I'd say Tess was pretty straight. But we come back to the same thing. Isn't it all a bit *convenient*? The prime minister needs to be cleared of suspicion and here, hey presto, is the means of doing it.'

'Possibly, yes.'

'We should still try to track Natasha Demidova down. I don't see how we can really assess her until we can see the whites of her eyes.'

'Let's start at the tennis club tomorrow morning. Callum, could you hire a car and make sure you're back at the hotel for breakfast at seven? We'll go from there.'

Kate could tell Julie had more to say. 'Go on, spit it out,' she said.

'There's something else you should know, which I've been toying with telling you. Andrew has a new asset in Moscow.'

Andrew Blake was SIS's undeclared station chief, working undercover as head of Chancery. 'He – or she – is codenamed Incisor, and came online about two months ago.'

'Just after I left.'

'Yes. Ian's all over it like a rash, of course, but Andrew's in the driver's seat right now, and will be until he heads back to London at Christmas. Incisor's intel has been pretty good so far, the main revelation being that Igor Borodin never entirely retired from the Service and continues to run some kind of special unit. Incisor arranges travel for its operatives and occasionally picks up gossip that way.'

'What does the unit do?'

'It seems to be Borodin's own vehicle, and was set up years ago, but we don't yet know its precise purpose. So far as we can tell, he doesn't have to answer to Vasily Durov, but directly to the Kremlin and the Russian president.'

'But if they wanted to convince us that the whole thing was a set-up from the start,' Callum said, 'this would be the perfect moment to feed us tales of Igor Borodin's own top-secret unit.'

Kate and Julie looked at him with new respect. 'You're learning fast,' Julie said.

'I presume you didn't bring your whites,' Callum said. 'So text me your sizes.'

They both looked at him blankly.

'We'll be less conspicuous if we're actually playing ten-nis, right? Instead of just poking around for no good reason. Miss Winkelman can make up the four.'

9

CALLUM TURNED OUT to be better at logistics than couture. By seven, he had hired a compact Peugeot and three pristine sets of tennis kit. But that was where he'd faltered.

'I look like one of the Ugly Sisters,' Julie said, as she emerged on to the hotel forecourt.

'I'm not a miracle worker,' Callum replied.

'You cheeky bastard.'

Kate could see what her friend meant: their outfits were on the tight side. Perhaps Callum had done that deliberately.

Tess Winkelman was waiting outside the club wearing a stylish pair of Ray-Bans against the bright morning sunlight. 'I've had to move heaven and earth to get you in,' she said. 'You're normally only allowed one guest, so I said you were all newly arrived diplomats looking to join.'

The courts were clay, and housed in a cavernous, heavily air-conditioned dome. 'We're at the far end,' Tess said. 'And

I hope you're not going to let me down. I said you were all serious players.'

As it happened, Kate's small Quaker school had been heavily focused on sport and she had pretty much excelled at them all. In her last year, she'd been captain of the First VI, and if that didn't quite put her in Tess Winkelman's league, it allowed her to more than hold her own against her opponent's ferocious serve and heavy top-spin forehand. Callum had no trouble keeping up either.

It was only Julie they had to play around. Kate's friend and protégée was a natural sportswoman with an easy athleticism, but tennis is a game of patience and practice and Julie had evidently had the benefit of neither. She darted and cursed her way around the court to precious little effect.

They passed an hour easily enough and, as luck would have it, Natasha Demidova turned up on the next court but one, pitting herself against a machine that spat balls towards her consistent and devastating backhand.

They were careful not to rush their own game and waited for the Russian to grunt her way loudly through a final dozen returns, pick up her tracksuit top and stalk away towards Reception.

Kate played out the point and suggested they call it a day. They shook hands and walked towards the changing rooms, in time to catch sight of their quarry speeding out of the car park behind the wheel of a blue Audi A5.

'Shit,' Kate muttered, under her breath.

'You want to hold off until tomorrow?' Julie said.

'No.'

Kate wheeled right out of Reception, said a curt farewell

to Tess Winkelman, who seemed briefly to entertain the idea of joining them, then ripped the keys from Callum's hand and installed herself behind the wheel of their Peugeot.

'You think she knew who we were?' Julie asked.

'Yes.'

'How come?' Callum asked.

They both ignored him.

'Turning left ahead,' Julie said.

Kate accelerated hard until they were close enough to sit comfortably on the Russian's tail. They swung down on to a road that curved around the edge of the Bosphorus and hurtled towards the 15 July Martyrs Bridge.

'She's going somewhere she can dry-clean,' Julie said.

'What's that?' Callum asked, from the back.

'To check she's not being followed – or, in this case, to work out who we are, who we work for and how many there are of us.'

'How does she do that?'

'Goes somewhere she can move from quiet places to crowded streets and back again. In the former, she works out how many of us there are. In the latter, once she knows how many pursuers she has, she can take a look at us and lose us if she decides she wants to.' Julie turned to Kate. 'She'll use the bazaar or İstiklal Avenue and Taksim Square – or maybe both.'

Kate thought of the last meeting with Lena in the Grand Bazaar before she had forced her aboard Igor Borodin's super-yacht. It had been Kate's call to recruit Lena, to bully and blackmail her into working for SIS and push her head first into the lion's den.

'I know what you're thinking,' Julie said. 'It wasn't your fault.'

Kate glanced at her friend. She was assailed suddenly by the visceral image of Lena's naked body stuffed in a wardrobe on the Greek island of Andros. Hadn't she, on some level, always known how it would end? 'I appreciate the sentiment,' she said, 'but we both know it was.'

'What's happening with Maja?' Julie asked.

Kate thought of the locket Lena had asked her to give her young sister in Belgrade once they'd made good on their promise to bring her into the UK. It was still burning a hole in her pocket.

'Still waiting,' Kate said.

'I bumped into your aunt outside Ian's office the other day. I asked her about it. She said, "Soon." '

'I'm keeping up the pressure,' Kate said. She didn't want to get into Ian's attempts to block the whole thing.

Julie had been right about Natasha Demidova's target. The Russian pulled into a car park close to the bazaar and emerged a few moments later on to Yeniceriler Street.

'Just wait here,' Kate instructed Callum, as she and Julie got out. 'We'll have to play tag,' she told Julie. 'I want her to know it's only the two of us, so don't make any effort to hide yourself. I'll go first.'

Clutching her bag to her right shoulder, Natasha's progress was hurried, broken, radiating nervousness. She'd thrown a pink cardigan over her tennis whites, but still stood out from the crowd. Kate wondered if they were being set up, but decided it was too late to turn back now.

The Russian swung into Çadircilar Street and strode through a profusion of stalls selling jeans, T-shirts and mountains of fake handbags, watches and designer apparel of every possible kind. Kate had to take an age selecting a denim jacket for her daughter as she waited for Natasha to emerge from the book bazaar opposite.

Julie brushed past her. 'Should we go in?'

'No.'

Natasha reappeared and hurried off, with Julie now taking the lead in her pursuit. They plunged through the Beyazıt Kampüsü Gate, past the moneychanger owned and run by SIS's Istanbul station chief, where Kate had tried to boost Lena's flagging courage before sending her to her doom.

It was a moment before Kate realized Julie had stopped to browse at one of the jewellery stores so she could take over again. She pulled herself together and strode on through the thronged alleyways. Her white and pink target wove nimbly through the tourists and shopkeepers trying to lure her into their dens.

A young man sidled up alongside her. 'Can I offer you something you don't need?' He had sallow features, a drooping moustache, much too old for his years, and a lopsided grin.

'Nice try,' Kate said.

'It has a proven track record,' he said.

'Not today, my friend.'

'But life is for living today, is it not? And I have something that would look peerless on that delectable wrist.'

Perhaps she was getting rusty, or blunted by the emotional burden of Lena's memory, but Kate was off the pace and suddenly afraid she'd lost Natasha. She brushed the man away and stopped at a crossroads, scanning the alleys around her, the excited hubbub of the crowds bouncing off the beautiful mosaic domes. She'd reached the central section of the bazaar now, where the stores were loaded with copperware of all shapes and sizes, and bashed into a young man hurrying along with a delicately balanced tray of coffee and apple tea.

She was recoiling from his curses when she felt Julie's reassuring presence at her elbow. 'Easy, Kate. She turned right ahead.'

Julie took the lead again and Kate breathed a sigh of relief as they hurried on. They watched Natasha browse in a silver store and, later, in booths selling inlaid boxes and painted glass. Julie let Kate catch up with her. 'My God, we look like bloody amateur hour. Why don't we just go and talk to her?'

'We need to wait until we're sure she's comfortable.'

They did as Kate instructed until Natasha installed herself in one corner of Şark Kahvesi, a coffee shop with patterned tablecloths and garish wallpaper close to the market entrance. The place was full of old men reading their morning newspapers beneath a couple of wooden ceiling fans.

Kate led Julie direct to the table.

'I ordered you Turkish coffee and some baklava,' Natasha said. 'I hope you're hungry.'

It was only when they sat down that Kate took in just how attractive Natasha Demidova was. She had a fine nose, Slavic cheekbones, long eyelashes and flawless skin. Her face lit up when she smiled.

'I thought your surveillance was so amateur, you must be Italian or French,' the Russian said. 'But then I thought,

Ah, no, two *British* intelligence officers, but on their own. Correct?'

'It was a pretty pointless game. I've never seen anyone in tennis whites try to lose themselves in a crowd.'

'Then how limited your experience has been. I can lose myself wherever, whenever and however I wish to.'

Kate bit her lip. Julie nudged her underneath the table.

'You *are* from British intelligence, I assume?' Natasha said. 'I've been waiting for you.'

'We're from a special unit set up to investigate the information you passed to Tess Winkelman. That's why we don't have back-up.'

'Just the two of you?'

'More or less.'

'I can see how seriously you are taking this.'

Kate couldn't stop herself bridling. 'We're taking your observations on security very seriously, which is why the unit is small and has travelled here without support.'

Natasha lit a cigarette and pushed the packet across towards them. Julie took one, but Kate restrained herself. The Russian rested her perfectly formed elbows on the table. 'You don't need me to tell you that Istanbul is crawling with every foreign intelligence agency on the planet, most of which know me well. So, whatever you want, get on with it.'

'We're trying to establish why you would share such secrets with a total stranger,' Kate said.

'Because they killed my lover. And I adored him.'

Kate felt the blood rush to her face and was only saved by the arrival of Turkish coffee and enough baklava to feed an army.

'And,' Natasha continued, 'I knew that a play-it-by-the-book diplomat like Tess Winkelman would do exactly as I asked and take the information straight to your prime minister.'

Kate stared at her coffee, stirring it carefully. She hadn't expected Sergei's lover to be quite so alluring in the flesh. 'How do you know they killed him?' she asked.

Natasha fixed Kate with a steady gaze. 'Trust me, he was as fit as a stallion. There is no possibility on God's earth that he died suddenly of a heart attack.'

Kate wondered if Natasha knew what had really happened that night on the train from St Petersburg to Moscow. Was she aware that Kate had been with Sergei moments before his death?

'We'd be grateful,' Julie said, filling the silence, 'if you could tell us everything you know.'

'You want me to repeat the same story?'

'If you would, Miss Demidova,' Julie said. 'Tess Winkelman is not an intelligence officer. We really need to hear it first-hand.'

'What can you do for me?'

Julie glanced at Kate. 'What are you looking for?'

'Asylum, if it comes to that. If I need it.'

'Agreed,' Kate said.

Natasha looked taken aback. 'You will need higher authority—'

'This unit was set up by the prime minister personally, and given all necessary measures. You have our word.'

Natasha stubbed out her cigarette and tapped painted nails on the table. Her hands, like the rest of her, were precisely manicured.

'Is asylum what you want?' Kate asked.

'I don't know what I want,' Natasha said, keen, suddenly, to get down to business. 'Let's just see it as an insurance policy. As you know, my role here is a cover. I am a mid-ranking SVR officer and I think you would best describe me as a protégée of Igor Borodin.'

'In what sense?'

'He made a point when he was chief of seeking out attractive young women for rapid promotion, at a price most of us were too young and naive to refuse.' Her bitterness, or anger, was almost palpable. 'I consequently spent more time than I should have in Moscow, paying that price flat on my back, but my reward was a position in Special Unit 61a, which reported directly to Igor himself.'

'Why 61a?'

'It was the office next to his suite on the top floor of the SVR building.'

'How many people worked there?'

'Perhaps forty or fifty, including support staff. Its work was highly secretive, with rigid boundaries between each section. I was brought in to work on Operation Alexander, which is what you have come to discuss, and which had, by then, been in the planning for some considerable time.'

'How long?'

'I joined the unit in 2015 and worked there for three years. I didn't have access to all the original case files, but I got the impression that the work dated back five years or more. Some of the people in my section were on long-term secondment to the unit.'

Kate considered again the convenient way information

appeared to come to her in choreographed patterns. No sooner had Julie told her about the SIS Moscow station chief's new agent Incisor and his allegations of a special unit run by Igor Borodin than here, apparently, was independent confirmation. Was this a window on the truth, finally, or just another turn of the misinformation dial?

'Although it was never discussed – indeed, it was expressly forbidden to talk about anything at all with other members of the unit, or even socialize with them – I had the impression that everyone in 61a was working on material that originated from or involved Agent Dante at the heart of MI6 in London.'

'Did the unit still report to Igor Borodin after he retired as head of the SVR?'

'Yes, primarily, though I think he and Durov worked together on it. Vasily was Igor's close ally anyway, so the truth is Igor never really retired. He became like a chairman, running the best and most sensitive material and leaving the hard grind to his successor.'

'Talk us through Operation Alexander.'

Natasha shrugged. 'I told Miss Winkelman about it. Other units were dealing with subversion in all the European democracies and in America, but because of Dante and his position in MI6 – and the quality of intelligence and insight he was able to provide us with – 61a was by far the biggest and most important unit of its kind, and Alexander was its most significant operation, with maybe half the staff working on it. By the time I arrived, you had already been identified as the principal conduit.'

She tried not to let her humiliation show. 'Why, if you don't mind me asking?'

'You were considered ambitious, single-minded, conscientious. And your unrequited love for Sergei Malinsky was viewed as an Achilles heel that we could exploit.'

The word 'unrequited' was like a blow to Kate's solar plexus. 'But I'm not sure I understand. Sergei was a GRU officer. Even if he'd been honest about our past friendship, how would the SVR have been aware of it?' The GRU was Russia's military intelligence arm and the rivalry between the two services was legendary. 'Or are you saying they worked together?'

'We hate each other, as you well know.'

'So how could the SVR have been aware of our past friendship?'

'I don't know. You had been identified as the conduit before I joined the unit, so I wasn't involved in those discussions. Maybe Dante recommended you. My job was to seduce Sergei and make sure he was aware that Igor Borodin was in the habit of hosting the cream of Russia's intelligence hierarchy on his yacht in the late summer every year. We were confident Sergei – and you – would do the rest.'

Kate thought of one of the prime minister's first questions to her in the South of France: who in the Service could have known of your friendship with Sergei?

The answer was very few. Yes, the friendship was technically listed in her personnel files, but not its depth and affection.

'But nobody foresaw the possibility that you would fall in love with him?' Julie asked Demidova.

'Exactly. I was sent to Istanbul, where he was based and, well . . .' She gave Kate a knowing look. 'You understand.'

'How come Sergei was posted to London?' Julie asked. 'The SVR can't have arranged that.'

'They already knew that was to be his next job. He had only a few months left in Istanbul by the time I arrived.'

'You must have had to work fast,' Kate said, and regretted it.

Natasha smiled at her. 'I don't think that becomes you, Mrs Henderson.'

Kate tried to smile back. 'Who is Agent Dante?'

Natasha shook her head regretfully.

'You said "his".'

'I think so.'

'Why?'

'I asked Igor about Dante once in one of our sessions. That was when he said "he", but I have no more to go on than that. Maybe it was a generic expression. In Moscow, all agents are generally referred to as "he".'

'You must have formed a view of who he *might* be, based on the type of material you were getting?'

Natasha started to tap her nails on the table again, staring over Kate's shoulder into the middle distance. 'I know he was recruited in New York sometime in the nineties.'

'How?'

'Because the only way I could piece together any clues as to his identity was from what Igor told me and the email traffic that referred to my own small part in Operation Alexander.' Her eyes flashed. 'Igor once let slip he had spent a lot of time in New York in the mid-nineties. I asked what he had been doing there and he just smiled. And then a couple of emails I had in one particular trail referred to some early intelligence Dante had provided on events in

Bosnia. A later email referenced the depth of material he had provided on the Americans' attitude to a particular UN resolution.'

'Not much to go on,' Kate said.

'If you had read the email trail, I think you'd have reached the same conclusion.'

'Do you—'

'I have notes.'

They stared at her.

'Not printed. That would be suicide. But stored in a notebook.'

'Could we—'

'I can give you an hour. I will meet you here at the same time tomorrow. Then I am done. And I want to know you will hold good on the offer of asylum if I ever need it.'

'Agreed.' Kate nodded. 'Agreed, of course.'

10

'HAVE YOU NOTICED,' Julie said, as soon as they were safely back in the car, 'that at every step of this business we strike what appears to be intelligence gold? I know we've worked at it, but it just falls into our lap every time and it *is* dazzling. Except that the real truth is like a mirage that fades further and further into the distance.'

'You drive,' Kate instructed Callum.

He handed her his phone. 'I'll need you to put it in the satnav.' Kate did as she was instructed. She gave him back his phone. 'Sounds like you had an interesting meeting,' he said.

Kate didn't answer. 'Do you see what I mean?' Julie prompted from the back. 'We come out here for Operation Sigma and it all kicks off. The prime minister has prostate cancer and is about to resign and one of the leading candidates to replace him is a Russian agent. Boom! Off we go. Then Igor Borodin is going to defect with a juicy sex video of our new PM and boom again!'

'I don't think I'd describe a video of him having sex with a group of underage girls in Kosovo as juicy,' Kate said.

'You know what I mean. And just when everything is completely settled and done, along comes another bar of gold. It's all been a hoax, orchestrated by Agent Dante, a very senior traitor at the heart of SIS. Boom again.'

'Agent Dante?' Callum asked.

Neither replied. 'Don't you think, Kate?' Julie prompted.

'In the spirit of full disclosure,' Callum went on, 'what did she have to say about Agent Dante?'

Kate turned towards him, since his question was a lot easier to answer than Julie's. 'She claims she's a protégée of Igor Borodin and had worked for a special unit he created called 61a to deal with the flow of intelligence from Agent Dante at the heart of SIS – and to run all the operations that stemmed from it. She suggested that everything we've seen in the UK – all of the operations Julie was just describing – have been the product of this unit, working hand in glove with Dante.'

'And who is Dante?'

'His identity is the greatest and most closely guarded secret in the Russian state.'

'But definitely a "he"?'

'She thinks so, but I thought her logic was pretty shaky on that point, so I wouldn't stake my life on it.'

'Perhaps it *is* Ian,' Julie said. She was talking to Kate, but it was Callum who responded.

'Why Ian?'

Kate sighed. 'Because the only concrete piece of information she was able to give us was that Dante was recruited in New York in the mid-nineties and some of his early intelligence appeared to relate to UK position papers on Bosnia.' She turned to Callum. 'And Ian was our man in New York during that period.'

Callum whistled to himself.

'But you see my point?' Julie asked.

'I do,' Kate said finally.

'Could you clarify?' Callum asked.

'Just when everything's calming down,' Kate said, 'and matters seem settled, they stir it all up again with another golden nugget that seems to suggest, a touch too neatly, that Agent Dante just happens to be the new chief of SIS.'

'And yet we've suspected Ian all along,' Julie said. 'Haven't we?'

They fell silent after that and, back at the hotel, Kate was grateful to be able to retreat to the relative peace and quiet of her room. She sat on her bed for a long time, then went down to have a cup of coffee at a table in the corner of the terrace. She watched a gleaming white super-yacht moor where Igor Borodin's *The Empress* had once been. It had three fake masts to make it resemble a tall ship.

Did she suspect Ian? Had she all along, as Julie had suggested?

Somehow she struggled to see Ian as a long-term traitor. But perhaps his neediness and insecurity were an act. He was clever enough, that was for sure. As he liked to remind people, he might well be the smartest person in the entire Service with a double first and cognitive scores that were off the chart. Too clever for his own good, Sir Alan had once said, and maybe there was some justice in that.

She sipped her coffee very slowly, trawling her memory for other signs over the years that she might have missed, but she kept returning to the question of how Agent Dante could have known that Sergei Malinsky was Kate's 'Achilles heel'.

She doubted Ian would have found enough in her personal vetting or recruitment files to reach that conclusion – then bet a whole operation on it. So that left either Stuart or Sergei himself, neither of whom was a palatable possibility. Or Sir Alan, of course. He had worked out very early on that Kate's friendship with Sergei was more significant than her personnel files seemed to suggest. But how?

Kate texted Fiona. She got a reply straight away. *All great here. Everything cool with Rose. Can't wait for you to be home.*

She tried the same with Gus. *All OK?* A few moments later, his reply made her smile. *Fine,* he said.

Finally, Kate pulled up Stuart's number. She stared at it for a long time. Was she really about to go down the road of suspecting him again, of letting doubt poison the reconciliation her children so desperately hungered for?

And what did she actually want? *Did* she hope for a genuine restoration of the love they'd once known? On that, she just couldn't get any consistent clarity. She had left France convinced that she knew what she wanted and how to get it, but doubt was creeping back in. Was it really possible Stuart had told his Russian handlers about her unconsummated love affair with Sergei and, if so, could he conceivably have offered it as a weakness to be exploited?

No, no, no. She found herself shaking her head. No, that was not possible. She could not – would not – go there again. She sent Stuart a WhatsApp message: *You OK?*

Never been better, he shot back. *How about you? Is it going to plan?*

So far, she replied. *You?*

Good, he said. *The Russians do want to meet. Any idea where?*

Kate thought about this, trying not to be irritated by the pressure of one kind or another that Stuart always seemed to provide. *Paris,* she sent back.

Julie joined her. 'I saw you talking to yourself from the window, mouthing no, no, no. Are you going mad?'

'Going?'

Julie was dressed in tennis whites. 'Are you heading back to the club for some reason or were you just taken by Natasha's uniform?' Kate asked.

'Young Callum is going to teach me tennis.'

'You're shameless.'

'We're only young once, Kate.'

'Well, be careful. I'm not picking up the pieces again.'

'Speak for yourself.'

Julie sashayed off. Kate drained her coffee. Stuart still hadn't replied and she suddenly had a desire to hear his voice. She called his number and walked down to the terrace by the water's edge. 'I can hear seagulls,' he said, as he answered. 'Where are you?'

'Not where I'd like to be. You?'

'You're kidding!' His laugh was still infectious. 'I've come to the conclusion Moscow is the biggest dump on earth. Paris sounds like a much better bet. I've just sent them an email. I'll let you know as soon as I hear back. When would suit you?'

'Next week, perhaps. Not before.'

'Okay. How are you? I mean, after . . .'

'You mean what should you read into our night of passion?'

'Yes. Something like that.'

'That we had very nice sex, for old times' sake.' That came out much harsher than she'd intended and she heard the hushed intake of breath at the other end of the line.

'I see,' he said.

'No, I'm sorry, that didn't come out quite right. I've just been sitting here trying to work out how much I want the reunion for my sake and how much for the children's.'

'And what answer have you come to?'

'I haven't. But in the end, maybe it doesn't matter. I don't think either of us can afford to let the children down again, so we have to go through with this now and make it work. That's what I think I've concluded.'

There was another long silence. 'Thank you, Kate,' he said. 'I mean, really, thank you.'

'See you in Paris.' She rang off and walked back to her room, aware that, when it came to Stuart, she really had absolutely no idea what she was doing. But she was learning that there were worse things to do in life than travel on instinct.

Kate changed, went to the gym and pounded the running machine for what felt like a very long half-hour. She liked running, but not on a conveyor-belt. It was the definition of pointless. She had only just got out of the shower when she had a message from Natasha Demidova. *Can't wait until tomorrow. Need to meet urgently. Same place. One hour.*

Kate tripped into her clothes and almost ran to the tennis court when she got an answer from neither Julie nor Callum. 'You need to pay attention to your bloody phones,' she said. 'We have to go now. And change, for God's sake.'

Kate drove. Fast. She and Julie left Callum in the car and made it to the rendezvous only three minutes beyond the appointed hour. The café was fuller than it had been earlier, mostly with old men smoking hookah pipes and chatting. Julie ordered apple tea, Kate Turkish coffee. The caffeine was starting to make her feel light-headed.

They waited. 'Christ, we really are sitting ducks,' Julie said. Kate was scanning the crowds thronging past from both directions. 'You think we should move further away from the door?' Julie asked.

'No.'

Kate spotted the man approaching from the right. He was young and dark, with a beard and round glasses. He had a hasty, uneven gait, accentuated by his attempt to conceal it. He was sweating.

Kate got to her feet. She looked around her for anything she could use as a weapon. 'What are you doing?' Julie asked.

'Incoming.'

Now Julie saw him too. 'This is fucking it,' she whispered. Kate expected the man to reach into his pocket, take out a gun and shoot them. There was nowhere to run, or hide, nothing she could do to protect herself, so she stood her ground and Julie did the same beside her. 'Follow me,' the young man blurted out, when he was almost upon them.

Kate stepped into the alley as he turned on his heel, but Julie gripped her forearm. 'We can't, Kate. It's suicide.'

'It's all right.'

'We don't know who the hell he is! They're trying to get us somewhere quieter!'

'We don't have a choice.'

'Of course we have a choice!'

The young man was already disappearing into the crowd again. 'You stay here,' Kate said.

She turned out of the café and it was a few seconds before she realized that Julie was with her. 'I'll follow, you hang back,' Julie said.

'No,' Kate insisted. 'My show, I take the lead.'

The young man took them on a circuit of the bazaar, too eclectic to be anything but an attempt to work out if there were more than two of them. Julie caught up with Kate as they emerged into an alley thronged with currency traders yelling prices into their phones – a poor man's Wall Street. They were all men, mostly middle-aged, and the air was thick with smoke and body odour.

At the other end of the alley, the young man picked up the pace. He was no athlete, but fear must have been powering his step, because he hurtled away from the bazaar and up to the Golden Horn Bridge. As they reached Taksim Square beyond it, the business heart of Istanbul, Julie came level with Kate for a moment again. 'I should call Callum,' she said. 'I think they'll take us up İstiklal Avenue.'

'Do it.'

Julie fell back. But she was right. For a moment, Kate thought the young man had got on to a tram just by the statue of Atatürk, but he emerged at the other side of it and she followed him all the way down İstiklal Avenue.

He slowed his pace now. He glanced into a café and looked as if he might stop at another serving elaborate Turkish desserts. Was he searching for someone, waiting for a contact?

He came to a halt at a restaurant with a giant slab of doner kebab by its entrance, but didn't take a seat at the table or look back towards Kate and, for the moment, she made no attempt to approach him. She got out her phone and, as if to check where she was on Google Maps, pulled to the side of the street.

She watched him discreetly out of the corner of her eye as the Turkish lunchtime shoppers flooded past, the secular and the religious, women wearing sunglasses and head-coverings, young men in baseball caps, jeans and T-shirts interspersed with those wearing more traditional forms of Turkish dress. This city wasn't just where east met west, but where every style of existence appeared to be fighting for its place in the sun.

Now he was approaching her. 'We're clear. Get into the car up ahead there.'

'We'll follow you.'

'No. You must—'

'That wasn't a suggestion.'

He shrugged nervously. Kate followed him towards a black Mercedes saloon parked just beside a restaurant on the far side of the road. Kate called Callum. 'Where are you?'

'The far end of İstiklal Avenue.'

'Come this way. Fast. You'll see a black Mercedes, parked outside a smart-looking Armenian restaurant. Park right behind it.'

'Got it.'

As Julie came up to join her, Kate said, 'We have to follow the black Mercedes. I've called Callum.'

He was there within seconds. Kate asked him to move to the passenger seat and got in to drive. The Mercedes pulled away and Kate sat closely on its tail.

11

'WHERE THE HELL are they taking us?' Julie asked.

They had been on the freeway heading out of the modern section of Istanbul for almost fifteen minutes and the car in front was picking up speed.

'We need to abort this, Kate.'

She didn't answer.

'We're here without back-up and God knows where these bastards are taking us.'

'I can let you out on the first freeway exit and you can make your own way back.'

Julie cursed quietly.

'You?' Kate asked Callum. 'There's no shame if you want out.'

'Of course not. We need to hear what she has to say.'

Silence descended as Kate concentrated on staying in view of the Mercedes ahead. The bright new skyscrapers of the European side of Istanbul dwindled slowly until they were out in the countryside, hemmed in by thick trees. 'They're taking us to Belgrad Forest,' Julie said eventually, eyes glued to her phone. 'Which seems like a good place to bury three foreigners.'

Julie was right. Twenty minutes later, they were through the main entrance gate to the forest and still struggling to stay on the tail of the speeding Mercedes, the afternoon sunlight now filtering through the thick canopy of thousands of sessile oak trees. 'This is where they buried Jamal Khashoggi,' Julie said, referring to the journalist the Saudis had cut up in their own embassy in Istanbul.

They reached a fork in the road and took the lower route to the bottom of an old dam. The Mercedes pulled up and the same man they had followed from the café got out and crossed the open ground towards them. 'He's nervous about something,' Kate whispered, as she watched his uneven gait.

'No prizes for guessing what,' Julie said.

Kate wound down the window. 'Follow this lower road beyond the dam,' the young man told her. 'You're looking for a grey Audi. It will be parked on the roadside a mile or two ahead.'

'Where are you going?' Kate asked.

'Back to Istanbul.' He returned to the Mercedes. It swung around and hurtled back the way they had just come. Kate glanced about her. A line of cars was parked close to the dam. A mother and three children with staves fashioned as swords approached one.

'Text her,' Julie said. 'At the very least, we should find out if she's here.'

Kate did as she'd been instructed, but no message came back.

'We have to turn around, Kate,' Julie said.

'Let's go on,' Callum insisted. He was a damned cool customer.

'Don't pay any attention to him,' Julie said. 'He's no idea what he's doing.'

Kate drove gently ahead and Julie slumped back into the rear of the car.

Kate checked her mirrors. No one in front, no one behind, just the silence of the great forest. She wound down the windows. A steady breeze rustled the leaves of the trees all around them.

They came around a bend in the road and there, parked ahead, lights on, was the grey Audi. Kate stopped. She pulled out her phone again and tried calling Natasha, but there was still no answer.

'This is a trap, Kate,' Julie said.

'Maybe.' Kate glanced in her rear-view mirror again. 'I think you're right.' She started to reverse on to the side of the road, so that she could turn around. Her phone rang.

It was Natasha. 'I'm in the Audi. I'm sorry. I had to check you weren't being followed. I think they suspect me. Park behind and get in.'

Kate ended the call. She peered closer to the mirror. It had started to spit with rain, so she switched on the windscreen wipers, but didn't drive any closer.

Her phone rang again. 'What are you waiting for? Come now, or I go.'

'I've no back-up. This could be a trap. If you're there alone, then you come to us.'

Natasha swore in Russian. The driver's door was opened and she stepped out. She had a leather satchel over her shoulder. She pulled a scarf over her head to shield her carefully curled locks from the rain and began to close the gap between them. She got about twenty yards and Kate was just preparing to climb out to meet her when there was the roar of an engine as a black Mercedes van gunned around the corner.

Natasha froze.

The van hurtled past Kate and her team and screeched to a halt beside the Russian. Kate tried to get out, but she felt Julie's hand on her shoulder.

Three men in balaclavas poured out of the back of the van. Natasha appeared to be reaching into her jacket for something – a gun perhaps – but the men were too swift. Kate saw the glint of the afternoon sunlight on the needle of a syringe as it was plunged into Natasha's neck. She collapsed instantly and was bundled into the van.

Kate slammed her car into gear and accelerated towards them, intending to smash into the van and force it from the road, but the closest man turned calmly in her direction and opened fire with a Heckler & Koch MP7, peppering her tyres and the engine of the car, so that she skidded off the tarmac and into the undergrowth.

Natasha was bundled into the back of the Mercedes, the driver gunned the engine and they sped away.

Kate got out and ran towards the Audi, but Natasha must have slipped the keys into her pocket. She sprinted back to her car and swung it on to the road. They got only a few hundred yards before the tyres started to shred, but they'd reached the car park. Kate and Julie ran along the line of vehicles until they located one they could hot-wire. Julie smashed the driver's window with a single tap in the corner – the weakest point – and was behind the wheel in seconds.

As she roared away, Kate made a decision. She pulled up the number for Zehra Sahin and dialled it. 'Kate,' the voice said, at the other end of the line. 'How nice to hear from you.'

'I need help.'

'I imagined as much.'

'We're in the Belgrad Forest. A potential target has just been abducted. We're here without back-up, answerable directly to the prime minister for reasons I'll explain to you one day. In an ideal world, if you can help, I'd prefer not to involve your father, but either way, it's imperative that nothing is passed back to SIS in London.'

'Understood.' Zehra's father Yusuf had been SIS's legendary station manager in Istanbul since the 1970s and Zehra was his heir apparent. She was as good as he was, if not better. And, between them, there was nothing and no one they didn't know in the tumultuous world of Istanbul's intelligence community. Kate reeled off the make and number-plate of the vehicle, the number of occupants and the identity of the suspected target. Zehra confined herself to a quiet whistle. 'Let's keep the line open,' she said. 'Hard not to include Dad, but I'll step into his office and seal us off from everyone else.'

Kate put her phone on the dashboard on loudspeaker. For a few moments, all they could hear was Zehra explaining the circumstances and parameters of the situation to her father, whose response was as calm and collected as Kate would have expected. He and his daughter were two of the most effective operators the Service was privileged to have at its disposal anywhere in the world.

They murmured quietly, tapping away at a keyboard. 'Looks like a team came in from Moscow this morning. Arrived at Atatürk by private jet via . . .' a long silence '. . . Odessa. Eight of them got off the plane.'

'Two teams?' Kate asked.

'I'd say so,' Yusuf said.

Julie had her foot flat on the accelerator. They hurtled up the slope to the main road. Julie barely touched the brake before they flew on to it.

'It's just clocked through a speed camera on the Istanbul highway at a hundred and sixty kilometres an hour,' Zehra said.

'What's the back-up team for?' Kate asked Julie, but it was only a split second before they had their answer as another black Mercedes van emerged from the siding.

Julie's instincts were razor sharp: she hit the brakes, swerved right and ducked behind the van so that it only clipped the front left-hand side of their own car. The impact was still shattering and they spun once and spun again.

Then Julie slammed the car back into gear and accelerated away, ahead of the Mercedes. 'Jesus, fuck,' Callum muttered, under his breath.

'You all right?' Yusuf asked calmly.

'We found the back-up,' Kate said, picking up the phone from the floor.

'Looks like they are headed for the airport,' Zehra said. There was another long silence. 'The rooftop camera is a little far away, but I'd say the plane has its engines running.'

Kate mouthed a silent curse as they all absorbed the brutal reality of this. 'You want me to talk to our friends in the police?' Yusuf asked.

Kate didn't answer. Inform the police and everyone in Istanbul would know what had happened and would be asking why, not least Yusuf's SIS superiors in London. Any chance at discretion and secrecy would be blown. But if the Russians were on to Demidova, they knew what was going on. And if they were aware, then Dante would soon know in London, too.

Her cover, such as it was, had been blown already. 'Yes,' she said simply.

Julie burned on to the highway bound for the airport. Within a few seconds, the battered old Citroën they had hot-wired was pushing through the 150 k.p.h. mark.

At the other end of the phone line, they could hear Yusuf talking to someone in Turkish. Halfway through, he broke off, and said to Zehra, in English, for Kate's benefit: 'Get going.'

He finished his conversation in Turkish, before offering Kate an explanation. 'Our Russian friends have bought cover with the police. Must have cost them a fortune. Who knew this Demidova was so valuable? I have told Zehra to take the boys and see what she can do. It will be close and we can't afford a shoot-out, but I will talk to our friends in MIT, see what can be done.'

'Thank you, Yusuf, as always.'

'I will have some explaining to do with your friend Mr Ian Granger if he gets to hear of this, but such is life. I could speak to someone in the prime minister's office here. Perhaps if—'

'No, it's all right.' Kate was aware how much political capital Yusuf was offering to expend and she was touched, but that would create an enormous crisis within SIS back at home, which would blow the last chance of shielding this from Ian and his colleagues.

Julie kept her foot on the accelerator as the minutes crawled by, and Yusuf calmly announced the Russian team's advance on the airport. 'This is crazy,' Julie said, after a while. 'What are we going to do? Try to bar the approach to the plane? They'll just shoot us and get on board.'

'I doubt their police cover involves a murder charge.'

'Maybe that just costs extra.'

They could hear the calls Yusuf was making in Turkish. It was probably ten minutes before he came back to them. 'MIT say they will look into this, but if the police decide to block the arteries of action, I don't think I can get there in time unless I go to the prime minister's office.' There was another silence. 'You are four or five miles behind them, so if they have a wave-through, I don't see how you can interdict.'

Julie asked Callum to navigate them to the entrance to the private terminal, but Kate knew they were counting down to failure now. Yusuf called out the progress in his steady, lugubrious way. The Russians were six minutes from zero, Kate's team twelve or more and Zehra and 'the boys' around the same. Neither could close in on the Russians.

Yusuf conversed with someone again in Turkish and conveyed that MIT were taking it seriously now and calling the chief of police, but Kate knew this was a lost cause. The Russians were two minutes from zero, then one – and then they were racing past the terminal and three men carried some kind of heavy-looking suitcase into the rear of the plane.

By the time Kate reached the airport, MIT had intervened and Zehra arrived to ensure the barriers were open, but all they saw as they roared on to the tarmac was the plane with the clues to Agent Dante's identity on board taking off into the rich red haze of a vintage Turkish sunset.

12

KATE REACHED HER desk in the makeshift office in Cambridge Street late in the afternoon of the next day and she was pleased to see that, waiting for her, in hard copy, were the files Shirley Grove had promised her.

She put to one side those relating to her former boss, Sir Alan Brabazon, the last chief of SIS, and focused instead on the ones that dealt with the Service's current head, Ian Granger. The top file was marked 'Personnel', and the one beneath 'Vetting'. Kate switched on her desk lamp, pulled up her chair and started on the former.

Ian Granger had been educated at Aylesbury Grammar School and Trinity College, Oxford, where he had studied modern and medieval languages. He had joined the Service as a new entrant in 1990 – on the recommendation of his Oxford tutor – and completed the induction period nine months later. After a brief stint in Counter-Intelligence as a junior officer, his first overseas posting had been in

Tbilisi, Georgia, in early 1992, where he had worked undeclared and undercover as a third secretary in the Chancery
section of the British Embassy there. After another brief
period working for the controller, North America, in London, he was transferred to New York in 1995, where he had
been promoted but was still working undercover as press
secretary for the British delegation at the United Nations. He
had clearly been heavily involved with the negotiations in
Dayton, Ohio, to end the war in Bosnia, which had perhaps
led to the communication with the SVR in Moscow that
Natasha Demidova had referred to in their meeting in
Istanbul.

So far, Ian's career had been predictable but unspectacular. An intelligence officer's great fear was to be detected
and exposed while working undercover, which was particularly debilitating and embarrassing when working in a
friendly country such as the United States. It tended to
limit future career options. Ian had therefore done well to
avoid detection and his personnel files were full of positive
annual assessments and reports from his superiors. But
equally there was nothing to make him stand out. It was
steady, satisfactory – but not the stuff of a future C.

However, that all seemed to change *after* his posting in
New York. It was a fact of Service life that you could make
your name in the most out-of-the-way places. So while an
outsider might assume you'd need to do well in Moscow to
cut your teeth as a Russia hotshot, it was equally possible
to do so in somewhere far removed from the Russian
capital.

And Ian appeared to be a case in point. After New
York, he had returned to a year on the Russia Desk at

Vauxhall – the personnel file recorded he felt his Russian language skills honed at Oxford were getting rusty – during which period he had brought on board the agent Irina, whom Kate had passed on to him from Istanbul. And then, after a year's immersive *Spanish* language training, Ian had been sent as the station chief in Santiago, Chile.

Why there? Well, this did and didn't make sense to Kate. On the one hand, it was an out-of-the-way posting for an ambitious young intelligence officer – particularly one who had recruited his first foreign agent. But, equally, it was a promotion – and quite a big one. The Service had only opened the station in Chile three years earlier and was to close it shortly after Ian left, but not before he had used his few years there to achieve a triumph of which Kate had previously been unaware and which seemed to go a long way to explain his subsequent meteoric trajectory.

Because the file clearly recorded that, in Santiago, Ian had managed to recruit a source in the Russian Embassy who had, as subsequent assessments confirmed with growing praise, gone on to be a significant player in the Kremlin's opaque power structure. The personnel file did not, of course, record whether the new recruit was in Russia's diplomatic service, intelligence service, or military, still less his or her identity. But it was the start of something. After that, Ian's career progressed steadily. He was posted to Berlin, Brussels and Paris – all plum assignments – with spells in London in between, before taking over the Russia Desk and eventually being appointed controller, Europe.

The files made only glancing reference to Irina, the translator in Istanbul, her recruitment and the debacle involving the German finance minister. It was clear that the agent in Chile – whoever he or she was – had made Ian's career.

All of which begged so many questions. How come Kate, as head of the Russia Desk, had been entirely unaware of this agent's existence? It was custom and practice for an agent's identity to be a secret beyond the immediate handling team but, even so, she couldn't imagine whom it might be, given the reporting out of Moscow that had crossed her desk.

Perhaps Ian had insisted the stream of information from this source came only to him after he was promoted to controller, Europe.

But there were other, equally pressing, concerns. Was Ian's recruitment of this agent just luck? Had he used the kind of intelligence skills that were internally legendary to spot, track and recruit someone whose potential for treachery might not have been picked out by others? Or had he known that the source was there for turning before he left London for Santiago? And, if the latter, could it have been a set-up by Ian's Moscow handlers to 'make' his career back in London and ensure that he was thereafter on an upward trajectory of ever greater force, with the access to more and more important secrets that flowed from it?

The agent in Chile had made Ian in a way Kate had never appreciated – and turned the course of his career. How easy it would have been for Moscow to make that happen.

It didn't prove he was Agent Dante, of course, but it gave her nothing to dismiss the idea, either. And the timeline worked: recruited in New York in the mid-nineties, as

Natasha Demidova had suggested, then super-charged by the recruitment of the agent in Chile.

Kate swapped Ian's personnel file for the one covering his vetting over the years. He had first, of course, been assessed upon entry to SIS, a process repeated every five years or so, or after any particularly difficult, complex or controversial assignment.

The first positive vetting contained detailed accounts of conversations with Ian's school headmaster and Oxford tutors. All praised his intellect, though the Oxford dons questioned his application and commitment, suggesting he was easily bored by assignments that didn't interest him. The headmaster gave a by and large positive account of his character and abilities, though he stressed Ian's weakness was a certain degree of social insecurity and the desire to be liked and respected by his peers. Ian's mother had nothing but praise for her son, whom she clearly doted on, and his stepfather almost nothing good to say about him at all. This, the assessor concluded, was pretty much par for the course in a broken family – including the social insecurity – and not to be considered a bar to his recruitment.

Subsequent vetting had been conducted only twice outside the five-year routine. Once was after New York, the second time after his assignment to Paris. Kate was not surprised to learn that, in both cases, the reason was reporting by 'colleagues' of barely concealed affairs with diplomats of other legations – a Czech in New York and a Dutch woman in Paris. The assessor in both cases took a lenient view, concluding that Ian's behaviour should be considered a private matter that ought not to impinge on his career progression.

Kate got up and went to make a cup of coffee. She had
sent Julie and Callum home with the instruction they
should all meet to regroup early tomorrow, Julie in the
meantime tasked to arrange a meeting with Ian's ex-wife.
So, Kate had the office to herself. She watched the machine
spit out the dark liquid and thought how typical it was for
the – no doubt male – assessor to conclude without prompting that Ian's affairs were a personal matter. She had
absolutely no doubt that a woman of the time would have
been judged differently and she wasn't completely certain
that that had changed.

She returned to the desk and switched files to consider
the career of her friend and mentor, the former chief of SIS,
Sir Alan Brabazon. He had been educated at Sherborne
School, where she and Rav had established he was a close
friend of the prime minister, and Manchester University,
where he had studied history. He had joined the Service in
1986 after writing a personal letter of application.

If anything, Sir Alan's career progression had been more
predictable and solid – more conventional, perhaps – based
on his unarguable social skills, emotional intelligence and
steely resolve. His first foreign posting had been to War-
saw in 1988, where he had worked undercover in the
Chancery section of the British Embassy. But he had then
moved on to Prague in 1990 and Moscow in 1993, by which
time he was the press secretary. There was a consistent pattern of reported recruitment of foreign targets in all these
locations, though little subsequent reference to them. Were
his successes less influential than Ian's, or was the latter
just better at blowing his own trumpet and making sure he
got the credit?

Sir Alan was apparently brought back from Moscow early to serve undercover in Bosnia with the SAS. After that, he spent two years in London on the desk that covered Italy and Spain before being posted to Pretoria for three years as the declared (to friendly countries, at least) SIS station chief.

He had moved back to London as deputy head of the North America Desk before being posted to Washington as station chief. This had led to the Russia Desk and spells as controller of Europe, then Counter-Terrorism before he was made C.

Kate sat back. Was it her own personal friendship with this man that made him so much less likely a suspect? There was nothing here – nothing at all – to hint at any possibility that he might be working for a foreign power, but perhaps he was too clever for that.

Kate got up. A thick bank of cloud had darkened the skies outside, so it looked like night was already closing in. She glanced at a copy of her own personnel and vetting files on the far corner of Shirley Grove's desk.

Surely that couldn't be passed off as a box-ticking exercise.

She got her coat, carefully locked the door of the apartment and walked out into the spitting rain. It took her half an hour to get home. As she passed her mother's nursing home by Battersea Park, she noticed that the light was on in Lucy's window on the fifth floor. And, just for a moment, Kate thought she had glimpsed her mother's face in the window, peering out into the gloom.

She did not go up to visit.

But the scene that confronted her at home presented different challenges altogether. Around the kitchen table sat

Fiona, Gus and Rose. They were FaceTiming Stuart in Moscow. And Rose's cautious welcome was warning enough. 'Have you heard?' Gus asked.

Kate dropped her coat into the armchair in the corner of the kitchen and glanced at Nelson, who rolled on his back in his basket, his own particular brand of welcome. 'Heard what?' Kate asked.

'Fiona came to school this afternoon and filmed the trial for Dad. All of it! It was so exciting.'

'He's been made captain of the First Fifteen,' Stuart said, beaming from the rectangular prism of their son's phone. Either the colour was off, or he had covered himself with fake tan. He looked most peculiar.

'He'll miss the first few games for sure,' Gus told his mother. 'But we've got a Sevens tournament in Sussex on the seventh of October, so we reckon he might make that.'

'I think I'm going to be in the school play,' Fiona said, not to miss out on the action. 'December the sixth, seventh and eighth – he'll definitely be here then?'

It was a statement, thinly disguised as a question, but the potential delay clearly troubled her brother. 'He'll be back before that. He'll be here in early October,' Gus insisted.

'Hi,' Kate said to her husband, failing to warm to the excitement of the scene – and acutely conscious of it.

'Hi,' Stuart said. 'There are no guarantees,' he told the children. 'You know that.' And Kate warmed to him for saving her the trouble. 'We've just got to take each day as it comes, and if your sister turns into a sports correspondent, I'll be able to watch all of your matches anyway.'

'I'm not sure I want to video everything,' Fiona said. 'My arm nearly fell off.'

'We're going to have a big Christmas party,' Gus said, which was particularly surprising, given that he had previously shown no desire whatsoever to hang out with his parents' friends. 'And we're going skiing in Courchevel at New Year.'

'Are we indeed?' Kate tried to smile at Stuart again, the warmth of a few moments before evaporating swiftly.

'And Corfu next summer,' Fiona said. 'Dad can't wait to see Jay again.'

'I bet.'

And so it went on. Kate tried her level best not to be riled by the elaborate nature of the plans her children and her husband had cooked up together, not least because they had avoided any hint as to how any of them might be paid for. She'd existed these past few months on her meagre savings, and the time was rapidly approaching when getting a job became a necessity, not a luxury. She made a mental note to check with Shirley Grove that she was being paid for the work she was currently undertaking, at least to the level of her Service salary.

It occurred to her later that Stuart might be mentally spending the cash he'd hoped to generate from putting her with his handlers in the SVR. But the Russians weren't stupid: they were unlikely to hand over anything until they had seen the colour of her own money.

The call ended and the children flew upstairs in the highest spirits imaginable. For a while, she and Rose contemplated each other over a bottle of white wine at the kitchen table. 'I'm not going to say anything,' Rose said, 'except I hope you know what you're doing.'

'Say away.'

'I don't understand how this sudden turnaround has been achieved. How are they under the impression that Stuart is about to return to this country?'

'I am not sure I told you. It was the price I demanded for taking a walk down Memory Lane.'

'And who agreed to it?'

'The prime minister.'

Rose whistled quietly. She shook her head. Kate waited for the rest, but she was pretty sure she knew what was coming. 'Are you sure that getting back together with Stuart is what you want?'

'You've seen how happy it makes—'

'Oh, I know it's what the kids dream of, though if you ask me, Fiona's beginning to have her doubts. Her enthusiasm waxes and wanes more than her brother's and there are moments when I think the hurt of his betrayal is becoming evident. I can understand, though, why you wouldn't wish to rip all that joy – or potential happiness, at least – from their hearts. But it's never going to work unless it's what you want, too.'

Kate refilled their glasses. They were both gulping it down. 'It is.'

'You don't sound very sure, if I may say so.'

Kate stared at the table, avoiding her aunt's penetrating gaze. 'The thought that their dad will never be able to return to this country is destroying them. Maybe it's even encouraging them to hang on to an idealized version of him. So I figure that if I have a chance to get him back in here, the rest will have to take care of itself.'

'It would kill them to have their hearts broken a second time,' Rose said.

Kate nodded. Rose was right, which was why this issue had barely strayed from her mind since she'd left the South of France. What moment of madness had led her to make those promises? 'I do miss him,' she said. It was the best she could conjure just now.

'I miss our old postman down in the country,' Rose said. 'It's not quite the same thing as being bound together for the rest of your lives, long after the children have left home even.'

'What would you do?'

'It's not my decision to make.'

'But . . .' Kate stalled. 'I mean, forgive me for asking. I can't imagine Simon doing anything of the kind, but did you ever have anything similar?'

For a moment, just the trace of a shadow shimmered in Rose's gaze before she quickly recovered her poise. 'I did spend many agonized hours discussing your father's situation after he discovered your mother had been having an affair with his best friend.'

The shadow, Kate concluded, was her aunt's fear that she was about to make the same mistake. 'You're saying he made the wrong choice by staying with her?'

'He did it for you. And I'm not sure it made him happy.'

'But—'

'I think you have to ask yourself if you've really forgiven him. If the answer is truly, honestly, yes – and you're certain you can find a way back to the love you once had – then, of course, you should carry on down this road. But if, as I suspect, the true answer is no – or even "don't know" – then I think you'd be most unwise to pursue a reconciliation, for the children's sake as much as your own.' Rose looked at her. 'I love you to pieces. You know that. But I'm just not sure you're the forgiving kind. And even if you were, it would be a huge ask.'

'I've made my decision. I've promised the children I'll give it another try. I can't go back on it.'

'I don't mind if you're doing this because you really want to,' Rose said. 'But I'll be upset if you made an impulsive gesture in the heat of a Bordeaux night and are too stubborn to face up to the fact it was a mistake.'

Kate didn't say anything to that. She realized that one of the reasons Rose was such a valuable force in her life was that she was willing to say things on occasion that no one else would dare to, except perhaps her mother, who could often be guaranteed to miss the point entirely.

'Infidelity is murder,' Rose said quietly. 'It destroys everything.'

It was said with such force that Kate wondered once again if there was a more personal resonance here than her aunt was admitting. But she found it hard to imagine Simon, a good, decent, loyal man if ever she'd met one, betraying the wife he so clearly loved.

'I hear you,' Kate whispered. 'I do hear you.'

Rose stood. 'I'd better be getting home. And I'm sorry to spring this on you, but I've arranged for Sir Alan to join Ian and me for breakfast tomorrow to discuss this attempt to block Maja's arrival here from Serbia. I know you're very busy, but I think it would help if you could be there.'

13

THE FOLLOWING MORNING, Kate arrived at MI6's grand headquarters in Vauxhall as an outsider for the first time since she was an inductee, a trainee intelligence officer, two decades before. Her aunt met and swiped her through the security pods. Sensing her unease, Rose offered a reassuring smile as they rode the lift to the top floor. 'Must be strange to be back.'

Kate nodded. She was dreading this meeting, for reasons she couldn't entirely place. They were met by the chief's butler and ushered into the wood-panelled dining room with its panoramic view of the river Thames, the Houses of Parliament and the grandiose buildings of Whitehall beyond it.

Sir Alan, the former chief, was already seated opposite his successor and the two seemed to have dressed to showcase their contrasting styles. Sir Alan was in one of the immaculately tailored suits that had been his hallmark, his only concession to retirement a thick white beard that made him look a decade older. Ian sat opposite in dark jeans and an open-necked shirt. He had drawn himself up awkwardly close to the table, with one suede Chelsea boot twisted across the knee of his other leg, as if attempting a new yoga pose. It was his new obsession, so rumour had it, since he told people he no longer had the time or inclination to train for the Iron Man competitions that had once been his most tiresome boast.

But he hadn't cut his long blond locks to fit his new responsibilities. Or learnt to do up his shirts, from which curls of long grey hair protruded. If the acid bite of setting eyes on a superior who had so often made her life difficult wasn't enough, this alone would have put Kate off her breakfast. She stuck to coffee. 'What are you up to, Kate?' Ian asked her breezily.

'Trying to get my life back on track.'

'Excellent! Kids all better?'

'In a manner of speaking.'

'I do hope we're still picking up the therapy bills.' He glanced at Rose, who nodded curtly. Ian had made great play when Kate left the Service of how her children needed 'proper help' to deal with the trauma of being kidnapped during Igor Borodin's aborted defection, which the Service would 'of course' pay for in perpetuity. Since it had gone wrong, he had of course forgotten all about Borodin's offer to defect, for which, when the prime minister's demise had seemed certain, he had briefly been a great enthusiast.

Ian's ability to tack to catch the passing wind was legendary. It was, Kate supposed, what many careers were made of.

'You look well,' Sir Alan told her. He gave her a sly wink

and she smiled back at him. He seemed to be enjoying Ian's preening more than she might have imagined. Perhaps his successor's vaingloriousness was obvious enough to lend him an air of absurdity, which he worked so hard to avoid. Ian hated not to be taken seriously.

'Alan has just been telling me how much he's been enjoying retirement.' Sir Alan offered his successor a flinty smile. 'Pottering around in the garden, lunch in the shade of the big beech tree by the river. Sounds idyllic.' Ian glossed over the fact that his predecessor was still wrestling with the loss of his wife of almost forty years to cancer. 'Not that any of us believe you would really retire,' he added, though he offered no clarification of what he meant. He looked across the table. 'We're keeping things ticking over here. Just carrying on in your own image.'

'Is that so?' Sir Alan said. 'I heard you were intent on remaking the wheel.'

'No, no. That hasn't been the message at all. Your sources fail you there, I'm afraid. We're just trying to tackle a – how can I put it? – somewhat cavalier attitude to the budget.'

Now it was Rose's turn to offer her boss an icy stare.

Ian really did have a unique ability to put people's backs up, Kate reflected.

'I seem to recall,' Sir Alan went on smoothly, refusing to take the bait, 'that only one section head was notorious for budget overruns. The controller, Europe.'

'Well, yes,' Ian conceded, 'perhaps there is a touch of poacher turned game-keeper, but I recognize that constant over-spends, however good the reasons, are putting terrible pressure on Rose and her team in Finance. And more to the point, given our track record . . .'

'By which you mean my track record,' Sir Alan said.

'Let's not get into that. I'm just not prepared to ask Number Ten or the Treasury for a subvention again. There's no excuse for us failing to observe basic budgetary discipline.' He took a mouthful of bacon and eggs and chewed without finesse. 'Which brings me to the issue at hand. I cannot authorize this Serbian girl's transfer here. And I won't.' ·

Sir Alan took off his trademark tortoiseshell glasses and cleaned them methodically. He held them like a weapon of war while Rose and Kate waited for him to eviscerate his successor. 'Ian, since you're new to your responsibilities, perhaps I can diplomatically remind you that our commitment to our sources is what sets us apart and makes us the envy of intelligence services the world over. We have neither the wealth of the CIA nor the wide degree of latitude in mores and methods of Mossad, or indeed our many enemies in Russia, China and North Korea. Our word is our bond. That is what we have. A global reputation for protecting our assets and taking their secrets not just to their grave, or all of ours, but history's too.'

'I'm not sure I need a rather pompous lecture from you on—'

Sir Alan leant forward. 'We gave this girl our *word.*' He looked, suddenly, as if he would rip Ian's throat out, moving from easy-going spymaster to visceral agent in a heartbeat. It was a side of her former boss Kate had rarely witnessed, but then she'd never heard anyone dare to talk to him in the patronizing and disparaging terms Ian had just used. Ian looked taken aback. 'Kate merely promised her *sister* that she would *attempt* to—'

'To be clear,' Kate said. 'Lena did not want to go on to that super-yacht. She collapsed in terror during our last meeting in Istanbul before she was due to go on board. The only way I could keep her on track was with the promise that, whatever her fate, I would make sure that we got Maja out of Belgrade and away from the dismal prospect that awaited her in life there. It was a specific, categoric promise.'

'I have flipped the IT upgrade on the first floor into next year's budget,' Rose said, 'so there is no longer an issue.'

Ian looked as if he would throw his breakfast at Rose, but she held his gaze. 'We've discussed the plan for the IT upgrade endlessly,' he said. 'We can't simply throw it all into the air just because—'

'I've informed everyone involved. They're perfectly relaxed about it.'

Ian's cheeks reddened. He liked to pride himself on being two steps ahead of everyone else in the great intelligence 'game' so the pain of being so swiftly and adeptly outmanoeuvred appeared almost physical. He pushed away his plate, took a sip of coffee, breathed in deeply and faced the window. 'You speak of our reputation,' he said slowly, before turning back to them. 'Well, then, let us be clear. It is a widely held view in this organization, and in many of our sister agencies around the world, that our handling of events over the last year has come close to making us a laughing-stock. You will acknowledge, I trust – at least in the privacy of this room – that I was opposed to the operation to bug Igor Borodin's yacht from the very start.'

'You authorized it,' Kate reminded him.

'Yes, but when the bombshell dropped, I didn't believe it. I said it was too convenient, that we were being taken for a ride.' There was a shrill timbre to Ian's voice now. 'The prime minister a Russian agent of influence? I mean, it was absurd!'

'I seem to recall,' Sir Alan interjected, 'that when Igor Borodin offered to defect with proof of the prime minister's treachery, you were all for it.'

'I had my doubts. They're on the record!'

'You oversaw the operation,' Rose reminded him. 'I went through every aspect of the budget with you. And you said that accepting the defection had been your idea.'

Ian gazed at her with barely disguised hostility. He looked like a cornered rat. But he had one ace in this game – power – and he played it now. 'That is the past,' he said. 'That we ran with this idea but never proved it has done more damage to the standing of this organization than anything else I can recall, and I now intend to move us decisively beyond it.' He looked at Kate. 'I will do anything I need to in order to protect the Service's reputation and good name.'

She wondered if he knew about her investigation already. Was that what had so riled him? And was this some kind of warning that she should expect the full weight of the Service to bear down on her if she went forward with it? He was the master of the coded threat, after all.

'So we can sit here all morning, but I'm afraid my decision stands. Lena, her sister, the super-yacht, Igor Borodin, his supposed defection and crazy allegations against the prime minister, or indeed members of this Service, are in the past. And the matter is closed.'

Ah, Kate thought. *Members of this Service.* Now his meaning was clear. He did know about her investigation and this was a direct warning to her.

Sir Alan was the first to move. He stood, folded his nap-kin and placed it on the table. 'Thank you for breakfast, Ian, and good luck. You're going to need it.' He walked to the door, followed swiftly by Rose and Kate. The butler fetched their coats. No one spoke until they reached the lift.

As soon as the doors closed, Rose said, 'I'm going to authorize it anyway.' She shook her head despairingly. 'Who the fuck does he think he is?'

Sir Alan smiled at her. 'Brave.'

'By which you usually mean foolish,' she said. 'But I'm done. Let him fire me.' The door pinged open at her floor and she flashed them both a smile and left them.

Neither Kate nor Sir Alan spoke again until they had reached the street outside the entrance. 'Don't tell me you were surprised,' he said.

'But why?'

He smiled at her. 'I'm sure you can work it out. Come down and have lunch with me sometime.' He walked away.

'Sir Alan?' He turned back to her. 'How did you know my relationship with Sergei was more than just a friend-ship? I mean, right back at the start, you came to my office and you spotted instantly that he was my source for that meeting on the yacht and you understood that I might have been susceptible to being misled as a result of my feelings for him.'

'Instinct,' he said. 'I've been in this business a long time. I meant what I said. Come down and see me. We'll talk.'

It was a long journey to see Ian Granger's former wife at her palatial surroundings in Wiltshire so Callum and Julie filled it by establishing, with great discussion and argument – and at some length – a 'definitive' list of the ten greatest films, TV series and songs of all time. Kate's contributions were *Mamma Mia, I Have No Idea* and 'Dancing Queen' – 'of course' – respectively. She didn't really understand this mania for creating lists. What was the point?

It seemed relevant somehow that Callum's favourite films were all spy yarns of the most exaggerated variety: '*The Bourne Supremacy, Casino Royale, The Bourne Identity*, in that order.'

They had met in the office just after nine, with Shirley Grove, and Kate had briefed them on the conclusions she had reached from her survey of the files the previous night. She didn't tell them of her breakfast meeting with Ian, though it had seldom strayed far from her thoughts. 'I'll leave you to explain what you've discovered in mine,' Kate told Grove icily, as she pointed at the file on the corner of her desk. Just for a moment, as she reflected upon Ian's evident determination to clear the Service's reputation, she wondered whether he and Shirley Grove might be working hand in glove. But wasn't she trying to resurrect the very subject he was trying to bury? Except, of course, having Kate publicly exposed as Agent Dante – a kind of criminal mastermind – would suit everyone.

Grove didn't dignify that with a response.

'It's not that anything in there proves Ian Granger is our man,' Kate had concluded. 'Merely that it provides quite a convincing narrative that he might be.'

Celia Granger had moved very fast since divorcing her husband, relocating her family and business to this bucolic site just west of Salisbury. The home was a handsome red-brick old rectory with wisteria climbing its façade, the business housed in a huge renovated barn on the other side of the drive. At the front door of the main house, a Filipina maid or housekeeper directed them to the reception area at the front of the barn, where they sank into low-slung sofas around a rattan and glass table furnished with fashion and lifestyle magazines of every hue.

The young receptionist offered them coffee, and a few minutes later, they were ushered into Celia Granger's office and installed in another low-slung seating area, which afforded a view of a cropped wheat field that sloped gently down to a copse and river in the distance. It was idyllic.

Celia finished her call and came over. She was an athletic woman with short, dark hair and bright blue eyes, dressed in yoga leggings and a thick white polo-neck with a gold necklace at her throat. 'Kate, how nice to see you again.' She turned to the others, who introduced themselves. Celia shook Callum's hand, then faced Julie. 'You're the young woman Ian had an affair with.'

It was said without noticeable bitterness or rancour, but Julie still looked as if she had been slapped, which perhaps she had, the blow all the more powerful for being delivered in such measured tones. Celia smiled at her, then retreated to the sofa opposite them, tucking her legs back as she leant forward to offer them all coffee.

'How's business?' Kate asked. Celia ran a mail-order and online sleepwear empire, which had once been one of Ian's boastful riffs. He'd set great store by having such a clever, successful wife.

'Booming.' Celia smiled again. 'I seem to be rather better at business than marriage.' She glanced at Julie, who was staring into her coffee, as if it was about to offer an answer to the meaning of life. 'But something tells me you didn't drive all this way to talk about my commercial activities. Perhaps you could start by telling me why your colleague here suggested secrecy was of such critical importance?' She was pointing at Callum.

'We've been asked by the prime minister to conduct an investigation outside the normal procedures within the intelligence services.'

'Into Ian?'

'Into the possibility we have a traitor at the heart of SIS.' Kate shrugged. 'You always struck me as a decent and highly intelligent woman, so I'm doing you the courtesy of telling you the truth and trusting that you'll see the seriousness of the situation.'

Even as she spoke, Kate wondered about her breakfast with Ian and his implicit warning. Had Celia tipped off her former husband about this meeting, or was it just coincidence?

'All right. Since you put it like that, I accept. I'll tell no one what transpires in this conversation,' Celia said. 'I don't have much of an appetite for the cloak-and-dagger world, for reasons you can probably guess at, so you can do me the favour of making this quick.'

Kate gazed at the woman opposite her, thinking again of the mystery men remained to her. Who would want to cheat on a wife like Celia? 'Maybe the easiest thing is if I share with you a working theory.'

'Go on.'

'We know we have a double agent working at the heart of SIS. We know that he or she has been in place for a long time, almost certainly from the mid-nineties. And we know that they have spent much of their career involved with Russia. But, as you will understand, whoever it is has been clever enough to cover their tracks.'

'Well, we can probably all agree that Ian is clever.' Celia smiled at Julie again. She was getting her money's worth here, that was for sure, and in the most elegant way imaginable.

'I spent most of yesterday combing through Ian's personnel and vetting files,' Kate went on. 'And while they don't provide any proof of anything, I found myself struck by the way his career changed course after that period in New York.' Kate thought it best to leave out Natasha Demidova's intelligence that Dante had been recruited in America during this period.

'Did it?' Celia asked.

'I think so. Before then, he was just another clever Oxford recruit. There was little to mark him out as a potential future chief. But after New York, he did a year on the Russia Desk – at his own request – and then you went to Chile, where he pulled off a significant coup that effectively made his career.'

'Did he?'

'He didn't give you any indication of the success he had achieved in Santiago?'

'Ian never talked about his work.' She smiled at Julie once more. 'It was the perfect way to hide less wholesome secrets.'

'The work he did in Chile appears to have been very significant. He gave you no hint his assignment had gone well?'

'None.'

Kate found this confusing. Ian seemed so prone to preening boastfulness that she found it difficult to imagine him keeping this potential career triumph from his wife, unless he had no longer felt the need to impress her.

'Look, I'll save you the trouble here. Ian is not your Russian spy.'

'With respect, Mrs Granger, I don't think you can know—'

'I can.' She nodded with boundless confidence. 'I'm not an expert in your world, it's true – thank God – but I know enough about human nature to be certain that betraying your country in any circumstances at any time is an enormous step that requires a certain kind of courage, which I can absolutely assure you Ian does not possess. He's clever, yes, insecure, definitely, and that makes him susceptible to the attention and flattery of others in ways I don't need to describe to you, but the idea of disgrace and even prison would so terrify him as to make the idea of him taking such a step inconceivable.'

Julie was nodding.

'You see,' Celia went on, pointing at her, 'even the lovely young Miss Carmichael here agrees with me. And she should know.' Julie's face coloured immediately.

'With the greatest respect, Mrs Granger . . .' Kate said.

Celia raised a hand. 'It's Celia, please. And I know what you're about to suggest – no doubt in your customarily diplomatic way. Perhaps a wronged wife is not the best person to lecture the world on her former husband's secret life.'

'I wasn't going to put it quite like that.'

'I bet. But I'm sure you're wondering if I was aware of my husband's many affairs?'

Julie was staring at the floor, as if hoping it would swallow her.

'It did occur to us,' Kate said tactfully.

'The answer is complicated, as they normally are, I'm afraid – and currently the subject of many hours of extremely expensive therapy. There is a difference between what your eyes may see and what your mind is willing to accept, a gap explained by your own past.'

If she'd been having a lot of expensive therapy, Kate thought, it was clearly working, since there was no doubt she exuded a sense of serenity. Perhaps it was the firm decision to move on from him, a resonance not lost on Kate.

'I came from a broken home with a philandering father and a mother who was determined not to see what was as plain as day to everyone else who knew us. But . . .' she sighed, the karma beginning to crack '. . . you don't need me to go into all that. So . . . yes, I guess I did know Ian was having affairs. Before we married, I convinced myself it was just a guy sowing his wild oats and it would all change once we'd exchanged our vows. And after our wedding, I would have done anything and everything to keep us together, even if it meant the pain of denying the evidence before my eyes.'

'I'm sorry,' Julie blurted out. 'Really, I'm sorry.'

'Think nothing of it,' Celia said kindly. 'If it hadn't been you, it would have been someone else – as it was in other times and places. The bigger question is what kind of fool puts up with it?'

Kate sighed inwardly. It reminded you how little we really know of others. Who would have guessed this attractive woman, who had built such an impressive business empire, would be travelling through life with so much psychological baggage?

But, then, wouldn't many have said the same about her?

'We understand your assessment of your husband's potential for treachery, Mrs Granger,' Callum interjected smoothly, 'and will certainly take account of it, but could we just ask you to focus on that posting to New York for a moment?'

Kate glanced at her new recruit, quietly impressed at the way he had steered the conversation back to safer ground.

'Of course. What would you like to know?'

'In retrospect, was there anything unusual about it? Anything at all you might think worthy of note?'

Celia considered this for a long time. She turned to the window and gazed out over the clipped stubble towards the wooded copse in the valley below. 'I suppose I would go through a pattern of acceptance and denial,' she said. 'About his affairs, I mean. I'd become suspicious and, for a while, jealousy would consume me, but then I would start to block it out until I could more or less convince myself it wasn't happening.' She smiled at Julie once more and, this time, looked on the point of tears. In fact, they both did. 'Our time in New York was particularly painful. We were newly married, so this was the first time the reality dawned on me that a wedding had not forced a leopard to change his spots.'

'He had an affair while you were there?'

'Yes, I think so. I mean, yes, definitely. A Czech girl. He played tennis with her.'

'A diplomat?'

'I doubt it. One of the women Ian worked with, whom I liked, later implied she was Czech intelligence.'

'Given that we know Ian did have affairs,' Kate said, picking her words very carefully, 'was there something you thought *particularly* unusual about this one?'

'The first of our marriage. The shattering of an illusion.' Celia shook her head sadly. 'But now I mention it, I have to admit it wasn't that. He just wasn't quite himself during the last six months in New York and I became convinced that he was going to leave me.'

'Had you ever thought that before?'

'No, and never since. Ian was extraordinarily good at compartmentalizing his life in that regard. These affairs were just sex to him, a bodily function like eating or sleeping. He always insisted our relationship existed on a higher plane than anything he had experienced before or would again. And I was fool enough to believe him.'

'But if this woman was an exception,' Callum asked, 'the obvious question is, perhaps, why?'

For the first time, Celia looked annoyed. 'How the hell should I know? Perhaps she did unusual things in bed.'

'But you said affairs were just sex,' Callum said. He glanced at Kate. Julie was still examining her feet with great intensity. 'So had you considered the possibility that you were right in that judgement and something else was going on there?'

'What do you mean?'

'Just that a Czech intelligence official operating in New York in the mid-nineties might easily have begun her career in the days of the old Soviet Union. So it's not a complete stretch to imagine she retained old loyalties and was tasked with trying to recruit an ambitious young officer like Ian to work for the Russians, is it? Perhaps one might even convince him he was going to be of great assistance to a new democratic Russia rising from the Soviet ashes.'

'Most of the Czech diplomats I met hated the Russians.'

'Yes,' Kate said. 'But I think Callum's point is that perhaps it was not betraying you that Ian had on his mind – as you've said, that didn't seem to cause him many dark nights of his soul – but his country, which, as you said at the start, would have consequences far beyond a divorce.'

'I just don't think he has it in him.' Celia raised her hands. 'I can't say more than that. I mean, is it *possible* that was what he had in his mind during those last few months in New York? Yes, I suppose so. I don't know if this stupid tart was some kind of honey-trap deployed by the Russians, but all I can repeat is that I don't think he has it in him to be a spy for Moscow. He's just not brave or stupid – or desperate – enough. And what would have been his motive?'

'Perhaps, newly-wed, he didn't want news of the affair to destroy his marriage,' Julie said. For the first time, she was looking directly at Celia, as if determined somehow to defend Ian from charges laid by his ex-wife.

'Well, all I can say is, if so, it was a fit of conscience that I don't think detained him before or has since.'

Kate stood, deciding to end the interview before it went off the rails entirely. 'Thank you for your time, Celia. I'd appreciate it if you could, as we discussed, refrain from letting anyone know we were here, including – indeed especially – your former husband.'

'I don't think you have to worry much on that score, do you?' She smiled again. 'I hope you hang him from Nelson's Column.'

Kate tried to smile back. 'One final thing. Would you, by any chance, recall the name of the Czech intelligence official?'

'Eva. I am not sure I ever knew her surname.'

14

'GOD, I FEEL a bit shit,' Julie said, breaking the silence that had held for about the first ten minutes of their return journey to London.

'And so you should,' Kate said.

'Mind if I smoke?'

'I do, yes.' Julie ignored her, took out a pack and offered one to Callum in the back, who declined. 'I meant it,' Kate said. 'Seriously, please don't smoke in the car. I'll throw up.'

Julie looked as if she would ignore the instruction, but eventually put the pack away.

'What did you think?' Callum asked, from the back. It was directed at Kate. 'It all fits, doesn't it? Every new piece of information seems to add grist to the mill of your working theory. You'd have to say he was probably recruited during those last six months in New York.'

Kate didn't answer.

'But what was his motive?' Julie asked.

'Just as his wife said. Fear of the affair being leaked and his marriage being undone.'

'But you just heard her say she more or less knew of his affairs, and a man who persistently, over decades, behaves with so little caution hardly strikes me as one who would contemplate flipping to the Russians because of a few rolls in the hay with a buxom lady from Czech intelligence.'

'If it is Ian we're looking for,' Kate said quietly, 'and that *is* still a big if, I think we're seeing another motive.'

'Such as?' Julie asked her.

'Insecurity, ambition. I've never met anyone who needs a place in the world and the esteem of his peers more viscerally than Ian. By the time of his posting in New York, he was five years into a career in the Service and there was little sign of the stardust he craved. He was a B list player, destined for a series of solid but unspectacular appointments.'

'So the Russians love-bomb him and he falls for it?' Julie asked.

Kate shrugged. 'They make him feel important. He's so talented, so overlooked. They would never make the mistake of undervaluing him. Maybe Igor himself flies over from Moscow to handle the final approach, as they wheel out the big guns for the seduction.'

'And perhaps there's money, too,' Callum said.

'His wife's rich,' Julie said.

'But she wasn't then,' Callum replied. 'I checked. And why be comfortable when you could be wealthy?'

The more Kate turned over the events of the morning in her mind, the more certain she was that she was right: if Ian had been seduced into working for the Russians, his fragile ego was the cause.

She only broke the silence to tell her companions that she wanted to make a small detour to the home of the former chief of the Service, Sir Alan Brabazon. Julie queried the wisdom of her visiting a potential suspect of their inquiry, but Kate insisted she knew him well enough to pass off the visit as a purely social affair. She dropped Julie and Callum for lunch in Stockbridge, a town on the bank of the Test river, and headed to the old mill-house hidden in the folds of a lush valley south of Winchester.

The electric gates opened automatically to a long and winding track, which led past grazing sheep to a wide gravel parking area in front of a red-brick house that sat sideways on a meandering stream. The garden was immaculate, clipped lawns sloping down to the water's edge, which was flush with water-lilies and wild flowers. The far end was dominated by a well-tended orchard, a series of raised vegetable beds and an iron and glass greenhouse.

Sir Alan and his late wife had often professed themselves devoted to the garden of their country house.

Kate stepped out of the car. The bright afternoon sun was filtered through the leaves of a beautiful, drooping beech. A table beneath it was covered with lichen, suggesting it was rarely used.

Kate knocked on the door. It was opened by the smiling figure of Mrs Evans, Sir Alan's housekeeper of many years. 'Mrs Henderson,' she said. 'This is a pleasant surprise. Sir Alan will be delighted.'

'He's not expecting me, I'm afraid.'

'There are some surprises he'll relish.' She stepped back to allow Kate into the cool flagstone interior of the hallway. 'Are Stuart and the children with you?'

'No. I was just passing on my own.'

'They're well, I hope?'

'Yes, yes.' Kate wondered if Mrs Evans was aware of Stuart's treachery. 'I mean Fiona and Gus are teenagers, so . . .' She smiled, as if that said it all.

'They're still delightful, I'm sure.'

'Possibly with strangers.'

Mrs Evans chuckled. 'Go through to his study. He's in one of the outhouses, fiddling around with that wretched old MG of his. I'll go and find him. Would you like coffee?'

'Yes, please,' Kate said.

She did as she was instructed, following the flagstones to the far end of the house. The study overlooked the bubbling brook beyond open windows. It was a dark room, with low ceilings, heavy with old beams and many hundreds of books, which filled every available inch of wall space. At one end a desk overlooked a flowerbed at the corner of the garden. It was groaning with files of the kind one used to find in Registry, before the Service had digitized its archives. She could clearly see one marked 'Top Secret'.

'That was quick.' Kate spun round to see her former boss silhouetted in the doorway. 'You're thinking I shouldn't have smuggled top-secret files from the office and you're dead right.' He stooped to kiss her. His hands were covered with grease.

'I meant to tell you this morning, you look well,' she said.

'I do not!' He gestured at the deep leather sofas in front of the fireplace. 'Take a seat. I just need to get this crap off my hands.'

Kate slipped into the armchair closest to the window and listened to the soothing gurgle of the water outside. She surveyed the collection of military history books arranged on the shelf and recalled how thrilling it had been to be here on their first weekend visit as a family, the sense that somehow, seated here with a whisky by the fire late at night, she had been admitted into an important inner sanctum.

Mrs Evans came with coffee and chocolate biscuits. 'Don't let him eat too many,' she said. 'I had to let out his trousers last week.' She smiled at Kate again. 'You look very well, Mrs Henderson. I asked about the children, but how is that charming husband of yours?'

Clearly, Sir Alan was not in the habit of gossiping about major developments at work to his housekeeper, which was perhaps encouraging, Kate thought. 'He's fine also, thank you.'

Sir Alan came in, still drying his hands. 'How's the MG?' Kate asked.

'The most infuriating machine ever made. I kept promising Alice that I'd get rid of it.' He placed the towel on the bookshelf, in front of a series of tomes about the Boer War. He sat opposite Kate. He certainly didn't look any thicker around the middle, though he lacked the air of suave charm that had once been the toast of Whitehall.

'I'm sorry,' she said. 'It must be so hard being here without her.'

He stared at his hands. 'It is hard not to think of the retirement we might have had together.' He shook his head. 'If I'd known you were coming *today*,' he said, 'I'd have tidied myself up.'

'You want to explain why you stole all those files from the office?' she asked, smiling at him.

'Ah, I *took* them before I left, so "stole" might be overstating it a touch.'

'Why did you remove them?'

Sir Alan leant forward to pour himself a cup of coffee. He chose three biscuits, then wasted a few seconds elaborately cleaning his tortoiseshell glasses. They didn't look much clearer when he put them back on. 'I was trying to rationalize the overall sense that I had been mugged,' he said. 'Which this morning only served to underline. But perhaps that's what all bitter old men do when they have nothing better to turn their minds to.'

'You're neither bitter nor old.'

'Oh, I wouldn't be so sure of that – on either count. Betrayal does leave a bitter taste in the mouth.'

She assumed he was talking about Ian, but it was a statement delivered with finality, as if a generalized reflection on the human condition. 'So what have you concluded?' she asked. 'From your studies of the past?'

He dipped a chocolate biscuit into his coffee. 'Did you know Ian asked for his assignment to the Russia Desk when he returned from New York?'

'Yes,' she said.

'And he then requested his posting to Santiago. A curious career zigzag, don't you think? I mean, why would an ambitious young officer seek out a relative backwater like Chile?'

Kate glanced at the pile of files on the desk. What were the chances of her and her former boss having reached the same conclusion at more or less precisely the same moment?

He smiled at her. 'Now you're wondering how you and I have come to the same answer.'

'I am kind of asking myself that, yes.'

'I'm retired, Kate, not dead.'

'That's not much of an explanation, if I may say so.'

'Well, I know about your inquiry, of course.'

'How come? It's supposed to be the most top secret of all government operations.'

'Yes, and I'm a potential suspect?' It was posed as a question, but she knew perfectly well he required no answer. He was smiling at her again.

She pointed at the files on his desk. 'But there's no way you could have got those out of the office after you retired—'

'I was fired. Let's not beat around the bush.'

'You must have taken them before you left.'

'I told you. I had the sense I'd been mugged.'

'You knew about Agent Dante?'

'I didn't have specifics, just a vague sense there was something I'd missed – and had perhaps been overlooking for years. But I'm aware of what you're investigating now and why.' He leant back in the leather armchair and crossed his legs. 'And, of course, I also know that I must be a target, so—'

'I wouldn't go that far—'

'Of course I am, or you wouldn't be doing your job properly. And since you're just about the most diligent intelligence officer I ever employed, I can rule out that possibility.'

'Am I wrong?'

He appeared to give this due consideration. 'No. I must be suspect, of course. And you should look into my past, just as others mine your own.'

'Others? Including you?'

'Not including me, no.'

She glanced at his desk. 'What conclusions have you reached from the hours you've spent buried in the files?'

Sir Alan leant forward and heaved himself up from the armchair. He went to his desk and rummaged around, returning with a thin pink folder, which he dropped on to the coffee-table in front of her. 'Bucharest, 1993,' he said. Kate read through it, scanning the pages before her at speed.

It concerned a young KGB officer called Katya Grigoreva, who had offered her services as a potential double agent for British intelligence. But it was not so much the description of the contact or ensuing assessment of her as the familiarity of the features in the photograph.

It had been a long time, but a good intelligence officer doesn't forget a face. 'Irina, the girl who approached me in Istanbul,' Kate said, looking up at him.

'Precisely.'

She thought about this. 'I don't get it,' she said.

'Yes, you do.'

Kate flicked on through the file. The woman who had passed herself off as Katya had been assessed by SIS's Bucharest station chief and rejected on the grounds of unreliability. 'So she tried again,' Kate said.

'Yes. But what had changed in the meantime?'

'Ian had requested an assignment on the Russia Desk, so was in a position to make sure that, this time, Katya – or Irina, or whatever her real name was – passed through the checks and on to our books.'

He got up again and returned to the desk. This time he

brought a thick collection of green files and dropped them with a thump in front of Kate. 'You've probably worked out by now that Ian went on to recruit a young assistant military attaché in Santiago, who is now General Menov, chief of the Russian General Staff.' Sir Alan moved to the other side of the coffee-table and leant against the fire-place. 'I've double- and triple-checked Menov's material, which has remained strictly for eyes only controller, Europe, and C, and concluded each time that it was reliable and genuine.'

'Menov was his calling card,' Kate said.

'Right!' Sir Alan slapped the brick chimney, in a display of frustration or anger that was quite out of character. 'We were all so dazzled by Ian's product that we failed to see we were being played in the most old-fashioned way imaginable. Menov's solid and genuine material bought Moscow two things: a guarantee that Ian's career would continue to progress to positions of ever greater influence and power.'

'And the certainty that any other material he brought to the table would be treated with the utmost seriousness,' Kate said, finishing his train of thought.

'Precisely.' Sir Alan faced her again. 'We were so impressed with Menov that we took our eye off the ball when it came to Irina's material. If Ian vouched for it, it must have been kosher. Their misinformation plays were begun in earnest there and then. And we've been eating them up ever since.'

'But why did Irina approach me?' Kate asked.

Sir Alan sat in the chair again and stared into the empty fireplace. 'I've been asking myself that,' he said quietly.

'The way it looks to me is this: they tried to get Irina on to our books in Bucharest, but didn't have any luck. They recruited Ian in New York, then got him back to London to a position where he could make sure the next approach was taken more seriously. It would have set off red flags to produce her in London, so better to have her approach a busy young officer working in Counter-Terrorism in Istanbul, in the full knowledge you would *have* to pass it on to the Russia Desk in London.'

'And once they've got it all set up,' Kate said, 'they give Ian Menov to act as his guarantee.'

'Yes,' Sir Alan said. 'Yes.'

'Is Dante real?'

'I think so.'

'Do you know about Incisor, Andrew's new agent in Moscow?'

'Yes.'

'Then don't you think it's all a bit *convenient*? Two things happen in tandem. A disillusioned SVR agent approaches a British diplomat in Istanbul to claim that this whole affair is a huge misinformation ploy conceived years ago with the help of a mysterious agent, Dante, at the very top of the Service. And, at the exact same time, a new agent comes on stream in Moscow with the intel that Igor has been running a special unit for two decades or more, handling the sensational material of a top source in London?'

'It is possible that it's a bit convenient, yes.' He nodded slowly. 'I do accept that. But it's also possible that, after years of flailing around and being comprehensively outplayed by our opponents, we're at last closing in on the truth.'

'Does Ian know about my inquiry?'

'I assume so. What else would explain his coded threat to you this morning?'

'You saw that too? I wondered if I was imagining it.'

'You weren't.'

'He was indicating he would use all the resources at his disposal to set me up as the culprit?' she asked.

'How else could you explain it?' Sir Alan paused. 'But it does add weight to the idea that we're finally closing in on him and he's feeling the pressure.'

'Do you think Rose will really authorize Maja's transfer to this country?'

'If I know her. She has nerves of steel.'

'Will he fire her?'

'No! You must know by now that Ian's bark is mostly worse than his bite. And if he's really the Moscow spy we think he is, he'll save his powder for defending himself. That, I think we can assume, he will do with all necessary ferocity.'

Kate's phone had been repeatedly buzzing in her pocket and she took it out to check who was trying to get hold of her in such a hurry. She noticed she had not one but five missed calls from her mother's care home. 'I'm so sorry,' she said. 'This is to do with my mother. They just don't usually call five times. You mind if I check?'

'Of course.'

Kate stepped out into the hallway. As she called back the care home, she noticed a turquoise scarf draped over the back of an armchair by an old mahogany dresser. It didn't look like the kind Mrs Evans might wear. It reminded her of one of Rose's.

'Mrs Henderson,' the anxious voice at the other end of the line said. It was Jane, the manager of her mother's care home. 'I'm afraid I have some terrible news. We went up to check on your mother half an hour ago and I'm so sorry to have to tell you she's passed away.'

15

KATE MANAGED TO arrange the funeral in five days. She told herself this was to do with the pressing nature of her current work assignment, not because she wished to hurry her final farewell.

Lucy was buried in the graveyard at the church of the Surrey village in which Kate had grown up. It was a blustery day with occasional bursts of sunshine and spits of rain, which seemed somehow appropriate for her mother's changeable temperament.

Kate went through the motions. She chose the coffin, planned the service and the wake in the nearby village hall, then issued the invitations, mostly verbally, working through her mother's telephone book to friends long forgotten. It was all-consuming, even if she did have the help of Rose and her children, and extremely lonely.

On the day, in the run-up to the service, despite the warm squeezes of affection from many good and decent people – a lot of them really old friends of her father, Jim – she was conscious of feeling absolutely nothing save for the faintest hint of relief.

Even as she watched her mother's coffin lowered into the earth and they bade their final farewells, she couldn't summon anything that vaguely resembled a tear. She told herself she was staying strong for Fiona and Gus, both of whom were visibly stricken with grief.

Kate turned away towards the village hall with a bewildering sense of otherness. What on earth was wrong with her? Who buries their mother and feels nothing in the process?

Other than that, the funeral was notable for the surprising nature of the guest list. Stuart had returned, having been given special permission to enter the United Kingdom for twenty-four hours by the prime minister via Shirley Grove, while Sir Alan Brabazon and Ian Granger had turned up uninvited, telling Kate at the entrance to the church that they wanted to be there to 'support' her.

Kate had no idea how Ian could even have found out Lucy had died, unless he had taken to surveying the deaths column of *The Times*, which seemed unlikely.

Stuart drove them from the church to the village hall in silence. He squeezed Kate's hand in the front of the car and she wished he wouldn't. But she didn't ask him to stop, or even catch his eye.

She waited inside the door of the hall and greeted the mourners as they filed into the drab interior, sipped champagne and ate canapés, which Rose and her husband Simon had organized and paid for. Since Simon was a very successful financier, both were expensive.

After the first few dozen guests, Kate grew tired of her obligations and took to circulating among those who had already filed in. She was mostly intent on avoiding people she didn't wish to have to confront today. Aside from Ian, and possibly even Sir Alan, they included Emma Johnson, the wife of the man Lucy had conducted an affair with throughout most of Kate's childhood. Their daughter, Helen, had been Kate's best friend until the affair had been revealed, after which they were never allowed to speak again.

Kate had not invited Emma Johnson and she was insulted that she had turned up. Once or twice, she caught Emma heading in her direction and quickly moved on.

It took almost an hour before Ian caught her alone. 'Kate,' he said. 'I hope you're bearing up.'

By this point, Kate had consumed quite a few glasses of Simon's fine champagne. A few too many. 'What are you doing here, Ian?' she asked.

'Just wanted to support you, old girl.' Ian was drinking squash and he swirled the remnants in his glass, then drained it. He'd thrown a jacket over his habitually casual attire, but he still looked like an overgrown student.

'That's too kind of you,' she said.

'Now, now. My secretary told me your mother had passed away. I knew you had a complicated relationship with her. I thought it might be a good idea to come and offer some moral support. After all, the Service owes you a great debt.'

Kate didn't know where to begin to dice this unlikely explanation for his presence here. 'It's decent of you,' she said easily.

'How are you?' he asked. 'We didn't really get to the bottom of that the other morning.'

'Fine.'

'We have a duty of care, as you know, not only during the years of employment, but afterwards, too. So if there's anything I or we can do together, don't hesitate to let me know.'

'I will, thank you.'

Kate was about to break off and go in search of more congenial company when he leant in closer. He had never been one to respect anyone else's personal space, especially when it came to the women he worked with. 'I just wondered what you were up to,' he asked.

'In what sense?' Kate was distracted by the sight of Sir Alan and Rose in deep conversation in the corner. She recalled the scarf she had seen in Sir Alan's house. Could it possibly be that Rose had also travelled down to see him that day and, if so, why?

'Well, I'm aware you left under something of a cloud. I've not had any other employer approach me to check a reference, which I have, of course, promised to provide. So I was just keen to ensure you're getting along okay.'

'I'm fine, thank you.'

'Good. Good.' He nodded. 'As I said, very happy to provide that reference – and even to help you find a job in the private sector if that would be helpful.'

'But?' she said. 'Because I'll take a wild guess that there is a "but" here.'

'I'd obviously wish to know if you were stepping back into territory that might impinge on our interests.'

'Your interests singular, or plural?'

'Well, without being pompous, dare I suggest it's the same thing?'

'Congratulations on your elevation, by the way,' she said. 'You've certainly earned it.'

Ian smiled at her. 'Characteristically ambiguous. I like that. And punchy as ever.'

'Get to the point, Ian.'

'That was the point. If there was a chance you might step on my toes, I'd like to know about it. I think you owe me that.'

Kate was minded to say she didn't owe him a damned thing, but as she broke away from the conversation all she could think about was who had tipped him off about her investigation. His wife, Shirley Grove, Julie?

She turned away, but that didn't take her into better territory. Emma Johnson had clearly been lurking, waiting for her chance. 'Kate,' she said. 'How nice to see you.'

'Thank you for coming,' Kate said mechanically.

'How are you?'

Kate stared at the woman. What did she expect her to say? And were they really, after all these years – after so much pain and heartache – going to stand there and exchange inanities?

Well, yes, perhaps that was the British way. And, if so, she could play with the best of them. 'I'm well,' she said. 'Fine.' And then as she gazed at Emma's concerned face, something broke inside her. It was not, after all, this poor woman's fault that her husband had betrayed his own marriage and ruined Kate's childhood. 'I hated my mother, so if you want the honest truth, I don't feel a damned thing today except relief.'

'But that in itself can be complicated,' Emma said, without missing a beat or appearing in any way surprised at the intrusion of raw honesty into the usual funeral small-talk. 'You've lost the chance of ever having a better relationship with her and that can be a traumatic realization, however much your rational mind tells you it was never going to be possible.'

'Maybe. How's Helen?'

'She's well. Married, with two children.' Emma smiled. 'Like you. I just had a chat with your kids. They're a great credit to you . . . I'm sorry your friendship was a casualty of those events. I hope you understand now why that was inevitable.'

If she was being truly honest, Kate hadn't seen at all why her relationship with Helen – her best friend – had had to be sacrificed, but she knew enough about the pain of infidelity to refrain from judging another woman's response to it. 'She missed you terribly,' Emma said. 'And I guess I'll carry the guilt of that to my grave.'

'I don't think there's much point in going over this,' Kate said. 'You were wronged. I don't blame you for any of it.'

'Thank you. That's kind,' Emma responded. Simon appeared at Kate's elbow. He introduced himself, but Emma didn't linger. 'I must let you talk to your other guests. It was nice to see you again.'

'Sorry, you looked like you needed help,' Simon said.

'Thank you. My mother had an affair with her husband, so she wasn't top of the list of people I wanted to see today.'

'Funerals have a habit of bringing people out of the woodwork. At my father's, not one but two mistresses turned up. I had to physically bar them from the wake.'

'One day,' Kate said wearily, 'I'd love to understand why so many human beings choose to endlessly complicate their lives.'

'Because they are easily bored, I suppose.' He shook his head. 'I always think people are divided between those who are drawn to emotional complication and those who prefer intellectual variety. The tragedy is when you mix someone from one group with the other.'

Kate smiled. 'That,' she said, 'surely counts as philosophy.'

Rose arrived. 'You don't look like you have drunk nearly enough.'

'I'm trying.'

'Was that David Johnson's wife?' She was looking at Emma as she gathered her coat and slipped out of the door.

'Yes.'

'Why was she here?'

'Guilt, I think.'

'About your mother?' Rose looked incredulous.

'Me.'

Rose nodded. 'Good for her, I suppose. Cutting you off was hardly fair.'

Kate steeled herself. 'Right, I must circulate.' She moved on. She drank several more glasses of champagne, until she felt as if she was actually floating through the wake, rather as her father might have done. He'd always known how to drink his way through an emotional crisis. She made small-talk with Sir Alan, who said quietly he'd been worried at her decision to step back into old territory and had wanted to be there to say she would always have his support in all aspects of her life. This almost made her cry.

The wake ground on for too long and she was exhausted

by the time they had cleared up the village hall and loaded everyone back into the car for London. Rose and Simon were absolute Trojans, insisting on quietly and seamlessly doing the lion's share of the work, and Rose's goodbye hug was particularly heartfelt. The only complication was that Kate had intended to drop Stuart back at Heathrow for his return flight to Moscow, but was too drunk to drive. They returned instead to Battersea in silence, both children lost in their headphones in the back and Kate half asleep in the passenger seat.

Kate ordered Stuart an Uber, aware he no longer had the wherewithal even to pay for a taxi, and they were left with an awkward few moments alone on the doorstep as they waited for its arrival. 'You going to be okay?' he asked.

She wanted to ask him what he'd meant by holding her hand, not once but several times in the course of the day, but managed to restrain herself. 'I'll be fine,' she said. 'It was good of you to come.'

'I wouldn't have missed it for anything. She was a difficult old bat, but she was your mother.'

The car arrived. Stuart plainly wanted to linger, to embrace, to engage in the kind of slow farewell only lovers can. But that wasn't where Kate was at, so to his visible disappointment she gave him a friendly peck on the cheek and stepped back towards her doorstep.

He smiled wanly, but took it like a man – and with a shrug, which seemed to suggest he accepted reconciliation was never going to be easy.

Gus, who had been lurking unseen in the doorway, rushed forward to embrace his father. And when he was finally released, Stuart asked, 'Where's your sister?'

'In a mood. You know how she is.'

By the time Kate had closed the front door on the emotional complications and confusion her former husband represented, she felt overwhelmed by tiredness. But after making a cup of tea and losing her son to Netflix, she went up to check on Fiona. Her daughter sat cross-legged on her bed, headphones on. 'I'm fine,' she said, without removing them.

Kate waited patiently, as she had learnt to do. Her daughter's cheeks were stained with tears.

Fiona eventually took off her headphones. Kate sat gingerly on the end of the bed, as if stepping on eggshells. 'You okay?'

'Fine.'

'Is it something to do with Dad?'

Fiona's phone buzzed with a message. She flipped it over, but not before Kate had seen it was from Fiona's boyfriend, Jay. Her daughter wiped another tear from her eye. 'Everything all right?' Kate asked.

The dam burst as Fiona convulsed with tears. Kate moved closer and wrapped her daughter in her arms, as she had so often when she was a little girl. It took some time before the truth spilt out. 'It was meant for his old girlfriend. He denied it, but I know it.'

'What was?'

'He sent me a WhatsApp message. *She's at a party on Saturday – some lame friend. How about we meet at your place, just like old times?* Kiss, kiss, bloody kiss. But it's obviously me who's at the party. I'd only told him ten minutes before.'

Kate's first thought was to wonder if Jay had done it deliberately as a way of fobbing Fiona off, but perhaps she'd just spent too long mixing with the likes of Ian. She tried her best to reassure her daughter and gradually the tears subsided. Fiona pulled back, leant against her headboard. 'I'm over him, anyway.'

'Are you?'

'Yes.'

'It's the oldest cliché in the world, but you're only sixteen. There are many fish in the sea.'

Fiona was staring thoughtfully at her hands. 'For you, too?'

'Where's that coming from?'

'Why did he have to do it?' Fiona looked up at her and, for the first time, Kate saw anger in her daughter's face. 'Why did he do it to us?'

'Dad?'

'Of course Dad.'

'Is that why you didn't come down to say goodbye?'

Fiona didn't give her an answer. 'How can you contemplate going back to him?'

Kate tried to think hard through the fog of alcohol. Her daughter's mood swings were so frequent and violent, she knew better than to trust this as a settled view. But it was a big change nonetheless. 'Sometimes we need to forgive people. I just don't know yet whether I'm capable of it.'

'Or if it's actually what you want?'

'That, too.' She leant forward and kissed her daughter's forehead. 'It's something we both need to sleep on. I'm sure things will be clearer in the morning.'

Kate went to her own room, brushed her teeth and slipped gratefully into bed. Her final thought was that it seemed highly unlikely she would be proved right. What chance was there that anything would seem clearer in the morning?

Kate awoke with a belting hangover. She got up, showered, dressed again and ministered to the children's needs before packing them off to school. She'd said to Rose she was returning to 'work' that day and would call her if she needed support on the home front. But before she could turn her attention to the concerns of Shirley Grove's inquiry, she had the small matter of an appointment with her psychiatrist, Dr Wiseman, to attend to. Vastly improved as her mental state generally was, she recognized the need to continue to tap into his apparently infinite wisdom.

So, at just a shade after nine she was seated in the deep leather chair in his office in Ealing, watching the shafts of sunlight dance through his thick curly hair from the slatted blinds behind his desk. He was writing again and she wondered how many of his neat A4 notebooks he had filled with details of her psychological torments and the history behind them.

Now that she knew him so well – or, rather, that he knew *her* so well – she got pretty much straight to the point. 'My mother is dead and I feel nothing,' she said.

He explored this for some time before piercing her gloom with an observation that perhaps ought to have been more self-evident. 'It's often more complicated to lose a parent we don't love,' he said.

'Oh, yeah?' she replied.

'Yes,' he said. 'Because with your mother's death has gone any potential of a better relationship, a reconciliation, a reckoning – or whatever it is that the wounded child within you really wanted.'

'A better mother.'

'That, too. I don't suppose you ever stopped hoping that that woman was in there somewhere. Now you'll never find her.'

Kate was silent for a long time. It was the observation Emma Johnson had astutely made at the wake. 'Stuart came over from Moscow for the funeral,' she said finally, as if it was a natural segue from what had gone before.

Dr Wiseman didn't blink. 'I thought he was banned from entry to this country.'

'He is. I negotiated an exception.'

'Why?' he asked.

'Good question.'

'What's the answer?'

He was tapping the tip of the pen against the top of the page, which she'd noticed he did when he was surprised at a turn the conversation had taken. It didn't happen often. 'I told you we'd made an arrangement that I would take the children to meet him in France or wherever else he could get to.'

'Yes. You thought it was important for their wellbeing.'

'Well, on one of those occasions, we slept together – or had some . . .' she stared at her hands '. . . sexual activity.'

'Why?'

'I don't know. The pull of the familiar, a desire to put the children first and give them the reconciliation they long for, a yearning to break free of the confusion of endlessly conflicted emotions.'

'A test?'

'Maybe.'

'A chance to re-establish your power over him, to punish him even?'

Kate didn't want to think of it like that. 'I do still love him.'

'And yet you cannot accept his betrayal, so a healthier part of you wants to move on?'

'It was a spur-of-the-moment decision. But it led to me agreeing to attempt reconciliation.'

'Is that what you want?'

'I don't know what I want. But I made the promise to the children, as well as to Stuart, so now I'm trapped. I don't think I can go back on it.'

Dr Wiseman put down his pen and straightened out his jacket. 'Let me ask you this. *Have* you forgiven your husband for his infidelity?'

'No.'

'Why not?'

'Because he knew what he was doing. He knew it mattered to me more than anything. It's not just the promises we made in a church in front of our friends and family, it's something we discussed often when we were younger, heart to heart, lover to lover, friend to friend. It was incredibly important to me, especially given what had happened to my family – but maybe to my character anyway. If you can't be loyal to someone you love and care about, if life is just a series of animal transactions, then it's meaningless, pointless, hopeless . . .'

'That's a lot of pressure to be placing on one human being.'

'Was I wrong to do so?'

'Not necessarily. I would say to err is human, but at the same time it isn't wrong to exchange a promise with a lover and expect him to keep his side of the bargain. That's in the nature of human affection. My question is not could one – theoretically – forgive someone, or should one do so, but merely can *you*?'

'I don't know the answer to that question.'

'Then you should not be considering reconciliation.'

'It's not as simple as that.'

'In this case, it is. I would suggest it isn't fair to either of your children – or even to Stuart – to pursue a reconciliation you know in your heart of hearts is impossible. It will open the door to the prospect of further heartbreak for all of you.'

Kate stared at the floor. Was that what she'd wanted to hear? 'But I made a promise to them.'

Dr Wiseman leant forward. He was smiling at her kindly now. 'You should give yourself time, Kate. There is no rush. If you can find it within yourself to forgive Stuart for his errors, then you can perhaps move on to assessing whether reconciliation is truly what you want. But if you cannot do the former, you cannot reasonably entertain the prospect of the latter.'

Kate glanced at the clock. Her forty-five minutes was up too soon, as always – and she'd yet to admit she'd returned to the same kind of work. She mumbled a thank-you and stumbled out into a deserted street.

She shuffled along a few paces and sat on a garden wall. She closed her eyes and let the sun warm her face. Did she forgive Stuart? Could she? Was reconciliation with him really what she wanted? She just couldn't understand why she didn't know. She'd grown so used to relying on strong instincts in life and here she was without any on the most important question before her.

She missed him, yes. But in the way we all mourn a relationship that has run its course, or in the kind of visceral sense that might force her to forgive and forget?

Her phone buzzed with a WhatsApp message from Julie. *Get in here fast. The shit just monumentally hit the fan.*

16

IT DIDN'T TAKE Julie long to fill Kate in – and by the time she had finished, the story was breaking on the TV screen in the corner of their makeshift office in Pimlico.

The prime minister had been dragged into another scandal that was unfolding with speed and force across the Atlantic in New York. Last night, a hedge-fund mogul called Malcolm Glass had been found dead in his Manhattan apartment having taken a lethal overdose of sleeping pills. Shortly after his maid had reported his death, the FBI confirmed it had been investigating him for many months for sex trafficking, including of minors, solicitation and a whole swathe of other offences.

The rolling news channels were already referring to him as the paedophile billionaire. But there was more. Early that morning, the FBI had added further details of what it had discovered in Malcolm Glass's New York apartment, which included videotapes of a number of rich and powerful people having massages and sexual contact of various descriptions with underage girls who had been trafficked to Glass's private Caribbean island – Paedophile Island, as it was already being dubbed – for that express purpose. And while the FBI was careful to underline that he had not been caught on video, they did confirm that Glass's records suggested that the current British prime minister, James Ryan, had been a guest on the island three years before, during his time as foreign secretary. He'd been flown there on Malcolm Glass's private plane at the end of an official visit to Jamaica.

'So what does this mean?' Julie asked, gesturing at the TV screen. Callum was next to her, sitting on the desk with his enormous feet on a chair.

'Nothing,' Kate said.

'It has to mean something.' Kate went to sit down. Julie came with her. 'I've tracked down the Czech girl Ian was screwing in New York. She still works for Czech intelligence, though I'm not sure of her role. She's back in Prague. I got her mobile number.'

'How?' Kate asked.

'The Americans. I tried Jason Snipe at Langley, which I thought was easier than alerting anyone in Vauxhall.'

'What reason did you give?'

'I didn't. I said it was a routine enquiry. He gave me something else too. They've long had her down as a probable Russian double agent within the Czech service.'

Callum whistled quietly. 'That sounds pretty big, doesn't it?' They turned towards him. 'There are just too many things stacking up against Ian for comfort.'

Kate's phone was ringing. She glanced at the caller ID

and decided to ignore it. The last person she needed to hear from right now was Imogen Conrad, the current foreign secretary, Stuart's former boss – and lover.

But Imogen kept calling. And Kate thought it better to put her off the scent by answering before she contacted SIS and demanded to know where she was. Kate had not spoken to her since she'd left the Service.

'Imogen, it's been a while,' she said.

'Yes, sorry about that.'

'I can't imagine why you're calling.'

'This is it, Kate. It's one thing too many. The Party won't stand for it. He's done for.'

'We've said that before.'

'This time is different. Downing Street isn't even bothering to deny that he was on this wretched bloody Paedophile Island.'

'What *are* they saying, out of interest?' Kate asked.

'Just that he saw nothing untoward. Now listen to me. I need whatever you've got. I'm pretty sure we have enough letters to force a no-confidence vote and I'm certain he'll lose.'

For a moment, Kate was too stunned to speak. The woman who'd seduced her husband, destroyed her marriage and arguably smashed up her career now expected her to do her bidding at the drop of a hat? 'I'm afraid I can't help, Imogen. I'm sorry.'

There was a brief silence. 'I thought you might say that.' She'd lowered her voice, so that it was richer and deeper, moving from political bruiser to seducer in no more than a heartbeat. She did that often, with not a trace of self-consciousness. 'But the man is a monster. You know it,

I know it. And now we both have a chance to do something about it. We just need some more details about that island – how long he was there, with whom, what exactly went on, you know the kind of thing.'

'I'm sorry. I really can't help.'

'I could order you to. I'm your boss technically, after all.'

Kate made her wait, enjoying herself more than she probably meant to. Since she'd been appointed foreign secretary a few months before, Imogen had not seen fit to reach out to the woman she'd called a friend when it suited her, as it did now. 'I've left SIS,' Kate said. 'I quit a few months ago after the debacle over that defector.'

There was a long silence. 'My God, Kate. I didn't know. I'm so sorry.'

'I shouldn't be. I'd had enough. It was time.'

'Were you fired? I could reinstate you.'

'No, I quit.'

'I am . . .'

Kate imagined her nemesis sitting in that richly resplendent office, staring out over Horse Guards Parade, scheming to get across the short stretch of tarmac that divided the foreign secretary's realm from that of the prime minister in Downing Street. 'I'm genuinely sorry,' Imogen continued flatly. 'I guess I should probably feel partly, if not wholly, responsible. If I'd known, I'd have tried to get you to stay. Ian Granger could do with some wise advice, in my experience so far.'

'Good luck with your mutiny.'

'No, wait.' There was a heavy sigh. 'Look, I should have called,' Imogen said. 'I'm sorry. It's really terrible to be in touch only when I need something, but the remit of this job is so damned huge it's taken every ounce of my time and energy reading in and travelling halfway across the globe while fighting to prevent Harry divorcing me. I should have got in touch to check how you were and I'm sorry.'

'I'm fine.'

'But I could do with some advice on this. You always know where the bodies are buried – or at least where to look for them.'

'I really can't help.' There was another silence. 'I'm sorry, Imogen, I have to go.'

'Please, Kate. I need you.' Her voice was imploring now. 'I'll make it worth your while if I get to Number Ten – any way you want me to.'

Kate was about to tell her former friend where to stick her offer when she thought better of it. What if Imogen was right and the coup she was mounting saw the prime minister rapidly shoved from office? How long would it take? A week, two at most?

And what would the prime minister's promises in relation to Stuart count for then?

'I knew I could rely on you,' Imogen said – as ever running ahead of herself. 'I'll pop around tonight.'

Kate didn't even have time to reply before Imogen had rung off. And she'd not put her phone back on the desk before she received a summons from the prime minister to Downing Street: *Come to Number Ten immediately*, the text read. *JR*.

Kate wasn't expecting a welcoming committee and she didn't get one. The prime minister's office at Number Ten was comfortably furnished, with a cream sofa, armchairs and a coffee-table beyond the broad desk, and enough bookshelves to pass as a library, but it was small and into it were crammed the prime minister and most of his immediate team, including Shirley Grove. Kate had brought Callum with her, at his suggestion.

James Ryan slouched against the side, hands thrust into his pockets. His cheeks were puffy and red, his dark hair tangled, as if he had purposely stuck it through a hedge for this meeting. He looked visibly weighed down by the cares of office. 'You've seen it all, I suppose,' he said, gesturing vaguely at the bookshelf, as if it hid a secret TV screen running news of his latest humiliation on repeat. Perhaps it did. 'They're shafting me as we speak.'

'Yes. I'm sorry, Prime Minister.'

'What do you make of it?' Grove asked Kate. She was the only one keeping her composure.

'Not much.'

'Isn't it another turn of the Russian dial?' Grove pressed.

'How do you mean?'

Grove looked pained, as though she was dealing with a difficult pupil. 'They've just found another way of setting up the prime minister, surely.'

Kate thought about this. It had not immediately struck her as likely, which suggested she was still struggling to believe in the prime minister's innocence. 'If it was Moscow, I imagine they'd have faked another video. It seems to be one of their specialities.'

'Who's to say that won't emerge?' the PM said.

'Could it?'

'For God's sake, Kate.' He walked around his desk and stared out of the window at the Downing Street garden. 'I should have picked someone who actually believed in my innocence to run this inquiry. It was Grove's idea to go for you.' He spun around. 'I'm screwed. Absolutely fucked.' He was looking directly at Kate now, as though this were all her fault. 'The chief whip tells me Imogen Conrad and her mutinous band are a day or two at most away from having enough letters to trigger a no-confidence vote. So that probably means I could be staring down the barrel of political annihilation in a week's time. You think you'll be able to prove I'm being set up by then?'

'I don't know, Prime Minister.'

'Well, can't you give me a progress report!?'

'All I can say is that we're working through things methodically, as you would expect.'

'So who is Agent Dante?'

'If he exists,' Kate said, but she regretted it. She could tell she was on the verge of pushing him too far. 'We have a suspect,' she reassured him. 'And I think we may be closing in on him.'

'Who is it?'

'I can't say just yet, I'm afraid. I don't think that would be fair.'

'How long until you can?'

She shook her head. 'I wouldn't want to put a timescale on it.'

The PM glanced at Grove and the sallow, slim man next to her, who Kate vaguely remembered was Downing Street's head of communications. 'We're going to have to leak it,' the PM said sombrely.

Grove sucked in her cheeks. The sallow man nodded sagely. Kate sensed his career depended on nodding a lot at what his boss had to say, but perhaps they were all like that. 'Leak what?' Kate asked.

'We have to get on the front foot,' the sallow man said. 'And we have to do it now. If the public knew about Dante, they'd be more inclined to view this as what it is: another plot to undermine the PM.'

Kate stared at him, dumbfounded. 'You absolutely cannot leak it,' she said. No one answered her. 'If you do that, whoever it is will cover his tracks and we'll never be able to prove what he's done to you.'

'If we wait any longer, it won't matter,' the PM shot back.

'Give me another week,' Kate said. She'd blurted out the timescale on instinct, with no forethought.

'I haven't got a week.'

'I'll get you a result by the night before the no-confidence vote, if it happens.'

'Are you sure about that, Kate?' It was Callum, who was leaning in close to her. 'I mean, I'm only an ingénu in these matters, I accept, but it seems a pretty complex inquiry to me.'

'If that's what it takes to keep it out of the public domain,' she said, 'then that is all I've got. Right?'

Callum didn't argue with her and neither did anyone else.

'Why did you go to the island?' Kate asked the PM.

'What island?' he asked.

Even Grove seemed startled by this protestation of ignorance.

'The one Malcolm Glass owned,' Kate said.

'Paedophile Island,' the sallow man chipped in. The PM

glared at him. He thrust his hands deep into his pockets again, as if he was going to find an answer there.

'I can't remember. It was years ago, for God's sake.'

'Three years,' Kate said. Now he stared at her. 'It would help to have some sense of how well you knew Glass and how he lured you into his web.'

'I don't bloody know,' the PM snapped. 'He was a friend of a friend. I met him in London originally. He seemed well connected, hanging out with fashion designers, actors, rock stars and even royalty. I just sort of bumped into him regularly. He seemed to know everyone.'

'And he invited you to join him on the island?'

'I sat opposite him at a dinner party held by a Party donor. I mentioned in passing I was about to head off to Jamaica. He said why didn't I come and stay on his paradise island. There would be some interesting people that weekend. He'd fly me over and back. I couldn't see any reason to refuse. I only told my office I was taking a few days off, but I didn't say where I was going or with whom.'

'Who was there?'

'Oh, I don't know. Mostly business people. A couple of American billionaires. An actor from some big American TV series. I didn't know any of them.'

'And what did you see?'

'Nothing!' The PM turned to face the garden again. 'Nothing at all! It was quite a boring weekend, to be frank. I should never have gone. Glass was starting to give me the creeps anyway.'

'Why?'

'I don't know. He was all over you like a rash.'

'Did you see any young girls?'

'Of course I didn't. It was a big place. You had your own bungalow and then there was a big airy central hallway where you could talk to a kind of receptionist and book into all kinds of activity from sailing to kite-surfing. No one mentioned anything about massages.'

He was still facing the garden and Kate was as sure as she reasonably could be that he was lying. Not for the first time, she questioned the wisdom of the path on which she had now embarked. Was there some special place in hell for those who defended the reprehensible and the guilty?

But she told herself she wasn't there for him, for his government, her country or anything at all, in fact, but the health and wellbeing of her family. 'Give me a week and I'll clear you,' she heard herself saying.

He turned to her. 'All right,' he said. 'But you'd better be bloody right, Mrs Henderson, or I warn you there'll be hell to pay.'

17

CALLUM KEPT PACE with Kate as she hurried along Downing Street. 'Are you sure that was a wise promise to make?' he said.

'Did it seem like we had a choice?'

Kate accelerated to try to kill the conversation, but she fairly quickly discovered the obvious flaw in this tactic: Callum's legs were so long that he needed only a single stride for two of her own. 'Why are you doing this?' he asked, as they swung on to Whitehall.

Kate waited until they'd woven through the tourists loitering in the sunshine outside the gate before she answered. 'Why am I doing what?'

'No one has explained to me why you left SIS, though I guess being lured into Agent Dante's web had something to do with it. So why are you doing this?'

'Does it matter?'

'It would help me to know. It might explain why you just made an undeliverable promise.'

Kate stopped. 'Callum, we're going to get along just fine if you do what I ask without issue or complication and *don't* ask me questions about my motives.'

'Ah, and if I do, what happens? I get promoted?'

As he towered over her, his handsome face creased with the faintest hint of a grin, she was aware for the first time of the true impact of his charisma. Young he might be, but naive he was not. 'If your true motive is revenge for being forced out of SIS, then it would be good to know,' he said. 'That's all.'

'It's not.'

'I'd understand if you wanted to bring Ian Granger down,' he went on, 'if he was the guy who forced you from the organization you'd devoted your life to.'

'He wasn't.'

'Has the prime minister promised you something?'

'Why do you ask that?'

'Because that's normally how he works. He rarely delivers on any commitment, as I'm sure you've worked out.'

Of course Kate knew the prime minister's word was worth almost nothing – and yet wasn't she, on some level, relying on it? 'So what do you think I should have said back there?' she asked.

'If you're asking my honest advice, I'd have held firm, warning against the leak but saying you'll deliver the verdict of your investigation whenever it's ready. He might well survive the no-confidence vote anyway – and, if he doesn't, whoever succeeds him is going to want to get to the bottom of this.'

'How public-spirited of them.' She started walking again. 'What do you really make of him?' Callum burst out laughing. 'What's so funny?' she demanded.

'He's a politician! I mean, if you really want to know, we'll be here for hours. He's selfish, but capable of altruism and generosity. He's egotistical, insecure, but bullish, even brutish – a suit of armour he's learnt to put on. He's emotionally incontinent and utterly unreliable, but needs to be loved in a way that is by turns endearing and pathetic. He's smart, cunning and likes to make bold gestures, though he's also capable of chronic indecision. He's funny sometimes, kind at others, but an absolute bastard when his back's to the wall. How long have you got?'

'Do you think he's innocent?'

'Of course.'

'Why?'

'Who in their right mind would even *try* to blackmail him?'

Kate didn't have an answer for that and she passed the rest of the journey back to their office deep in thought. Maybe Callum was right. Who would ever think James Ryan a suitable candidate for blackmail?

Julie had been back to SIS Headquarters in Vauxhall to print off a copy of the top-secret file on Ian's Czech lover, Eva Svobodova, which was now on Kate's desk.

She sat down, pulled her desk lamp closer, opened the file and tried to pay attention to the woman before her. It was a welcome escape.

Eva had been beautiful, without question. Not that this was a surprise: by and large, Ian had good taste. She had grown into a handsome woman with fashionable steel-rimmed glasses. She had begun her career in Prague in 1989, the same time, more or less, as Ian Granger had started out in SIS in London – just as the old Soviet Empire had begun to fall apart. New York had been her first foreign posting, a plum assignment for a young Czech agent, where, like Ian, she'd worked undercover as a press attaché in her country's UN delegation. Three years later, she had been transferred to Washington, where she was still undeclared as a press attaché at the embassy there.

After that, she had moved to Santiago in Chile. Kate checked her notes to find that Eva's time there overlapped with Ian's by six months. She was then sent on undeclared to Paris and then declared to London. She was currently head of the counter-terrorism unit in the Czech Foreign Intelligence Service in Prague.

Kate picked up a pencil and returned to the section relating to Eva's time in Santiago. Every one of her other postings had a few paragraphs describing her perceived duties, role and activities – usually written up by the SIS resident head of station – but her time in Santiago was blank.

Had Ian not bothered to write anything up about his former lover? Or had he been covering his tracks? Kate made a note on the side of the page to check with Julie as to whether the document had been recently edited inside SIS – and, if so, by whom. She put the file back on Julie's desk and returned to check some of the newspaper websites to be sure of the Malcolm Glass story, with its many grisly details of what had taken place on 'Paedophile Island'. Then she headed for the door.

Kate practically ran home, keen suddenly to be away

from it all. She cooked supper – a form of therapy that never failed – and lingered at the dinner table with Gus, Fiona and her boyfriend Jay. He was dancing around Fiona like a gadfly. She looked as if she might punch him at any moment. 'Is it true the prime minister is a paedophile?' Gus blurted out, after they had finished eating.

'I don't know.'

'He's a sleazy creep,' Fiona said, a remark that seemed intended for her wayward boyfriend. Kate had warmed to Jay over the past year, but it was surely time for him to be shown the door.

'I'm not sure that makes him a paedophile,' Jay said, and Fiona shot him a warning glance.

Kate's phone buzzed and, before she could turn it over, everyone had seen that it was a message from Stuart. 'Is that from Dad?' Fiona asked, though she knew very well it had been.

'What does he want?' Gus asked.

' "Coming under some pressure. They want to meet this week," ' Fiona said, displaying an impressive ability to read upside down at speed. 'What does that mean?'

'I'd better not go into it.'

'I thought you were going to be honest with us.'

'Not to that degree.'

There was a brief, tense silence. Fiona glared at her mother. 'You said we were all in this together,' she said eventually. 'We have a right to know if he's causing more trouble.' Now it was Gus's turn to shoot his sister a warning glance. Or was it just surprise at having lost an ally?

'There are some things it's better for you not to know,' Kate said quietly.

'Like what?'

'Like the pressure Dad is under from the people who blackmailed and recruited him in Moscow, or the plan we've both agreed to deal with it.'

Gus looked up. His face had been transformed. 'You have a plan.'

Kate was reminded that teenage boys wanted to know only that things were going to work out all right. Unlike his sister, he had no desire to probe for the details. 'Yes, we have a plan.'

'Will it work?' Fiona asked, as her mother reminded herself for the umpteenth time that her daughter's episodic bouts of aggression were really just concealed anxiety.

'Yes,' Kate said. 'It will.'

'Are you sure?' Gus probed.

'Yes, I am.'

Then Kate deliberately changed tack, asking Gus how his rugby team was shaping up. As she had predicted, Fiona grew bored very quickly and hauled Jay off to her room. He looked as if he was expecting punishment, and Kate found herself praying that Fiona would take the plunge and send him packing. It might allow a little peace to descend.

Shortly afterwards Gus ran out of steam discussing the ins and outs of Compton House rugby. Kate had just enough time to wash up (though she was slightly unclear why she was doing it) and pour herself another large glass of wine before Julie and Callum turned up for the discussion she'd not had time for in the office.

Like Callum, Julie was more than a little surprised at the promise Kate had made to the prime minister. But she said she'd come via SIS to check Eva Svobodova's file again and established that Ian had edited it six years before. Kate filled Callum in on the context.

The three sat in silence as Kate and Callum absorbed that information. 'But why would Ian do something so unsubtle and so certain to be traced back to him if he really was Dante?' Callum asked.

'Because there was something in it that would have incriminated him,' Julie said.

'But he wrote it up,' Callum said. 'At least, I assume he must have done if you said he was the station chief in Santiago at the same time she was there.'

'Not necessarily,' Kate clarified. 'They only overlapped for six months. Maybe the report on her was written up by his successor.'

'But why would he have waited so long to edit it?' Callum asked.

'Maybe he didn't know what was in it until then,' Julie said. 'Perhaps he just wanted to wait until long after his time in Santiago before he would risk covering his tracks.'

'Or he might have wanted to clean up before he was made C,' Kate added. 'Who was his successor?' she asked Julie.

'Pete Whaley.' They shook their heads sadly.

'Where is he now?' Callum asked.

'He was killed in Tora Bora,' Julie said.

'So what do you want to do?' Callum asked. 'How do we move beyond supposition to evidence? We have a decent circumstantial case against Ian Granger, I understand that, but how do we get to actual evidence?'

Kate swigged her wine and tried to suppress the desire

to ask for a cigarette. Julie and Callum had already made one quick trip to the patio at the back of the house, where Kate knew Fiona also sneaked for illicit fags. Sometimes it was a pain in the neck having to be the grown-up in the room. 'I think we should go to Prague,' she said.

'As soon as we do that, Ian will know we're on to him for sure,' Julie said.

'Possibly. But the way he suddenly turned up at my mother's funeral suggests to me that that ship has already sailed. So, let's just suppose it was Eva who seduced, black-mailed, bribed or otherwise persuaded Ian to work for Moscow. I very much doubt she remained in the picture, or took the lead role in running him for any length of time, which means – at worst – that she'll merely pass the details of our approach back to Moscow.' Kate shrugged. 'Igor Borodin is too smart to respond to that in a knee-jerk way, but it will demonstrate to him that we're on his trail and getting closer. Under pressure, teams make mistakes, as we've learnt many times to our cost.'

'And if she was just his lover,' Julie said, 'she'll alert him back here.'

Kate thought Julie was missing the point a bit, but didn't say so. 'If you assume that Ian and Eva remained on good terms, then, yes, we gain nothing from a trip to Prague, bar alerting him and possibly Moscow to the fact that we're investigating his past. But my observation is that Ian doesn't handle women or his affairs well. So he may have broken it off badly, in which case Eva may have things to add to our understanding. I'll go with Callum and be there and back in forty-eight hours at the outside.'

Julie seemed about to protest, so Kate said, 'I need you to

do a deep dive into the files. See what you can do to trace through every tiny step of Ian's history. Eva's time in Chile may not be all he's attempted to clean up.'

Julie nodded to indicate that this made sense, though she still looked disappointed at missing out on a trip to Prague and, glancing at Callum, Kate was fairly sure she knew why.

She sent them both home and went round to her aunt's Chelsea townhouse. The front door was slightly ajar, so Kate walked into the hallway and then immediately wished she hadn't. There were raised voices from the kitchen.

'I'm sorry,' Rose said.

'You always are,' Simon replied.

'Please . . . I don't want to rake over the past.'

'Nor do I. The question is whether the past is behind us.'

'Of course it is. We agreed that we need to look forward. And that is what I am trying to do.'

Kate retreated rapidly and rang the doorbell. It was a while before Rose answered. 'I'm glad you came.'

'That sounds ominous.' Kate followed her aunt into the handsome kitchen at the rear, with its view of a small but beautiful garden, carefully lit to enhance its effect. 'Everything all right?' Kate asked.

'Of course.' Whatever the argument had been about, Simon had disappeared and Rose was determined to put on a brave face. 'Wine, whisky?' she asked.

'Tempting, but I'm fine, thank you.'

'Tea?'

'No.'

Rose took out a mug and made herself a herbal tea as the

kettle came to the boil. 'After we had that breakfast meeting with Ian, before your mother died, I went down to
Alan's house to discuss how we deal with the fact that Ian
is not going to let the past lie. Alan said he thought Ian
would launch a full-scale internal inquiry into you and
your conduct, and I'm afraid he's been proved right.'

Kate wondered why her aunt and Sir Alan should have
been so concerned about Ian raking over the past, but she
suppressed the thought immediately. This investigation
was beginning to make her start at shadows.

'This morning, he outlined his working theory to the
management committee. There is, he said, likely to have
been a high-level mole working at the heart of SIS for a
great many years.'

Kate sat. Was Ian buying time by launching a search for
himself? It might give him the excuse and time to hoover
up all available evidence and destroy it.

'But what troubled me was the outline he drew, that it
was likely to be a woman, recruited in the mid-nineties. It
seemed certain, he said, that it was also someone who had
spent much of her career working on Russia.'

'So me, basically?'

Rose sat opposite her. 'Alan's view is that the investigation has two purposes: systematically to find and destroy
evidence that would prove Ian's guilt, while pointing the
finger – circumstantially, at least – at you.'

'Sir Alan must have told you about Dante?'

Rose nodded. 'He's suspected a mole for years. It's no
surprise that more evidence has emerged that one exists.'

'What do you think I should do?'

'You have no choice. Find Dante before he or she manages

to destroy the evidence of their treachery. Or walk away and hope for the best.'

'I have a week at most. Then the prime minister pulls the plug and it becomes all too easy for everyone to lay the blame on me.'

Rose leant forward and gave her niece a tender kiss. Kate held her aunt tightly. Suddenly, she needed all the support she could get. 'Everything all right with you?' Kate asked again.

'Of course. Why wouldn't it be?'

'Oh, no reason. Just . . . checking.'

Kate made the domestic arrangements for the children, bade her aunt farewell and drove home, where she found Fiona sitting nervously with the new head of SIS, foreign secretary Imogen Conrad, and Kate's half-Vietnamese former deputy in the Service, Suzy Spencer. Imogen already had a bottle of wine open in front of her, which was the first of many ominous signs. Fiona, sensing perhaps that the temperature had just dropped ten degrees, bolted for the door. Kate wished she could do the same.

18

'IT WAS IMPORTANT to bring Ian into this,' Imogen offered, as her opening gambit, without greeting or apology.

Ian raised his hands. 'I've made it clear I'm merely a neutral observer. I can't be seen to take sides between the foreign secretary and the prime minister. That simply isn't in my remit.'

But he didn't need to explain why he was there. Ian had developed a tummy in the last few months and had the sleek, well-fed air of the avuncular father figure he now affected to be, his once unkempt blond curls tightly combed back behind his ears. One didn't have to search far for the cause of his new-found contentment. Suzy looked as if she would curl up in his lap at a moment's notice, though it would take more than a promotion and love to bring a smile to those pinched, narrow cheeks. Ian must have been eating for both of them, Kate thought uncharitably. Perhaps he had less need of Iron Man competitions now he had no superiors in the office to try to impress.

And, of course, she needed no explanation for why he might have chosen to break protocol and get involved in an essentially political matter between the prime minister and the foreign secretary. If nothing else, Ian was a master at knowing which way the wind was blowing. 'This is the last straw, Kate,' Imogen said. 'Even you can see that.'

'What is?' she asked, though she knew perfectly well.

'Paedophile Island. This man Glass is a monster. His behaviour is disgusting, shameful, abhorrent, but what really disgusts me is that he clearly got away with abusing young girls for years because he was incredibly rich, no doubt dangling his many powerful friends in front of police and prosecutors if they ever got close to him. If you read the stories, it's clear you couldn't go to that island without getting a keen sense of what was happening there. Everyone admits there were suspiciously young-looking girls all over the place. So James went. And he almost certainly partook in whatever sordid activities were on offer, or at the very least was aware of other people doing so.'

Imogen was staring at Kate, waiting for an answer. 'I'm not sure what you want from me,' she said.

'You're investigating him,' Imogen said, as if Kate was having a brain bypass.

'I've left the Service.'

'You've been set up in a special investigation unit reporting to Shirley Grove,' Imogen said. 'Everyone in Whitehall knows that.'

Kate tried to keep her temper.

Suzy was glaring at her, as if being left in the dark about this new unit was a personal insult to her. 'It would have been courteous to inform us of what was going on,' she said, glancing at Ian. 'We would undoubtedly have been able to help.'

Kate felt giddy as she stared into exactly the kind of swirling waters of Whitehall she had most wanted to avoid. How little she missed them. 'I can't talk about what I may or may not be doing,' she said finally.

There was a stunned silence. Imogen leant forward and took another enormous slug of wine. She placed her elbows firmly on the table, the glint in her eye a blend of righteous zeal and naked ambition. 'It's perfectly obvious to me that you've been right all along, Kate. That is all we're really saying here. We always knew James had loose morals, but I'm not one to throw stones into that pond, as we all very well know – and neither are many of my colleagues. However, this is something different. One, having a paedophile as prime minister is of a different order of magnitude entirely from a merely priapic one. Surely even you can see that. And two, it stands to reason that, given the evidence you were looking at before, he must surely have been turned by Moscow as a result of these proclivities. I mean, if they hadn't done so, they'd have been missing the opportunity of a lifetime. He is guilty and he must go, for the good of the country.'

'Is he, though?'

There was another long silence. They stared at her as if she had just lost her mind. Kate was reminded that when Ian and Suzy had thrown in their lot with the changing guard, they had done so with conviction. 'What do you mean, *is he*?' Suzy asked. 'I thought it was your firmly held conviction.'

'The Service devoted a lot of time, energy and expense to attempting to prove it, Kate,' Ian reminded her. 'In Istanbul at the start of the whole affair and then with Igor's attempted defection, which I knew at the time we should have gone through with.'

There were so many things Kate could have said at this point: that the defection had collapsed because the Russians had kidnapped her children; that Ian, Suzy and the Service generally had effectively demanded she totally reject any suggestion of the prime minister being a stooge for Moscow as the price for her leaving SIS without a board of inquiry into her own conduct.

But what was the point? The prime minister's fortunes had withered and he now, finally – as they all did – stood on the brink of annihilation. The Party was swinging behind Imogen Conrad, and Ian and Suzy were happy to fit the truth to this new reality. Only Imogen seemed genuinely troubled by Kate's hesitation. 'I thought you were absolutely convinced of his guilt,' she said.

'I was.'

'And now you're not?'

'I'm more hesitant.'

'Why?'

'Because the prime minister has promised to let Stuart back into the country if she carries out this investigation and declares him innocent,' Suzy said, with a triumphant smile. It was all Kate could do to resist punching her.

'Is that true?' Imogen asked.

'I need to go over everything once more,' Kate said. 'For

my own peace of mind. His argument is that he may be many things, but certainly not a paedophile. And it's true that if Moscow wanted to create a long-term misinformation ploy he would be the perfect target.'

Kate could tell Ian was torn. Since this very conclusion had been his consistently held belief from the start, it was requiring all his strength to resist informing Kate that he had told her so. Now that the political wind had changed so had his convictions.

Imogen held the floor. She was the coming force. 'Listen, Kate. You know how much I admire you,' she said. 'Tomorrow it will be announced that we have enough letters in for a vote of no confidence. It will be held next Wednesday and I'm pretty sure we're going to win. It might be a bit nip and tuck, but the Party is now over the James Ryan phenomenon. He's a tarnished, spent force, with an electorate that once thought of him as something different, and if we want to win again, we have to forge a new direction. I've been around long enough to be certain he's finished. If you carry on with your investigation, whatever he may have promised you, he will use whatever slender straws in the wind you can find as hard evidence that he's the victim of a monstrous international conspiracy.'

'But what if he's right?'

Imogen was struggling to keep her temper. 'He isn't. You know it. I know it. Ian and Suzy know it. And it's time for all of us to do our duty.'

Kate could think of few things more unlikely than Imogen being motivated by anything as quaint as doing her duty but she picked a different target. 'I thought Ian was only here as an observer,' she said. Ian gave her a withering look and she regretted the cheap shot immediately. But exposing his transparent political manoeuvres was a temptation she could never resist.

'What I'm really asking is, are you with us or against us?'

Although she was well versed in Imogen Conrad's colossal political ambition, Kate was nevertheless a bit shocked by this. She hadn't expected her to make it quite so tribal. She wondered what Imogen's often-cuckolded husband Harry thought of her new determination to rise to the very top.

Kate thought long and hard before replying. 'I'm not for or against you, Imogen, as you of all people should know. I'm just trying to get to some form of truth here.'

'How very noble of you,' Ian said. He stood. 'Good luck, Kate.' He moved to the door, Suzy with him, as if they couldn't wait to get away. Imogen appeared torn, but followed her new acolytes, a little sheepish as to how this had turned out. Kate tidied up, washed and put away the glasses, then went up to bed. Before she turned off the lights, she sent a message to Stuart: *Tell them I'll meet the day after tomorrow in Prague.*

And another to her old friend from the SIS ops division, Danny: *Hi Danny, sorry to contact you out of the blue. Any chance you could slip out for a coffee early tomorrow morning? I have a favour to ask and, inevitably, time is not on my side.*

Danny pinged a message straight back: *Anytime. Where and when?*

Kate picked a coffee house not far from the makeshift office in Pimlico and switched off the light. As a testament to her new state of mind – and, to be fair, the medication she was on – she went out in seconds and slept deeply.

19

THE HEADQUARTERS OF the Czech Foreign Intelligence Service, UZSI, were located in a nondescript grey suburban office block with a side-extension that resembled a collapsed chocolate box. After much internal debate, Kate had decided that the best course of action in approaching Ian's former lover Eva Svobodova was relative honesty. She and Callum had briefly toyed with the idea of claiming they were conducting another round of positive vetting as a result of Ian's new appointment as C, but if Eva was half the intelligence officer she was supposed to be, she would certainly check this out. Much better to say they were conducting an unspecified investigation on behalf of the Cabinet Office and offer her the cabinet secretary as a contact point.

Shirley Grove's credentials were serious enough to deliver a smiling and friendly Eva to Reception that grey afternoon. She took them to the café on the first floor and they sat in the corner overlooking the road. 'I assume you have been to Prague often enough,' she said, as she placed their coffees in front of them and took a seat opposite.

'Never,' Kate said.

Eva gestured at the road outside. 'Well, it has better views.'

'I'm sure we'll get to that.'

'How about you?' Eva asked, smiling at Callum in the way most women seemed to.

'I studied here for a year,' Callum said.

'Nice,' Eva replied. 'Then you can show your colleague around.' Eva leant forward, elbows on the table. 'What can I do for you?' She was wearing a chic grey suit with a very faint check, a cream blouse and large gold hoop earrings. She had tumbling, wild hair and could have passed as Julie's older sister. Ian clearly had a type.

'I don't think you'll be surprised to learn that we're here to talk about Ian Granger,' Kate said.

'Why wouldn't I be surprised?' Eva asked, without returning Kate's smile. She had the kind of relaxed wariness common among intelligence officers the world over.

'You've probably heard he's just been made the new chief of the Secret Intelligence Service,' Callum said.

She switched her steady gaze to him. 'You are also with SIS?'

'No. I work for the prime minister.'

'So this is positive vetting?'

Aware he was already drifting out of his depth, Callum deferred to Kate. 'Not exactly,' she replied.

'What, then?'

'It's probably easier if we don't outline what we've been asked by the prime minister to investigate,' Kate said.

'Easier for you or me?'

'Perhaps both.'

Eva sipped her coffee. She leant back and crossed one perfectly tailored leg over the other. She was thicker-set than in the SIS file photographs. 'We wanted to ask you about Ian,' Kate said. 'I'm very sorry not to be more specific as to our reasons why, but we'd ask you not to discuss what we're about to talk about with anyone at all, either inside your service or out.'

'You don't ask much.'

'I'm sure there may be a time when the prime minister or I can return the favour.'

Eva weighed this. If she'd checked out Shirley Grove's credentials and those of this investigation with the Cabinet Office in London, then she was bound to assess this as a promise with some potential. Favours could be useful in this business. 'All right,' she said, leaning back and spreading her arms, as if to welcome them in. 'What is it you want to know?'

'You first met him in New York?' Callum asked.

She cracked a smile. It transformed her face, imbuing it with sudden life and warmth. '*That*'s your opener?'

'His wife suggested you were lovers,' Kate said.

'I bet she did.'

'*Were* you?'

'What do you think?'

Eva's gaze was fixed on Kate now they had finally locked horns. 'Well,' Kate said, sipping her coffee and then leaning back in her chair. 'Since she spent a lifetime trying to pretend Ian's wandering eye was fixed solely on her, I'd say you can hardly have been subtle about it.'

'He told me I was the love of his life and he was going to leave her for me.' She smiled again. 'So what a naive fool I was, eh? You'd think an officer in this business would know better.'

'How did you meet him?' Callum asked.

'Oh, some cocktail party or other. He was saying he needed a new tennis partner, because the French press attaché was leaving. I said I'd step in, provided he could beat me in a singles game. He didn't, but I relented and became his partner on the court and off.'

'You knew he was married?'

'Of course. He wore a wedding ring.'

'Uncomplicated sex?' Kate asked.

'At first, perhaps. But . . .' She spread her arms again. 'Why do you want to know this?'

'I assume it can't have been a coincidence that you both ended up in Chile?'

'He proposed to me on my last night in New York. We moved heaven and earth to secure a posting in the same city so we could work out the details.'

'What happened then?'

Eva gazed at her, genuinely confused. 'What happened was that I discovered the hard way that Ian was not as brave a man as he liked to make out. As the days became weeks and then months in Santiago, it dawned on me that his prevarication was about more than just the fine details. So I asked to be transferred home early. We didn't part as friends.'

'Have you spoken to him since?'

'He's called me from time to time. I don't answer.'

There didn't seem much doubt about Eva's bitterness,

which still had a sting to it even after all these years, and Kate wondered at how any woman could think Ian capable of loving anyone but himself.

'I suppose this is exactly what you expected to hear,' Eva added.

'Yes,' Kate agreed.

'You can't have come all this way to talk about whether or not he's ever going to leave his wife?'

'As a matter of fact, he has,' Kate said. 'Or, to be more precise, she finally booted him out.'

'He'll be devastated.'

'Why do you say that?'

'She was like his mother, the security blanket he couldn't do without.' Kate looked confused. 'Surely you have worked *that* out already?' Both Callum and Kate shook their heads slowly. 'Ian got no love at all from his mother and nothing but the back of a hand from his stepfather, whom he detested. His adult life has been consumed by the search for love, affirmation, approval, affection. If he has hidden that from your internal psychological profilers, then you need to seek better ones.'

'We don't have access to his files.'

'Ah, because he is the chief now.' She shrugged. 'I see your dilemma. Look, I am only going to tell you what you already know. Ian is clever – perhaps one of the cleverest men I have ever met. He has an uncanny knack of being several moves ahead of everyone else and accurately predicting how an individual, or an organization – or a country – is going to react. I thought he had a quite brilliant mind. And, when he wanted to be, he was immensely charming and funny. But that hunger for love undoes him, and it is why he will never really leave his wife, even if she boots him out. I wouldn't bet on that remaining the status quo.'

'Do you think he was susceptible, given his erratic personal behaviour, to some kind of foreign approach?'

'*Ian?*' She shook her head. 'Don't be ridiculous. The idea would terrify him. The consequences – even the thought of them – would literally make him pee his pants. If you want an able administrator, a brilliant diplomat, a mind capable of seeing around corners, then, my God, he is your man. But if you want bravery or principle, then forget it. It takes a peculiar kind of courage to betray your country – and, believe me, Ian does *not* have that.'

'I presume you know that the word among some foreign services is that, at the time of your New York posting, you were a probable KGB agent?'

'Ah! Now I see it.' She leant back again and crossed her legs once more. 'You mean the CIA, of course. And, yes, I am well aware of the file they have on me at Langley and so are my employers. I suppose your theory is that I recruited Ian while we were in New York together.'

'It's one possibility,' Kate said.

Eva snorted with what appeared to be genuine incredulity. 'And so, having recruited him, I arranged that we should both be posted to Santiago at the same time – a fact easily confirmed by even the most casual survey of your internal files, I am sure – making me the most incompetent KGB officer in the history of the organization? Is that really your working theory?'

Now it was Kate's turn to lean forward. 'No,' she said emphatically. 'Which is why I'm here. I don't think Ian has the courage to betray his country either. But I need to be sure. Completely, absolutely certain.'

'You're hunting a mole,' Eva said.

'I can't tell you what we're doing.'

'And you came all this way to strike him out?'

'I'm following every lead I can.'

Eva was silent for a long time. Eventually, she nodded. 'In that case, I can help. Ian Granger is many things – able diplomat, as I have said, capable intelligence officer, liar, cheat, adulterer. But I would stake my life on the fact that he is not a Moscow stooge. You will need to look elsewhere.'

She stood abruptly. 'I'm sure you can see yourselves out. I'll know where to find you when that favour falls due.'

20

THEY WERE SILENT in the back of the taxi until Kate finally roused herself. 'I'm going to need a tour of central Prague, on foot. Pick a route where we move from crowds to empty streets and back again.'

Callum looked confused. 'What do you want to see?'

'I don't care.'

'You're interested in art, history, music?'

'I don't give a damn what you show me. I think we were being followed by two cars playing tag from the airport and one of them – the grey Prius – is behind us again.' Callum was about to turn around when Kate prevented him. 'Don't look back.'

'Okay,' he said. 'Who would be following us?'

'If I knew that, I wouldn't need you to act as my tour guide.'

'All right,' Callum said, smiling at her. 'You asked for it.' He leant forward and spoke briefly to the taxi driver, who nodded. A few minutes later, they were deposited outside a tall Gothic tower. 'The Powder Gate,' Callum said. 'Built by Vladislav the Second to add prestige to the adjacent Royal Court, which never really worked because the king fled riots in the Old Town centre a few years later and hid in the castle.'

'I'm not a fan of Gothic architecture or royalty.'

'Then you're going to find Prague a great disappointment. It is one of the – maybe *the* – great Gothic masterpieces, though a lot of it is overlain and intermixed with the Baroque influences of the Counter-reformation.'

'Explain.' Out of the corner of her eye, Kate watched the Prius glide on past them, without slowing. Two young men in the front did not glance in their direction. Perhaps she was mistaken.

'Well, I guess you'd say Prague's golden era was when the Holy Roman Emperor Charles the Fourth chose to make the city the site of his imperial residence and determined to make it the most magnificent in Europe. I'll show you the Charles Bridge in a minute. But after that, Prague became one of the hotbeds of the reform movement, led by Jan Hus – even you might have heard of him. He was burnt at the stake as heretics tended to be in those days. So when the Habsburgs take over, you get a strong counter-reformation led by the Jesuits, which is why you get all this incredible Baroque architecture overlying the Gothic, as if they were trying to obliterate all signs of what had gone before.'

'Fascinating. Let's get moving.'

They walked over the cobbles, weaving between thick crowds of tourists. 'This is Celetná Street,' he said, 'which follows one of the oldest trading routes in eastern Bohemia. The name comes from the plaited bread rolls that were first baked here in the Middle Ages, but the reason so many tourists are here is because it was part of the Royal Route all the way from the Municipal House up to Prague Castle.'

It was a pretty street, sure enough, the houses with pastel façades and graffiti, inscribed for posterity in damp render, and uneven cobblestones that must once have rattled to the sound of horses' hoofs, but now dealt with nothing more onerous than thousands of American trainers.

Callum took her away from Celetná Street to the Basilica of St James, which he informed her had been rebuilt in the Baroque style after a fire in 1689 allegedly started by agents of Louis XIV. 'Don't tell me you actually were a tour guide?' she asked.

'It was easy money as a student.'

'How come you were a student here?'

'We could choose to spend a second year abroad, so I came to Prague.'

'You were studying Czech?'

'History. Most of the courses were in English, but I did learn Czech.'

They were in front of an impressive Rococo building now. 'This is the Kinsky Palace,' he said, 'which was where the Communist leader Klement Gottwald effectively launched the Communist *coup d'état* in 1948. Do you actually want to know any of this stuff?'

'Just keep on talking.'

They emerged into the Old Town Square just as the sun

slipped beneath the Gothic spires of the Church of Our Lady Before Tyn.

The square was crowded with tourists waiting for the famous astronomical clock to strike the hour. A piano player entertained some adults in one corner, while families with children were clustered around a man dressed in a giant panda suit and a clown blowing bubbles into the still evening sky. 'I love the south side of this square,' Callum said, with something approaching rapture. 'Most of these houses have Romanesque or Gothic origins, but they're such a jumble of beautiful overlapping styles.' He took her closer. 'This is my favourite, the Storch House.' Kate looked up at the beautiful paintings that adorned its façade.

Callum glanced at his watch. 'You should probably see the clock strike.'

They walked over to the other side of the square and waited with the tourists in front of the town hall. 'All right,' Kate said. 'Apart from the obvious, why is it called the astronomical clock?'

'Because as well as the time, it displays the movement of the sun and moon through the signs of the zodiac, and of the planets around the Earth.' They watched as the beautiful, elaborate and ornate clock began to strike. 'Now you see the procession of the twelve Apostles,' Callum said. 'I must have witnessed this a thousand times, but I still love it.'

Kate had lost interest in the clock again, because she was nearly certain now that the man loitering by the entrance to Melantrichova Street back on the south side of the square was the short, slight, dark-haired man of Middle Eastern appearance she had seen passing them in the

passenger seat of the Prius at the Powder Gate. It was notori-
ously difficult for surveillance teams to pass themselves
off as tourists without fair warning, especially of the kind
that milled slowly around central Prague. And he was
failing in the task. 'Okay, rapture over,' Kate said. 'Let's
move on.'

'Where do you want to go?'

'Just keep the tour ticking over. I'm making some progress. And let's speed up a bit.'

As they moved down the tight, winding Charles Street,
with its pretty houses, Baroque façades and stucco reliefs,
speed was easier said than done. The tourist throng was
thicker here and slower moving, all the way on to the
Charles Bridge, with its magnificent view of the castle
above. 'Let's wait,' Kate said. 'Tell me about it.'

'I thought we were in a hurry?'

'Do as you're told, Callum.'

He gave a barely perceptible sigh. 'What do you want to
know?'

'The standard tour will do.'

'All right. Two striking Gothic towers. The Old Town
Bridge Tower was an integral part of the foundations. The
Malá Strana Tower, which was built a bit earlier, was originally used as a watchtower. The whole bridge is obviously a
masterpiece, commissioned by Charles the Fourth, and the
backdrop to most of the dramatic events in the city over cen-
turies and, these days, plenty of films you'll have sat through
with your kids.' He was recovering his enthusiasm quickly.
'Some of these statues are masterpieces.' He strode forward.
'This is Braun's *St Luitgard*, which, if you ask me, is one of the
finest of its kind. This is a copy, mind you. The original

statues are all in a museum now to preserve them.' He took her to lean over the bridge towards the waters of the Vltava river below. He pointed at another statue. 'Bruncvik, a mythical Bohemian knight – Prague's answer to King Arthur.'

'Did he draw a large sword?'

'Yes, and is said to have helped a lion fight a seven-headed dragon. He and his army are certain to rise and save Prague in its most desperate hours.'

'Like during Nazi rule, you mean? Or the long period when the Russians were in charge?'

'He seemed to sleep through those bits.'

Callum started walking again, until they reached the castle side of the bridge. 'This is Malá Strana, founded by King Ottokar the Second by joining a group of villages together.'

'Speed up again, Callum,' Kate said.

'Who are they?'

'I don't know. I can't work it out.'

'Why would anyone be following us?'

'Just keep walking and talking while I try to find an answer.'

Callum did as he was instructed, leading her along Mostecká Street to Malostranské Square, dominated by the Baroque edifice of the Church of St Nicholas. Kate urged him on and they climbed up Nerudova Street, past smaller Baroque townhouses, and turned right at the top towards the spectacular sight of Prague Castle.

Kate was pretty certain who her pursuers were by now, but she was no nearer to determining what country or organization they represented and why they were following her. 'Is there a café or restaurant nearby?' she asked.

'Don't you want to see the castle?'

'Later.'

'There's a place called Kuchyn. An old friend took me there just after it opened in July. You basically order by walking through the kitchen.'

'Sounds great.'

Callum led her to the restaurant on the far side of the square and they took a seat at a long oak trestle table on the terrace at the rear where the sun was setting behind the dome of the Church of St Nicholas, bathing the old town in an amber glow. 'Some view, huh?' he said.

They ordered beer, then wandered into the kitchen to peer into great copper pots to place their orders for the main course. Kate was halfway through her rabbit when Callum broke off from reminiscing on his time in Prague. 'The guy in the corner is either a spy or a drug dealer.' Kate was about to turn. 'Don't look around.'

'Why do you say that?'

'Instinct.'

'Well, we know you are new to the spying game, so tell me why he might be a drug dealer?'

'It doesn't matter.'

'It does.'

'I learned more about the Prague mafia than I wanted to know.' He shrugged. 'You got any further working out who is following us?'

'Not yet,' Kate said. 'Maybe it doesn't matter.'

'The expression on your face tells me it definitely matters.'

But they didn't have to wait long for an answer. A few moments later, a middle-aged man in a leather jacket –

balding, but fit and lithe, with a huge Tag Heuer on his wrist – slipped on to the bench beside Kate. 'Pete,' she said, nodding to herself. 'I should have guessed it was you.'

'I'm sorry, Kate,' he said. 'I knew you'd be sweating, but we're under the watchful eye of your former deputy, Suzy Spencer, so I had to wait until she left the control room.'

'Where are you set up?'

'I can't tell you that. I just wanted you to know who we were, so that you didn't worry.'

'I can think of lots of reasons this would make me concerned, Pete.'

'It's a watching brief, that's all. Nothing more.'

'Does one of you want to tell me what the hell is going on?' Callum asked.

Kate looked at him. 'Pete works in the SIS Operations Department. The men who have been trailing us are our people.' She turned back to Pete. 'Authorized by Ian, I assume?'

'I can't tell you that, Kate. I'm sorry.'

She faced Callum again. 'I don't think Suzy would have the guts to authorize this kind of operational expense on her own, so it either came from Ian or was signed off by him. The difference is academic.'

Callum looked more surprised by this than he should have done. 'We have the direct authority of the cabinet secretary and the prime minister,' he said, as if this should answer all potential challenges.

Pete shrugged. 'We miss you,' he told Kate. 'You're in good hands,' he told Callum. 'She's the best.' He stood. 'I'd better get going. She'll be back in the control room in a minute and she doesn't miss a trick.'

'Thanks, Pete. We'll be out of here tomorrow and we've nothing else going on bar a night on the tiles, so I should enjoy the sights.'

'Will do,' he said. And then he sauntered out.

'A night on the tiles?' Callum asked, once he was gone.

'Why not?' She smiled at him. 'And you shouldn't look so surprised by all that. It does your street cred no bloody good at all.'

'Well, I am surprised. We're conducting an investigation under the direct authority of the prime minister. They've absolutely no call to be interfering with it in any way.'

'How do you know Shirley Grove didn't authorize it?'

'It's possible. But why would she do that?'

'Because I'm a suspect. You heard her. So I investigate Ian, while she looks into me. That's how it's going to work. The bigger question is whose side you're on.'

'You have to ask?' He leant forward, placing his elbows on the table. 'Besides, Grove didn't authorize this surveillance.'

'How would you know?'

'I've worked with her a long time. She's pretty straight.'

'In this kind of investigation, no one is straight. Rule Number One.'

'She is. And so am I. Which means that only Ian could have authorized us to be tailed. I don't think it reflects well on him.'

'And yet everyone we encounter who knows him intimately is of one view. He does not have the courage to be an agent of an enemy power.'

'I thought it was weakness we were looking for, not courage.'

'Perhaps a peculiar combination of both,' she said.

'Anyway, I have some things to take care of tomorrow morning before our flight, so you'll have a chance to catch up on your old haunts.'

Callum looked at her oddly for a moment, then drained his glass. 'All right,' he said. 'But before we get to that, you promised me a night on the tiles. And I haven't got really hammered in Prague for a very long time.'

21

AND SO IT was that Kate found herself more or less forced into the most unlikely event of her recent life: a bar crawl of central Prague, with the impossibly handsome young assistant she had acquired in this latest twist of the intelligence dial.

They began in earnest in a place called Katyna, a restaurant-cum-bar housed in a former bank in the Old Town, just the other side of the Charles Bridge. They sat in the back at a chrome table beneath a cavernous ceiling, served by a slim waiter with a thin pencil moustache who brusquely ticked off each new delivery on a sheet in front of Callum. Kate started with a pilsner, which was about as far as her taste in beer had ever gone, but Callum grew didactic and impatient and started ordering for her, so that she progressed on to black beer, which bore no resemblance whatsoever to stout, and *výčepní*, or draught, which was weaker, and finally to extra malty *kvasnicová*.

They talked easily, so that the night spun past in a blur. Callum loomed over her, leaning forward on the table, so that his face was close to her own, and drawing her in every time she pulled back, like a moth to a flame. He was very funny, incredibly handsome – had she noted that already? – and about as charming as any man she had ever met. He didn't look, sound, or feel like the relatively young man he actually was, so that the chunky age gap seemed to melt into the soft Prague night.

He asked her what she had been like at university. Bookish, she'd said, but he didn't believe her and she gradually offered up snippets of her past: her terrible fashion sense, questionable taste in music and a penchant for really intense, late-night conversations by a fire with a bottle of whisky beside her. 'Wild,' he said.

She threw the question back at him. He admitted to having a remarkably well-developed fashion sense, amazing taste in music, a thirst for Moscow Mules and a reputation for all-night partying in the lively night scene to the extent that he was lucky to scrape a two:two. 'Plus,' he said, 'I smoked a tonne of weed.'

'I noticed a cannabis shop just around the corner,' she said. 'Maybe we should go and buy some. That will definitely convince Suzy Spencer and Ian that I'm a Russian spy.'

'How long were you married?' he asked.

She was taken aback. 'That's a bit personal.'

'Aren't we getting a bit personal?'

'Are we? I don't think so.' His gaze was fixed on her. 'A long time,' she said finally.

'They say you were childhood sweethearts.'

'Who is they?'

'Julie.'

'We met at Cambridge, so not really childhood sweet-hearts, no. But we have been together a long time.'

'Have been, or were?' She frowned at him. 'You were together, or you are?' he clarified.

'That *is* a bit personal.'

'Just asking.'

'Well, don't.' She pushed the beer away from her. 'How about you?' she asked, in a clumsy attempt to change the subject.

'Single,' he said, and gave her another of his mega-watt smiles. Damn, she thought. Wrong question.

'What – like forever single? Single as a state of mind?'

'Serial monogamist.'

She tried not to meet his eye. 'Well, I suppose there are worse things to be.'

'With a taste for older women.'

'Jesus!' She burst out laughing with the shock of it. 'Wind your bloody neck back in, office junior.'

'I'm not really an office junior, though, am I?'

'You are!'

'I thought we were partners.'

He was smiling at her again and it was beginning to annoy her now. 'My, you are a cocksure son of a gun.'

'All right,' he said, raising his hands in mock surrender. 'I've had three serious girlfriends. Two years, one year, two years. The last one broke my heart.'

Kate stared at the nearly empty beer glass in front of her, really wishing she hadn't drunk so much now. 'All right, I didn't need to know that. We should go.'

'You asked.'

'Did I? This conversation isn't going to plan at all.'

'Really? What was the plan?'

'You're bamboozling me!' Kate's phone, which she had left on the table, buzzed with an incoming message. It was from Stuart. *You here? All set for tomorrow?* She flipped the phone over, but not before Callum had seen and read the message.

'The business you have to attend to tomorrow?' he asked.

'Not really your affair.'

He smiled at her again. 'Whatever you say, partner.' He drained his glass and tried to catch the waiter's eye. 'One more for the road,' he said, glancing at Kate.

'No!'

'I thought we were having a night on the tiles?'

'We've had one.' She picked up her phone and put it back into her handbag. 'Believe me, this qualifies as about five nights on the tiles when you get to my age.'

'Yeah, right,' he said, still waving the waiter over. 'Two more *kvasnicová*,' he told the man.

'No,' she said. 'Seriously.' But the waiter turned away and, strangely, Kate did not get to her feet. Was she too pissed? 'We have to go,' she said.

'We don't.'

'We do. We absolutely do.'

But she still didn't move and it gradually dawned on her that what was keeping her fixed in her seat was not encroaching inebriation – though, God knows, she was very drunk – but the power of his smile. 'This is like sorcery,' she muttered to herself.

'Relax,' he said.

'No. That's an even worse idea.' She pushed herself to

her feet. 'Give me a moment.' She picked up her bag and disappeared towards the Ladies. Once out of view, she leant against the wall and breathed in deeply. What the hell was she playing at? She took out her phone, pulled up Stuart's message and stared at it, as if this act alone would bring her to her senses. She replied: *All set. See you in the town square at noon and then fifteen minutes later, by the astro-nomical clock.*

She waited, drumming her fingers impatiently against the wall behind her. Stuart replied: *They insist on setting venue.*

No, she replied. *In the Old Town Square or the meeting is off.*

Roger that, he replied finally. *I'll tell them.*

Kate slipped the phone back into her pocket and went into a cubicle. She had a pee, then sat with her head between her legs as her vision swam. It reminded her of the terror of being pregnant on the St Petersburg to Moscow night train after her few minutes of passion with Sergei. But it had been worth the wait. She finished, straightened and went to stare at herself in the mirror while she washed her hands. The woman who gazed back at her seemed older than the one she thought she knew, but perhaps that was the impact of the booze again.

She returned to the table. 'I need to turn in,' she said. 'You finish up.'

'Don't be stupid,' he said. He stood, scooping up his khaki cotton jacket from the seat beside him.

'We should probably pay,' she said.

'I have.'

'Thank you.' She led the way out of the restaurant to the square beyond and was confident that after the exchange with Stuart and the memory of her time with Sergei on the train – in which she had strangely blotted out entirely the terrible aftermath – she was back in control. And she remained so, until she stumbled on the first step of the hotel staircase and he caught her arm, then her hand, which sent a sharp snap of electric current right through her.

At the turn of the stair, he slipped his hand into hers.

On the landing above, he turned her in the semi-darkness and stooped to kiss her against the wall by the old-fashioned lift. She might have said no – perhaps she had that much wit about her – but she was old enough to know that her body sent out precisely the opposite message.

Was she making up for a steady, conservative youth? Or still punishing Stuart? Or trying to double down on the thrill of that night with Sergei?

Whatever the answer, the only thing she knew for sure was, at that moment, despite the booze, she wanted this very badly indeed and her abiding memory of the minutes that followed was of her sitting across him as she scraped her nails through the soft hair on his chest and threw her head back in absolute ecstasy.

22

SHE AWOKE IN his room in a tousled, but empty bed. She dressed, feeling intoxicated and sluttish in about equal measure, and hurried back to her room, where neither a shower nor her thumping hangover could quite drive out a deep contentment. Christ, she thought, as she looked at her face in the mirror, smudged with last night's make-up, why was all that not a cause of regret?

Callum was waiting for her at the breakfast table. 'I see you spared my morning blushes,' she said. 'Nice touch.' And she meant it, too.

'You were snoring.'

'Not so charming.' She waved over the waitress and ordered coffee. 'I'm not going to throw any allegations at you,' she said.

'That's big of you.'

'I was seduced, fair and square, and I don't unfortunately regret a single second of it.'

'Good.'

'But it's never going to happen again. And you will be a gentleman and keep it to yourself in perpetuity.'

'Well, on the latter, of course. On the former, if you say so. But why make a promise we may not keep?'

'Because we damned well will keep it.' She was glowering at him now. In the cold sobriety of dawn, she meant it, and it was irritating that he thought last night's sublime charm would work as well in the harsh light of day.

'All right,' he said. 'I get it.'

'Do you?'

'Yes. Yes, I do.' The waitress brought Kate's coffee and she eyed the breakfast buffet warily. Her head hurt. Callum leant back and smiled at her. 'It was some night, though, right? You are one hell of a woman.'

'I assume that's how all your nights on the tiles ended in Prague.'

'That's beneath you.' It wasn't, of course, but it was a reminder that if you wanted your cease-and-desist message to stick, you had to give up flirting. She went and filled a plate with fresh fruit and tried to sober up in more ways than one.

'Our flight isn't until five,' Callum said, 'so I thought I'd show you around Karlstein Castle, since you love Gothic or, in this case, neo-Gothic architecture so much.'

'I have business to attend to. I'll meet you here at three, so we can share a taxi to the airport.'

'Oh, yes, your husband,' he said, deflated.

For a moment, Kate was confused. But she recalled Callum catching sight of the text from Stuart the previous night. 'Yes,' she said.

'Fair enough.'

Callum left her, strolling away across the breakfast room with his usual loping insouciance. He was infuriatingly cool.

After she'd eaten, Kate washed her face again, feeling worse than she had, and put on some make-up. She glanced through a basic tourist guide she had procured from Reception, then set out just after ten, walking northwards into the drizzling rain.

Dry-cleaning – checking you were not being followed – was difficult, time-consuming and laborious on any day, but particularly so when operating alone and with a thumping hangover. Kate had chosen a simple, winding route through Josefov, the old Jewish Quarter, in an attempt to convince Suzy Spencer's watchers – and anyone else who might be on her tail – that she was engaged in nothing more dramatic than some essential sightseeing in the few hours before heading to the airport.

Josefov, which is encircled by the river and the Old Town, was an enclosed ghetto in which the city's Jews had once been confined, before being gradually cleared out in the nineteenth century. Those who were left were murdered during the terrible days of the Holocaust.

Kate started by the river at the St Agnes of Bohemia Convent, then circled to the corner of Bilkova and Elišky Krásnohorské, where a large apartment block with a few simple repeated geometrical shapes on a plain façade stood out from the flowing art-nouveau decoration of many of the surrounding buildings. She stood in front of this striking example of the cubist architecture that was briefly popular in Bohemia and Austria both before and after the First World War.

She took a picture on her phone and moved on to the Jewish Museum, then the Old Jewish Cemetery, with its crooked gravestones and Hebrew inscriptions.

She ambled past all the natural tourist sights of Josefov and made a point of moving through crowded areas, then more deserted backstreets, stopping frequently to take a picture or browse in a shop.

By the time she headed back towards the Old Town, she was puzzled by her conviction that neither Suzy Spencer's team nor anyone else was watching her.

Which begged the question: why not? If she was a target yesterday, why was she not today?

She had intended to catch the tram to Vysehrad, thinning the pursuers by stringing out their resources and doubling back in a taxi, but she could no longer see the point. So, she was back in the Old Town Square early for her meetings and wiled away twenty minutes with a coffee while admiring the Rococo splendour of the Kinsky Palace.

She took in the occupants of the square in a steady, methodical way, sweeping from one side to the other and back again. If the Russians hadn't been watching her already this morning – and she had to face the possibility that she was losing her touch – they certainly would be now.

At five to twelve, Stuart entered the square and she watched him for two or three minutes as he glanced nervously up at the astronomical clock, then at the tourists around him.

Why was he so on edge?

Kate paid for her coffee and approached him. He had his back to her. 'Hi, Stuart,' she said easily.

He spun around. 'Kate!'

'Were you expecting someone else?'

'No, no.'

They embraced. Kate hugged him tightly as she very carefully slipped the package she had received from Danny before she left London into his coat. 'I've just put a burner phone in your pocket with a battery strapped to the back. If you ever get a message from or about one of the kids, saying they have a fever or are unwell, throw your old phone away, move some distance from it, put the battery into this one and switch it on. It has an encrypted app called Signal and I will communicate with you via that. Got it?'

She released him, stepped back. 'Yes,' he said.

'Sure?'

'Yes, of course.'

'Are you all right? You seem nervous?'

'That's because I am. This spy business might be second nature to you, but I can assure you it isn't my natural territory.'

'It'll be all right.'

'Will it?'

She touched his arm. 'Yes. Trust me.'

He hugged her again. 'I love you. Do you know that?'

'I do, yes.' She gently separated herself from him.

He was staring at the ground, avoiding her gaze. 'You never say you love me back, do you know that?'

'I'm not really in that head space just now,' she replied.

He looked at her, his gaze an agonizing clash of hope and despair. 'What can I do to make things right?'

'Nothing. We're doing everything we can. I'm not saying

that everything we talked of in France is null and void, I just mean that I'm about to engage with your new over-lords and I need every wit I possess about me. That's all.'

He seemed unsure as to whether to accept this reassur-ance, if that was indeed what it was. 'I understand,' he said, though his demeanour made it abundantly clear he did not.

'It will be over soon,' Kate said. 'I promise you that.'

Stuart turned away reluctantly. 'They said I wasn't to be around for the meeting,' he said. 'But good luck.'

'Thanks.'

She watched him go, feeling a vague and queasy sense of guilt as she recalled last night's visceral sex with a man practically young enough to be their son.

She kept her gaze on Stuart's hunched gait until he had turned out of the square, then swung back towards the astronomical clock as it struck the hour.

Now that she had a few moments to think about it, Kate was aware of a slight flutter of nerves in her stomach. She was playing with fire and she knew it. But the agent who approached her was about the last candidate she might have expected in the tourist throng: a homely woman in beige slacks and a blue cardigan, with a warm smile and a chunky gold bracelet adorning an outstretched arm. She looked like a wealthy American tourist, which was per-haps the point. 'Mrs Henderson?' They shook hands. 'I am Nina.' She gestured at the square around them. 'Did you have somewhere in mind?'

Kate pointed at the café she'd frequented earlier and they crossed the cobbles to sit beneath an awning that shielded them from the sun that had finally broken through the noonday cloud. They ordered. 'I have never been to Prague before,' Nina said. 'But now I wonder why not.'

'You're based in Moscow, I assume?'

'Yes. But I spent most of my career in Europe – France, Germany, Brussels.' She smiled. 'Not what you might call hardship postings.'

It was difficult to guess the woman's age, but Kate placed her in her late thirties or early forties. She had an easy, calm manner, perhaps why she had been chosen for this task in the first place, and a lopsided smile that lent her a certain charm, which had been more or less entirely absent from every other SVR operative Kate had ever encountered. 'We'd better get to business,' Kate said. 'Some of my former colleagues have been watching me here in Prague.'

'Yes, we saw.'

'This morning?'

'We have not seen them today. We naturally wanted to be sure you were here without the cavalry, so were out yesterday. What were your colleagues doing on your tail?'

Kate weighed what to say, despite having thought of almost nothing else all morning. 'We're hunting Agent Dante. I've been brought back to head an external investigation, reporting directly to the prime minister.'

'Who is Agent Dante?'

'I think you know the answer to that. And if you don't, your superiors in Moscow certainly will.'

Nina tilted her head to one side, as if considering how much to admit. Her gaze never left Kate's face. 'Please carry on,' she said.

'We've narrowed the search down to two final suspects. But both men – and possibly others at the heart of what we might loosely call the British establishment – would find it easier to have the woman who was ultimately hoodwinked into starting this ball rolling as a public scapegoat.'

'You? If true, it makes this meeting a risky one.'

'A calculated gamble.'

Nina nodded slowly. For the first time her gaze left Kate's face as she swept the square from one side to the other and back again, much as Kate herself had done earlier. 'What do you want?' Nina asked eventually.

'Ten million, new identities for myself, Stuart and the children – and a new life somewhere outside Russia in a country of my choosing.'

Nina nodded again, as if this was more or less what she had expected. 'And in return?'

'My flight will ensure I'm identified and publicly exposed as Agent Dante. The British establishment will have its scapegoat and you will see a threat to your source removed. In addition, you will have access to every piece of knowledge about the Service and its operations that I have accumulated in my career.'

The waiter brought their coffee. Nina lit a cigarette and offered one to Kate, who had to exercise a lot of self-restraint to resist the temptation. 'The issue we have with this offer,' Nina said, 'is that every single psychological assessment we have of you on file suggests that you would be the very last known officer in SIS likely to succumb to any proposal we might make.'

'Then why are you here?' Nina wasn't smiling now. 'I'm not going to sell myself to you,' Kate went on. 'I'm in a corner. You have Stuart. You're not going to release him. You know that, so do I. I therefore have a choice. My family or my country. And I'm prepared to bet your psychological profilers are clear which way I'll jump on that one.'

'Actually, they say you would believe you are smart enough to preserve your loyalty to both.'

Kate's respect for the work of Moscow Centre crept up a notch, but it didn't help her here. 'You won't release Stuart, so my choice is limited.'

'But is he what you want?' Nina wondered. 'You don't strike me as the kind of woman who would bet her house a second time on a proven adulterer.'

'He's the father of my children.'

'And that's enough? For you, I have my doubts.'

'I'm here because you said you wanted me to come and work for you. Well, now you know what I want and need. We're closing in on Dante in London and I'm not operating alone. Much longer and there will be no turning back. So we have a few days at best to make a decision.'

'What evidence do you have?'

'I can't and won't tell you that. Not yet.' Kate stood. She didn't want to give this woman any more. 'It was good to meet you,' she said, as she walked away. She didn't look back.

Kate was lost in thought as she approached her hotel on the fringes of the Old Town. How would the men of Moscow Centre respond to the news that she was closing in on Agent Dante?

A few seconds later Kate got her answer when a black Mercedes screeched to a halt beside her. A man hit her from behind and she felt herself propelled towards the opening rear door. She let out half a cry before the assailant had a hand over her mouth. She bit his fingers savagely, twisted, so that she just avoided his attempt to force her directly into the back, the edge of the door smashing into her spine.

Another man was racing around the car. She thrust with the heel of her palm towards the assailant's chin, but he parried. He grabbed her hair again and smashed her head on to the roof of the car.

She felt her vision blur and her knees weaken. The second man kicked her legs from beneath her. Her head was almost in the car. She heard a howl of rage somewhere close. 'Bastards!'

One of the men swore in Russian as he was clattered from behind and fell clumsily on top of her. Through the pain of blurred vision, Kate caught sight of Callum, his long arms twirling. He retreated before the men could fell him, ran on to the bonnet with two great strides and smashed the windscreen with a well-placed kick.

Now it was the turn of the driver to swear in Russian. Callum jumped to the cobbles on the other side of the car, yelling his head off in Czech.

One of the men was still trying to force Kate into the back of the car, but he was distracted by Callum's shouts and a growing crowd: Kate was able to get a sharp elbow into his groin. He groaned and grunted, but she wriggled from under him. As he straightened, she swung away from him and now the heel of her palm to his nose delivered the desired result. He cried out in pain and staggered backwards.

Knowing he was no match for the Russians in a fight, Callum had retreated, but the moment the driver doubled back he used his considerable bulk to slam into him from behind again, sending him tumbling to the cobblestones.

The crowd was thickening and some were joining Callum's cries for help. The first assailant faced Kate, a stocky, balding man with dense stubble and a swarthy complexion. He looked Georgian or Bulgarian and made one more attempt to subdue her, coming in hard. But Kate was more than a match for any man one to one and, this time, he retreated, barking an order to the driver before both of them barged through the crowd and disappeared.

Kate leant back against the wall, misjudged it and slipped to the ground. Anxious onlookers crowded in. Callum forced his way through them, kneeling before her. 'Are you all right?'

She nodded.

'I'll get an ambulance.'

'No.'

'Kate, you've got blood all over your face!'

'It's a graze.' The pain seemed to be coming from everywhere – her back, arm, face. 'I don't need an ambulance.' She pushed herself to her feet.

'Don't be an idiot,' he told her. But she pulled him close. 'Do as I say.'

She started hobbling away. He came alongside her and offered his arm. She used it to steady herself. 'Are you sure?' he asked, as they pushed through the bewildered onlookers.

She waited until they were clear, before she answered. 'We don't need close questioning by the authorities, as I'm sure you can work out. Move fast.'

Her body might have been screaming at her to stay and rest, but her mind had other ideas. They went to their rooms, checked out immediately and had left the hotel by the rear entrance before the police or anyone else caught up with them. They walked a few hundred metres and climbed into a taxi for the airport.

As soon as the doors closed, she asked the question that had been at the forefront of her mind. 'What were you doing following me?'

Callum looked surprised, even shocked, at the question. 'I was just walking back to the hotel,' he said. 'You thought I was tailing you?'

Kate didn't answer. Her mind swam with questions and they passed most of the rest of the journey – to the airport and indeed back to the UK on the plane – in uneasy silence. But she discovered as they arrived in London that she had much bigger problems than what Callum might have been up to.

Two women in dark suits were waiting for her beyond immigration. 'Mrs Henderson, would you mind coming with us?' said one.

'We're from the Security Service,' the other chipped in, as if that much was not obvious.

'Good for you.'

'We have the Metropolitan Police on standby to intervene if you do not cooperate.' They nodded at two uniformed officers watching them warily from twenty yards away.

'Ian Granger,' she muttered, 'you are one sorry son of a bitch.'

23

THEY TOOK KATE to an interview room, its grey lino floor and beige walls matched by the pallid expressions of the women who faced her from the other side of the table. They introduced themselves. 'I am Jane Williams,' the older, dark-haired one said.

'And I am Emma Young,' her younger blonde companion added.

The door opened and Suzy Spencer walked in. She took a chair from the back of the room and sat just behind the two women from the Security Service, as if to distance herself or indicate that she was in charge of these proceedings, or possibly both. She crossed one long, slim leg over the other and eyed Kate without expression or comment.

Jane Williams took a thick file from her briefcase and opened it on the table in front of her. She had chunky forearms and big hands, which looked as if they were capable of packing a punch. Emma Young fidgeted beside her and kept tucking her blonde curls behind her ears. She was pretty in an angular kind of way, with cadaverous cheeks and piercing blue eyes. 'What were you doing in Prague, Mrs Henderson?' Williams asked.

'I don't believe I'm obliged to answer your questions.'

Williams rewarded her with a thin smile. 'We're aware that you know your rights, Mrs Henderson. But we're investigating the possibility that there is a foreign agent at the heart of SIS, codename Dante.'

'I don't work for SIS.'

'Indeed. And you're quite at liberty to refuse to assist us. But I should warn you that, if you do not cooperate, we will be forced to ask the Metropolitan Police to place you under arrest and the rest of this interview will be carried out under caution.'

'Under arrest for what?'

'Espionage.'

Kate leant forward, trying to conceal her disquiet. Could this really have been Grove's doing? And why undermine her investigation in this way, unless the real purpose was, as Kate had once feared, to fit her up as a convenient scapegoat? 'Well, this is funny,' she said, 'because I've been tasked by the prime minister himself to carry out an investigation into the very same Agent Dante. So who does your authority stem from?'

Williams didn't flinch. 'We're confident of our mandate, Mrs Henderson.'

'I asked who your authority stems from.'

'The law. As I said, we're quite happy to call for the police and conduct this interview under caution, if that is what you would prefer.'

Kate glanced at Suzy, who was staring at the floor. She had to admit that the blithe confidence the two women opposite her exuded was unsettling. Could it really be that the prime minister or Grove had authorized *two* investigations? And, if the intention had been to fit her up from the start, why go to the trouble of forcing her to conduct her own inquiry? It made no sense. 'What were you doing in Prague?' Jane Williams repeated.

Kate sat back. 'I'm afraid that's classified.'

'You were conducting interviews related to the inquiry you believe you've been empowered to pursue?'

'I have the prime minister's instructions in writing.' As she said it, Kate recalled that these had been requested but not yet delivered. She quietly cursed her own sloppiness.

'We can keep going around the houses here, Mrs Henderson,' Williams said. 'Or we can go the police route.'

'That's not going to change the fact that what I was doing in Prague was classified. And if you're in any doubt about that, I suggest you call the prime minister yourself.'

Williams rewarded her with another thin smile. 'You met a senior member of the Czech Foreign Intelligence Service.' She took a photograph from the pile of papers in front of her. 'And then an agent of the Russian Foreign Intelligence Service.'

The picture showed Kate sitting with the SVR operative who had introduced herself as 'Nina'. And now she genuinely cursed her own carelessness. How could she not have spotted Suzy Spencer's watchers on her tail? She glanced at her former deputy, who had a glint of triumph in her eye. 'We have identified her as Tanya Mikhailova. She is the deputy director of the London Desk in Moscow Centre.'

'I'm afraid my work in Prague was classified.'

'Not to us.'

'Above your pay grade, Ms Williams.' But even as she said it, Kate was aware that she was not going to be able to patronize herself out of the corner she'd marched herself into.

Williams opened her arms. 'Must we go around the houses each time, Mrs Henderson, or could we just get on with this?'

'Let's get on with it,' Kate agreed.

'We can't see what reason you would have to meet your handler at short notice and at considerable risk in Prague unless it was to update her on how the search for Agent Dante was proceeding.'

'You mean the search for myself?'

'Precisely. But you would need a scapegoat, of course.'

'Who do you think I have in mind?'

'That is not a subject of this discussion.'

Kate shook her head. 'Look, I understand you're trying to do your job here, Ms Williams. We both are. But I'm sure you will appreciate that I do not feel at liberty to discuss what transpired in Prague, or in any other part of my inquiry, without the express permission of the man who authorized the investigation, the prime minister himself.'

Kate saw the flicker of doubt in the blonde girl's eyes. She did not have her colleague's poker face.

Whoever had given them the authority to sit there, it was not the prime minister. And that meant it was probably not Shirley Grove either, which only deepened the mystery. How had they discovered the existence of Agent Dante?

Unless this was the work of Dante, desperately trying to

halt the investigation that would inevitably end with his exposure and ruin.

'I believe,' Williams said, 'that it is your current working theory that Dante has helped mastermind the greatest mis-information play we have ever witnessed, all of which began with you being duped into bugging a conversation on board Igor Borodin's super-yacht.'

'No comment. I've told you I'm not going to get into the areas our inquiry is considering.'

Williams passed the file to her blonde colleague, who turned the pages with long, slender fingers, then pulled out a sheaf that was stapled together. 'We'd like to ask you some questions about your former contact, Sergei Malin-sky.' Suzy Spencer looked up from the floor and gave Kate another smile of triumph, in light of which Kate mentally braced herself for what was coming. 'Were you aware of his position within the Russian intelligence hierarchy?'

'Not precisely, as I have said many times.'

'But if you had to guess?'

'I don't guess.'

'Please answer the question, Mrs Henderson.'

'In our last conversation, he did not deny that he was a member of the GRU.'

'Yes,' Young said. 'A very senior one.' She pushed across a still photograph of Sergei sitting with the head of the Rus-sian military intelligence agency and the Russian president at the Sochi Winter Olympics in 2014. 'I believe some of our colleagues showed you the video this still photograph has been taken from during the investigation they conducted into the death of your former deputy, Ravindra.'

'We're going over old ground here. I knew Sergei was a

senior member of the Russian intelligence hierarchy. I didn't know precisely which agency he worked for at the start, but I trusted him. That was why we took seriously his tip-off about the meeting on Igor's super-yacht and decided to attempt to bug it accordingly.'

'But you later managed to clarify that he was a senior operative of the GRU?'

'He never confirmed as much, but that was my understanding, yes.'

Emma Young tilted her head to one side, as if a thought had just occurred to her. She had a studious quality, and Kate sensed she was new to this kind of interrogation, but still confident of the hand she had to play. 'Would you mind just talking us through once more your relationship with Sergei and how this tip-off came about? I'm sure you would agree it is really central to our assessment of this entire affair.'

Kate was about to refuse, but something about their poise was unsettling her. She wanted to force them to reveal their hand now. 'We met while I was studying Russian in St Petersburg. We became friends, not lovers as is sometimes alleged.'

'But you lost touch after you left?'

Kate could see what Young was driving at. She sighed. 'Yes, it's true, he wanted more than friendship and I was then firmly hitched to the man who became my husband, Stuart. I could not, or would not, reciprocate Sergei's feelings. But we didn't part on bad terms. We remained extremely fond of each other. We understood that our parting at the end of that summer was a permanent one and we would not remain in touch.'

'And you didn't see him again until he approached you
at a social function in London?'

'That's right.'

'He was clearly a diplomat attached to the Russian
Embassy. You had no reason to guess that he was a member of their intelligence apparatus?'

'I had my suspicions, but I wouldn't put it any higher
than that.'

'And they were confirmed when he gave you this
extraordinary piece of information – that Igor Borodin
regularly hosted get-togethers for some of Russia's most
senior intelligence officials on his super-yacht in the
summer.'

'Yes.'

'Were you surprised that Sergei offered you this information?'

The more Kate was asked, or considered, this question,
the less she liked it. The way she had taken it at face value
so quickly did not reflect well on her. 'He later explained
the context. He'd been posted to Istanbul prior to coming
to London. The consulate there had been forced to intervene after a young girl who had been on the yacht claimed
to have been raped by a Russian man.'

'But were you not a little startled that this . . . *friend* you
had not seen for years and years suddenly offered you such
an extraordinary tip-off?'

There was no way around it: she should have been. And
they all knew it. 'Look, we've been over this time and
again. I hadn't set eyes on Sergei since I left Russia. It was
nice to see him again and his sincerity didn't seem to be in
doubt. I concluded, in consultation with my superiors,

including Ian Granger . . .' she glanced at Suzy, who still gleamed with impending triumph '. . . that it was worth a shot. If our operation succeeded and we managed to get a bug on to the yacht, we would treat the intelligence we picked up on its own merits.'

'And what a bombshell it was,' Williams said.

'Yes, but easily verifiable. We concluded that if the prime minister *did* turn out to have prostate cancer, then the Russians clearly had a highly placed source.'

'Very convenient,' Suzy Spencer said, from the sidelines. Everyone else ignored her.

'So you really had no contact from Sergei Malinsky in the period between your departure from Russia as a student and your reunion in London?' Young asked again.

'No.'

'None at all?' Williams asked, sceptical. 'No friendly message, letter or postcard?'

'None.'

Young nodded, as if her section of this interview was concluded. Williams took the file back from her and turned a few more pages. Kate had the sense they were enjoying this, but not as much as Suzy Spencer. 'After your probation period,' Williams said, looking at the file, as if its contents were news to her, 'your first posting was to work undercover at the consulate in Hong Kong.'

'If that is what it says.'

Williams smiled again, like a cat playing with a mouse. 'Stuart accompanied you?'

'Yes.'

'He was also able to secure a job in the consulate?'

'In the trade delegation, yes.'

Williams nodded. 'Since then you've been based in London?'

'Yes. The trajectory of Stuart's career made permanent location abroad difficult.'

'You spent a long time in Counter-Terrorism?'

'After Nine/Eleven, it absorbed a lot of the Service's time, energy and effort, and understandably so.'

Williams turned the pages. 'Eight months in Lahore.' She looked up. 'That was where you met your former deputy, Ravindra?'

'Where is this going, Ms Williams? If you were watching me in Prague, you'll be aware that I had to fight off a potential abduction by a Russian snatch squad, which would be a strange turn of events if I really were Agent Dante – and thanks for the assistance, by the way, if you were on my tail.' She meant that for Suzy, who was now failing to meet her eye. 'So just get on with it.'

Williams looked at her, unruffled and unhurried. 'You travelled extensively in your time in Counter-Terrorism, did you not?'

'Of course I bloody did. There was a war on.'

Williams pushed a sheet across the table. 'You attended a counter-terrorism conference in Sofia in 2012.'

Kate glanced over the piece of paper, which was a print-out of her travel schedule of the time, including her flight and hotel details, along with her security pass number for the conference. 'Yes,' she replied, unsure as to where this could possibly be heading.

Williams took another photograph from the file and put it before Kate. It appeared to depict Sergei in a group of men entering the conference hall.

They waited while Kate absorbed this. Suzy Spencer leant forward. 'I hope you're not going to try to tell us, Kate, that you attended the same conference as your former lover and managed not to bump into each other? Or, still more incredible, that you have forgotten you saw him there?'

Kate held up the photograph. 'Where did you get this? Who took it?' Her mind was doing somersaults.

'I'm afraid we're not at liberty to disclose that,' Williams said.

'How do you know it's genuine?'

'We're a hundred per cent sure it is not faked,' Suzy said. 'Unlike much of the material you have been presenting to us in the last eighteen months.'

Kate shook her head. 'To answer your question, yes, I'm absolutely sure I didn't see Sergei at this conference. I mean, if I had, why on earth would I lie about it?'

The answer to that was obvious and their silence made the point well enough. 'It seems more than a touch convenient that it's turned up just at this particular moment, wouldn't you say?' Kate asked.

'That's not the inference we have drawn from it,' Williams said.

There was a noise from the corridor, and a few seconds later, Shirley Grove burst in. She was wearing a raincoat that made her look bulkier than she really was, her face and hair damp from the weather outside. She looked flustered, even angry, her cheeks flushed. 'What is the meaning of this?' she demanded.

Suzy was on her feet, like a scalded cat. 'We have authorization!' she said.

'From whom?'

'We are following due procedure under the law.'

'Are you out of your minds?' Grove asked, staring at them in cold fury.

'We are investigating a case of possible treason,' Suzy said, sounding defensive and uncertain now, as Williams and Young seemed to retreat into themselves, evidently unwilling to charge to Suzy's defence. Kate wondered if Ian had told his lover that they had more top cover for this ambush than was the case.

She tried to hide her own sense of confusion as to where Grove really stood. Could it be the case that she *had* set this up and her outburst here was no more than a charade?

'Mrs Henderson is leading an investigation at the direct instigation of the prime minister,' Grove thundered, 'who, last time I looked, was still the democratically elected leader of this country – with all the legal and natural authority that flows from it.' Grove turned to her. 'Mrs Henderson, you are free to go.' She swung back towards Suzy. 'As for you, Miss Spencer, and your friends here, one more step out of line and it is you who will find yourselves under arrest. *Is that clear?*'

Grove was damned impressive when riled. She seemed taller, more imposing. Kate followed her out. 'Bloody jokers,' Grove muttered, as they headed back towards the baggage reclaim area and the exit. 'Ian Granger's overplayed his hand this time. You wait until the prime minister hears of it.'

Grove offered Kate and Callum a lift and suggested Kate hop into the back with her. As soon as the doors were closed, Grove turned to her. 'I'm sorry, Kate. I got wind of it too late.'

Kate was gazing out of the window at the damp streets and the lights of the traffic refracted through the rain on the glass. 'The Security Service knew about Agent Dante.' Kate turned back to Grove. 'How?'

'I don't know.' She shook her head emphatically. 'Truly.'

The car was silent but for the hum of the engine and the beat of the rain. 'What did they ask you about?' Grove went on.

Kate considered how much to tell her. Was Grove friend or foe? As this affair wore on, it was harder and harder to say with almost everyone involved. She looked at Callum's dark curls brushing the ceiling of the car. Was it possible that he had told someone about Dante?

'Ian and his acolyte Suzy have done a great deal of work to try to fit me up as Dante.'

'What kind of work?'

'They presented me with evidence that Sergei had attended a conference I was at in Sofia in 2012.'

'I don't understand why that is significant.'

'Because I told them I hadn't seen Sergei between the time I left Russia as a student and him turning up in London.' Grove was still frowning at her. 'If I was Dante, they would naturally want to assemble a pattern of clandestine meetings with contacts over a period of years. But I absolutely did not see Sergei at the conference, so either the still is faked, or he was there and I just didn't run into him.'

'But the Russians might have been thinking far enough ahead to put Sergei in exactly that position for exactly that reason and instructed him not to make contact with you.'

'It's possible.' Kate didn't want to think about the level of complicity and premeditation that implied on Sergei's part. But perhaps that was her blind spot.

Grove was silent for a long time. 'What do you think Ian's motivation is?' she asked finally.

'If he's Dante, then it's naturally to cover his tracks. And framing me allows him to do that. If he isn't Dante, I guess he's hedging his bets. "Proving" that I betrayed the prime minister all along would allow him to curry favour in the event the PM survives Imogen's attempt to get him out of Number Ten.'

'Which he will.'

'Maybe.'

'He's a born survivor.'

'No one survives in politics for ever, though, do they?'

Kate filled in Grove on what had happened in Prague. She didn't want any more of a post-mortem with Callum for a whole load of reasons, so she got out of the car early, saying she had to head home. Instead, she took a taxi to Imogen's house to pursue an idea she'd been toying with during the flight home.

It was late by the time she got there and the night and the weather had closed in, the rain billowing down the street in successive gusts of wind. So it was a moment before she identified the man scurrying out of the entrance to a waiting Mercedes.

But as she stepped back into the shadow of the taxi to avoid being seen, she caught a glimpse of Ian Granger, his face damp with rain.

24

KATE WAITED UNTIL Ian's car headlights had disappeared around the corner before she knocked on Imogen's door. A young woman with the brusque pretension to grandeur that marked out so many political advisers answered. 'Yes?' she asked, with barely concealed disdain, as if she had just discovered dog excrement on the heel of her shoe. She was blonde and pretty with oval glasses.

Kate disliked her instantly. 'I'm a friend of Imogen's.'

'Are you from the *Mail*?'

Kate smiled. 'No, I am not from the *Mail*.'

'The *Sun*?'

'I am not from any newspaper. My name is Kate Henderson.'

'Wait here,' the girl said imperiously, and closed the door in her face.

'How to win friends and influence people,' Kate muttered

under her breath, as she turned back to the street. There was no sign of any waiting press.

The minutes crawled past and Kate was about to call a taxi and go home when the door opened behind her again. 'Come in,' the girl said, without explanation or apology for her attitude or the delay. 'We had a couple of journalists trying to blag their way in earlier,' she said.

Imogen was at the kitchen table with half a dozen men and women sitting around her, poring over charts of names. Her husband Harry was the first to greet her. 'Kate!' He came over and gave her a polite peck on the cheeks. The fact that Kate's husband and Harry's wife had once had an affair might have brought them together, but seemed only to have pushed them apart. Harry rarely exuded the easy geniality of their first acquaintance, these days, and politely kept his distance.

'Kate!' Imogen boomed. She strode over to offer a more effusive kiss. Imogen generally strode everywhere. 'How nice to see you. It's going well! We have the numbers for the no-confidence vote. We've just given the story to the morning papers. And we're pretty sure he's going to lose it.'

Kate was tempted to say that she who wields the sword rarely wears the crown but managed to hold her tongue. 'Do you have a few minutes?'

'Of course! For you, always.' Imogen led her through to the adjoining sitting room and closed the sliding double doors. She moved to the curtains and tugged them shut also. 'We've had a couple of reporters here this evening,' she said, sounding frankly thrilled to be so much the centre of the attention. 'Drink?'

'No, I'd better not.' Kate thought of how much she had overdone it last night in Prague, the after-effects of which were still with her.

'What's up?' Imogen asked, dropping down into the sofa. She was wearing a cream skirt, which served to high-light her long, tanned legs. She looked ravishing, on any analysis, and Kate felt a sting of fury at the way in which Stuart had succumbed to her.

'I've considered what you said.'

'About what?' Imogen asked.

'You requested my help. I'm happy to do what I can, but I need something in return.'

Imogen raised her eyebrows. 'Wow, trading. That isn't like you. Have you been spending too much time around politicians?'

'Possibly.'

'What is it you want?'

Kate fidgeted. Imogen swigged from the large glass of white wine she had brought with her. 'You sure I can't get you something?'

'No,' Kate said. 'I've just been away for a few days. I really need to go home. I wondered if I could get access to your office tomorrow morning and all the files that are connected to it. I'd probably need to bring someone with me.'

Imogen looked puzzled. 'I'm sure the answer is yes.' She raised her hands. 'I have nothing to hide. But why?'

Kate hadn't given enough thought as to how to frame this. But the only way to engage Imogen was to suggest it would further her own ambition. 'If we're to bring down the prime minister once and for all, I need more evidence.

And I think I might find it through the files I can only access in your office.'

'From his time as foreign secretary, you mean?'

'Yes.'

'Deal!' Imogen leapt up again, as if, business done, she was anxious to get back to counting the number of her supporters. Kate waited until she was at the door before she asked her final question. 'Have you seen Ian recently?'

'No,' Imogen said, without looking round. 'Why?'

'I'm just trying to work out which side he's on in all this.'

'Professionally neutral, he says. Repeatedly.' Imogen hesitated before opening the double doors again. 'I think it's probably best to avoid any gossip about what you might be doing there. Could we do this early tomorrow morning?'

'Of course.'

'How long would you need?'

'A couple of hours, at a guess.'

'Let's say we meet at six a.m. I'll see you outside my office.'

Kate said her farewells, and during the cab ride back to Battersea she called Danny to ask for his assistance in the morning. She caught the hesitation in his voice this time and she apologized for asking so much of him without explanation. She was aware she was stretching friendships to breaking point.

The same could be said of Rose, who was in bed in the spare room but not asleep by the time Kate got home, her bedside light visible beneath the door. Kate knocked and went in quietly. Rose put down her book. 'Welcome home, traveller,' she said.

'I'm sorry I'm so late.'

'All is well. Fiona is at Jay's house. Gus went out like a light. I think all the rugby training is tiring him. He doesn't even have the energy to game when he gets home.'

'Wonders will never cease.' Kate came to sit on the end of her aunt's bed. One of her mother's landscape paintings was the only adornment to a plain, drab room that overlooked the main road at the front. She had been meaning to do it up for years. 'I must admit I thought the relationship with Jay might have gone south by now,' Kate said.

'I think their ardour has been rekindled, somehow.'

Kate smiled at her aunt. 'We'd better not ask how.'

'Did you have a good trip?'

'It was eventful, which seems to be the story of my life, these days.'

'I sometimes worry that you're a bit too fond of the drama of interesting times.' It was said without rancour, in the style Rose had perfected of reflective – and astute – psychological observation.

'Maybe I was, but not any more. I want it to be over now.'

'And how will it be over?'

'I have some ideas. I mean, there are theories, but I need to find the evidence.'

Rose closed her book. 'Well, good luck with that. In the meantime, I have good news. Maja arrives here tomorrow with her new parents. We've rented a house in Croydon. And found both the parents jobs. She'll start school here in a few weeks' time.'

'Christ. What did Ian say?'

'He doesn't know.'

Kate burst out laughing. 'You sly fox. How did you manage that?'

'I've flipped it into next year's accounts with only minor dishonesty.'

'He'll go absolutely mental.'

'I certainly hope so.' Rose was smiling back at her.

'He'll fire you.'

'I doubt it. He's not as brave as he likes to make out, as we have often discussed.'

Kate looked at her aunt. 'Thank you,' she said. She went to hug her. 'Thank you so much.'

'I'm going down to meet them in their new home tomorrow night. You can come with me, if you'd like.'

'I'd love to.'

But as she lay in bed and tried to sleep, it was not joy or anticipation or even hope that gripped her, but Lena's pale, frightened face as she'd steeled her to go undercover on that yacht in the days before she had been so brutally murdered.

25

THE FOLLOWING MORNING, Danny was like a cat on a hot tin roof outside Imogen's office. 'My God, you get me into some dodgy scrapes,' he said. 'I don't know why I always say yes to you.'

'Blind loyalty is a much underrated quality.'

'Well, this is the last time.'

'You've said that before.'

Danny paced. 'You sure this really has the PM's backing?'

'Yes. But if you want to cut and run, I'll understand.'

Danny didn't – and wouldn't, as they both knew from long experience. And a few moments later, Imogen arrived clutching a cup of coffee and the red box with her overnight papers. 'Sorry, I just had to get my morning fix,' she said, holding up the coffee. She led them into the palatial grandeur of her office and over to her desk at the far end, with its spectacular view of Horse Guards. 'Christ, some office,' Danny whispered, taking in the red leather furniture, antique bookcases, circular globe map of the world and assorted detritus of Britain's imperial past.

Kate put her bag down on the desk. 'We're going to need your log-in,' she told Imogen.

The foreign secretary's breezy confidence evaporated. 'What do you mean?'

'We need to search the system. If Danny tries to break in, there'll be the mother and father of all witch hunts.'

'But they'll be able to trace it back to me.'

Kate stood her ground patiently. 'This isn't a tracing-back-to-you situation. We're looking for evidence. It either exists or it doesn't. If it does, we can find various ways of hiding where we got it from.'

Imogen had segued to wary politician and looked deeply reluctant. 'I'm not sure I can do that. It doesn't feel right.'

But Kate had come too far to give up. 'Imogen, the reason I'm standing here is that *you* said I had a moral duty to try to find the truth about the prime minister. So that is what we're doing. We need your log-in.'

Imogen weighed this. 'All right,' she said. 'Step back, I'll log in and leave it. That way, well, at least I can deny I gave you my details if it ever comes to it.'

They did as she suggested. Imogen logged in, picked up her box and went to sit on one of the red leather sofas. 'I'm here if you need me,' she said.

Danny took Imogen's chair and Kate pulled over another to sit beside him. They leant in towards the screen. Danny searched the system for 'Jamaica', which brought up a vast array of documents that had no bearing whatsoever on the prime minister's official trip there during his time as foreign secretary. It was laborious work scrolling through them and it was clear that all were related to Imogen's period as foreign secretary and thus connected to her log-in only.

Danny tried to access the Foreign Office's internal travel department, but seemed to be finding a constant stream of dead-ends. 'I don't think I can do this without being an administrator.'

'There must be an archive,' Kate said.

Danny shrugged, but there was. He searched 'Jamaica' there, too: 6,112 documents. 'Christ,' he whispered.

He started scrolling through them despairingly. 'What are we even looking for?' he asked.

Kate sat back in her chair. It was like searching for a needle in a haystack, except that it was more complicated than that since they weren't even sure if they were looking for a needle or something else entirely.

Imogen was no longer sifting her red boxes. She was glued to her phone and texting furiously. It was only a few more minutes before the first call came in, and Danny's attempt to find something relevant in connection with James Ryan's trip to Jamaica in the archive was accompanied by the sound of Imogen cooing down the phone to MPs she was attempting to woo. 'He *doesn't* listen,' she said, to more than one. 'You're quite right. *That*'s what needs to change.'

Kate had long since learnt that when a backbench MP complained that Downing Street was not listening, he or she meant that the prime minister and his team were not listening to *him* or *her*.

Between calls, Kate interrupted. 'When you go abroad, who arranges your travel?'

Imogen looked at her in confusion, as if the question had been posed in Spanish. 'What?' she asked, her mind in the faraway reaches of her ascent to ultimate power.

'When you travel, who arranges it?' Kate repeated.

'My team,' Imogen said airily.

'Who in particular?'

Imogen thought about this, as if it was the most difficult question she had faced all year. 'Erm. Stacy. She's the assistant private secretary.'

'What's her surname?'

'Er . . .' A longer pause. 'Evans. No . . . Hughes. Yes! Stacy Hughes.'

'And she liaises with Travel?'

'Travel?'

'I assume she doesn't book your air tickets herself.'

'No. You mean the travel department here?'

'Yes.'

'I suppose so,' Imogen said. 'I must admit, I've never really thought about it.'

Not the only thing you never reflect on, Kate thought. 'Was she here before you arrived?'

'Yes, I think so.' A light suddenly flooded Imogen's crowded mind. 'Actually, no. Now I come to think about it, someone said James had been shagging the previous girl.'

'What was her name?'

'I don't know. I'm sorry.' Imogen was immediately lost to her political battle for power. She switched on the TV on the wall opposite, turned up the volume and began to flick through the morning news programmes. Most were focusing on the upcoming vote of no confidence in the prime minister, with running tallies of confirmed supporters, for and against. There was also a great deal of speculation about who, apart from Imogen, might run if the prime minister lost.

'Look in her inbox for a "handover",' Kate instructed Danny. He did as she'd asked and it didn't take them long to find an email that told Imogen Stacy Hughes would soon be taking over duties, including arranging her travel, from Petra Willis.

'If she left,' Kate asked Danny, 'would they put her email account into the archive?'

'Maybe email archive,' he said.

He went in search of it. They were having more luck now. It turned out that the foreign secretary did have access to the email archive and Danny managed to find the contents of Petra Willis's account: 9,212 emails had been sent and almost double that received. He searched 'Jamaica' and, with a few false starts, eventually found what they were looking for.

He opened James Ryan's travel arrangements for his trip to Jamaica. There was a detailed account of his flights, combined with a schedule of meetings and functions covering every hour of daylight while he was there. At the end – after lunch with the Jamaican prime minister on the final day – the schedule merely referred to: *at own arrangements. Depart at 1500 hours on flight JZ 216 from Norman Manley International, Kingston.* Two days later it had the details of the inbound flight from the unspecified destination and the connecting BA flight back to London Heathrow.

The accompanying email, from Petra to James Ryan, said only: *Have fun. But not too much! Xxx*

'Is there anywhere he goes that he doesn't find someone to shag him?' Danny asked.

'What was that?' Imogen yelled across.

'Nothing,' Kate replied. And then to Danny: 'Apparently not.'

'I don't see what it tells us, though,' Danny said. 'I mean, he went off somewhere on a private plane while he was in Jamaica. So what? We knew that.'

'Is there a way you can see if anyone has checked through this before us? If anyone else has accessed this exact part of the archive?'

'Followed the same trail, you mean?'

Kate nodded.

'Not unless I can log on as an administrator or hack in, which we've agreed is a bad idea, and even then . . . Well, I couldn't guarantee it.'

Kate looked across at Imogen, still scrolling furiously through messages on her phone. She toyed with the idea of asking her if she would order the duty officer in Computer Support to hand over the administrator codes, then had a better idea. 'Just try a search,' she said. 'Of names. Maybe someone just requested it. I mean, why go to the trouble of breaking in when you're senior enough to demand something without any real questions being asked?'

Danny shrugged to indicate he got the logic of it. He tried Ian Granger first, but without any luck. But when he entered the name Alan Brabazon, a single email came up from Petra's 'sent' folder: *Dear Sir Alan, I hope this is what you are looking for. Do call again if I can do anything else, Petra.*

Attached to it was the file containing the foreign secretary's travel arrangements to Jamaica.

Kate studied the date. The email had been sent four months *after* the Jamaica trip had been completed.

Danny looked at her.

'Christ,' Kate said.

'Is that what you were looking for?' Danny asked.

'Maybe,' she agreed, as she reeled from the implications of the words on the screen before her. Until now, she hadn't wanted to acknowledge how much she desperately needed the finger of guilt in this investigation to point towards Ian Granger, her nemesis, not her friend and former mentor, Sir Alan Brabazon.

Was it really possible he was Dante?

'Fucking hell!' Imogen shot to her feet. She flicked the screen back to ITV, where they were reporting news that 'allies close to the prime minister' had told *Good Morning Britain* that 'the endless succession of fake news scandals about the PM's past has been orchestrated by an Agent Dante working at the heart of MI6, whose identity is now being urgently sought by the Security Service'.

'What the hell is going on?' Imogen shouted.

Kate stared at the screen, wishing the news it imparted – now running in a ticker tape along the bottom – could be reeled back in. Her own phone buzzed. It was a text from the prime minister himself. *Please come to Number Ten immediately. James Ryan.*

26

TEN MINUTES LATER, when she was shown into his study, the prime minister was standing with his back to her, gazing out at the Downing Street garden. A red box was open on the ancient wooden desk, its contents spilt across the leather top like the detritus of some undergraduate essay research.

He turned. 'Kate,' he said. He looked as if he had aged physically, his cheeks puffy, his hair greying at the temples, but regressed mentally, his hands in his pockets and his shoulders sloping. He had a steaming mug of black coffee on the windowsill beside him, which he did not appear to have touched. 'It's a bloody business,' he said.

She didn't enquire which bit of this affair he had in mind, though there were plenty of candidates.

'Don't you think?'

'Yes, Prime Minister.'

He didn't look as if he would welcome an interrogation

into which aspect of her investigation he might have been referring to. 'I'm sorry,' he said. 'I just had to.'

'Had to what?' she said, though she knew what he had done. She just wanted him to admit it.

'I leaked it, of course.' He waved airily at the outer office. 'I mean, they did. Dark arts and all that.'

'I assumed as much.'

'I know I said I wouldn't.' He nodded, as if genuinely troubled, though why a man who was a byword for perfidy should care about this broken word was a mystery. 'But the chief whip tells me I'm going to lose next week. The tide is turning against me. The team were convinced I needed a powerful counter-narrative to change that and this was the only one they felt might do the trick.'

'And, after all, it is the truth.'

He frowned at her. 'I thought you'd be furious.'

'I find I've got to the age where fury is overrated.'

'I wish I had!' He was gazing out over the garden again. 'I'd like to roast Imogen Conrad over a roaring fire.'

The image of Imogen being roasted was unfortunate on too many levels to contemplate, so Kate let it pass. 'Could I talk to you about something, Prime Minister?'

'Of course.' He tried to smile at her, but it came out as a grimace. 'Don't tell me you've found the wretched blighter!'

Kate pointed towards the seating area on the other side of his desk, as though this were her office. But he meekly complied. He fell into the sofa with a dull thud. He wasn't growing any lighter. 'I feel as if I'm just getting started,' he said. 'That's the absolute bugger of it.'

She let him settle. 'Could you tell me about your friendship with Sir Alan Brabazon?'

He looked as if he had been shot. '*What?*' he spluttered.

'You were great friends once. It would help me to know about that period.'

He shook his head ruefully. 'He told you, did he?'

Kate wondered why he was making such a meal of this. It wasn't the world's best-kept secret that they had been at school together, though few perhaps knew that two of the most powerful men in the country had been in the same year and boarding house – and, more than that, had been the very best of friends. Inseparable, one of their contemporaries had told her. 'You think he was so upset with me when we fell out that he's spent the rest of his life working out a way to destroy me?' He shook his head. 'You're going to have to do better than that, Kate.'

'You did fall out?'

'Why on earth would it matter now?'

'We're at the stage with this, sir, where everything matters. We spoke to one contemporary who said you were inseparable for much of your school career.'

'I wouldn't go quite that far. We weren't shagging each other, if that's what you're driving at.' Why, Kate thought, did everything with this man have to come down to shagging? 'Boarding school in those days was a rather brutal experience,' he went on. 'You needed a sense of humour to get you through. We bonded over that, and I suppose we were close for a while.'

'Until when?'

'Look, Kate, does this really matter?'

'I have no idea.'

'All right. We fell out in the sixth form because I found his attitude towards my romantic activities a trifle priggish.

Alan never found a moral high ground he wasn't determined to mount.'

'Would you care to elaborate?'

'Not much.' She leant forward, ready to press further.
'All right!' He flung his hands up in exasperation. 'I was a
bit of a bounder, no question. I wasn't too good at letting
one girl know I'd had enough of her before moving on to
the next. I rather enjoyed my reputation, but he had a sister
at the girls' school next door of whom he was very protective and . . .'

'You had an affair with her?'

'Worse than that. I'd been to Amsterdam one half-term
with a friend from home and managed to pick up some
crabs.' He grinned sheepishly. 'You know . . .'

'I'm familiar with what they are. And you gave them to
his sister?'

'I'm ashamed to say that I did.' That would do it, Kate
thought. 'You asked,' he said.

'I did.'

'But I don't think a contretemps over his sister requiring
a shameful trip to her GP quite justifies a lifelong revenge
tragedy, do you?'

Perhaps not a lifelong one, she thought. But, still, it
would explain a splintered friendship. 'Did he have a
weakness?'

'He was bloody ambitious.'

'That's not normally considered a weakness.'

'It depends how much you want something. When I
think of the establishment, or what people mean by it, I
bring to mind Alan. He was head of house, his older
brother, his father and his uncle were all head of school.

They called his older brother Thrasher, because he wielded the cane with a merciless power that shocked even his contemporaries.'

'What about Sir Alan?'

'They banned boys beating other boys five years before we got to the school. His older brother had been there at the same time as mine and they hated each other. Look, all I'm saying is that Alan *believed* in it all.'

'What, exactly?'

'*Dulce et decorum est.* The whole good-men-and-true nonsense. That's his weakness. If anything had gone wrong and threatened his position at the heart of life's inner sanctum, if something had challenged his inherent sense of self-worth or his right to occupy the moral high ground, that could have pushed him off the rails, but nothing else.'

Kate glanced at her phone. She'd just received her third text from Julie in as many minutes. *Need to speak to you. J.*

'Duty calls?' he asked, smiling sheepishly at her once more.

'Yes, sir.'

'What's going to happen, Kate?'

She stood, still turning over the idea that had occurred to her in the dead of night. Was the risk involved suicidal? And, if so, did she really have any choice now? 'We're going to find Dante,' she said. 'And we'll do it in the next few days. This can't go on any longer for either of us.'

'If you manage that,' he said, 'I'll make you the bloody Queen.'

She smiled back at him. 'No, thanks.' She walked slowly towards the door, but turned as she reached it. They'd got beyond the point of half-measures or hesitation. She had to go all in. 'I need you to do one more thing.'

'Anything.'

Kate hesitated only a moment longer. 'Please ask Shirley Grove to contact Andrew Blake, who is technically our head of Chancery at the embassy in Moscow.'

'But really our man in the Russian capital?'

'Yes. Grove needs to make sure she speaks to Andrew himself on a secure line. No one else. Not a secretary or an assistant. She must ask him to call you personally from the secure section of the embassy on a highly sensitive matter that he must not discuss with anyone else, particularly within SIS.'

'All right. What do I tell him?'

'You explain. You say there is a matter so sensitive it has to be run by you from Downing Street, outside all normal channels including within SIS, though you can mention that you've hired me to run the investigative team. You tell him you've been made aware of a new cultivated agent his team has brought on stream called Incisor. You say you're going to have to ask him to task Incisor with something sensitive and difficult. He will politely refuse, before you even explain what it is. When you press him, he will deflect. When you insist, he will refuse point blank.'

'Why?'

'Because I would and so would any self-respecting station chief or agent handler, particularly if the source in question was one he or she had cultivated.'

'What do you mean, "cultivated"?'

'Someone you'd spotted, groomed and then reeled in. It's a difficult, subtle process, in which a strong personal bond is normally forged. Hell would freeze over before you'd allow any politician to start messing about with your agent, and Andrew is a good operator.'

'So then what do I do?'

'You say you entirely understand his reservations, but this is a matter of national security and you're afraid you're going to have to insist. You'll accept whatever terms and conditions Andrew may set, but you have a single task that must be put to Incisor direct. He will have made some promises to his agent that ultimately must be delivered by the British state, so at this point Andrew will be wondering just how far you'll push it. Then he'll try to stall. He'll say it's practically impossible. He'll claim he doesn't have enough guaranteed clean skins in his team in Russia to scope out a face-to-face meeting at short notice, and if teams cannot be sent from SIS in London, then he'll regretfully have to leave it for another day.'

'I tell him we can't wait for another day?'

'Yes, but more than that, you let him know you'll be sending a team from London to take care of that operation.'

'Where am I going to find such a team?'

'I'll go, with my colleague Julie.'

'Christ, Kate. You're going to Moscow? Is that wise?'

'If we want to get to the bottom of this, I'm not sure I have a choice.'

He nodded, as if impressed. 'Roger that. I assume you know what you're doing. You seem very clear how this is going to pan out with this fellow Andrew.'

'Any case officer would do exactly the same. You'd move heaven and earth to keep any politician a million miles away from an agent, so we have to convince him these are exceptional circumstances. He'll immediately come back to you and say it would be impossible to work with an outside team, whoever it is. At that point, tell him you're going beyond your area of expertise and schedule a virtual meeting tomorrow at which Julie and I will be present. In all likelihood, he'll continue to fight it, but it'll be harder with me there to bat his points back one by one and, in the meantime, he and his team will do some emergency groundwork just in case they find they can't wriggle out of it.'

As Kate walked down the stairs to leave Downing Street by the back entrance, she was already starting to have regrets. And when she got to the office, Julie had similar misgivings – and then some. 'Are you out of your mind, Kate?'

They stood around the espresso machine. 'Andrew will refuse to have anything to do with us,' Julie said.

'Of course.'

'There's no way he'll activate contact or permit it on a politician's whim.'

'We're going to parcel it up as a matter of national security. And he'll have promised Incisor the earth – perhaps even safe conduct to the UK when the time comes – and he'll have to be wary of going against the prime minister's directly expressed wish, even if his political future is in the balance.'

'He'll stall, he'll sabotage.'

'Yes, but he may in the end calculate that it's worth this single risk, depending on Incisor's current status.'

'He'll claim he only contacts him via a cut-out.' Julie shrugged. 'And it's probably true.'

'Yes, but there will be an emergency procedure for a face-to-face. We're just going to have to persuade him to activate it.' A cut-out was a middle man or woman, used so that handling agents rarely if ever had to make direct contact with the source. A 'diplomat' seen to be contacting an architect, or an engineer, or a journalist might not in itself be suspicious – and neither would it be so for that person then to be seen with the ultimate third party.

'We won't be able to clean the route on our own,' Julie said.

'No, but – whatever he says – he'll have some facilities, agents he's confident are clean. Combine that with the two of us and I think we can get him over the line.'

'It's a suicide mission,' Julie opined.

'Possibly.'

'If all our original instincts about this were correct, if the prime minister *is* Moscow's man in London, then we're walking into the jaws of the dragon.'

Kate took her coffee and went to sit on the balcony, bathed in bright autumn sun. She felt jaded, even a little sick.

'Look, let me tell you where I've got to,' Julie said, as she seated herself opposite. 'And see whether it changes your mind.

'I went through every bloody entry that Ian and Sir Alan had ever written, in the entire course of their career. And I could find very little beyond what we already knew, apart from the fact that they both file a mean, pithy report, and appear to have had more than their fair share of successes along the way. But I thought there had to be more than that. So then I tried to look at access . . . I can't ask Danny for assistance any more, but there is a woman called India in Tech Support I had a thing with once.'

Kate wondered how many people in the organization Julie had had 'a thing' with over the years.

'I said I was working directly for the prime minister, which she didn't believe until I got Grove involved.'

'She helped you?'

'Yes. She did.' Julie opened her handbag and pulled out a sheet of paper. 'This is the result. There have been five instances of someone other than Ian accessing and editing his material in the last ten years.' She looked up at Kate. 'Three involved Sir Alan and two you – or someone using your log-in and security clearance.'

'What was changed?'

'We couldn't recover that. It had been wiped from the server.' Julie's gaze was fixed on her. 'Is there something you need or want to tell me, Kate, before we go any further?'

Kate had no idea what to say to this. How could someone have accessed her log-in? It ought to have been impossible, as Julie well knew. 'I have no idea what's going on. Someone trying to frame me, I suppose. Did you determine the dates the files were edited?'

'Yes. Five years ago and three in Sir Alan's case. Three years ago for you.'

Before Operation Sigma. Before this nightmare began. How could that possibly make any sense at all? 'I can stop now,' Julie said. 'I'm your friend and I owe you that. But if we go on, I don't know where it all ends.'

'You think it's me?'

'I have to be open to that possibility. This whole affair just gets weirder and weirder. I'm not going to lie to you, I'm out of my depth.'

'Or it gets simpler.' Kate looked at Julie. 'Thank you.'

'For what?'

'Telling me. You could have gone to Grove, to Ian – to any of them.'

'I'm your friend, for God's sake.'

'But this is beyond our friendship and we both know it.'

'Nothing's beyond friendship, Kate. In this business, it's frankly all we have.'

'Maybe.' Kate drained the dregs of her coffee. If nothing else, this latest twist solidified her sense that she needed to make a bold play now to settle the matter once and for all. She could no longer carry on in this twilight world of twisted half-truths. 'I *am* going to Moscow,' she said quietly. 'I have to bring this to a conclusion. I can't ask you to come with me.'

'But why? What on earth are you going to find there?'

Kate turned her hands over in the sunlight, examining the wedding ring that was still resolutely in its rightful place. Or was it? 'We're never going to find evidence here in London. Dante has had all the time in the world to lay a thousand false trails and he's going to lead us a merry dance for just as long as we allow him to. It's quite a few years since I worked with Andrew Blake, but he's nobody's fool. If this new agent Incisor is real – and we have no reason to suppose he isn't – there's an outside chance that he, or she, will be able to give us the concrete proof we need.'

'How?'

'You said Incisor works for Igor Borodin's special unit, among others, arranging travel schedules?'

'I guess, but so what?'

'Igor runs agents the old-school way and with the

minimum risk possible. But if Dante is the strategist we think he is – and senior enough to have a mind worth picking – then Igor will have wanted to get alongside him every year or two.'

Julie nodded. 'All right. So if we can find Igor's travel schedule, we can overlay it on our own files and . . .' She trailed off as she considered the implications. 'Actually, I did check out with Travel who went to Washington or New York during the year Dayton was being negotiated, just to see if anyone else could have been filing those Bosnia reports we were told about in Istanbul.'

'Sir Alan?'

Julie nodded. 'Three trips to Washington, but every time he was over there, he came back via New York.'

'If Sir Alan or Ian was in the same place as Igor once or twice in a decade, that could be a coincidence,' Kate said. 'But more than that and we have our man, I'd say. If we can get Igor's travel schedule, we can nail this once and for all.'

'That's smart,' Julie said eventually. 'Really smart. But I'm going to come with you, no argument. We've been through too much to turn back now.'

'No.'

'Yes, Kate. Otherwise it's no deal. You cannot do this on your own. And we'll need to take Callum, too. He can do the driving.'

'Absolutely not. He's not a pro—'

'We need bodies on the ground, Kate. He can come in with me and we can give him a limited role, but we need him.'

'This is my show. I cannot allow you—'

'I'm not going to negotiate. Not this time. It's probably

suicide as it is, but doubly so if you attempt it on your own. You have no idea what you may or may not find when you get there. You must have more than one of us to watch your back.'

Kate couldn't fault the logic of this, but she was damned if she was going to let her friend take the risk. 'I can manage.'

'No, and that is final. You need both of us.'

Kate sighed. It was unarguable that it would be easier, and probably safer, with someone to watch out for her, though Callum's inexperience made it questionable as to whether he would prove help or hindrance. 'I've got an Australian passport I was given originally in my days in Hong Kong so I can use that, but you don't have an off-the-grid identity, as far as I know, and Callum definitely doesn't.'

'I'll sort that for him and me overnight, don't you worry. And we'll both need to be on the set-up call with Andrew. We'll go in separately.'

'I was thinking Minsk, then by road.'

'All right. I'll square Callum and we'll get to work on a different route and back story.'

'I'll speak to him. I don't want him to feel he has to—'

'He'll do it. Leave him to me.'

Kate neglected to ask what made Julie so sure Callum would wish to risk his neck to assist either of them, but she doubted very much she would want to know the answer.

27

IT WAS EARLY afternoon by the time Kate reached the Old Mill in Hampshire. She found Sir Alan sitting at a table in the shade by the river, polishing his household silver. 'Forgive me for asking,' she said, as she slid in beside him, 'but isn't that what you employ a housekeeper for?'

'It's her day off.'

'It could perhaps wait.'

'I'm tired of fixing the MG,' he said. 'Besides, I'm retired, a lonely, useless old widower. What else am I to do?'

His chin was covered with white stubble, his tortoiseshell glasses smudged, his shirt missing a button. 'I'll spare you the violins,' she said. She pointed at his chest. 'Mrs Evans is certainly capable of sewing a button back on to your shirt.'

'You've come to arrest me?'

Kate gestured to her non-existent back-up team. 'I hope you're going to come quietly. Otherwise I'm in all sorts of trouble.'

'Wait there.'

He dispensed with his silver cloth and the rose bowl he'd been polishing and stalked away towards the house. Kate gazed at the effervescent waters of the brook and the bees zigzagging through the lavender on its nearside bank. She glanced at the rose bowl, first prize in the Leicestershire open tennis championship of 1911. 'My grandmother,' he said. 'She was quite the player until she became an alcoholic.'

He was armed with a tray, upon which were two plates of beef, a salad, a bottle of red wine and two glasses. 'She always insists on making up for two, just in case I have a guest,' he said.

'What if I'm not hungry?'

'Then you'll join me out of politeness.' He poured two glasses of wine and handed her one. She didn't dare refuse. 'You think he'll hang on?' he asked.

'The PM?'

'Who else?'

'I guess you could be talking about Ian Granger.'

'Oh, God, that cockroach. Well, he'd survive the nuclear apocalypse. No, I mean the prime minister, of course.'

'Honestly, no,' she said. 'Though he might stand a chance if I can find Agent Dante by the time of the no-confidence vote next week.'

'And how are you progressing on that front?'

'Oh, you know . . . Getting closer.'

'Hah!' He was grinning from ear to ear. 'Teasing me! This . . . this is what I've missed. So you *have* come to arrest me?'

'You seem very sure you're guilty, if I may say so.'

'By now, your candidates are few. And I venture I look the likeliest of them all.'

'Why do you say that?'

'Ian, or whoever else we're looking for, has spent a very long time planning this. If he hasn't laid a trail directly to my door and beyond I'd be frankly disappointed. And perhaps it has enough feints and sleights of hand to keep even you interested.'

Kate really wasn't hungry, but neither of them touched their food. She was grateful for the wine, though. 'You know what troubles me honestly,' she said. 'The question I keep coming back to?'

'Why you?'

'Not so much that.' She shrugged. 'Hard as it is, perhaps I just have to accept I was picked for my credulity.'

'Hardly,' he said. 'Better candidates there by the dozen.'

'How did Dante know about my friendship with Sergei? It's a key pillar of this entire operation. How did he know my instinct would be to trust what Sergei told me and not ask all of the many questions that should have automatically come to mind?'

Sir Alan finally turned to his food. He cut and ate with measured precision. 'I knew, as you have already pointed out,' he said at last.

'But how? I'm not sure I'm satisfied with how you spotted that connection so easily in my files.'

'Instinct. Not so much what was in your file, but what you left out. One does develop a sense of these things, you know, after a lifetime in the Service.'

'You knew that before the operation in Istanbul or afterwards?'

'Afterwards.'

'But that doesn't track,' Kate said. 'Whoever set this

thing up knew about my relationship with Sergei years previously – long enough ago to have him attend the same counter-terrorism conference in Sofia in 2012 and deliberately avoid me. Ian wasn't even head of the Russia Desk by then, let alone controller, Europe. How would he have seen that potential in my files?'

'He might have done, if he'd gone looking for it. And Dante *was* searching, I'll wager.'

Kate put her wine down. She was tired of his intellectual jousting. If this was a world he wished to cling to, like the dying light, it was one she wanted to leave behind her. 'Shall we stop playing games?' she asked. 'Why don't you finally tell me what you really think?'

He concentrated on his food with consummate deliberation.

'And why is it I always get the sense you know more than you're telling me?' she added.

'Suspect, not know.'

'Then tell me what you suspect.'

He sipped his wine and chewed his food. He dabbed the corner of his mouth with a napkin and seemed once or twice on the verge of sharing something with her. But then the moment passed. He imperceptibly withdrew. 'I suspect Ian Granger was a Russian plant even before he joined the Service. I think the KGB was never as down-and-out in the aftermath of the fall of the Soviet Union as we once thought. The most reliable and subtle officers – Igor Borodin at the forefront of them – never lost faith in better days and a return to the old ways.'

Kate didn't believe him and the disillusionment was crushing. All those years of looking up to him, of modelling her career on his sinewy steel, charm and intelligence, and yet here they were, one to one, cutting to the quick, while she listened to him lying to her.

Sir Alan as Dante? Was it truly credible? And if not, what was he hiding from her? 'Please help me,' she said. 'You've always looked after me and I have everything on the line here – Stuart, my children, my sanity . . .'

He didn't meet her eye. 'I have helped you, Kate.'

'What are you not telling me?'

He raised his head, back to that flinty gaze. 'I'm offering you what I believe, the product of years of steadily unravelling the web that Ian Granger has woven.'

'Why did you access and edit some of his files?'

'I didn't. Any more than you have.'

'How did you know about that?'

'Because . . .' he gave her a wintry smile '. . . it's perhaps time for you to acknowledge that, wherever this road takes you, it's to a place I have been before.'

This glimpse of the intellectual arrogance that had often been gossiped of, but which she had never experienced, was like a slap in the face. Was that what he intended? To put her off her stride? 'Why did you ask James Ryan's assistant private secretary at the Foreign Office for his travel plans to Jamaica?'

She appeared to have surprised him. But he recovered quickly. 'The same reason as you, I should imagine.'

'And yet your request was made four months after the trip. Why would you have been interested at the time, unless you were planning to use the details to set him up?'

Sir Alan finished his food slowly and carefully and put his knife and fork together. He drained his glass and poured himself more wine. 'Check,' he said, smiling at her. 'If not quite yet checkmate. You'll need more than circumstantial evidence, as well you know.'

She met his gaze. 'But the thing is, I just don't believe it's you, which leaves me to wonder about the truth you're protecting.' She shook her head. 'Because the only thing I'm absolutely certain of is that you've already got to the end of this maze and have the answer.'

'Perhaps you're looking at the answer,' he said. 'And just don't want to believe the evidence of your own eyes.'

There was a long silence as she tracked the progress of a bumble bee. How liberating, she thought, to have a life of such simple purpose. 'Rose said she came down here after that breakfast meeting with Ian to work out how you could both protect me.'

'She did. And she was right to. You're his target, his get-out-of-jail-free card. Whitehall wants to hear that you're Dante. It solves every problem in one go.'

'So what conclusions did you reach with her?'

'We agreed to intensify our efforts to prove Ian is the man we seek.'

Kate wasn't sure she believed this. 'You and she have been friends for a long time?'

'Yes.' He nodded. 'If Alice was a domestic rock, Rose performed the same role in my life at work and I make no secret of it. As head of Finance, there's little she's not privy to and I found her advice invaluable. She's shrewd and loyal, everything that a man like Ian is not, which is why I doubt she'll survive much longer.'

Kate stood very slowly. 'Thank you,' she said. 'This has been helpful.'

28

ROSE HAD ARRANGED to wait for her by the metal gazebo at the heart of Wandle Park in Croydon. She sat in a cream raincoat with a steel flask of tea. She had on a pair of incongruous grey Bose headphones and was evidently lost in the music, eyes closed, so that Kate had to tug at her sleeve to get her attention. 'My God,' Rose said, whipping off her headphones. 'I'm sorry, I was miles away.'

Kate took a seat beside her. She picked up Rose's phone from the bench. 'Bose headphones, Spotify, eighties playlist . . .'

'Fiona and Gus made it for me.'

Kate had never heard either of her children listen to the music of the 1980s and she wondered how much else about their lives with Rose she didn't know about. 'Great headphones,' she said, holding them up.

'Simon bought them.'

'He really is a very generous man.'

'He is.' Rose held up the flask. 'Tea?'

'I think we should get on with this,' Kate said. But Rose poured her some anyway. Kate sipped. As the evening chill descended, hurried by a cutting breeze, the warm, sweet tea was welcome.

Kate glanced around her. They were the only people sitting on the benches that circled the gazebo and the park was more or less empty but for a few lone dog-walkers hurrying home before the angry dark clouds overhead dumped their contents on an unsuspecting city. 'This is going to be a good moment,' Rose said.

'I'm dreading it.'

'Well, that's foolish, if I may say so. You've single-handedly given this young girl a new life and I am sure she'll be very grateful.'

'It's hard to forget that I killed her sister.'

Rose reached out to take her hand. 'Time to look forward, not back.'

The sincerity, the love, in her aunt's eyes was unmistakable. 'It's hard to look to the future when I'm still trying to make sense of the past,' Kate said.

'Then bring it to a conclusion and move on. Because that's long overdue and we both know it.'

'I have to go away tomorrow. I do genuinely think it will be for the last time.'

'You've found your answer?'

'Getting closer.'

Rose smiled. 'I suggested the kids come and stay with us anyway, so don't worry about it. I wish I could help you, my girl. Because I think all this risks dragging you back down into the abyss.'

'Yes,' Kate said simply. 'It does.' What was the point in denying such a self-evident truth? And to Rose of all people, with whom all deception seemed pointless.

'What is it?' Rose asked.

'I just think I've been such an idiot,' Kate said. 'That's what really gets to me. I always thought I was smart and capable, but I'm starting to feel I've been manipulated like a five-year-old child.'

'In what way?'

'Every time I feel confident of what happened, that I can see the truth, that I have the coordinates of the confusing terrain, the compass goes haywire and I'm suddenly utterly lost again. It's as though I'm passing through the intelligence equivalent of the Bermuda Triangle.'

Kate finished her tea and tipped the dregs on to the gravel by her feet. 'What really troubles me,' she said, 'is Sergei. These past few days, I've been obsessed by trying to work out who in SIS could have been aware of the true nature of my friendship with him.'

'Why?'

'Because the entire operation was predicated on me trusting his motives. And there is no way Igor Borodin would have gone to such lengths unless he was damned sure I'd swallow it.'

'So it had to be someone who knew you well enough to be certain of that connection,' Rose said.

'I was thinking that. But then I had another idea, which was a lot more disturbing.'

'Which was that Sergei was not an unwilling pawn of his bosses in Moscow, but the architect of the entire business?'

Kate didn't answer, but this was precisely the fear that had consumed her on the journey back from Sir Alan's home in Hampshire. How could she have been so naive? She had even considered the possibility that his death in that train carriage in Russia had in some way been faked. After all, had she taken the trouble to check his pulse and ascertain beyond doubt that he was indeed dead?

Rose put the top back on her Thermos and placed it in her bag. She stood. 'I don't have an answer to that question. And I don't suppose you're going to find one either, any more than, at this stage, you're ever going to sift fact entirely from fiction in this case. The Russians are now so good at confusing the very nature of truth that I'd say you'd be better off moving on and making a success of the rest of your life.' She offered her hand. 'But there is a young girl half a mile away whose world you've totally transformed and that's the kind of truth we all need more of.'

Kate took her aunt's proffered hand and hauled herself wearily to her feet. They walked the half-mile to the small terraced house in silence, through the commuters hurrying home before the rain set in. Thunder rumbled in the distance.

They hesitated by the newly painted front door, their feet by a mat that proclaimed its welcome in large, untarnished black letters. Rose knocked. They heard voices inside. Rose gave Kate an uncharacteristic wink and Kate returned her smile. 'Cheer up,' Rose said. 'Not everyone gets to save a soul from a life of purgatory. It might even be enough to impress St Peter, when the time comes.'

'I'll need something.'

'So will I.' Rose smiled at her again as the door was opened by a slim, neatly dressed man of indeterminate age with thick glasses and skin scarred from adolescent acne. The woman who came into view behind him wore the nervous smile of all arrivals unsure of the welcome their new home will offer.

They introduced themselves as Alexander and Zara and their servile gratitude immediately grated. What on earth, Kate thought, did any of them really have to thank her for?

The couple led Rose and Kate through to the small kitchen at the rear, where a Formica table groaned with sandwiches, biscuits and juices. At the end of the table, Maja sat with her back to the light, her gaze firmly on the floor beneath her feet. 'Maja,' Zara said, 'this is Rose and Kate, the ladies who helped you.'

Maja barely lifted her gaze. 'Maja!' Zara admonished, but Kate raised her hand. She took a seat at one side of the table and Rose the other.

Maja was pretty, with her sister's blonde hair and vivid blue eyes. She was still every inch the child and Kate found herself thinking of the video of the prime minister cavorting with three young teenage girls in Kosovo. Why had she been so quick in recent days to accept that really was a fake? She reminded herself not to allow her investigation to be limited by a failure of her own imagination.

'Please help yourself,' Zara said. But neither she nor Alexander joined them at the table. 'Perhaps you could just give us a minute,' Kate asked them.

She waited until they had left the room and pulled the door quietly shut. 'Hello, Maja. My name is Kate and this is Rose. Do you know who we are?'

Maja gave them a barely perceptible nod. Kate took a

plate and filled it with sandwiches. Rose did the same and they offered the groaning platter to Maja who tentatively followed suit.

None of them ate.

Kate tried to catch the girl's eye. 'Maja, your sister worked for us. She did so to help you. We tried everything in our power to keep her safe, but we couldn't save her. We couldn't be sorrier about that. But you should know that she took the risk to ensure you would have a better life, and we'll keep the promises we made to her now and in the future.'

Maja brushed her stick-thin legs against the chair, like a child half her age. She still hadn't raised her gaze.

'We've found you a good school. When the time comes, if you wish, we'll make sure you're offered financial help to go to university. We'll do our best to help you into employment. Alexander and Zara will take care of you, but we'll always be in the background, ready to offer any assistance you might need.' Kate took a business card from her pocket and pushed it towards Maja. 'This is my mobile phone number. Call it at any time and I'll do my level best to help.' Kate glanced at Rose, who nodded in encouragement. 'We recognize that this is never going to bring your sister back and I can't tell you how desperately sorry we are about that. She was a brave young woman and she risked her life to give you a better future. I hope we can persuade you to grasp it with both hands.'

The room was silent, but for the sound of Maja's trainers scuffing against the chair legs.

'Maja?' Rose asked kindly.

Maja met Kate's gaze. 'What happened to her?'

'She was working for us undercover,' Kate said. 'She got a job as a nanny to some very influential enemies of the British state and the people she was watching found out who she was and I'm afraid they killed her.'

'Did my sister make a mistake?'

'No,' Kate said. 'The errors were all on our side.'

'Is that why you're paying for me to be here?'

Yes, Kate thought. 'No,' she said. 'We're trying to be true to the promise we made to her.'

'How did she die?'

'I don't think you'd want to know that.'

'Did they hurt her?'

'It happened very quickly,' Kate said. 'We were looking for her and they were trying to get away from us.'

Maja examined her hands. 'She loved me.'

'She did. Her only concern was for your safety.'

'No one else has ever cared for me.' She looked up again. 'And no one ever will.'

'I hope that's not true,' Kate said. She glanced towards the door and the couple beyond it.

'Perhaps they tell you they look after me,' Maja said, following the direction of Kate's gaze. 'But they only care about the money.'

Kate had never seen a young girl look so bereft, so alone.

'Do Alexander and Zara not treat you well, Maja?' Rose asked.

She sighed. 'They feed me.'

Kate met Rose's gaze once more. She wanted to promise the girl the world, but she'd learnt the hard way that glib pledges sometimes came with unforeseen and unpredictable costs. 'You'll have to stay here to go to your new school,' Rose said, 'but we won't abandon you.'

Maja shrugged. She must have learnt not to believe in promises.

'You've never been to England before,' Rose went on. 'It can be very beautiful at this time of year. So how would it be if I pick you up tomorrow evening and you come to stay with my husband and me in the country for the weekend?' She pointed at her niece. 'Kate's children will be with me. They're a little older than you, but at least there will be someone under the age of fifty. I could drop you back here on Sunday evening, in time for your new school.'

Kate and Maja stared at Rose, for different – or, arguably, the same – reasons.

Maja didn't answer. And Kate swallowed the many questions that the gesture prompted. She didn't get to ask them until Rose had squared the logistical details with Maja's carers and they had stepped into the chill autumnal wind outside. 'Are you sure –' Kate began, as soon as they were safely beyond earshot.

'– that was wise?' Rose finished for her. 'Of course not. But you saw the poor girl. She has no one.'

'She's my responsibility.'

'No,' Rose said. 'Financially, practically, she's the Service's burden, as you well know. But I played a significant part in getting her here, so emotionally, she's as much my responsibility. Besides, I'm having her for the weekend, not adopting her.'

'But she's very damaged. If we start to open this door—'

'I'll make sure Fiona and Gus are protected, don't worry.'

'That wasn't what I meant and you know it. You're a bloody saint. That's the truth.'

Rose draped an arm around her niece's shoulders. 'I do like a challenge and I'm getting to the stage in life where new ones are not easy to come by.'

They didn't speak again until they had climbed into Rose's car. 'Did you ever think of adopting?' Kate asked. 'You have so much love to give.'

Rose breathed out. She looked, for just a moment, as if she might cry. 'I'm sorry,' Kate said. 'I didn't mean to—'

'It's all right.' She tried to smile at her niece. 'Dr Wiseman has spent years telling me it isn't a crime to talk about it.'

'Why didn't you?'

'Oh, I don't know. We'd been through so much pain by then. I think both Simon and I needed to find peace.'

'The miscarriages?'

'Everything. The years of trying, both of us wanting it so badly, the times it went wrong and we lost . . .'

The rain came in hard, thrashing the windscreen. Kate sensed her aunt was on the cusp of telling her something, so she waited.

And the silence stretched out.

'I'm going to tell you something, which I suspect you've already worked out but are too discreet to probe. I mean it as a cautionary tale.' Rose put her car keys on the dashboard, as if abandoning any attempt to run away from this. 'The years of trying and trying again to conceive put phenomenal pressure on my relationship with Simon. In addition to the emotional toll it took on us, he was working hard and so was I. It's the oldest cliché in the world, but I drifted too close to someone.'

'Sir Alan?'

'Yes. We'd been friends for a long time but, very briefly, it turned into something more than that.' She paused. 'Neither of us could live with the deceit, so we agreed that he would confess to Alice and I to Simon. As you will imagine, it was by some distance the worst conversation of my life, except discussing my miscarriages with our doctor. I've never seen such hurt. The pain I'd caused . . . it broke us both.'

'Did he leave you?'

'For a while. But in the end, after we'd both been through more pain than I could possibly describe, he came back and said he wanted to forgive and forget.'

'But it's impossible to do either, which is why you don't want me to get back together with Stuart.'

'Simon has tried – I mean really, *really* tried. And I love him all the more for it. But I can't say he's ever forgiven me and I don't blame him. I don't deserve a second chance.' She looked at her niece. 'There is no going back.'

Kate stared at the rain. This explained so much and opened up as many questions. 'I know,' she said finally.

'Do you?'

'I think so, yes.'

Rose gripped her wrist, took the keys and started the car. They drove all the way home to Kate's house in Battersea in uneasy silence. Rose turned off the engine again as she parked outside. 'Try not to think too ill of me,' Rose said. 'I'm not sure I could bear that.'

'I'd never think worse of you,' Kate replied, though even as she said it, she was not precisely sure it was true.

'I know what your mother's betrayal of your father did

to you. I'm not naive enough to think this revelation will land without impact.'

Kate looked at her aunt. 'You're not my mother and you never will be. What happened between you and Simon or even you and Sir Alan is not my business.' She hugged her aunt and put her hand on the door lever. But she hesitated again. 'Are you sure he confessed to his wife?'

'Yes, quite sure.'

Kate was thinking of the prime minister's description of Sir Alan's dominance of the moral high ground. 'It couldn't have been used to blackmail him?'

Rose shook her head. 'No, not least because Alice did a better job of forgiving him.'

Kate walked away, stopping to gather herself at the front door as she put the key into the lock. Not my business, she told herself. Just not my business.

But the evening had one more surprise in store, in the shape of Ian Granger hunched at the kitchen table, nursing a mug of tea. There was no sign of either of her children. 'Fiona let me in,' he said apologetically.

Kate took off her coat and hung it up. She flicked the kettle back on. She turned to face him. 'This is a bit of a liberty, Ian.'

'I've forced the Security Service to call off its dogs,' he said.

'There's enough deception in that single sentence,' she replied, 'to keep me occupied for months.'

'I'm offering an alliance.'

'For what purpose?'

'Finding Dante. Bringing this to a conclusion. Look . . .' He put his tea to one side and leant forward, elbows on the table. 'The Security Service think it must be you. Indeed, I'd go as far as to say they're obsessed by the idea. But it can't be you, as I've now told them many times.'

'Why not?'

'Because I don't think even your worst enemy believes you're bad enough to expose your husband as a spy and have him exiled to Moscow to the heartbreak of your own children.'

'Unless it was to deflect suspicion from me and in preparation for the day when I'm finally exposed and have to flee to Moscow myself.'

'If you're Dante and have survived more than a decade, perhaps two, at the heart of the Service, I don't think you'd assume your days were numbered.'

'All right, but it could be you. Indeed, on some measures, it probably *is* you. So how is an alliance going to work?'

'Because there's only one person at a senior level within the Service who has been sceptical of the claims of this operation from the start. Who was it who argued for caution over the recording of that bugged conversation on the super-yacht? Who worried we might be being set up? Who didn't want to take it forward? Who doubted Igor Borodin's veracity as a defector and didn't want to go through with it?'

Until it looked like it might be a success, Kate thought, at which point you were all over Borodin. But she made her tea in silence. Ian indisputably had a point. 'So what alliance do you propose?'

'Come on, Kate.' He sounded exasperated. 'You know Sir Alan is Dante. Who else could really have pulled this off over so many years? He spotted the vulnerability created by your relationship with Sergei years ago and tipped off his paymasters so that they could start to work out how to exploit it. Who else could have so skilfully manipulated the passage of events so that I would emerge as a key suspect?'

You did that all by yourself, she thought.

'I know what you've been doing, Kate. I can see how it looks. My career takes off after that period in New York. I request an unlikely posting to Santiago and Menov lands in my lap, arguably the best agent inside the Kremlin we've had in modern times.'

'You have to agree it looks suspicious.'

'Of course, but now I'm going to tell you something that I bet you don't know. Who was it, do you think, who first encouraged me to apply for that posting in Chile?' There was a long silence as this sank in. 'Yes, Alan Brabazon.'

'On what basis?'

'Oh, he dressed it up well enough. He's much too smart to leave any hostages to fortune. He suggested we play squash in the RAC Club and he took me for a drink in that wood-panelled bar in the basement afterwards. Had I heard about Santiago, he asked. Always good to be one of the first into a new station, the chance to really make your mark. A bit out of the way, I suggested. I was worried I'd be seen as a B-team player of limited ambition, tagged with a preference for the dreaded "lifestyle" postings. No, no, he said. That was to misunderstand the Service. The way to get noticed was to make a true success of an unlikely prospect. Besides, Chile was one of the chief's new ideas – make a go of that and you're set for rapid and certain promotion.'

'Which is pretty much what happened.'

'Yes. He had plans for me, as the debacle over the German finance minister and that fake sex video was to demonstrate. But since he'd encouraged me into that debacle, too, I started to be more wary and suspicious of his enthusiasm for me.'

'Yet he's gone and you're here.'

'Yes. I'm pleased to say he underestimated me.'

'And your political skill?'

'If you want to put it that way.' He stood. 'I've said enough, Kate. I'm not asking you to sign anything in blood. I've called off the dogs. You probably won't believe it cost me a fair degree of Whitehall capital, but I've done it. The Security Service have re-nosed their investigation and you're in the clear. I'm just asking you to consider keeping me in the loop. If we work together, we can finally close the net on him and start to limit the damage he's caused to the Service and the country.' He put his mug by the sink. 'Thank you for the tea.'

He moved towards the door, but turned back. 'How are you getting along?'

The question he's been trying to resist, she thought. 'I'm making progress.'

'Typically elliptical,' he said, with a weary smile. 'You don't change, Kate.'

'Neither do you.'

'Indeed not. But I've seen this clearly from the start. Or at least from before the time of the operation on Igor's yacht. You'd have to grant me that?'

'I would, yes.'

He hesitated, as if reluctant to leave it there. 'Just think about it, that's all I ask.'

'I will.'

But as the door closed, so too did her mind on that particular subject. She went up to bed, fatigued beyond measure and desperate for sleep. Her final thoughts that night settled on the necessity for the journey she was about to make. She had, now, to move this once and for all beyond conjecture to truth.

29

DESPITE THE MEDICATION she was on, Kate managed only a few hours of broken sleep in a torturous night of tossing and turning. The decision to bet the house – and very probably her life – on this trip to Moscow had seemed bold when she'd made it, but bad and indeed mad in the dead of night.

By eight, she had been summoned to a meeting in the Cabinet Office Briefing Room. She instructed Julie and Callum to join her there at nine. And just after that, the prime minister swept into the anteroom, with its bank of screens, Shirley Grove hot on his heels. They patched through to Moscow on the encrypted line and were faced with the stony expressions of Andrew and his two female deputies, neither of whom Kate knew.

As Kate had predicted, Andrew put up the fiercest possible resistance. He confirmed that Incisor was a cultivated agent and the officer who had taken control of his

grooming, approach and recruitment, Jilly Peters – whom
Kate knew from Counter-Terrorism – had just been sent
home after they started to suspect she was under close surveillance by their enemies in the FSB, Russia's internal
security service. Incisor was nervous, spooked even, and
they now only dealt with him through a cut-out. There was
no mechanism to task him: it was a one-way informational
drop-off. They were simply reliant on what Incisor chose
to give them.

The prime minister intervened. What had Incisor been
offered, he asked, in return for his services? Or was he just
an idealist?

As Kate had predicted, Andrew began to give ground
here. He acknowledged Incisor had been promised safe
passage and complete security in the West after a period of
two years, if the information he provided continued at the
level they had agreed. The prime minister jumped in again:
'That sounds like a mighty expensive promise, if you don't
mind me saying so. Hard to conceive of how it would be
worth it if he refuses to help us on a matter of vital national
security.'

Andrew and his colleagues looked as if they had been
punched by the blunt nature of this threat. They appeared
on the verge of calling out the prime minister on whether
this was a matter of national security or merely of his career. But discretion got the better of them.

Andrew fell smoothly back on his second line of defence:
doubts over whether the cut-out was really effective
enough for the timescale and nature of the task in hand.
He gave a little ground in terms of secrecy in order to shore
up his broader strategy. He confirmed the intermediary

was a journalist for *Izvestia* who was a keen amateur swimmer. In an early-morning club he attended on a Monday morning, he swam with the young woman to Andrew's right, who had once toyed with becoming a professional. On Thursday mornings, he swam with Incisor at a different pool close to Gorky Park. Messages and information were passed in a bag left in a locker. 'But,' Andrew went on smoothly, 'the journalist and Incisor have been spooked by our decision to send Jilly Peters back to London. They would likely not respond if they were suddenly confronted by a new message with any dramatic request.'

Now it was Kate's turn to jump in. 'You must have an emergency procedure for a face-to-face?'

'Yes,' Andrew conceded hesitantly. 'But I have to say, Kate, we assess that now is absolutely not the time to exercise it – at least, not without a grave threat to our agent.'

'Sometimes the potential reward justifies the risk,' the prime minister said. 'So I'm afraid we'll have to insist you activate the emergency procedure. If there's a risk to Incisor – and I accept there may be – I take full responsibility for that decision and any potential consequences that may arise from it.'

For a long time, Andrew seemed about to refuse point blank and Kate had no doubt he would have done so in any other circumstances. But the prime minister's direct order made his position difficult and everyone in the room knew it. Grove kept her eyes fixed on Kate.

Andrew Blake withdrew to his third line of defence, which involved the practicable impossibility of arranging the meeting without unacceptable risk to Incisor in the timescale available, given the number of clean 'facilities' agents they used in Moscow who were certain to be free of suspicion by the FSB.

The prime minister was growing still blunter. 'But Mrs Henderson here is a field agent of at least your experience, or greater, is she not?' Andrew had to concede she was. 'Right, then,' the prime minister said. 'I accept your reservations. I understand the problems you're working with. So I hereby appoint her as commander of this operation. You will assist her in so far as you can, but she will have control of the preparations and events on the ground in Moscow. You will make sure she has the procedure for triggering an emergency meeting and she will handle it from there. Your reservations are noted, but if she's confident she can bring in the resources to manage this safely, then I'm afraid that's good enough for me.'

At this last hurdle, Kate was briefly certain Andrew would refuse or offer to resign, or both. But he must have been more ambitious than she'd imagined – or more certain than he'd let on that he could manage events on the ground safely for Incisor – for he moved on without a beat to begin the process of detailed planning. As she had predicted, he and his team must have been up half the night working on it, because their preparation was exceptionally thorough.

The prime minister excused himself with a glint of triumph in his eyes and Andrew gave Kate and Julie the details of how they ran Incisor. He lived in a flat by Gorky Park, between Leninsky Prospekt and Donskaya. Each morning, he left the house at 6 a.m. to walk through the park and across the bridge to an open-air swimming pool called Chaika, or Seagull. On Thursdays – when he swam as part of a morning club – they managed the exchange of information through a leather bag left in a locker three along from his own in the changing room. If SIS wished to communicate with him on any but the appointed day, a yellow car would be parked outside the swimming pool, alerting him to the need to check the locker in question.

After his swim, he would return home, pick up his dog and take it for a walk around Gorky Park. If SIS had requested an emergency meeting, it would 'clean' his progress all the way to the pool and back, then through the park to a café called Ostrovok, where he was in the habit of drinking his morning coffee and reading a paper. If he wished to trigger an emergency meeting, he would take a different cut-through from Leninsky Prospekt. Andrew punched up a photograph on the screen they shared. 'It leads past a restaurant called Kafe de Marko here.' He switched photographs. 'If everything is proceeding as normal, he takes his usual route here.'

'Is there not a danger in meeting so close to home?' Julie asked.

'We don't think so. We devised this system with him. He was adamant he wanted something that could be meshed into his daily routine. We're a long way from SVR Headquarters here, and few of his colleagues live in this area – which is why he moved here. He's something of a loner and has assured us he doesn't know any of his neighbours. There's no immediate prospect of bumping into anyone he knows in this part of the city.'

It was an agent handler's recurring nightmare: the possibility of a random coincidence in which either the source or, worse, the handler bumps into someone either knows in the middle of a sensitive operation.

'We haven't attempted a meeting with him since we set him up,' Andrew said. 'And since then, we're down to two facilitators. So we're going to need your help. I suggest you and Julie take the park. We're more familiar with the top-ography around the pool and the journey to and from it. The park is more straightforward. And it leads into the meeting itself. You think you can handle that?'

'Of course,' Kate said. 'Will he be expecting to see one of you?'

'No. We've made very clear to him that he's dealing with a system not an individual or a series of them. You will say, in Russian naturally, that you're waiting for a man called Boris, and would that be him by any chance? He'll smile and say, no, he's sorry, he can't help you there – but you're welcome to join him while you wait. You'll take a seat and say that Boris is *very* late.' Andrew leant forward towards the camera. 'I want a promise from you, Kate.'

'Of course.'

'I assume you're not going to inform me of the nature of the request you'll make of Incisor.'

'I'm afraid not. It's just too case sensitive, as I think the prime minister outlined.'

'All right, but I would like this certainty, that if Incisor is in any way reluctant to carry out the task or hand over the information you require, if he thinks it's too sensitive or dangerous, you don't press the matter. I've always prom-ised him that we'd do all we could to avoid putting him at risk and he is, understandably, of a nervous disposition.'

Kate wasn't sure she could give this pledge, but what choice did she have? 'Of course. I would never do anything to put anyone unnecessarily at risk,' she said, thinking of

Maja last night, the death of her sister Lena and the fact that this sentence – which she might once have uttered with conviction – carried no weight whatsoever, a fact of which Andrew must be acutely aware. How had she, always so careful in all things, managed to gain a reputation for being reckless? 'But I do have to warn you that the stakes are very high,' she said. 'And there's nothing any of us can do about that.'

Andrew didn't look satisfied, but he had clearly made his pact in this matter, if not peace with himself for failing to respect his own principles and instincts. 'All right,' he said. 'I need to get on. I'll leave you to hammer out the final logistics. Kate, we can pick up when everyone else has finished on our psychological assessment of Incisor.'

After that they were on the call for a further two hours. Andrew's assistants took them through the route to the pool and back step by step and landmark by landmark. Then they worked through the park. In order to keep anyone watching him on their toes, Incisor varied the route of his morning walk in this section and didn't always leave by the same exit. The park was normally busy by the time he arrived, even in the depths of winter, so if you combined it with the route to the swimming pool and back, there was enough light and shade in anti-surveillance terms – busier sections giving way to quieter ones and then the reverse – for it to be workable, if, Kate thought, less than ideal.

Finally, they dealt with the issue of communications. Julie had prepared this and they had two series of phone numbers for the two parts of the operation – the initial meeting and then a drop-off a day or two later of whatever information Incisor might have to impart. Kate and her team would power up the appointed phones at six on the Monday morning and power them off again as soon as the meeting had been completed. If Andrew's team was confident that Incisor was not being watched or followed as he returned home to pick up his dog and walk in the park, there would be no communication at all and Kate would merely pick up and handle it from there. If there were to be an issue, Kate would receive a message: *Sorry, our dog needs to go to the vet. Can we reschedule?*

Incisor would still proceed to the café, but there could and should be no approach.

Julie had a lot of further questions – she had a forensic operational mind and a grasp of detail that was second to none – and they were on the call until she was satisfied she had all the answers.

Once they'd rung off, there were still the not inconsiderable issues surrounding their own team: how did they get safely in and out – and how did they communicate once they were there?

Kate said she was going in via Minsk, Julie that she would take Callum – who had sat spellbound through the entire briefing – the longer route via Riga. She had arranged a series of phones to be used in successive rotation. The first would be before the day of contact, the second on the day of the meeting only, the third between the rendezvous and the point at which Incisor might hand over whatever information he had gathered, and the final one for the journey out of Russia.

There was a great deal more and, by the end, even Kate's concentration was beginning to flag. But there was one further curve ball to deal with. Towards the end of the discussion, Julie began to fret at their ability to pull off an operation with so few resources and so little back-up. In the middle of something of a tirade, Grove intervened: 'I'll come with you.'

They all looked at her in stunned silence. It was a while before Kate realized she was serious and the suggestion required a response. 'You can't,' she said.

'Why not? Julie was saying you have no one to run proper back-up, to take the role of point man, as she put it. Well, unless I'm mistaken, that doesn't necessarily have to be someone from the intelligence community, does it? It could be a civil servant who is resourceful and experienced.'

'No, I'm sorry,' Kate said. 'We don't have the time to deal with all the reasons why this is not a good idea. I—'

'I have an Irish passport in my maiden name, which I kept for superstitious reasons, but I don't have to invent a very deep cover story. I can come in with you as a friend or lover on a weekend jaunt as a tourist to Minsk and Moscow. If something goes wrong, I can simply rock up at the embassy and throw myself on the mercy of the ambassador, perhaps with Callum, if necessary. He'll have little choice but to help us and, while there might be something of a diplomatic rumpus, I don't think we'll spend the rest of our lives rotting in a Siberian gulag. We have the advantage of being genuinely clean skins, which, as I understand it, is what this operation lacks.'

'We can't carry anyone else,' Julie said, as much to Kate as to Grove. 'Callum can drive. He has a reasonable degree of deniability. He'll say he's my boyfriend and was duped. With enough diplomatic muscle, you could dig him out of a hole, but we can't afford to have anyone else who—'

'But the same goes for whoever plays the point man, surely. You can keep me at a distance from the operation itself. I step in if there's a problem, or you have an issue getting the material Incisor gives you out of Russia. From my analysis of everything that has been said, it is you and Kate who are most vulnerable here. There is every chance the Russians might twig who you are.'

There was a certain logic to Grove's argument that even Kate couldn't fault. Operating in hostile countries, there was often a place for the bumbling amateur, who was either disposable or of sufficient diplomatic standing to be protected from executive action on the ground, but she had neither the time nor the energy to do the groundwork required. 'I'm sorry,' Kate said. 'I understand your argument, but I'm afraid the answer is no.'

'I think you misunderstand me, Mrs Henderson,' Grove said. 'It was not a request, but an order. Given what is at stake for all of us, I want to oversee this operation at the sharp end and this is not a matter for negotiation, I'm afraid.'

It was the second time in only a few days that Kate had witnessed the steel, even the menace, in Grove's soul and she saw it clearly enough to concede without further argument. They debated the remaining logistics for a further hour, then separated.

Kate did not see Grove again until they met at the airport, Kate having gone through the laborious process of ensuring she wasn't watched by her own side with a long walk to her gym and a swift exit to a taxi via the basement. The flight and their passage through immigration in Minsk passed without incident or much conversation, and before long they had hired a car, left the drab airport, with its reminders of Belarus's Soviet past – not least the old airliners parked out front – and hit the road for the long journey east. But throughout, Kate could not get one question from her mind: just why had Grove been so insistent she come on this trip?

She turned over the possibilities. She sifted what she knew of Grove's career as a civil servant and the potential ways in which it might have been interwoven with SIS, either formally or informally. She had been at the Foreign Office with the prime minister, yes, but she had never, as far as Kate knew, had any dealings with SIS in the years prior to that.

Was it conceivable that Grove was somehow Dante? Or that she was connected to him and determined to cover up his crimes?

Or, to put it another way, was the purpose of joining them on this trip to ensure that Incisor's secrets never saw the light of day?

As the rain ceased and the last rays of evening sun illuminated the pencil-thin lines of silver birches by the highway, Kate wondered if, in allowing Grove to join them, she had simply signed her own death warrant.

30

THEY SPOKE LITTLE on the journey. Grove drove, while Kate was absorbed in what Andrew Blake had told her on the final call the previous day.

He'd finally admitted that the cultivation of Incisor had not been the work of Jilly Peters, though she had overseen it. The approach had been masterminded by another officer, Max von Braun, who had also now left Russia and returned to SIS in London.

Von Braun was gay, single and had been a frequent visitor to a club called Central Station, which thrived despite the, at times, extreme hostility of the Russian state and many of its citizens. One night, he had met a shy man who had boldly announced he worked for the Russian Foreign Ministry, but had become notably evasive when pressed as to exactly what he did or even whether he worked in the monumental Stalinist Gothic Foreign Ministry building just by Smolenskaya.

Von Braun had not pursued the matter and certainly didn't accept Incisor's offer of a ride home. But he went to Central Station more often after that, with Andrew's encouragement, and managed to fall into conversation with his new friend a second and then a third time.

On a fourth occasion, the man had been drunk – very drunk – and had grown more inebriated and incoherent in the course of their conversation. Von Braun had offered to drop him home. Incisor had at first accepted, then vehemently refused, as if he had momentarily forgotten himself. And through a largely rambling and elliptical account of why he was so beside himself with fatigue and worry, he had given von Braun the impression that there was some issue with debt, perhaps – if his body language was anything to go by – of the kind that keeps you awake at night, more because of the people it is owed to than the scale of the undertaking.

After that, Max von Braun had withdrawn, but not before telling Incisor that he was inherently sympathetic. He was a rich man, he said, who had quite often helped members of their community in trouble, particularly in Russia where ignorance and prejudice were so widespread. He asked if Incisor would like to meet somewhere in daylight hours for a sober discussion – a business talk – about how he might be able to help.

Incisor seemed both intrigued and repelled by the idea. Just as he had with the lift, Incisor accepted and then backtracked as von Braun tried to set a time and place to meet. So in the end, he had handed over a business card with a new, off-grid, mobile that he kept for such a purpose – then left.

It was a week before a message came through. And since von Braun turned on the phone only once a day – for security reasons – and the instruction was to meet him in a section of the Sparrow Hills by Moscow State University, he had been forced to drive hard to get there on time.

For a long while, he wondered why he'd bothered. He waited and waited at the designated rendezvous and only as he was about to disappear again, an hour later, did Incisor appear.

They walked and talked for a further hour and, although on this first occasion, Incisor still gave little away, von Braun was able to build a sufficiently strong relationship in subsequent meetings to winkle the truth – or the story the man wanted to tell – out of him.

Von Braun was naturally sympathetic. He needed no instruction on how tough it was to be gay in Russia and had heard many stories of prejudice and abuse – indeed one could argue that it was impossible to be gay here without one. Incisor's father had been a former Soviet Army officer and vicious bigot, who had once beaten his son severely enough to require a hospital stay for the singular sin of wearing his mother's lipstick.

After that incident, Incisor had done everything in his power to hide his sexuality for many years. He married an unkind girl, who quickly suspected the truth and took to taunting him for his inability to sustain erections during intercourse. Instead of leaving him, she decided to blackmail him to fund her prodigious shopping and gambling habits. Incisor drifted into white-collar crime and debt, in both cases with the kind of people you most wanted to avoid in Russia or anywhere else. His eyes glimmered with the kind of desperation that comes from knowing you're only a heartbeat away from being discovered at the bottom of the Moskva river.

Von Braun made him wait. It was only on the fifth or sixth meeting that Incisor was terrified enough of impending doom to admit that he worked for the Russian Foreign Intelligence Service, not the Foreign Ministry. He withdrew again after that confession and almost ran for his car, but he came back the following week and on this occasion admitted that he worked in a section of the Travel Department that arranged logistics for the service's most senior executives, including Igor Borodin and the operatives of Unit 61a, which Incisor said the (technically) former chief ran as a private empire.

By now, Andrew and Jilly were directly involved, consulting with Ian and Suzy in London. Ian signed off on a very expensive offer: the settlement of all Incisor's debts plus safe passage, a pension, house and offer of employment in London, if he was able to complete two years' service.

It was the kind of deal they gave only to a select few and Kate had wondered at Ian's decision to sanction such expense. Was it just ambition?

Since then, Andrew said, the flow of intelligence from Incisor had been solid, if unspectacular. He had a good handle on gossip within the SVR, which was sometimes useful but largely provided confirmation or overlap of what they were hearing from other agents. He had been able to provide few details on the movement of Borodin and others because they had barely left Moscow in recent months.

And Andrew had outlined another problem: the settlement of Incisor's debts had not seemed to alter the impression they had of a man under severe pressure in more ways than one. Three weeks after he'd been made operational, they had grown sufficiently concerned that von Braun had been compromised that both he and Jilly – who had also met Incisor – were sent home. They had since communicated solely in the pre-agreed way and had avoided all face-to-face meetings. The intelligence had slowed to a trickle.

'So he'll be bloody nervous,' Andrew had told her. 'You'll have to offer him immediate free passage if you're going to ask him anything that is remotely dangerous or difficult. I don't think there's any chance he'll accept unless the prospect of release from his torment is immediate.'

That made sense, but Kate had known damned well there was no prospect of her or her team arranging a difficult and dangerous extraction at such short notice. She'd eventually forced Andrew to admit that he had a plan, as she'd known he must. He'd said he couldn't possibly go through with it without help from London: he just didn't have the resources. She'd persuaded, then wheedled and in the end almost begged. And he'd finally agreed, provided he had her promise it was 'with the prime minister's full authority'.

She had no doubt Andrew would extract a price at some point down the line and she didn't blame him. She was about to plunge in with size ten boots and blow up an agent and operation that might well have been the sum total of his work in post, with the credit and benefits not guaranteed to accrue to him or any of his team.

It had been a lot to ask.

They'd almost reached Smolensk now, the sun setting behind the blue and gold dome of a Russian Orthodox chapel in the corner of a flat wheat field. 'We should get something to eat,' Kate said.

'I thought you were never going to speak,' Grove replied.

'Sorry, had a lot to think about.'

They had the only phones they'd brought with them powered down, the batteries out, so Kate took out a map and guidebook – their cover story was that they were tourists, after all – and navigated them to a restaurant called Temnitsa by a section of the fortified walls of Old Smolensk, just next to the Dnieper river.

Inside, it looked like an old Russian merchant's house, a solid brick structure with high ceilings and ornate furniture. They were offered a table in front of a giant fireplace with an enormous oak lintel and red-brick surround. The fire was not lit, but a row of candles above it burned brightly. It was a romantic setting, which was not quite the mood Kate had been striving for. 'You think he'll live?' Grove asked, as they surveyed the menu.

'Who?'

Grove looked at her, puzzled. 'Navalny.'

'Oh, yes.' The big news that morning had been that Russia's main opposition leader had been poisoned on a flight from Siberia, then rushed to hospital. It didn't take a detailed knowledge of world affairs or Russia to identify the culprit.

'Have you met him?' Kate asked.

'Navalny?'

'No, sorry, the Russian president.'

'Yes, twice. With the prime minister, of course.'

'What was your impression?'

'Low cunning. A not inconsiderable ego. I mean, he's personable in private and direct. He knows what he wants. But he does what it says on the tin.'

'Meaning?'

'Well, if you were to get your average sixth-form history student to write an assessment, I don't think it would be very different from the summary I might come up with having spent several hours in his company.'

'What do you think he really wants?'

Grove thought about this. The waitress came and they ordered some wine. Grove waited until the woman was out of earshot. 'Russia is not very strong, financially, militarily. As you know, it's no match for the West. At least, not yet. So our assessment is that he wants to undermine our way of life, our democracy, to foster dissent and division and argument, so that we turn inwards.'

'And he can rebuild the Russian Empire?'

'Yes, but what do you think? You're the expert, after all.'

'Well, he's had a good run. In retrospect, the way he was given a free hand in Syria was pretty startling and may have some long-term consequences. He's secured his Mediterranean base and he's having a good go at getting a second in Libya, so, yes, the more he can distract us and encourage us to argue among ourselves, the more he has a free hand to rebuild his empire, which will probably end up with a focus on financial and military muscle. I don't think we should doubt his ambition.'

'Our assessment is really that we're in a new Cold War on two fronts,' Grove said. 'Russia is a more consistent, more undermining and irritating threat. But the real danger of a hot war is in China, where the ambition to control the South China Sea and surrounding region is now beyond argument. If there is a war in the next ten years, it will be in Taiwan.'

Kate nodded. On this, in truth, there could be little argument. The waitress arrived with the wine and noted down their order. Kate was due to take over the driving, so she restricted herself to one glass. The last thing she needed was to be stopped by the police at any point on this journey.

'What are you going to do when this is all over?' Grove asked, when they were alone again.

'Oh, God, I don't know. Sleep.'

'I mean for work.'

Kate shook her head. It was true she probably ought to have a better idea of how she was going to pay her mortgage in the coming months. She was certain she wouldn't be able to rely on Stuart. 'What about you?' she asked Grove.

'I'll leave with the PM and, since that may be imminent, I've been giving it a bit of thought. Some kind of consultancy, I imagine.'

'What kind?'

'Leadership, reputation. I've talked about starting something with Callum, since we have complementary skills. Perhaps you should join us. Then we could add security to our portfolio.'

Kate smiled. For the first time since they'd left London, she thought of Callum and Julie in a car together making their own journey across to Moscow. She had to suppress an unwelcome pang of sexual jealousy. 'You don't look enamoured with the idea,' Grove said.

'I wouldn't say that. I've heard worse.'

Grove smiled back at her. 'That's what I call enthusiasm. Think about it. It might work well for all of us. A couple of the richer Party donors are interested in backing us, so we could be up and running quickly.'

Kate did think about it, but not for long. Her mind drifted back to Incisor and the job that awaited them in Moscow. After dinner, she drove on through the pitch-black night, the moon barely ever visible behind thick banks of cloud that rolled across the Russian hinterland.

They were still several hours short of dawn when they reached the capital's almost deserted streets, the Stalinist Gothic splendour of the Seven Sisters buildings and other Moscow landmarks ghoulish in the first slivers of moonlight since they'd left Smolensk.

Kate was relieved to find the key, as promised, in a lock in the porch of the tiny Airbnb apartment she had rented in Arbatskaya. They walked up the stairs and said a brisk goodnight before Kate flopped face down on the bed in the room closest to the front door. She was asleep before she'd summoned the energy to undress.

31

GROVE WAS ALREADY awake and sitting by the window when Kate got up, so she showered and changed quickly and they walked out to a nearby café called Brusnika for breakfast. It was a Scandinavian-style bakery of pine, glass and exposed red brick. It was bright and cheerful, with colourful abstract paintings on the walls and brightly painted pipes on the ceiling.

They both had coffee, toast and jam as Kate explained the purpose of the day, which was to ensure that they were not being watched. 'If anyone spotted us on the way in, I'm hoping I'll catch them on our tail today. We won't have time to carry out more than a cursory check tomorrow morning, so we'll be locked in the apartment after this. Buy whatever you need to keep you going here.'

They returned to the flat with sourdough bread, cheese, water and ham from a neighbouring supermarket. Then

Kate led Grove on a tour of central Moscow that she'd planned meticulously and committed to memory before they'd left London. She began by Kropotkinskaya Metro station, weaving through gardens that surrounded the Cathedral of Christ the Saviour. 'It looks suspiciously new for an ancient cathedral,' Grove said.

'It is. Stalin blew up the original in the nineteen thirties. It's a replica.'

They paused by a statue of Tsar Alexander II, as any tourists might. 'Then why didn't he blow up this?' Grove asked.

'He wasn't so averse to the traditions of autocratic rule.'

They turned left on to the Moskva river embankment and walked up to the Borovitskaya Tower, one of the entrances to the Kremlin. 'That's where the president goes in when he's in Moscow,' Kate said.

They walked on through Alexander Gardens, past strolling families and idling tourists. They took in the Kremlin's walls and turrets, the fountains full of characters from Russian fairy tales, the monuments to the cities that had held out against the Nazis – Kursk, Leningrad and so on – and the tomb of the unknown soldier. They stopped beside the statue of Marshal Zhukov, the defender of Stalingrad, astride his horse just outside the historical museum. 'You seem very relaxed,' Grove said. 'Am I missing something?'

'Have you ever been to Moscow before?'

'Once, with the PM, right at the start of his time in Number Ten.'

Kate led Grove on past the new Kazan Cathedral – another reproduction of an iconic building smashed up on the orders of Stalin – and then through Red Square to cross the river. She took Grove on a tour of Zamoskvorechye so lengthy that even the normally stoic cabinet secretary began to grumble about how much longer this would take.

They returned to the apartment in Arbatskaya with Kate as confident as she reasonably could be that no one had been alerted to their presence in Moscow. They idled away the rest of the day, eating an unappetizing meal, talking about children and the early part of their careers, and playing cards. Grove had had the foresight to bring a pack.

The following morning, Grove left first and took the car to a pre-agreed point at the far end of Gorky Park. Kate set out on foot. She accepted that any attempt to dry-clean her route – to check she was not being followed – at this time in the morning, with Moscow still shrouded in darkness, was likely to be incomplete and she was relying on the work she had done the previous day.

The sky had cleared overnight, so the first rays of dawn light warmed her cheeks by the time she walked past the grandiose Museum of Culture at the entrance to Gorky Park, a bright white building that looked as if it might have been modelled on Berlin's Brandenburg Gate.

Kate swung to the left and walked down an avenue lined with lime trees to the boating lake, which was as still as a mill pond. Its catamarans and pedalos were peacefully tied up, the sun glinting off the water.

The last time Kate had been to Gorky Park, with Sergei on a trip to Moscow, it had been a sad, decaying relic of the Soviet regime, with shabby amusement arcades. But since then it had undergone a major refurbishment. Gone were the rusting metal speakers that had once blared out Soviet propaganda, the gaudy advertising boards and tacky novelty lights. In its place was a neat, well-kept park, which owed less perhaps to its original architect, the Soviet Melnikov, and more to the original aristocratic owner of the Neskuchny Estate, who had once planted a large botanic garden on land now enveloped by the park.

Kate zigzagged, as a tourist might, walking past the fountains opposite the museum and on towards the Moskva river, where the traffic was already building up.

By the time she had completed her first circuit, the park was busy with morning dog-walkers, runners, commuters and children racing around on bikes and scooters, perhaps taking the slow route to school. She had switched on the phone assigned for this morning's operation and, as she circuited back past the museum, it pinged with a message for the first time. It had no words, merely a picture of a bearded young man dressed in leather jacket and jeans who was roller-blading along a pavement. Kate understood exactly what was meant by it: the Moscow team suspected him of being part of a surveillance unit.

Along the river section, Kate passed Julie for the first time. They did not meet each other's gaze.

Shortly afterwards, her phone throbbed again. *En route.*

Kate worked tirelessly, sweeping to and fro across her field of vision, trying to spot anyone whose presence might be unusual or unexplained – anyone who was not settled in the easy routine of their normal morning business. She walked with purpose, as if making more than one circuit was an exercise routine, and she had timed her final lap so that she ought to reach the entry point of Leninsky just a few moments behind Incisor himself, but it was a moment or two before she picked him out.

He wore a fawn jacket and dark slacks and followed a

black Norfolk terrier on an extendable lead. Kate's phone throbbed again. It was a message from Julie: *Roller-blades has exited park. Now clear.*

There was a reply from one of the Moscow team. *Clear.*

Kate wiped a bead of sweat from her forehead, though it was not a warm morning. She tried to dry her palms with the inside of her jacket. She held back, let Incisor get ahead, at one point even stopping for a moment to fiddle with her watch, as if checking her rate of progress or pulse rate.

She could see no evidence that Incisor was being followed.

Kate picked up the trail until she reached the Ostrovok Café, where he sat at a table overlooking another boating lake, his dog curled up at his feet.

She took a seat opposite him. 'I am very sorry to bother you,' she said, 'but I am waiting for a man called Boris. That wouldn't be you, by any chance?'

He smiled at her. 'No,' he said. 'But you're welcome to join me while you wait.'

Kate did as invited. 'He is *very* late,' she said.

Incisor nodded. He waved at the waitress and a pretty young girl flitted over. 'A double espresso,' Kate asked the girl in Russian. Incisor surveyed the menu and then ordered, which gave Kate a moment to study him. He was very thin, with drawn, hungry cheeks and a tattered brown moustache. His fawn jacket was grubby and his cotton shirt and slacks might have been hangovers from the Soviet era.

He waited until the waitress was out of earshot before he turned back to her. 'Are you from the embassy?' he asked, in English.

'No.'

'London?'

'Yes.'

His bright green eyes were vibrant, even startling, in direct contrast to the down-at-heel air of every other aspect of him. 'What do you want?' he asked.

He glanced at a young couple strolling past. They appeared to be deep in conversation but Kate waited until they were also out of earshot before she replied. 'We need you to complete one task that is of vital national importance to the United Kingdom. If you do it, we will consider your obligations to us discharged and immediate steps will be taken to fulfil all promises made to you.'

He reached down to stroke his dog, carefully glancing about him. Kate watched a family of ducks drift past on the pond opposite, confident that if there were an issue, Julie – who was keeping watch outside – would let her know. 'You have a London team here for security?' he asked.

'For extra security, yes.'

'Clean skins?'

'Yes.'

'Are you sure?'

'Yes.'

He nodded and seemed to relax a little. His shoulders sagged. 'What is it you want?' he asked.

'We'd like Igor Borodin's travel records from the year Unit 61a was set up until the present day.'

He had taken a packet of sugar from the metal container on the table and was turning and turning it nervously in his fingers. 'You don't want much, then?' he asked, with a rigid smile. She waited. 'Any paper trail is impossible,' he said. 'It would be too risky. But my memory is very good, even photographic.'

'I need the detail, not the hard evidence.'

'Ten million.'

Kate didn't know whether she was more surprised by the speed of his capitulation or the scale of his demand. 'Three,' she said.

He didn't blink and she had to admit he had an impressive poker face. 'The extraction plan involves not just me but my sister. We will have to remain in hiding for the rest of our lives. We will never know a moment's peace.'

'Andrew has already agreed we will take care of your security. You will receive a house, a pension.'

'This is the most sensitive information in the most secret organization in Russia. They will not rest until they have killed me.' His gaze was fixed upon her once more.

'I'm sure that's true,' Kate countered, 'but we have learnt from our mistakes. They will never get close.'

'But we must have a life. The two of us. Seven million.'

'Four,' Kate countered. Whichever way she'd imagined this conversation going, it was not to a multi-million-pound negotiation for a deal she, in truth, had no authorization to make.

'Six,' he said.

'Five. And that really is our final offer. I came here with the authorization to do whatever it took to make this happen, but there was no expectation that you would ask for a settlement on that scale. If I agree to more than that, I can't vouch for our ability to deliver it.'

The waitress came with their coffee. Incisor tried to smile at her, but it came out as a pained grimace.

He smacked the packet of sugar three times against the table and tipped it into his coffee. He did the same with another, then stirred it in, scooping and turning the liquid with a teaspoon. An agent, Kate thought, of superstitious rituals.

A young man came past on a scooter. At the last moment, he looked in their direction in a manner that might have been accidental but felt deliberate. Was he trying to catch Kate's eye or perhaps that of the waitress behind her? Kate turned, but the girl was nowhere to be seen and the deck outside the café was otherwise empty.

Kate tried to disguise her reaction, but Incisor had seen it and his body language altered immediately. He sat up straight, pushed away his coffee, uninterested. He glanced about him nervously again and stroked his dog, as if looking for reassurance. 'It was nothing,' she said.

'He was too interested.'

'He was checking me out, but not as a potential agent for a hostile power.'

'He—'

'Trust me,' she said. 'I've been on enough stakeouts and clandestine meetings in hostile environments all over the world to know for certain that only self-confident sexual predators make eye contact with total strangers.' He didn't seem reassured and she wasn't so sure she was either.

'I can't do it,' he said. He put some roubles on the table. 'Tell your masters in London I can't do it.'

'Wait a moment.' He was about to get up when she gripped his forearm. 'Sit down,' she instructed him.

His resistance seemed to evaporate. His shoulders sagged again. 'You shouldn't overreact and neither will we,' she said. 'I'm offering you everything you ever wanted here. If the pressure of your secret existence is getting to you, here is a chance to end it. With one bound, you will be free.'

Kate recalled the last time she had used that line, with Lena, in Istanbul and Greece. Had she believed it then? Perhaps. But all she had managed to achieve was to send the poor girl to certain death and she wasn't any more confident this would end differently. 'You don't believe it,' he said.

'I do,' she replied, with as much confidence as she could muster.

'No,' he said. 'It is too dangerous.'

Kate leant closer. 'You don't have a choice. If you want what has been promised to you, it is infinitely more risky to attempt to keep up this double life for another two years and we both know that. This is swift and decisive, one strike and you're out – and a rich man.'

He took another sugar packet. He hadn't touched his coffee. Kate let his silence play out. The sound of the morning birdsong appeared newly deafening, as did the chatter from the family of ducks on the water. 'They will have alarms,' he said finally. 'I don't know how to beat them.'

'How does the internal security system work?' she asked. 'And on what realistic timescale?'

'If I trigger an alarm, it would appear in Tech Support. The duty officer would alert his supervisor, who would speak to the senior officer in Travel. He in turn would pass on his suspicions to one of the senior executives in 61a, who would alert Borodin himself.'

'They'd put you under surveillance straight away?'

'Of course,' he said.

'An internal team or the FSB?' The FSB was Russia's internal security agency, the equivalent of the UK's MI5.

'Internal.'

Kate watched him as he weighed the choice: another two years of terror or a swift and dramatic roll of the dice? She could tell he was toying with an idea. 'Is there a way through?' she asked, keen to tease it out of him. 'We can act as swiftly as is required.'

He turned the packet faster and faster until it seemed to irritate him, too, whereupon he took to tapping it against the side of his mug of coffee. 'Today I start a week of night shifts. They are long and boring. Senior members of 61a rarely arrange travel outside office hours. Sometimes I take a walk around to chat to other officers. There is a community ready to share our gripes about the graveyard shift and what it says about the progress of our careers.'

He shrugged. 'The shift ends at six, but by the last few hours, we're all counting down. It is not uncommon for the officers to sneak away a few minutes early and even more usual for those coming in to be late.'

'Go on,' Kate said.

'If I were to seek this information between five forty-five and six fifteen in the morning, it's just about conceivable that the alarm might fall between the cracks, or at the very least that the confusion and lethargy between shift changes might delay action for half an hour or more.'

'Doesn't a security alert trigger immediate action?'

'In theory. But some things have not changed much since Soviet times. It is a bureaucratic organization and ambitious men – particularly those who want to spend less time on the night shift – are wary of bothering their superiors. They would want to investigate first. It would take time for the message to be passed up the chain of command and, in the intervening period, no one would dare cut corners.'

'So, as long as we began the extraction process immediately, we could be one step ahead of them?'

'It's possible,' he said.

Kate didn't wait for him to have second thoughts. She needed to take the idea and run with it, to turn a proposal into fact. 'I'll tell Andrew this morning that your extraction will need to begin at six tomorrow morning, as soon as you've passed the information to me.'

'I will bring it with me.'

She shook her head. 'It can't work like that. You're asking us to spend a great deal of money and shoulder enormous risk—'

'Risk for you?'

'For all of us. I need to be sure I have the material before we can go through with it.'

The waitress brought his food: eggs on toast. He ate it methodically, as if wanting to buy himself more time. 'Why do you want this information? How can it help MI6 to have the travel records of the former head of the SVR?'

'We're looking for an agent at the heart of SIS called Dante. We think he is the principal, if not only, source of information for Unit 61a. He has helped Borodin and his acolytes create and implement the greatest disinformation campaign we have ever seen, which has systematically undermined the reputation of our prime minister and democracy.'

'Your prime minister will pay anything, then, for his name to be cleared?'

'We've narrowed the hunt for Dante down to two

suspects. If we can overlay Borodin's travel schedule with theirs over a long enough period, we feel the truth will be clearly evident.'

He nodded. 'I will leave the office early at five minutes to six. I will drive to my apartment, then walk through the park and along the Moskva Embankment. My sister will be with me. I will stop and ask you for a light. I will slip a USB with the information into your pocket. We will proceed to the swimming pool, where the extraction process will begin with the procedure I have agreed with my handlers here.'

'I thought you said it was dangerous or impossible to download material.'

'There is danger in any event. This way, our contact is reduced to a minimum. Agreed?'

'Yes.'

And before she could probe any further, he was up and gone.

32

KATE SENT ONE more burst of communication to relay what had been agreed, then took out her phone battery, threw the SIM card into the river and walked back to Arbatskaya.

Grove was already in the flat and they settled in for a nerve-shredding twenty four hours.

Kate went to bed early that night, but her sleep was fitful and she eventually got up and installed herself by the window of the small sitting room to gaze out over the city's rooftops. She was so lost in thought that she didn't notice Grove's presence until the cabinet secretary had dropped down into the seat beside her. 'Can't sleep?' Grove asked.

'I never have, before an important day in a hostile country. You just go over and over everything, wondering what you might have missed.'

'And what could it be here?'

Kate examined her wedding ring. 'I didn't see any tell, formal or informal,' she said quietly, as if talking to herself, which perhaps she was.

'What do you mean by that?'

'If Incisor was worried or wanted to alert us to anything or delay the meeting, he would have been carrying the dog's lead in his left hand. That's the agreed signal. But aside from that, you can often tell if an agent is under pressure as they approach from the ease or otherwise of their gait. I didn't spot any signals in Incisor on the run-in, but he was nervous in that café. He fidgeted and kept glancing around us, which he will have been instructed to avoid doing, because it sends a sure signal to anyone who might be watching.

'Then there was the guy who scootered past. As he drew level, he looked up and right at us, as if he knew we were likely to be there.

'And, finally, I don't understand why he changed his mind about the method of handing over material. Initially, he said he could only memorize it and pass it on to me verbally, but he then switched to a download.'

'I thought that was because he knew he'd set off an alarm either way and at least this method would be quicker.' If Grove was nervous, she was doing a much better job of hiding it.

'But it also leaves me with hard evidence if I'm caught,' Kate said. 'Enough for a long stretch in a Russian prison.'

'You think that's why he changed his mind?'

'In the dead of night, it seems more than a possibility.'

After that, Grove tried to reassure her, but there was little point. It was an intelligence officer's gift to doubt their own judgement and everyone else's motives and it was a process that, once begun, rarely went into reverse.

Kate returned to bed, but not to sleep, and only the onset of dawn and the approach of the climax of this affair settled her nerves. She drank black coffee for breakfast and tried to dry-clean her passage as best she could on the walk to Gorky Park. It was a bleak morning, the sun struggling to break through thick banks of dark cloud, gusting hard with spitting rain so that those who had ventured out at this hour often had to tilt their heads into the wind.

It was not ideal weather for this kind of assignment. Who stops someone to ask for a light in a howling gale?

Kate tried to push the niggling doubts from her mind. She'd made her call and rolled the dice. Now they would land where Fate decreed.

She passed Julie halfway through her first circuit of the park, but her protégée gave no sign that she'd seen her and Kate marched on purposefully. They locked eyes on a second circuit. All clear, Julie appeared to signal. *This is it.*

Kate hoped the nervousness evident in Julie's gait was not mirrored in her own. She breathed out, tried hard to relax. Morning exercise in the park: no more. She pushed on harder.

But on her third and final circuit, she could see no sign of Incisor. She slowed, as if her exercise routine was coming to an end and she was warming down.

He should be here, on this stretch by the river.

Walk on, her instincts told her.

Something has gone wrong. *Abort.*

But she lingered, stopping to watch a tugboat lumber up

the Moskva. The wind strengthened, the rain thickened. Kate looked down the path.

Where was he?

She could hear Julie's voice in her head. *Get out of there, Kate.* She knew her protégée must have failed to clock him entering the park on her circuit and would have instantly abandoned the mission, as all procedure and logic suggested she must.

But Kate was rooted to the spot. She leant against the wall and watched the tugboat, trying to suppress a wave of nausea. She glanced left, then right.

There was no one here.

Why was it so deserted?

She could hear Julie's voice screaming in her head now. *For God's sake, Kate, abort.*

She finally dragged herself upright again and, with leaden feet, she continued on her route.

She couldn't abandon him, not now. What if he'd been delayed and was hurtling towards her?

Kate knew she needed to leave the path, to swing left and hurry out of the park to the rendezvous with Grove, after which she had to leave Russia by the swiftest route possible. She thought of how calm and collected Grove had been. Had she set them all up here?

Kate was on the verge of doing as the voices in her head so urgently demanded when she spotted Incisor emerging from behind a line of trees. He was alone, walking swiftly, his gait rigid.

He hurried towards her, before she could panic enough to run. 'Have you got a light?' he demanded, his eyes wide with fear. She took out the lighter, he held up his raincoat against the wind. The handover was clumsy – a left hand shoved hard into her inside pocket.

She steadied him, lit his cigarette. 'It's all right,' she whispered. 'Good luck.'

And then he was gone. She resisted the temptation to glance over her shoulder.

With each pace beyond him, she was seduced a little further into the belief that this had worked – that burning a hole in her pocket was, finally, the evidence she needed to get her life back.

She breathed a sigh of relief, closed her eyes, tilted her head towards the sky and felt the rain on her cheeks.

There was a cry. Before she could prevent herself, she swung around. Two men in leather jackets were looking over the wall to the river, but there was no sign of Incisor anywhere.

The men shouted for assistance. One was speaking into a radio. *FSB*, she thought. *We're blown.*

Much later, Kate would find it hard to describe the events of the subsequent minutes. Some atavistic mixture of fear, instinct and long experience took over and propelled her out of the park to the cut-through off Leninsky Prospekt where Grove was supposed to be waiting.

And when she realized that Grove wasn't there, she didn't miss a beat. She just kept walking, with the ease of a woman strolling to the shops. She thrust her hand into her jacket pocket and, with long, nimble fingers, installed both the new SIM left there for this purpose and the battery. She called her daughter. Fiona answered, her voice sleepy. 'Mum . . .'

'Hi, Fi, I need you to do something for me. Please don't

ask any questions. Text Dad right now and tell him Mum thought I should let you know I'm feeling pretty under the weather.'

'But why would I—'

'Just do it, please, right now. And then everything will be fine.'

'Mum, is everything okay?'

'Do as I ask, now.' Kate curtailed the call. She texted the number she had given Stuart in Prague, via Signal. *Meet you by Paveletskaya metro ASAP. Come on foot. Leave behind everything else.*

She disassembled her phone. She dropped the SIM into a drain and the rest into a bin.

She walked on to Paveletskaya. She waited by the Metro, watching the commuters pour out on to the street like an incoming tide. It was raining still harder. She took in her surroundings bit by bit, trying to still the questions flooding her mind. Had the FSB spotted that she was the handler? Where was Grove? Had she blown the entire operation?

Kate sectioned off the square around her, sweeping each part of it in turn to make it less conspicuous that she was trying to seek out any potential surveillance. But by the time she saw the reassuring figure of Stuart emerge from the throng in his trademark jeans and black leather jacket, she was pretty sure she was not being watched and her heart leapt.

She let him pass, then approached him from behind, slipping her arm in his. 'Just keep walking,' she said.

'Christ, Kate . . .'

'Don't say anything.'

She could tell it required all Stuart's self-restraint to resist demanding what the hell was happening and she didn't blame him. They walked south on Dubininskaya Street.

Kate set the pace, more or less a march. She took a winding route, weaving from busy thoroughfares to quieter residential streets and cut-throughs. And finally, she found what she had been looking for: an old, beaten-up Fiat. She approached the side closest to the pavement, wrapped her fist in her coat and smashed the window with one brief, well-aimed punch to the corner. She got in, slipped over to the driver's side and instructed Stuart to get in beside her.

She ripped the ignition leads from the underside of the dash and hot-wired the car. She accelerated away, holding the leads together to keep the car in motion and only releasing them for a split second to change gear.

'Where are we going?' he asked.

Kate didn't answer. She kept glancing from the road to the side and rear-view mirrors. 'Kate?' Stuart tried again, but she was too absorbed in her task. It started to rain harder, which made it more difficult to see if anyone was on her tail. The minutes crawled by. They drew clear of Moscow and the traffic thinned. Kate didn't allow herself to relax.

'Are you going to tell me what happened?' he asked. 'Or at least where we're going?'

'Georgia.'

'*What?*'

'An operation went wrong, but I have what I need. With any luck, it'll take them a while to work out that I was the recipient. When they do, they'll expect me to make the short run to the border with Belarus or Lithuania. They won't imagine I'll take the long route south. And I know Georgia. If I can get us there, we have a decent chance of making it all the way home.'

'What operation?'

'It should prove who has been betraying us.' She looked across at him, trying to decipher the strange look on his face. Was it consternation, fear or regret?

He turned to the window. 'Are we going to make it?' he asked.

'I don't know.'

He wiped the condensation from the glass. 'What do you mean? Who's been betraying us?'

Kate wondered why that had not been his first question. 'We have an agent at the top of SIS who's been working with the Russians for years. It was almost certainly his idea to recruit you as a decoy.'

'Who?'

'We've narrowed the search down to Sir Alan or Ian Granger.'

'Christ,' Stuart muttered. 'And whoever it is knows you're here?'

'If they didn't before, they will now.'

Stuart was staring at his hands, turning them palm down, then up again, as though he was about to strangle her and contemplating whether he had the strength, physical or otherwise, to do it. 'What went wrong with the operation?' he asked eventually.

'They closed in on our source after he made the transfer.'

'So you have the material?'

'Yes.'

'What happened to the source?'

'I don't know.'

She waited, more absorbed now in the danger he might represent than in who could be tailing her. Long gone was the regretful, remorseful, loving Stuart of her recent acquaintance and fond memory.

'What happened to your back-up?'

'She disappeared.'

Kate took it as a good sign that he didn't enquire who it was. Perhaps he just assumed she had come with Julie.

Stuart settled back into a brooding silence. It was half an hour before he spoke again. 'We'll never get out of Russia,' he said.

'We might.'

'We're both destined to die here, leaving our children as orphans.' He looked at her. 'And I'd love to claim it was your fault, but we both know who is to blame.'

Relief flooded her. Not for the first time, she had mistaken self-loathing for some kind of looming threat. 'I think you have to accept,' she said, 'that we're both pawns in this game. And that it was devised long ago by someone who has been able to out-think us at every turn.'

'When you work out which one of those bastards it was,' he said, 'I hope you chop them into a thousand tiny pieces.' He shook his head. 'I never liked either of them – a snob and a social climber.' He looked at her. 'They'll catch up with us. We have to face that fact.'

'Maybe,' she said.

'You think we can outwit them?' He was smiling at her again.

'*Maybe.*' She smiled back.

'You look wired for bloody sound,' he said. 'So let me know when you want to relax enough to let me drive.'

After that, the day closed in with a steady gloom that Russia seemed to have made all its own. Fog alternated with sleeting rain. Visibility was negligible and Kate used the unexpected cover of the weather to turn off the main road, wait a while and come back on to it again. But she wouldn't give up the wheel.

In Voronezh, she piloted her way into a grim estate full of Soviet-era apartment blocks and forced Stuart out of the car. 'What are we doing?' he asked.

'We need to change transport.'

Kate made him walk a mile or more, in which the view didn't change markedly. She alighted on a beaten-up Lada Vesta. She didn't have to break the window and they were on their way again in seconds. The next time they had to fill up with petrol, Kate agreed to let him drive, though she refused his request to repair to the ugly steel and glass diner for something to eat.

She settled into the passenger seat, watching the rain hammer the windscreen. 'How could you see anything?' Stuart asked, leaning into the glass.

Driving was absorbing work and neither spoke as the battered Lada rattled on southwards and into a night that crept imperceptibly upon them. Kate slept for a while and awoke as they approached Rostov-on-Don. She insisted they change cars again, switching one old Lada for another. They took it in turns more frequently in the long hours of the dead of night. And as she awoke with a start from a fitful sleep, she saw Stuart smiling at her. 'Man, you like to sleep talk,' he said.

She rubbed her face, sat upright. 'What was I saying?'

'I don't know. A load of absolute gibberish.'

Kate tried to ease the ache in her neck. Ladas were not made for sleeping, or for much else, come to that. 'I can't believe they're not following us yet,' Stuart said.

'No, but waiting for us, possibly.'

'There've been no roadblocks.'

'Yet. Besides, there's still the border.'

'You want to park up, leave the road and cross on foot?'

She looked at him. 'I wouldn't put it past the Russians to have mined it.'

'In the middle of the Caucasus?'

The idea of going on foot had occurred to her, but it would slow them down considerably, which carried risks of its own. Besides, the Caucasus represented hostile terrain even at the best of times. And they were certainly not equipped for a long trek in inclement weather. They slipped back into a prolonged silence. Kate found herself thinking of how comfortable she felt on these long journeys with Stuart in stressful circumstances in a hostile country. Was it just the solace of familiarity? Even now, she couldn't be sure it was love that kept her coming back to him.

'Give it time,' she whispered to herself.

'Give what time?'

'Nothing.' He looked at her once more. 'Nothing.' She tried hard to return his smile. 'We'll be all right.'

'Will we?' he asked.

'Yes,' she said. But it was a question with many nuanced levels of meaning. She made no attempt to give answers to them all and he didn't press her.

Kate tried to suppress the sense that their relationship

was condemned to exist in a hard-to-define space between old love and new beginnings. She thought of Fiona and Gus tucked up in bed far away, in London. She knew well enough Fiona would have been panicked by the call Kate had made from Moscow. 'Do you think the kids are all right?' Stuart asked, as if able to read her mind.

'They will be when we're safely home.'

'How are we going to get across the border?' Kate did not answer. 'I assume you're here with a fake identity and passport, but unless you brought one for me, I'll have to go through on my own account.' She felt his eyes upon her. 'Don't tell me you've failed to consider this because I won't believe you.'

'I have thought about it,' she said.

'And?' he asked, when she failed to elaborate.

'I don't have an answer.'

He tapped his fingers against the steering wheel. 'I'll get out of the car just before the border and hitch back to Moscow. I'll try to leave another way.'

'If you don't cross with me now, they'll never let you leave Russia. And since we won't be allowed back in here, you'll never see any of us again.'

'I've committed my crimes. Perhaps now is the time to pay for them.'

'A heroic offer, but no cigar, I'm afraid. It would kill the kids.'

'And you?' He tried to force a smile. 'Would it kill you?'

She didn't – perhaps couldn't – answer that.

'I've been thinking,' he said.

'That sounds ominous.'

'I know you, Kate. I've loved you for two decades. And

I've tried to convince myself on the long nights in Moscow that the woman I love is capable of the forgiveness I need. But, in my heart of hearts, I'm certain you're not.'

'Stuart—'

'It's not a criticism. I know you've tried, are *trying*. I see the pain of the effort in every last gesture. And I want you to. God knows, I'm willing you on. But I *know* you. You're fiercely proud, loyal, decent, honest. You would never betray someone you love. Ever. Under any circumstances.'

'You make it sound like a flaw.'

'No, I don't. It's a hard taskmaster, but it's the essence of your humanity. It's who you are. It's why I love you. So we can go on in this twilight world where I beg and you try, but it's never going to work and, deep down, I think you know that.'

She didn't offer him the denial he so obviously still hoped for.

'Letting you go on is the last service I can provide you, the final proof of my love. And I'll do it without any expectation—'

'No,' she said. 'You might sacrifice yourself for me as some kind of twisted penance but not for the children. They don't deserve to pay that price. We cross together or not at all.'

The honesty of his appraisal of their fractured relation-ship punctured the air of claustrophobic intensity inside the car and she leant her head against his shoulder. He put an arm around her. 'Friends?' he asked.

'Always.'

Her head slid down into his lap and, within moments, she had drifted off to sleep again.

By the time a bump in the road awoke her, slivers of dawn sunlight were already illuminating the craggy peaks of the Caucasus Mountains. They stopped for petrol one more time, then Kate took over the driving.

They started to climb towards the border. The road deteriorated, and so did their mood. 'In all seriousness, do you have a plan?' Stuart asked, failing to mask the tension in his voice.

'Of sorts.'

'What is it?'

She was reluctant to explain, confident it would sound still less convincing when said out loud. 'When they worked out that it was me in Moscow, they will have started going through the records of all Russian border crossings to try to determine how I came in and with what identity. But the photograph in my passport is quite old, so there's a possibility they'll miss it. I don't think they can know that I'm with you. So it's conceivable you're not on a high-alert list . . .'

He was staring at her as though she was mad. She'd been right: it sounded even less convincing when said out loud. 'They won't expect us here,' she said, more firmly. 'So we have to use that. I have a large supply of roubles and dollars. I'm going to put some big bills in my passport. In the confusion that this elicits, I may have to drive for it. Then it'll depend on how alert they are and how good my evasion skills are.'

Stuart's pallid face lost what remained of its colour. 'Well, I'll say one thing for you,' he said, when he had regained his composure. 'Life is never less than interesting.'

She put her hand over his. 'It will be all right,' she said, projecting a confidence she didn't feel.

Nothing about the trip to the border did anything to calm their nerves. There was a queue of lorries parked on the side of the road waiting to cross that stretched back for ten miles or more. Progress even for cars was achingly slow. It took them two hours to reach the first checkpoint, where a policeman waved them through with only a cursory glance at their raised passports.

It was another half an hour before they were driving towards the low-slung grey buildings of the main border post. The approach and, as far as Kate could tell, the exit were surrounded by high white fencing and low crash barriers. 'It's like Checkpoint Charlie in the bad old days,' Stuart muttered.

It was an impression Kate couldn't argue with. For the first time, she questioned the wisdom of taking such a long route out through one of the world's heavily militarized zones. But she banked still on an element of surprise. This was surely the last place they would expect her to cross.

Eventually the single-file queue split to allow access to four different booths. They inched forward until Kate was alongside a lugubrious middle-aged man sitting in a heavy winter coat behind the glass. He was Russian, obviously, though looked Georgian, with thick wavy dark hair, swarthy features, magnificent bushy eyebrows and a thick moustache. He didn't return her grin. She was grateful she'd thought better of trying to bribe him. 'We're very low on petrol,' she told him in Russian, as she handed over their passports. 'Any chance you could tell us how far it is to the Georgian side of the line?'

'Three kilometres,' he grunted. 'No petrol station there.' Kate glanced at Stuart, who was staring at the floor beneath his feet. Three kilometres on a winding mountain road qualified as a suicide drive. 'This is madness, Kate,' Stuart muttered.

She didn't demur. But what choice did they have?

Kate watched as the cars at the other booths moved off and were replaced. But the officer at their cubicle just stared at the screen in front of him, as he had been doing ever since he'd first swiped their passports through.

Time crawled by. Kate looked straight ahead, trying to project a nonchalance she certainly didn't feel. 'Get ready,' she muttered, under her breath.

The Customs officer stood. 'Stay here,' he instructed. He stalked across to the low-slung grey stone building that appeared to act as the headquarters. As soon as he had disappeared from view, Kate began to accelerate gently.

Stuart glanced over his shoulder. It was only a few seconds until the officer re-emerged from the building opposite. And as he shouted an indecipherable warning to the armed guards sleepily leaning against the walls around him, Kate stamped hard on the accelerator.

Bullets shattered the rear windscreen. She hurtled down the narrow lane between the fence and the central crash barriers, pushing the beaten-up Lada for every ounce of its feeble horsepower. The barrier marking the official limit of Russian territory loomed. Two soldiers were rushing to stand in front of it, rifles raised. 'Get down,' Kate yelled.

Stuart appeared frozen, so she took hold of his hair with her left hand and yanked his face down towards the steering wheel a split second before bullets shattered the front windscreen and ricocheted off the bodywork.

The car hit the crash barrier, bounced into the fence, but

kept its momentum. Kate sat upright again. She accelerated away just as another slew of bullets tore through the car, whistling past her head.

They were out in no man's land; three kilometres of road winding down to the Georgian side, with a static queue of bumper-to-bumper traffic coming in the opposite direction.

At least one of the tyres must have been shot out. Kate had to fight to keep the car level as the rubber eventually shredded, then spun off.

Stuart straightened, looked behind them.

Kate kept her foot down, still wrestling to keep the car in the narrow gap between the queue of traffic coming towards them and a precipitous drop on the other side of the road.

They approached a tunnel. The car slewed towards the edge of the tarmac and it was all she could do to fight it back on course. She missed the wall at the entrance to the tunnel by centimetres.

'Anyone there?' Kate asked.

'Not yet.'

The noise of the wheel rim against the tarmac was deafening. Kate slowed a fraction, then swung the car at the last moment into the front of a lorry that had been inching slowly forward in the queue on the other side of the road. Stuart exhaled in panic and shock. Kate unclicked his seatbelt and her own and grabbed the lapel of his leather jacket, wordlessly dragging him out of her side of the car.

Kate charged at an SUV waiting behind the lorry. A frightened man and woman stared at her in horror. 'Get out!' she yelled. She ran to the driver's side. The man locked the door.

Kate smashed the window, unlocked the door and yanked him out. His wife screamed. As the man tried to fight back, she punched him in the stomach hard enough to wind him. The woman was out of the car now, reaching for her child, who was screaming in the back.

Kate got into the driver's seat as the lorries and cars around them hooted in protest. No one got out to help the stricken family.

As soon as Stuart was in, Kate turned the car around, slamming carelessly into the tunnel front and back as she made the tight turn. She accelerated away. As she did so, the jeep sent to pursue them smashed into the side of the stricken Lada they had abandoned.

But she had wedged it sufficiently that it did not dislodge. 'What's happening?' Kate asked Stuart.

He turned around. 'They're shunting the Lada,' he said hesitantly. 'Hitting harder.'

The tyres of the SUV were flat and Kate had to fight the steering wheel, which pulled hard to the right.

They burst free of the tunnel.

Kate closed her mind to everything but the twists and turns of the road ahead of her. She was doing seventy or eighty on a route in which forty was already much too fast.

Every time Stuart tore his eyes from their pursuers, he braced at the road hurtling towards them.

They passed in and out of tunnels. And still the queue of traffic on the other side was solid and stationary.

'They're closing,' Stuart said, failing to keep the panic from his voice.

'How many?'

'One jeep.' She waited. 'No, two,' he said.

They entered another tunnel. Kate hit a pothole, lost control of the car. It smashed into the wall, bounced back into the line of vehicles opposite and hit the wall a second time. One of the tyres had burst.

Within yards, the screech of metal on tarmac was piercing. Kate lost control of the car again and it slammed into the line of traffic coming the other way, spun once and was again wedged between a truck and the wall.

Kate needed to give Stuart no instruction this time. He clambered out behind her. Up ahead, she could see the barrier finally of the Georgian border. 'Run,' she said.

They sprinted out of the tunnel. It was two hundred metres at most to the barrier. Kate glanced behind her as the lead jeep shunted the car blocking its passage.

Stuart tripped. She doubled back to help him. He tried to get up, but yelled in pain. 'My ankle.' He was groaning. She put his arm around her shoulder and yanked him to his feet. 'No,' he said, hobbling in agony.

'I'll carry you!'

He crouched down on his good leg and tugged her down towards him, his face close to her own. His gaze was steely. 'If you stay, we will both die. Go!'

'No!'

He pulled her closer still. 'Do it. For Fiona and Gus. For us. Or I will never forgive you.'

'No, Stuart—'

'Do it!' The force and passion of his voice propelled her, staggering, away from him.

Kate ran on. Her vision narrowed to the barrier ahead. All she could hear was the rasp of her breathing.

A hundred metres.

She looked back. Stuart had turned around. He stood in the middle of the road, as if he could stop their pursuers by the power of his will. She shouted his name, but no sound came out.

The jeep that had been chasing them finally shunted free and scraped past the abandoned SUV. Within seconds, it was roaring towards them.

Kate ran again. She thought with cold desperation of their children, so far away and about to be made orphans.

There was a cry ahead. A truck sped through the barrier. It was also full of heavily armed soldiers. 'Kate!'

It was Danny, leaning out of the window.

Kate glanced behind her again. Stuart still stood resolutely in the centre of the road. She stopped, turned and watched in horror.

She shouted his name.

The jeep slowed for a moment. There were shouts, then gunfire. Stuart was hit, first by the bullets, then by the jeep.

He was tossed aside, like a rag doll. The jeep roared on towards her.

But Stuart had done enough.

Kate tried to run to him, but Danny was out of the truck and had his arms around her.

The Georgian soldiers fired a hail of bullets into the air, then formed a protective ring. 'There's nothing you can do, Kate,' Danny whispered, as she stared at Stuart's inert body by the roadside. 'He's gone.'

Danny dragged her into the back of the Georgian vehicle. The Russians were screaming and shouting. One was running towards them yelling dire warnings. The driver of the Georgian truck slammed his vehicle into reverse and they hurtled back towards the barrier.

And then they were across and into the shelter of a car park behind the Georgian Customs post. Danny helped Kate down from the truck, but she fell to her knees in the dirt. 'It's over, Kate,' he murmured, as he held her. 'It's all over now.'

33

KATE THOUGHT THEY looked like expectant parents and perhaps that was no mistake. It was a shade after eight in the morning and they had been smuggled by Julie into SIS Headquarters in Vauxhall via the garage entrance. She had escorted them to a small office on the second floor where Danny was waiting nervously by a computer with access to the mainframe.

He had inserted the USB stick Kate had brought back from Russia and now they waited for the computer to run a match with the travel records of every SIS officer of the last two decades.

Kate glanced up at the prime minister, who was flanked by Callum and Julie. He looked as if he was waiting for a judge to pass a sentence of death.

Absent only was Shirley Grove, whom the Foreign Office was still trying to extract from Moscow: she had been the only member of the team arrested. She had denied everything, of course, and since there was no proof against her, the prime minister appeared confident she would be home in days, even if it cost them a concession or two in the meantime. Julie and Callum had made it out without incident, and Kate owed her life to Julie's guess that her friend would opt to run south and subsequent decision to alert London to that fact.

They were still negotiating for the return of Stuart's body.

Only Incisor's fate remained unknown, another weight on Kate's already burdened conscience.

She kept her eyes fixed on the screen, where the search bar moved with excruciating slowness.

There was a single match.

Danny hit the return button and there it was: the answer, the revelation of who was Dante.

Nobody moved or spoke. Kate felt giddy. She tried to stand, but dropped quickly into the chair again. Someone coughed.

In the silence, you would have heard a pin drop.

No one met her eye.

Eventually, she felt Julie squeeze her shoulder. 'I'm sorry,' she whispered.

'Good God, Kate,' the prime minister said. 'That's a bit of a bugger.'

Kate dared not look at any of them. Beside her, Danny stared resolutely at the screen. 'You'll require some time to get things in order,' the PM said. 'I understand that.'

Kate stood. She needed to exert some control here, to stop her head spinning. She had barely slept in the twenty-four hours since her return, and the conversations she'd had with her children had been the worst of her life. She couldn't think straight, as though she'd been repeatedly punched in the face. 'Yes,' she said. 'Thank you.' And then, when no one spoke, she added, 'I appreciate that.'

'I'll stay with you,' Julie said.

'We'll have to talk to the Metropolitan Police,' the prime minister added. 'And I'm afraid there must be due process and a trial. The record must be set straight, in all its lurid detail. But I owe you the courtesy of a little space.'

'Thank you,' Kate said, still unable to look at him – or anyone else in the room.

Kate took her jacket off the back of the chair, then followed Julie out into the corridor and down the stairs to the garage. Once or twice, she had to steady herself on the wall or the stair-rail. Callum came with them and climbed into the front passenger seat beside Julie. 'I'm afraid we have to wait for the Met,' he explained.

No one spoke in the ten minutes they had to sit there, or during the drive afterwards. When they arrived at their destination, Callum said quietly: 'I'm so sorry, Mrs Henderson. But we've been instructed to give you only ten minutes.'

Kate nodded. What more could she have asked for?

She got out of the car and crunched across the gravel to an iron side-gate. She found her aunt Rose sitting in a wicker chair, drinking her morning coffee, a copy of *The Times* open on the table in front of her. She didn't wish her niece a good morning, still less begin with any kind of excuse. She raised the cafetière before her. 'Coffee?'

'No, thank you. We don't have long.'

Even as she waited for her aunt to offer some kind of

explanation, Kate wondered why she had come. What kind of answer could stem the raging storm in her heart?

'I knew it was only a matter of time before you got here,' Rose said eventually. 'And the worst of it was that there was nothing I could do about it.'

Kate sat. 'You'll want to know why?' Rose suggested. When Kate didn't offer an answer, Rose shrugged. 'You asked me why Simon and I didn't adopt. The answer was that I couldn't bear to raise someone else's child, having chosen to destroy my own.'

She waited for that to sink in. 'Simon and I wanted a child so desperately, each in our own ways and for our own reasons. He longed for a boy – someone he could come out here and play cricket with in the summer – and a girl to be the apple of his eye. He'd have spoilt them both rotten. And we tried.' She shook her head again, a tear creeping on to her cheek. 'My God, we tried.

'My physical affair with Alan was brief, but somehow – miracle or curse – I got pregnant. It was after a period in which I'd been managing the logistics and finance for a big operation in Bosnia. No matter how much I tried to twist the dates and times, there was no conceivable way it could have been Simon's.'

Kate waited once again for her aunt to deliver the killer detail, but it never came. She filled in for her: 'You had an abortion.'

'Yes.' Another tear rolled down Rose's cheek.

'And Igor Borodin found out?'

'Yes.'

'You couldn't bear to tell Simon the truth?'

'I'd already confessed to the affair and he had taken me

back. I had seen how much it had cost. I knew this would kill him.'

'And what do you suppose it will do to us?'

Rose had no answer, for surely there was none to give. Kate had so many more questions yet none at all. It was done. It was *finished*. The Met, in their diligent, plodding way, would no doubt wheedle out the rest and Rose was smart enough to plead guilty to spare herself the humiliation and disgrace of a long trial.

Kate thought of when and how she would tell Fiona and Gus of this latest hammer blow, less than twenty-four hours after she had informed them of the loss of their father.

Would they even survive it?

Who could any of them turn to in their grief?

Kate stared at the grass beneath her feet, as if it was visibly shaking beneath her. How often had she sat here in the shade over the years? On how many days had she been grateful for the peace, love and consistency that Rose and Simon had offered? And now, like so much else, it had turned to dust. 'What about Lena, and Rav, and Sergei, and Stuart in exile in Moscow?'

Rose met her gaze, those pale blue eyes filled with tears. 'I know that nothing I say will ease the sting of my betrayal. But all I can tell you is that the first step is so easy,' she said. 'They ask for such small things. I somehow convinced myself that I could give them inconsequential detail. I tried many times to wriggle out of it, but in the end, I couldn't manage the alternative, which was to tell Simon the full truth of what I'd done. And once you've taken those first tentative steps, Igor never allows you to look back. He's a man without mercy.'

'I can't – I won't – offer you sympathy or understanding, still less forgiveness.'

'I would never ask you to.'

They were silent, but for the sound of the wind in the trees. It tugged at their hair. What was there left to say?

The two plainclothes Met officers had appeared by the side gate. They walked slowly across the perfectly manicured lawn, a verdant green now in the bright early-morning sunlight. Rose stood. She adjusted her dress. 'Goodbye, Kate.'

'Goodbye.' Out of the corner of her eye, she could see her aunt following the officers back to the gate. She would not – she could not – bear to turn around to watch her go.

Epilogue

Three months later

IAN GRANGER WAS like Tigger on steroids. He bounced into the SIS dining room on the top floor and it was all Kate could do to stop him throwing his arms around her. She put a hand on his shoulder and offered him her cheek. 'So good to see you,' he said, as she sat the other side of a table laid for two. 'Not bad, eh?' he said, gesturing at their surroundings, including the butler who was waiting to serve them breakfast, as if she had never been there before.

No one sitting there could dispute the sentiment. The wood-panelled room afforded a view of the river in both directions so that it looked as if you might hit the House of Commons with one well-aimed stone throw. Whoever had designed this building had known his business.

Ian wore a tweed jacket with a bold purple check, black jeans and scuffed suede Chelsea boots. He hadn't bothered

to clip his blond curls and she was surprised that a sartor-
ial style she had long viewed as a cry for attention had
survived his elevation to one of the most powerful jobs in
the country. She acknowledged to herself she might have
maligned him, in more ways than one.

He sat, made a fuss of flapping out his napkin and set-
tling it on his lap. There was already fruit, cereal and toast
on the table. The butler offered eggs, bacon and more, but
they both declined. Ian poured her coffee. 'White?' he asked.

'Black.'

'I should do the same.' He patted his expanding midriff.
'I need to lose a few pounds. This job's no good for your
bloody waistline, I'll say that. I don't know how Alan managed to stay so lean.'

From worrying about you, Kate thought.

'So, here we are . . .'

Kate smiled back at him. It was hard to resist his infectious self-satisfaction. And who could blame him? Now
cleared of all suspicion, he had the time and space to settle
into the job he'd always wanted. Even for a man as insecure as Ian, there could be no real dispute that he had
arrived – in every way that mattered.

'Did you hear that Celia and I are back together?'

'I hadn't,' she said truthfully. 'But that's good.' And inevitable, Kate thought, for all Celia's protestations of distaste.
She was tempted to ask what had become of Suzy, but saw
no point in rubbing Ian's nose in it. Suzy would no doubt
have been dispatched back over the river to her former
bosses in MI5, with her tail between her legs. She might
think a little harder in future before shacking up with her
boss.

'How are the children?' Ian asked.

Kate shrugged. This was neither the time nor the place to get into the devastating impact of Stuart's death and Rose's betrayal on Fiona and Gus, though in truth she had been surprised by the stoicism they had displayed, as if no longer surprised or shocked by anything the world could throw at them. 'Time will tell,' she said. 'We've stuck together.'

'And you. How are you?'

'In what sense?'

'I heard Shirley Grove has you in doing consultancy work for the Cabinet Office. Sounds ominous. Planning some big shake-up of the whole system?'

Ah, so that explains the sudden invitation to breakfast, Kate thought.

'But that's not why I asked you in here,' Ian corrected swiftly.

'She's just helping tide me over financially until I can find another job. I have a mortgage to pay and two children to support and London isn't getting any cheaper.'

'Oh, quite. It's a scandal.' Ian poured himself some coffee and stirred it thoughtfully. 'The lawyers say your aunt is certain to plead guilty, which is a relief to us all. I'm so sorry for the burden it must have placed on you, Kate. What with that and poor old Stuart . . .'

You have no idea, she thought. 'Is there any news on Incisor?' she asked, to change the subject.

'I'm afraid not. It doesn't look good.' He straightened up, ready to get down to business. 'Look, Kate, I'll cut to the chase. I asked you in here because we need you back. This denouement with Rose . . . I don't need to tell you it's a bad bloody business. Morale is at rock bottom. We need to rebuild and I'll require all the talent I can lay my hands on.'

'I'm afraid I have to stop you there, Ian.' She gestured at her surroundings. 'It's very kind of you to ask me in here and give me the royal treatment, but I'm honestly done. I'm not sure what I'm going to do with the rest of my life, but I'm certain I've had more than my fill of Igor Borodin's wiles and schemes, which you have been too polite to remind me you saw through quite clearly from the start.'

'Well, yes, but I doubted myself when he offered to defect, if you recall. Besides, it's not going to serve any of us to beat ourselves up on how we should have known better.' He took a large mouthful of toast. It had enough jam on it to feed an army. No wonder his midriff was thickening. 'I wasn't talking about Russia. I agree with you there. I'm looking at the more dangerous and long-term enemy. China. That's where the next war is going to come from and we both know it. You began your career in Hong Kong, you know the territory. So I'd like to bring you back as the head of our China Desk. We have some talented young staff, interesting operations, but we need a cool head to give them focus and direction and, in my opinion, that has to be you.' He looked at her steadily. 'I should perhaps add that the prime minister is *personally* very grateful.'

Generous of him, under the circumstances, Kate thought, given that she had been the one who had first fallen for the smears that came within a whisper of destroying him.

A respectful automatic 'No' was on her lips, but somehow it never came out. Perhaps it was just the surprise: whatever she'd expected here, it was not this.

'I—'

'Don't give me an answer yet.' He raised both arms, as if physically to prevent her. 'I know if I push you, you'll decline. And we need you, Kate. We really do.'

She wanted to say no. She was certain she should, indeed must, not least because she could think of no reason why Ian would want her back here.

Kate took some fruit from the platter in front of her and pushed it around the plate. They fell to talking about children, London's schools and, in the end, the lingering autumnal weather. Ian was clearly thrilled that he'd got her to the door without a definitive refusal and she was bizarrely touched by it. What was happening to her?

He kissed her goodbye and she took the lift down to the ground floor, then walked back out into the sunshine.

She set out for home, glancing at the wedding cake of a building behind her. On how many occasions had she looked back certain she had left for the last time?

Kate quickened her pace. Was she tempted? Perhaps. She had promised to think about it and she would. She acknowledged to herself how hard it was to get this work – this life – out of her psyche.

Her mood lightened with each step. She walked through the park and found two familiar figures strolling in the morning sun, their ancient beagle Nelson between them. He had a spring in his step, these days, and she knew the feeling.

Kate watched Fiona put her arm around her brother and draw him to her. Her daughter's steadfastness and maturity had been the stand-out revelation of the past few months.

Kate watched for a moment. She called.

They turned and smiled. And she found herself running to join them.

Acknowledgements

My wife Claudia has been my partner in life and writing for almost thirty years now, so my most heartfelt thanks are, as always, to her. And I've been working for almost as long with the very brilliant Mark Lucas and Bill Scott-Kerr, so a big thanks to them, and to Eloisa Clegg and the fantastic and dedicated team at Transworld.